Crazy Little Thing Called Love

RAEES & ZINNEERAH'S
PLAYLIST

MK·60·6 M3KI 1991

1. somebody to love by queen
2. while my guitar gently weeps by the beatles
3. rosanna by toto
4. (feels like) heaven by fiction factory
5. time after time by cyndi lauper
6. every little thing she does is magic the police
7. be my baby by the ronettes
8. heaven by bryan adams
9. is this love by whitesnake
10. all the man that i need by whitney houston
11. love of my life by queen
12. we've only just begun by carpenters
13. can't take my eyes off you by frankie valli
14. fly me to the moon (in other words) by frank sinatra
15. crazy little thing called love by queen

CONTENT WARNING:

This book explores sensitive themes, including detailed mentions of past domestic violence, detailed mentions of child abuse, depression, PTSD, anxiety, and a depicted panic attack. Additionally, our FMC, Zinneerah, has severe vocal cord paralysis. Although she has the ability to speak later in the story, she also uses ASL to communicate. To make it easier for readers, ASL dialogue will be italicized throughout the text. Her thoughts, as well as Raees', will also appear in italics, but the context will clearly distinguish between ASL and their inner reflections.

While the characters are Pakistani, there is no Muslim or Desi representation in this book. The characters' faith and practices are subtle and personal, rather than central to the story. If this doesn't align with what you're looking for, I completely understand and encourage you to explore other books that might better suit your preferences.

Thank you for your understanding, and I hope you enjoy their love story if you choose to continue.

For Mama

In another universe, you are a little girl whose dreams are nurtured and whose heart is held with gentle, patient, and unconditional love.

I'm sorry this universe couldn't give you that.

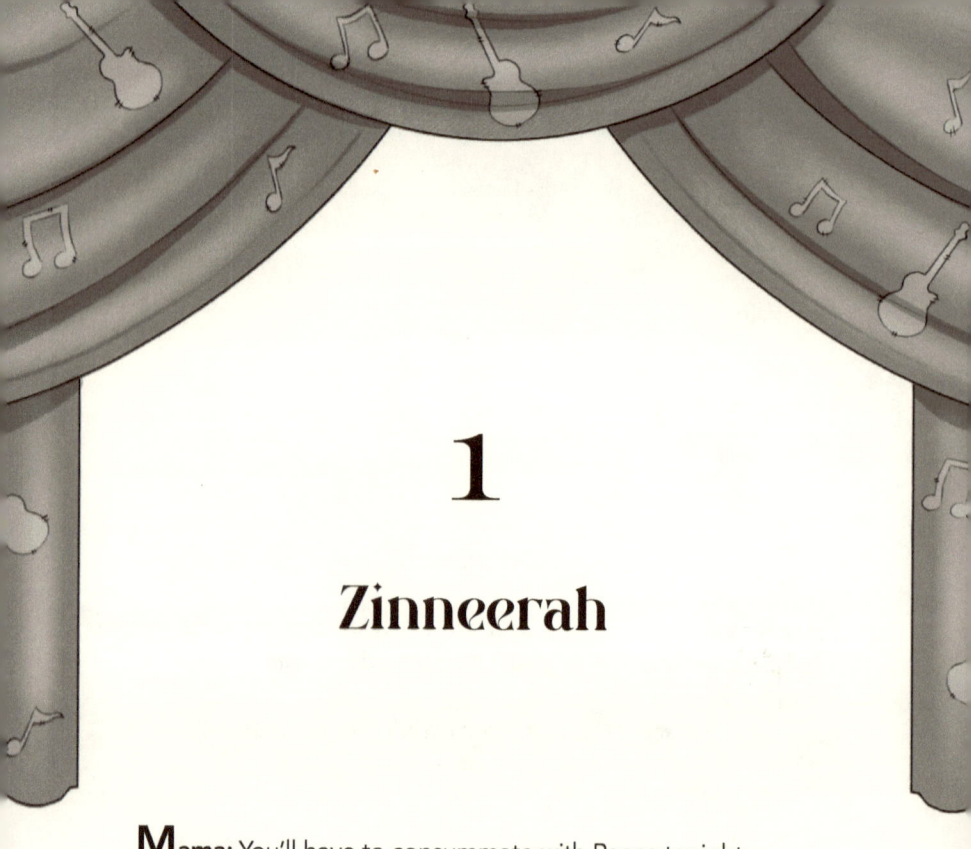

1

Zinneerah

Mama: You'll have to consummate with Raees tonight, Zinneerah.

That's the first text I receive while I stand in the middle of my new bedroom's, new bathroom in my new detached suburban home.

How thoughtful of her.

I graze my thumb back and forth over the grey bubble, focused on the words 'consummate' and 'tonight.' I wish I could smudge the letters on my screen, but they demand action. Action I won't be getting tonight.

Consummate.

How do I sign that word? Do I want to sign it? I've read enough to know that legality doesn't hinge on a single act, but societal expectations love to clutch its pearls over these things.

Maybe I could delay, find an excuse tonight, and buy some time to gather my courage.

But what if that creates more tension between us? What if it signals a lack of commitment or willingness? What if Raees wants to consummate?

No, he isn't like that.

I've seen enough of his character during our arrangement, the year I made him wait before agreeing to be his wife. He's always been patient with me—never pushing beyond what I'm comfortable with.

So, he'll understand now, right? I mean, I can't just assume. It's not about saying no; it's about how it might shift things between us.

Unless I'm misjudging.

Maybe I am.

Maybe I should have talked about this before.

But what if that makes it awkward? I don't want to end something that's just started.

Enough, Zinneerah.

Another concern to keep me up tonight, I guess.

Slipping out of that monstrous lehenga that felt like carrying a mountain on my hips, along with the scratchy jewels that left red marks on my skin, I carefully lay them on the cold counter.

After triple-checking the bathroom door lock, I step into the shower.

The steam envelopes me like a suffocating embrace. My eyes dart around, landing on the unexpected bench nestled in the corner of the stall.

Sitting on it, I curl into myself, knees drawn up to my chin, feeling the heat seep into my bones. The scalding water hits my skin like a thousand needles.

I sniffle softly, tracing the mehndi patterns on my palms. The henna artist's words echo in my mind, praising my stillness during those three spine-aching hours of her process.

In my old apartment, I'd spend hours staring at the wall, counting the seconds as they slipped away.

Tick, tick, tick.

I stand up slowly from the bench, my heart racing as I start to rinse the stiffened curls of hairspray from my hair. The shampoo and conditioner Raees' mother picked out are the exact ones I used back when I lived with Dua.

Interesting. Did my sister give her a list of my must-haves?

Once out of the shower, I wrap myself in a towel, and open the drawers of the bathroom counter with trembling hands, bracing myself for what I might find. And surprise, surprise—my familiar cleanser, moisturizer, toothbrush, and essential hair oil, all neatly arranged as if they've been waiting for me.

I don't have Dua's elaborate skincare rituals; her shelves are overflowing with serums and masks. My essentials fit neatly in a corner, much like my presence in our once-shared space.

I carefully apply oil to my hair, starting from my scalp and going all the way down to my knees. Abbu used to love braiding or styling my hair when I was younger, always fulfilling my demands with a smile. I've let my hair grow out for him, as a way to pay tribute to all the effort he put into it.

Each time I weave a plait, I'm honoring his memory.

Slipping into my black nightgown, the hem tickling my toes, and the long sleeves shielding my arms all the way to my fingertips, I finish my bathroom routine with a quick brush of my teeth.

There was a hollow point in my life, around twenty-four, where I couldn't muster the strength to even shower or tend to basic hygiene. Dua had to step in for the tiniest tasks, and on the rare occasion when she was tied up with her studies, Shahzad had to bathe me.

Most nights, I couldn't tell whose hands were running the loofah down my back, or soothingly massaging my scalp, or prying my jaw open to brush my teeth.

Time was fiction during those endless, numbing two years.

When I clutch the door-knob, twisting it slowly to peek out, I spy Raees adding extra pillows on my bed. He adjusts them around like a fortress and dusts his hands over the comforter, analyzing his cleanliness.

For a minute, he buffers.

His foot taps a rhythm on the wooden floor, a syncopated beat that matches my heartbeat. "Which side does she sleep on?"

The answer sticks in my throat like glue. *Left side.*

Instead, I slip out quietly and shut the bathroom door with a soft click.

Raees spins into view, and like always, my breath catches at the sight of him. It's been ages since my stomach fluttered like this, but today, it's like those butterflies want to burst out and paint every inch of his timeless face.

He's so . . . handsome.

His hair, a mix of onyx waves and whispers of gray around his temples, frames his face perfectly. Broad shoulders and a muscular, but lean physique that catch every woman's eyes. And that jawline, sharp like a diamond, paired with his full lips and those honey-brown eyes protected by thin, black-framed glasses.

I remember how he squinted during our wedding, struggling to see the crowd. It made him seem distant, like he was scrutinizing everyone, maybe even me.

But I know it's just his terrible eyesight. I hope he doesn't find me lacking somehow.

"I've set the bed for you." Raees's baritone cuts through the air like gravel on a quiet road. He's probably used to speaking loudly, addressing crowds of students day in and day out.

I glance up, nodding in response, my eyes inadvertently drawn to the Ralph Lauren logo on his sweater, a distraction from the awkward silence that follows.

"Was everything in the bathroom to your liking?" he asks politely.

My head gives a small nod.

He adds, "My room's down the hall if you need anything," and I nod once more, a gesture that has become my default response.

With a dip of his head, he politely exits the room, leaving behind trails of his sandalwood scent.

I close the door, my fingers automatically checking the lock multiple times, a habit born out of my anxious mind's need for reassurance.

Being in a new environment has me homesick. It's a newly renovated house, after his mother bought it last month and handed it to us right after we signed our wedding papers. Ammi couldn't contain her joy, Dua managed a strained smile despite losing her roommate, and Shahzad still has his qualms, even though Raees hasn't done anything to provoke my brother into shooting him between his brows.

I curl up on the left side of the bed, picturing Dua on my right. We used to sleep like this, whispering about her dates with Zayan or her struggles to secure a journalism internship since Raees vouched for her. What if she's feeling alone now? What if she needs someone to talk to? Should I reach out? I don't want to bother her if she's winding down with Zayan.

I close my eyes.

For two long years of my recovery, I found myself staring up at the ceiling on that cold, unforgiving floor, no soft blankets or comforting pillows to ease the pain in my body.

Dua respected my need for space and claimed the couch as her own makeshift home. There was a tiny, living part of me, buried in the cavities of my chest, that screamed for my sister's company, for her small body to spoon mine.

Yet, I stayed silent.

Maybe Dua misunderstood my empty gazes and lack of words as a signal to keep her distance. Even if she hadn't, I would have still silently pleaded for her to stay away. I couldn't bear the thought of anyone, even family, invading my fragile space.

Every morning, Shahzad would come to check on me, gently lifting me off the floor and placing me back onto my mattress. Sometimes he would lie down nearby, separated by mere meters, while other times he would join me on the floor.

I crane my neck up from the pillows and gaze at the polished, wooden ground of my new house.

The ghosts are still here. The old patterns and habits, lurking just below the surface. Even in this new setting, they're still with me. It's strange, to be offered a comfortable king-sized bed, a large space to aimlessly wander around as I please, a bathroom with a bench installed in it. Raees and his family gave me all this, but it's almost too good to be true.

It's hard, so hard, to quiet the doubts that whisper in the canals of my ears. But I have to try. I have to believe that I can find peace in this new life, that I can continue healing the wounds and build something beautiful, something real.

So, I close my eyes, clutch the blanket tighter, and breathe. Deep breaths, just like Dr. Olivia taught me.

This is your home now. This is a safe space you'll be sharing with your husband. He is a safe man. He will not hurt you. This is a safe space that belongs to you, too. This is your home now. This is a safe space you'll be sharing with your husband. He is a safe man. He will not hurt you. This is a safe space that belongs to you, too. This is your home now. This is a safe space you'll be sharing with your husband. He is a safe man. He will not hurt you. This is a safe space that belongs to you—

The melodious singing of birds slowly awakens me from my sleep.

Sleep?

I *slept*?

In a new environment?

My nose wrinkles as I take a deep whiff. Cinnamon. One of my favorite spices travels up my nostrils and spreads like wildfire around my brain. I can almost taste its flavor on my tongue.

I stretch my limbs, realizing I slept stick-straight for eight hours without tossing and turning. Eight hours in a place that isn't my old apartment. It feels like a small victory. This is a safe space, my brain assures me, and I nod, slowly swinging my legs off the bed.

I pull back the heavy black-out curtains, instantly greeted by the toasty embrace of the sun. With a deep breath, I unlatch the balcony door, letting in the crisp morning air tinged with the scent of freshly mowed grass from the neighboring yards.

Below lies a shimmering, blue pool I'm debating on putting to use. Can I swim without panicking? Absolutely not. But I would like to dip my toes in the shallow end to cool off. Besides, it's been ages since I've visited a pool, back when I was just a little girl splashing around in the shallow end.

I go through my morning routine, cleansing my face and brushing my teeth until they gleam. My fingers weave my hair into a crown braid atop my head, letting a few strands fall to soften the angles of my face.

The shadows beneath my eyes have healed with time, and the bronze hue of my skin is a friendly reminder that *you are no longer a corpse, Zinneerah.*

Dragging one of my three suitcases onto the tiled floor, I unzip it and take out an ivy-patterned maxi-skirt and a simple black long-sleeved shirt. I change in the bathroom, tracing the small scars and marks scattered across my stomach, thighs, and back. Then, I give myself a long look in the mirror and whisper, "This is a safe space."

Stepping down the stairs, I let the familiar morning sounds guide me: the kitchen faucet running, and the muted chatter of a CP24 news reporter blend into the backdrop.

As I reach the bottom step, I catch a glimpse of my husband around the corner of the open kitchen, wrestling with a stubborn jar of strawberry jam. His concentration is split between the jar and the sprawled newspaper on the island counter.

An *actual* newspaper.

I've never seen anyone read the paper under the age of seventy. In fact, I thought we, as a society, had collectively agreed to ditch the newspapers and move onto tablets by now, but I guess Raees missed that memo.

"What? He retired?" Raees mutters, engrossed in whatever article he's squinting to read despite the glasses. His fingers grip the jar's lid, muscles straining against his dress shirt. I tear my gaze away, fixing my eyes on the ceiling, where each line resembles the outlines of countries on a world map.

My heart flutters like a caged bird as I gaze down at my hands, noticing the faded crescent marks embedded on my henna decorated palms.

Something odd catches my eyes in the design as I hold my palm in front of me.

Amongst the delicate ivy and blooming flowers, there is a letter 'R' subtly hidden within the artistry.

It was just Dua and my mother in the room with me when I was getting my henna done, and this little trick is definitely my sister's doing.

"You win," Raees declares.

I pivot my head back only to see him abandoning the jar on the counter, sullenly munching on his golden, buttered toast without any toppings. He pours himself a steaming cup of coffee into a ceramic, green mug, and then adds three tablespoons of sugar. After a thoughtful sip, he shakes his head in mild dissatisfaction and reaches for a fourth spoonful.

I stand with my jaw hanging slightly open, hoping that he doesn't hail from a bloodline cursed with diabetes.

Raees moves fluidly around the L-shaped kitchen. He tidies up his newspaper, scribbles something on a notepad, washes his dishes, attempting once more to salvage the strawberry jam jar with no success.

I find myself hiding behind the wall, hidden from his view, aching from the strain of trying to stifle my smile.

Only when I hear his footsteps fade away do I tiptoe into the kitchen, picking up the notepad with his excellent cursive writing.

The refrigerator and pantry are stocked with ingredients. I've

bought cookbooks and left them on the kitchen island.

I survey the three towering stacks of cookbooks lining the kitchen counter. How ironic that my husband, a digital journalism professor, is thumbing through physical newspapers and flipping through the pages of old-school recipe collections.

And I like it.

I really like it. I like it to the point I smile and finish the last bit of his note.

Feel free to take a tour of the place. I'll be home by six.

Placing his note in my pocket, I scrounge the fridge and pantry and realize, very slowly, that it's only packed with snacks and frozen foods I like. Potato-garlic perogies, curly fries, taro flavored milk in tetra packs. I pause, considering the possibility that maybe Raees also avidly enjoys the niche taste of taro flavored milk. I must be completely in over my head to believe he went out of his way to buy everything I like.

Then again, maybe not. The stacks of sugar-free oatmeal cookies are a dead giveaway.

With a carton of my beloved taro-milk in hand and a trio of oatmeal cookies tucked away for later, I decide to explore the nooks and crannies of the house.

First stop: the basement.

I make my way downstairs, opening the first door to an indoor gym. The equipment stands patiently to sweat out my worries. Yeah, no. Never.

The second door belongs to the home theater, immediately drawing me in.

Sinking into one the plush, red cushions, I let out a sigh, my fingers tracing the grooves of the armrests.

I chuckle softly, shaking my head at the DVDs lined up neatly nearby. In this age of streaming services, Raees' love for physical discs and newspapers is kind of . . . No, actually, it is adorable.

Heading over to the glass cabinet, I start browsing through the discs.

Has Raees always been drawn to the macabre?

From the *SAW* franchise to *Texas Chainsaw Massacre* to *Silent Hill, 28 days, Insidious, Resident Evil*—it's an endless alarming collection of goriness and my all-time favorites.

A small smile tugs at my lips as I carefully place them back in the cabinet. At least we have our movie tastes in common.

Next, I explore the living room, drawn specifically to Raees' family pictures.

His mother, Rosy Shaan, is a well-known and respected real estate agent in Toronto, in charge of housing many A-list celebrities and sports figures. Sahara has collaborated on numerous projects with Rosy Aunty. My cousin once mentioned that Rosy reached out to her specifically when looking for vacation home rentals in Italy, long before Raees and I crossed paths.

During our weekly calls, Sahara had nothing but glowing praise for Rosy Aunty, assuring me that she would make a wonderful mother-in-law should I choose to accept Raees' proposal.

A smile tugs at the corners of my lips as I gaze at a photo of toddler Raees with his ruddy, chubby cheeks squished by his older sister, Ramishah, a diabolical smirk on her lips.

When she first set foot in my apartment with Raees and Rosy Aunty for the proposal, it felt like the arrival of an excitable puppy. She dashed around, exploring every corner, fiddling with Dua's collectible figurines, while my sister nervously bit her nails.

Ramishah insisted on a tour, only to peek into our walk-in closet and casually rearrange the clothes strewn on the floor. Then, she started dispensing skincare tips, which Dua eagerly noted down in her phone's app. If the advice was coming from a dermatologist whose skincare line was a luxury item, sold in high-end stores for the price of a vital organ, then I, too, made a mental note to pay attention.

Ramishah is more than just a friend; she's like the older sister I never had. She's the kind of person who would sneak out with you for a late-night fast-food run or throw a punch at your bully without batting an eyelash. I'll never forget the story she told me about how she met her husband Harry in high school—by breaking the bones of his bullies and becoming his closest friend.

As I continue down the wall of frames, I can't shake the feeling of emptiness that washes over me.

It's like my family's history is a puzzle missing half its pieces. Whatever photographic evidence Baba held dear from our childhood is collecting dust in one of Mama's old suitcases, buried in some forgotten corner of our home in Lahore.

I've thought about asking Mama to hand over those photos, to let me piece together our past, but the thought of reopening old wounds is too daunting.

So instead, I cling to the one tangible memory I have—a faded photograph from my middle-school graduation, where Baba stood proudly by my side. It's a small piece of our story that I keep safe in my wallet.

My phone decides to interrupt the moment.

Doo-Doo: if u see pitchforks and fire torches outside your house tonight, don't say i didn't warn u.

I raise a brow.

Me: Why?

Doo-Doo: the professors in my program found out about your husband's relationship status. they're interrogating him like he's in a courtroom. poor guy. he looks like a tall, helpless puppy.

She sends me a picture of Raees surrounded by a trio of professors, two female and one male. Looking at the photo, I can't help but agree—he does have that lost puppy look about him.

Me: Make sure he doesn't get eaten alive.

Dua's quick response pops up, complete with a thumbs-up and a heart emoji.

I snort at the picture again before pocketing my phone and carrying my breakfast out to the balcony upstairs.

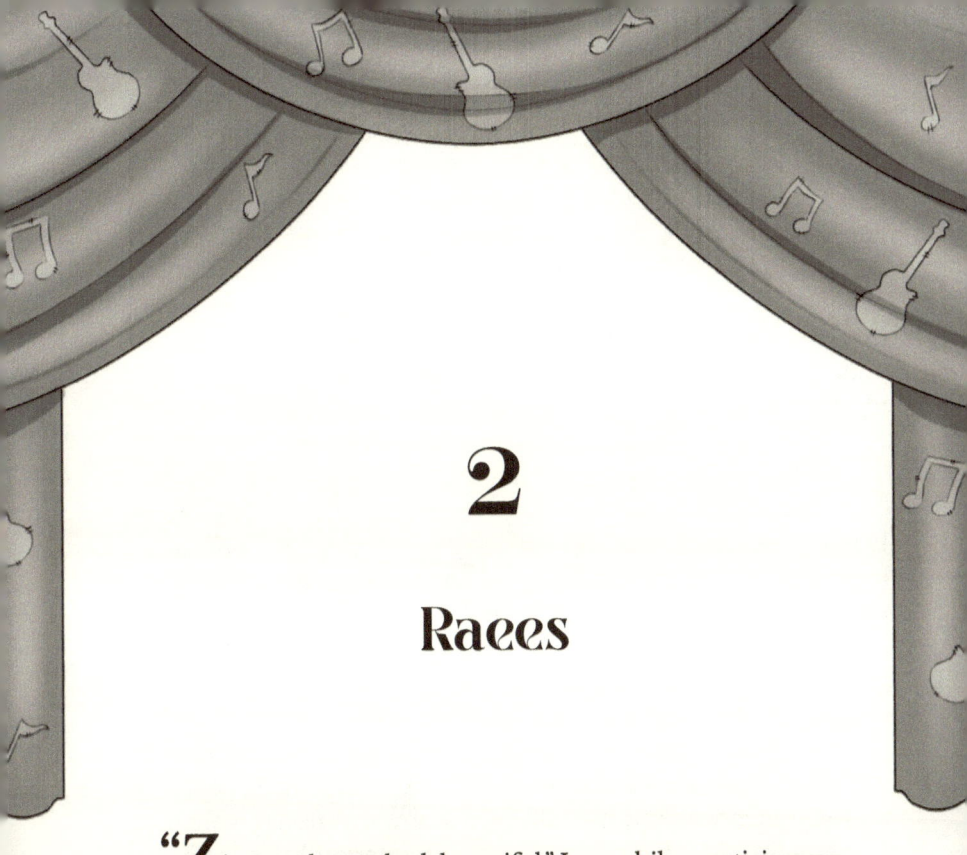

2

Raees

"Zinneerah, you look beautiful," I say while practicing my sign language in front of my iPhone's camera. *Or maybe.* "Zinneerah, you are the example of beauty. You make me question why I exist—"

Three knocks rap at my door.

Oh, for the love of God.

I don't have any office hours currently and students remember to book weeks in advance due to my high-scaling rate of attendees. My office is a revolving door of re-graded midterms and re-taken quizzes, all because, as the folklore in the literature department goes, "You're the professor who separates the wheat from the chaff, Raees."

Paradoxically, my classes have the lowest dropout rates.

I close my ASL textbook with a snap and slide it into my messenger bag. "Please, come in."

Dua peeks in. "Hey, Shaan bhai."

I offer a warm smile and motion for her to take a seat. "It's 'Professor' on campus, Dua." I power up my computer screen and clarify, "And it's Raees bhai for you. 'Shaan' is my mother's family name."

Looking a bit puzzled, she questions, "Huh?"

I chuckle lightly. "Unconventional, I know. But after my parents' divorce . . . my mother chose her maiden name again." Brushing aside the topic of my family's nomenclature, I lace my fingers together on the desk. "So, what brings you here today?"

"The internship. Do you have any news for me?"

"Not yet, I'm afraid."

"Dammit." She runs her fingers through her short, light-brown hair in frustration. "Okay, no worries. It's just my second-year spring term. I'll focus on improving my GPA and refining my transcript to an outstanding level. Then Anne won't have any option but to finally send that acceptance email that's been sitting in her drafts folder gathering digital dust bunnies."

Annie Lawrence, a fellow alum from our days at Saint Lawrence University, has carved out quite the career as a prominent sports journalist. While she's a master at keeping up with emails, being go-to for my students seeking internships, it seems my messages about Dua's internship at her publication have mysteriously landed in her junk folder.

"Since I'm already here, I might as well ask about Zinnie," Dua mentions, idly playing with my name plaque. "How is she?"

Avoiding me.

"She's doing well," I reply.

"Did she sleep at all?"

This morning, I made a quick stop by her door, just to make sure she was all right, to see if she had adjusted to her new surroundings. Instead, all I heard was the unmistakable sound of deep snoring. She's quite a sheltered soul, so seeing her settle into her new bed, her new room, in our new, larger house, filled me with a sense of pride for both of us.

Dua chortles. "Just give her some time. Trust me, once you crack her shell, she's a riot and surprisingly clingy."

"I'll take your word for it." I start gathering my things, eager to catch up with Zinneerah later. "How are you managing solo?"

"Oh, I'm good. Sure, I miss Zinnie's company in the apartment, but I've been prepping for this since you showed up at our door with that proposal last year." She absentmindedly fiddles with her jacket zipper, sliding it up and down. "But Zayan, my boyfriend— I don't know if you know him?"

"Hard to miss SLU's volleyball sensation, Dua."

She lets out a dry chuckle. "Yeah, well, he's crashing over whenever he can, so I'm not exactly drowning in solitude." Stretching her arms above her head, she rises from her seat and snags her backpack, a colorful array of pins and keychains adorning it, from the floor. "Listen, as your sister-in-law, I want to let you know that this marriage will test your patience. You've already shown it by waiting a year for Zinnie to say yes, but the real test begins now."

I arch an eyebrow. "You make it sound ominous."

Dua's expression is contemplative. Her throat works a gulp, fingers gripping tightly onto her bag straps. "My sister, she's . . . she's strong as steel yet delicate as glass. Her resilience is unmatched, but her heart, it's vulnerable. It's in your hands now, Raees bhai, so please, please don't drop it."

My heart races against the confines of my chest. That's the last thing—scratch that, it's not even in the realm of possibility.

Breaking my beautiful wife's heart is simply out of the question. I've been the epitome of patience for nearly six years now. I wouldn't dare rush her into picking up the pace in our marriage. I'll wait years, decades, even centuries if it means catching a glimpse of her breaking out of her cocoon or feeling her hand graze against mine.

She's not just my wife; she's my universe encapsulated in one person.

Dua's suppressed laughter breaks me out of my running thoughts. "Oh, yeah," she muses, "I always knew you were the chosen one, Professor." She twirls on her heel and heads out of my office.

I lean back in my chair, idly spinning my wedding ring around my finger. "Damn right I am.

The drive back home from campus takes approximately twenty minutes. If I could, I'd break a few speed records just to get to my wife's side ten minutes sooner.

Ramishah helped us set up a security app on our phones that technically screams, "Honey, I'm home!" It's like having a virtual guard dog minus the barking. Shahzad insisted on private cameras all around our property when we met up for coffee in May.

Was I dying to escape the suffocating intensity of his thirty-minute glare? Absolutely.

But I also needed to make a lasting impression on him, so, naturally, I complied with his security demands. Plus, I've noticed my wife has this nervous energy and flinches at the slightest intrusion into her personal space.

Take our wedding, for instance. Whenever kids leaped onto the stage and let out joyful squeals, Zinneerah would visibly shrink. Or when her well-meaning relatives showered her with blessings that involved cheek-pinching and awkward hand-kisses—it was like she was dodging bullets in a social minefield.

Zinneerah was squirming in her seat, teetering on the edge of a full-blown panic attack. Being her husband, I took matters into my own hands, discreetly signaling my mother that we were off-limits to everyone but close family. Thank goodness for that intervention because the moment the pressure eased, my wife's complexion became much less pale.

Pulling into the driveway, I steal a quick glance at my reflection in the rearview mirror.

Hair? Check. Breath? Minty fresh. Glasses? Smudge-free.

All set to make a good impression on my bride.

I step into my house, met by an eerie silence. Slipping off my shoes, I head to the kitchen and notice the notepad exactly where I left my message. Did she read it?

"Zinneerah?" I call out, peeking into the living room, and scanning the backyard.

No sign of her.

Her bedroom door remains shut tight, and I'm not about to play detective and barge in. The security app is blank about any house exits, so she's definitely hiding in here somewhere.

With a resigned sigh, I opt for a hot shower and a change of comfortable clothes.

Afterwards, I venture down to the basement—the final frontier. And what do I hear from outside the door? Sounds of a slasher film.

A smile bends at my lips. Looks like you've found your favorite horror collection.

Now, I must confess, anything involving clowns on tricycles, masked killers, or zombies sends shivers down my spine. But my lovely wife? She's a card-carrying horror aficionado.

Quietly, I push open the theater room door and spot her in the back row, head tilted to the side, dark eyes shut in a peaceful sleep amidst the on-screen carnage. A packet of oatmeal cookies rests on her lap, a sprinkle of crumbs on her clothes.

Taking off my glasses to blind myself from the splattering human guts, I quickly turn off the massacre and flip on the lights, adjusting the dimmer with a twist.

I crouch down beside her. The glint of her diamond ring sends a jolt through me, preparing my heart to burst into a shower of celebratory confetti.

"Zinneerah?" I whisper.

She is out like a light. Completely out.

I recall how drained she looked at our wedding, barely touching her food at the buffet. Of course, her mother's constant nagging about her posture and unenthusiastic interaction with relatives and their rehearsed pleasantries didn't help either.

Walking over to the laundry nook, I grab a blanket and return to her side, unfurling it and draping it over her form from shoulders to toes. Her socks sport tiny white skulls. Cute.

I pause, admiring the sight before me.

My hand hovers mid-air, fingers quivering as if tickling the ivories of an invisible piano.

Zinneerah wakes up.

I startle at the sudden rush of fear coursing through me and instinctively take three steps backward. "My apologies," I blurt out.

She doesn't bat an eyelash.

Her eyes, as dark as midnight, dart between the hand I just retracted and my flustered expression.

"Have you had anything to eat?" I ask, trying to diffuse the awkwardness.

Zinneerah yanks the blanket off her frame and tosses it aside.

"Is everything all—"

She snatches her oatmeal cookies, shooting me another bone-chilling glare before vanishing from the room like a breathtaking phantom.

I collapse into her vacant seat, burying my face in my hands. "Shit."

3

Races

My wife isn't an early bird.

Meanwhile, I'm rising with the sun at six, pounding the pavement on my morning run, followed by a stint in my home gym, and preparing a hearty breakfast fit for champions by eight. In my mind, she's gracefully sipping Earl Grey or wandering around the piano room.

Except, wishful thinking is my specialty, leaving me stranded on the back patio with my lecture notes, distracted by the ripples in our swimming pool.

Goddammit.

Isn't this just a fine mess I've gotten myself into? I mean, seriously, what was I thinking last night, playing the part of the gallant knight and almost brushing her hair away from her face?

She was like a startled deer during our first meeting, all wide eyes and nervous energy, perched on the edge of her couch as if she had an eject button ready to launch her out of there at any moment.

Our families had left us to our devices in her apartment—the obligatory ritual before any arranged engagement.

Zinneerah avoided eye-contact, her eyes fixed on her trembling fingers entwined in her lap. I mirrored her silence, my own stare locked onto the window before us. As minutes stretched into an hour, my mind swirled with thoughts of a future with her as my wife.

The next day, I cried.

Happy tears, of course.

My mother delivered the news that Zinneerah wished to see me again. And so, for a blissful week and a half, we shared a comfortable silence. She seemed more at ease, lounging on the couch, absentmindedly tracing the lines on her palm with her thumb. Every now and then, she'd steal a glance my way, acknowledging my smile with subtle nods—

Creaks of a wooden door yanks my gaze upward, straight to Zinneerah's balcony.

Speak of the angel.

The sun seems to play favorites as it bathes her rich brown skin in its golden glow the moment she steps out. Black, long strands dance in the breeze, framing her face like a dark halo, and with a flick of her bony fingers, she tucks a stray strand behind her ear, leaning against the wrought iron railing.

My breath catches as our eyes lock.

Electricity shoots up my spine, propelling me to my feet as if she were some heavenly being perched on a pedestal. If a glance could be a lifesaver, it would be my wife's.

I offer a hesitant wave.

Clutching her cardigan tight around her, she twirls back into her room, leaving me to slump back into my chair, drumming my fingers against my chest in a futile attempt to contain the wild beat of my silly heart.

The Global Media and Journalism program has carved its own niche, founded in a run-down arts building beside one of Saint Lawrence University's myriad extravagant STEM buildings.

While SLU is renowned for its top-notch engineering programs, our GMJ program is no less formidable. 'We don't teach journalism; we mold warriors of the media battlefield', like it says on one of the many dramatic murals in our building.

Second year, however, is the litmus test where the weaklings are unceremoniously weeded out.

The remaining funds have found their way to revamping the ice-rink for the struggling hockey team and a new football field, despite our less-than-stellar track record in both sports. But it's the volleyball squad that continues to hoist the banner of glory for SLU.

Anyway, I handle the first and second years with Mass Media journalism during spring term, thirds years with Influence of Digital Media in the fall term, and later the fourth years with specialized journalism regarding the environment and scientific research every spring.

With the start of the spring term, many undergraduates from various programs have chosen Mass Media as an elective, including eager first and second years looking for a quick head start. They often assume it's an easy course, but according to my previous students, I'm notoriously the toughest grader. My profile on RateMyProfessor.com is proof enough.

Despite this, I walk into a lecture room filled with ninety-seven students, who quickly silence themselves and prepare their laptops.

"Morning, everyone," I greet, receiving a dull, half-hearted response. Fair enough. It's nine in the morning, and sitting through a three-hour lecture after a weekend of frat parties and vomiting on our mascot, Gary the Goose's, statue is pure torture.

Dua sits in the very front, grinning ear-to-ear and seemingly the most awake on behalf of every other student. However, a closer look reveals the assistant position is starting to wear her out. Her usually round face has become slimmer, and, without meaning to sound rude, she's developed heavy, dark circles under her eyes. Her brown hair is tied back in a bun resembling a bird's nest, and I can't tell if that stain on her sweater is chocolate or something worse from cleaning up after the players.

I adjust my glasses and flick on the projector with the remote, displaying the slides. The weariness in the air dissipates as I clear my throat, and every colorful eye is now focused on the PowerPoint, fingers poised like guns, ready to fire away on their keyboards.

After class, I head over to Studio 365 to get a caramel latté. The place is almost empty, with only two girls hurriedly working on an assignment in the corner booth and an elderly man reading a magazine by the window.

"Slow day, huh?" I tap my card on the payment device.

"Too slow," Penny replies with a sigh. "Boss is cutting hours and thinking about selling the place. I think we could turn it around if we attract more students. Just look at this place."

She gestures to the sparse decorations, scratched floorboards, dirty windows, and stained beige wallpaper.

My eyes drift to the corner where they used to have open mic nights. The booth next to it is where my ex-fiancé admitted she'd gotten drunk, and cheated on me with a stranger at her bachelorette party.

But it's also where I first heard my future wife singing, her voice cutting through the apologies rolling off my ex's tongue.

So, yes, this café holds a special spot in my heart. I'll be damned if Martin sells it off to some jerk who'll turn it into a dispensary.

And besides, the coffee here is top-notch.

With my latté in hand, I leave a generous tip and head back to campus, finding a bench that overlooks the clock tower where the music department resides.

"God, I still can't believe I'm married to Zinneerah Arain," I mumble to myself.

It was six summers ago, when I was a nervous wreck on my first day as a professor, palms sweating, legs bouncing uncontrollably, lips parched as if I were lost in my own desert.

Everything was perfect. The sun hung high in the sky, burning through the clouds and over the students sprawled out on the grass.

Amongst the many was Zinneerah. It was only my second time seeing her since my breakup the week prior. I considered it a stroke of luck or perhaps a sign. She sat there, slightly slouched, with her black acoustic guitar and composition sheets scattered before her. The wind played with her hair, twisting it in the perfect dance, rendering her almost otherworldly, irresistible, *calling*.

I'd fled the scene as quickly as I could and spent the remaining minutes in an empty lab room.

God, what I wouldn't do to see her sitting in the grassy field with her instrument and music sheets.

As I rise from the bench, I steal one final, longing glance at the spot beneath the oak tree where she sat, before making my way back to the faculty building for my evening lecture.

When I get home around eight, Zinneerah's in the kitchen. As I walk in, she glances at me with worry, while she nervously chews her bottom lip. Something's on her mind, and I would cut out my kidney for her to confide in me.

"Did you have dinner?" I ask, noticing the empty pots and the absence of any inviting aroma wafting through the air. Maybe she just didn't feel like cooking tonight. Unless she can't cook. "Would you like me to make something for you?"

Her fingers move gracefully as she mouths, "I'm sorry."

For a moment, I contemplate whether I should reveal that I am fluent in ASL, or if I should wait for a more opportune moment, when she's in a better frame of mind.

"Whatever for?" I ask, setting my bag down on the kitchen counter. She's standing near the pantry door, stocked full of her favorite snacks from top to bottom, with mine squeezed in wherever there's space. My wife has a penchant for snacking, so what? "Is this about last night?"

There's a tiny quiver in her chin as she signs "I'm sorry" once more. I long for her to meet my gaze, but as I watch tears cascade down her cheeks and her hands tremble violently as she wipes them away, my heart aches.

"Zinneerah, is it all right if I come close to you to tell you something?" I ask gently. She nods, and I approach, keeping a respectful distance. "Please don't ever apologize to me for anything ever again. I should've made myself known last night before awkwardly watching over you. It was foolish and irrational, and I promise I won't do it again."

For a brief moment, she lifts her lashes, and my soul shatters at the sight of her tear-streaked eyes. She was already crying before I arrived, and I desperately hope it's not because she's blaming herself for something that wasn't her fault in the first place.

"I promise," I whisper, "to ask your permission when and where it's necessary. It wasn't my intention at all to make you uncomfortable. I sincerely apologize for it."

A nod, and a weak thumbs-up.

I release a relieved breath through my nose. "Is there anything I can do to—" I stop mid-sentence, gesturing to my eyes to indicate her tear-streaked ones. "A tissue? Would you like a tissue?"

She nods.

I quickly retrieve two tissues and hand them to her. She thanks me, using them to dab at her eyes and blow her nose.

I stifle a smile behind my fist. "Are you feeling a bit better?"

She nods again, her expression grateful.

"Good," I say with a smile. "If you need anything else, just let me know, okay?"

As she walks past me to dispose of the tissues, she gives a small bow of her head.

"Wait—" I start, but Zinneerah scurries back upstairs before I can finish.

I slump, bumping a defeated fist against my palm as her door shuts and locks.

Goddammit, Raees.

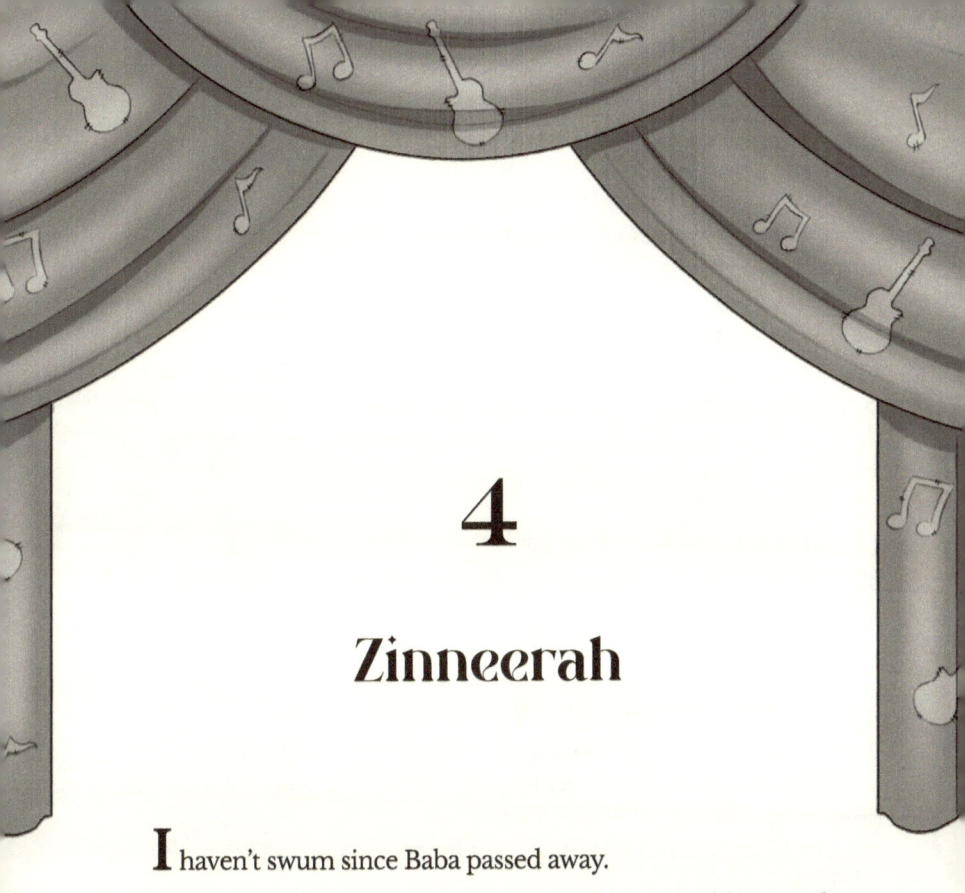

4

Zinneerah

I haven't swum since Baba passed away.

Each weekend, it was our ritual: Baba taking my siblings and me to the lake, where we'd lose ourselves for hours under the scorching sun or skip stones over the rippling waves. Shahzad would bravely dive into the deep end to practice swimming, while Baba would give Dua piggy-back rides in the water. I'd linger in the shallow end or perch on a weathered rock, feeling like a mermaid soaking up her daily dose of Vitamin D.

But now, standing here by the swimming pool, my towel draped over my arm and my satin bathrobe concealing the one-piece I reluctantly wear, it's as if a floodgate of memories has burst open. What once was will never be again.

As I slip off my bathrobe, I take care to neatly fold it on the lounge chair before hesitantly dipping my toe into the water first, feeling the chill seep into my bones. Despite it being July, the pool remains icy. But the thought of standing on the scalding concrete barefoot any longer is unbearable.

Summoning all my courage, I slowly lower myself into the pool, one leg at a time, until I'm standing in the shallow end. It's embarrassing for me to cling to the corner, but, hey, I refuse to compromise my safety for the sake of pride.

Swimming has never been my forte, and I'm not hell-bent on mastering it now. I find a certain peace in the stillness of the water, content to watch the world around me unfold. The majestic oak tree, the squirrel darting up its trunk, the birds soaring overhead, and the rustle of leaves provide all the distraction I need.

This is nice.

This house is nice. This pool is nice. The kitchen and its pantry are nice. The basement is nice—

The basement.

I frown at the memory of two nights ago. Raees meant well, I'm sure, but I couldn't handle his close proximity, or how his hand obstructed my view. My initial reaction was to fear the worst—that he might lash out at me for dozing off instead of preparing dinner. I should have been a more considerate wife, and prepared a meal for both of us. After all, I had survived on oatmeal cookies all day while he toiled away on campus, likely forgetting to eat in between his busy schedule.

Please don't ever apologize to me for anything ever again. I should've made myself known last night before awkwardly watching over you. It was foolish and irrational, and I promise I won't do it again.

God, I'm an idiot.

I'm an unreliable idiot.

This is a safe space, I repeat to myself like a mantra. *My husband is safe and dependable. I chose him because he makes me feel secure. He respects my boundaries, always asking before he gets too close.*

Last night, he meant no harm. I should have calmly signaled for him to announce himself if I'm asleep.

But instead, I panicked and fled.

At first, running away felt like the only option, but I'm better now. I don't need to run anymore.

In this house, I am safe.

I am safe with Raees.

After spending an hour in the pool, I finally step out and wrap a robe around myself, drying off as I make my way to the kitchen where I left my phone to charge—

And there he is, Raees Shaan, making coffee.

He turns to greet me, cheeks slightly puffed from the taste of the brownies I'd baked earlier. Small crumbs cling to the corners of his perfect lips, and a few more dot his cashmere sweater.

"Hi," he greets me through a mouth full of chocolate. "I'm sorry. That—Give me a minute." His words are slightly muffled as he aggressively chews, his fist covering his mouth and his foot tapping anxiously as he struggles to swallow.

What a dork.

Raees clears his throat and faces me, clasping his hands behind his back. "Did you have a good swim? Not that I saw you swimming. No, I would never do such a thing. You've returned from the backyard . . ."

I nod absentmindedly, but my attention drifts to the hint of chocolate smeared on the side of his pearl-white teeth. Moving downwards, my gaze lingers on the curve of his broad shoulders, the way his shirt stretches over his mesomorphic torso. His hands, large and, well, very handy-looking, gesture as he speaks . . . about something.

I break out of my blatant staring when the coffee pot begins to bubble.

"—and I know—Oh, give me a second." Raees reaches for his green mug on the third shelf of the second cabinet, the highest one, and pours the black, bitter liquid into it. Three tablespoons of sugar follow, as always, along with sweetened oat milk. He stirs it all together with a spoon before bringing the rim up to his lips, taking a long, satisfying sip. "Ha . . . I make the best coffee."

I point to the tea bags contained in a jar then to myself.

Suddenly, he's eager to share some random tea facts while I rummage the fridge for the strawberry jam jar. "You know, some teas, like Pu'er, actually improve with age? It's like fine wine, but with tea leaves. The longer it's stored, the more complex and richer the flavor becomes."

I find the jam jar and turn around with it.

He chuckles. "Believe me, that thing will not open—"

I pop it open.

Raees' jaw drops, his shock shifting between the glass jar and its lid. He doesn't scoff or roll his eyes at my potentially bruising his pride. Instead, he smiles wide. I avert my eyes, not wanting to start mirroring his expression. "I knew you were stronger than me, Zinneerah."

My lips twitch. *Zin-nheer-ray*. Not Zin-*nay*-rah, or, Zin-*nee*-rah. An unnecessary 'nhee' sound in the middle, but somehow, I don't know how, he makes it work. Even my siblings don't place much emphasis on that mid-syllable.

"May I take the jar?" He extends his hands. "Or you can place it on the counter? Whatever you're comfortable with."

I stick to the latter, feeling a flutter of anxiety as I watch for any signs of impatience or frustration on his face.

Nope. He just flashes that boyish grin again and takes the jar, attempting to open it. After a couple of failed attempts, he passes on the fifth try.

"It's a little tough."

I tap the counter, signaling for him to hand it back to me. He does, and I close the lid over it, my gaze flickering up to meet his before focusing back on the jar. He watches intently as I apply a bit of downward pressure and twist the lid.

"Oh," he drawls, adding another bright chuckle. "Like opening a medicine container. Can I try again?"

As soon as I set the jar on the counter, he swoops in and takes it, effortlessly following my instructions. The lid pops open under his touch, and the sheer joy on his face leaves me breathless.

His eyes, a warm golden-brown, crinkle at the corners with age, his thick lashes almost hiding them from view.

A smile spreads across his face, stretching from ear to ear, and the sound of his deep, smooth laughter fills the room, wrapping around me like a warm blanket and slowing the frantic beat of my heart.

He's saying something, his lips moving in that familiar way, but I'm too focused on them to really hear the words.

"Zinneerah?"

I blink.

"Where did you go?" His bends down slightly to meet my eyes. I instinctively take a step back, feeling like a tiny boat sailing towards a whirlpool. "I'm sorry." He quickly straightens up and shakes his head at himself. "It's a habit."

I shake my head in disagreement.

Seriously, it is. He's just being himself, with his gentle gestures and towering presence. A safe man. I know he won't hurt me.

Raees scratches the top of his brow with his thumb. "I apologize, Zinneerah." A soft smile lays at his lips. "I'm widely known in my family for breaching personal space. According to my sister, physical touch is my love . . ." His voice momentarily falters before he smoothly redirects the conversation, gesturing towards the now-vacant plate of brownies. "Those were very delicious."

I prepared a half-dozen for us. He ate them all. How do I tactfully suggest he consider moderating his sugar intake?

"Dua tells me you enjoy baking," he continues, shifting his weight from one foot to the other. "If you want, I can take you to this store nearby. They have everything for baking. A store dedicated to baking stuff—baking *equipment*, I mean. For your baking needs, of course."

There's a nervous energy about him, evident in the way he fidgets and avoids meeting my gaze, and strangely, we both seem to avert our eyes simultaneously.

I touch my chin with my fingers and pull them away, mouthing, "Thank you."

He takes a minute to unravel my words, then nods. "You're welcome. The offer will always be on the table."

There's an awkward pause.

Until I break it. All I have to do is point at myself, then point upwards.

His smile falters, granting me space to leave. "If you need anything, just knock on my bedroom door."

I resort to a sigh when he leaves.

God, he's got a sweet smile.

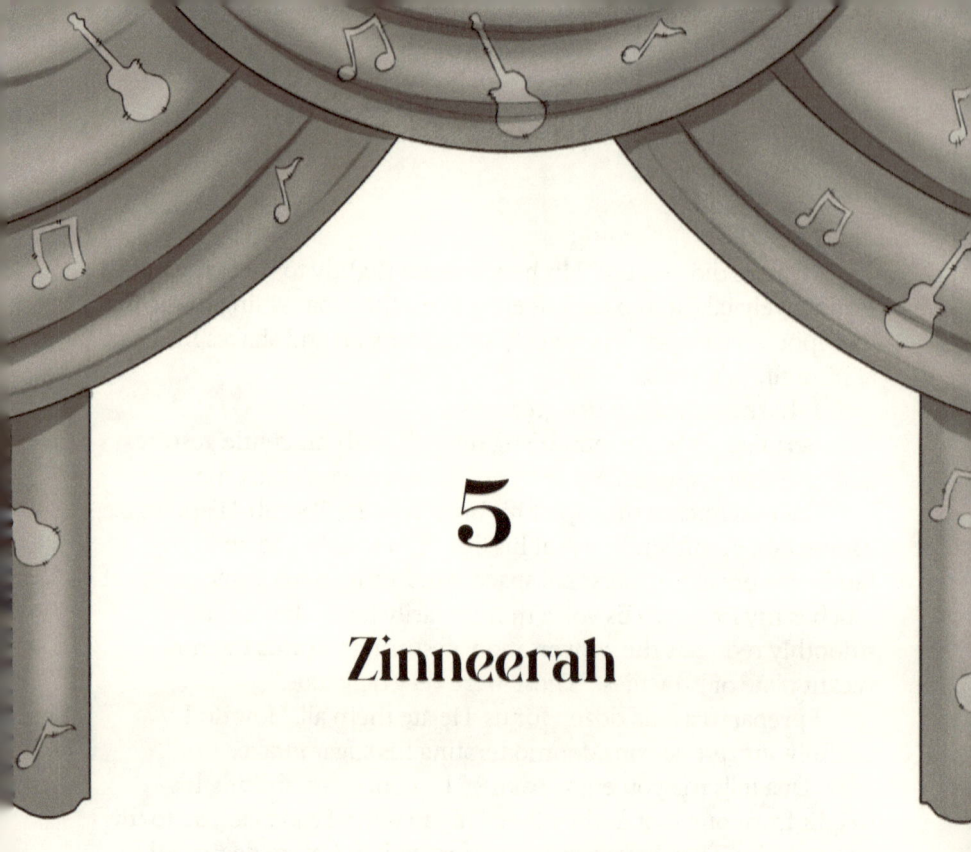

5

Zinneerah

Waking up to a text from your ex-fiancée isn't exactly the best start to the day.

Unknown: Hey, it's Saira. Saw your wedding pics on Facebook. Congrats. She's gorgeous.

I don't recall blocking her number or on Facebook, though I guess that would've been immature, I suppose. Even after she cheated on me just before our wedding and then drunk-dialed me during her bachelorette party, confessing her regrets.

Unless she's gotten herself a new number.

"Doesn't matter." I groggily rub my eyes and swipe away from my text messages, turning my attention to my email and daily schedule. A midday lecture awaits, followed by a flurry of office hours appointments. Then, there's the pressing task of grading my students' essays on the influence of digital media on politics.

The essays have been disappointing thus far—a good dozen or more caught by the university's plagiarism detection software, and another five with suspiciously similar sentences that warranted immediate action and a lengthy disciplinary email. The remaining submissions, while generally knowledgeable, often lack a compelling thesis.

I can already sense the frustration of those who are likely to fail, furiously typing negative reviews about me on that dreaded RateMyProfessor website.

I power down my phone and plug it in, getting ready for the day ahead.

Zinneerah is downstairs, fixing herself a mug of Earl Grey. I always make sure to announce my presence a bit louder on the steps, just in case she startles at the sound of me entering the kitchen.

Her eyes linger on me for a moment as she lifts the mug to her lips, painted a soft, dark brown.

"Going somewhere?" I inquire, noticing the coffee pot is ready. She brewed coffee for me? Oh, my god. A victorious smile tugs at my facial muscles as I turn to catch her response.

"Grocery store," she mouths, signing the word 'food shopping'.t

"Grocery store?" I repeat. She nods, and I pour myself a mug, reaching for the sugar container. "Alone?"

Zinneerah's black eyes are glued to the tablespoons of sugar I put in. I have a sweet tooth and a knack for caffeine—it's best to mix the two ingredients together.

I close the container and stir the mug, opening the fridge for the—"The creamer's finished?"

Food shopping, Zinneerah signs again. *I go.*

"We can go later in the evening when I'm back. Maybe grab some takeout if you'd like?"

She shakes her head, firm with her decision.

As much as I'd like to argue, I rest my case and take out a brownie from the dish. She scrutinizes that, too. "Is something the matter? You keep monitoring what I'm eating."

Zinneerah's scrutiny dissolves into anxiety in an instant. She flails her hands in front of her, head shaking. She even takes a few steps back.

I tilt my head at her. "I apologize, Zinneerah. I didn't mean it in a way to make you feel bad. I was genuinely curious." God, I need to work on my tone. I sounded like a jerk when she was only peering at my sugary intake. She studies me like I'm an impossible equation every time we're in the same vicinity, but that's just her way of understanding someone without tiring out her hands. My wife is quite observant and I should really stop calling her out on it.

Together, she signs, her eyes trained on the floor.

If I had a tail, it would be wagging violently. "Really?"

Yes.

I lick the excitement off my lips and warm them with the coffee my wife boiled for me.

I'm sorry, she signs.

"For wh—"

She takes her tea and hurries off to her bedroom where she usually likes to sit on the balcony and think about whatever is on her mind.

"Goddammit, Raees." I bang my head against the cabinet and sigh.

Someday, I wish, she might even share her thoughts with me.

Professor and Associate Dean of English Language and Literature, Mrs. Nicola Holmes, enters my lecture hall after it's been wiped out by my students.

Yes, introducing her with that title is necessary.

I stand up in a flurry of nerves. She's here for a serious topic of discussion if she's in a white pantsuit, gray hair slicked back in a bun, and frown lines carved near her lips.

Oh, she's here to slaughter me.

"Professor Holmes. I didn't know you'd returned from your sabbatical so soon."

Her smile is far from sweet. "How could I not cut it short when I heard that you, my dear Professor Raees, are a married man."

The thing with Holmes is that she's taken multiple opportunities to set me up with one of her three, literature genius daughters. I've refused each time because having higher-power doesn't mean I should accept every proposition she offers. Especially one as intimidating and critical as a marriage. Hell, she even tried to poke me for questions when I was engaged, but I didn't disclose any details—especially after it ended.

Rolling her eyes, she yanks my left hand, studying the silver band around my ring finger.

I seek her approval, even now. She was my mentor back when I was slogging through my Master's program—later on, she advised me through the harrowing process of my dissertation. There was even that time she bought me a sandwich from the vending machine when I pulled an all-nighter grading papers. The bread had mold on it, but still, it meant something.

"Who's the lucky girl?" Holmes asks, perching herself on the edge of my desk.

I hand over my phone, letting her swipe through the wedding album that's entirely dedicated to my wife. "Her name is Zinneerah," I explain with a smile. "Zinneerah Arain. Dua Arain's older sister." I pause, regretting the impending reaction. "Who, incidentally, is one of my . . . students?"

Her icy blue stare cuts to me. "You're married to your student's sister?"

Yeah, I assumed this would sound unethical despite that there isn't anything that's unethical about our relationship. "Professor, this is *that* Zinneerah. The singer? Studio 365?"

Holmes's eyes narrow as she returns her focus to the screen. Her breath catches as she swipes through the pictures faster, zooming in on Zinneerah's face. "How?"

"Fa—"

"Do not say 'fate,' Shaan."

"I'm sorry."

Rubbing the nape of my neck, I begin recounting how everything with Zinneerah unfolded naturally, from Dua's introduction to the moments that felt less orchestrated and more like life aligning on its own terms. As I speak, I watch Holmes carefully, her face softening. Her initial disappointment fades, and something friendlier takes its place. By the time I finish, she's already stepping forward, inviting me into a hug that somehow lasts an eternity.

"Now, listen closely." She fixes me with a pointed look, her index finger raised in warning. "Do not, under any circumstances, let this marriage lead to any favoritism in your classroom. Are we clear?"

Amusement lifts one end of my lips up. She's already rolling her eyes. "Wasn't I your favorite, Professor?"

"You were the least annoying, yes."

I suppress a chuckle, not wanting to break her serious facade entirely. "Well, Dua is a remarkable student. She's been proactive, taking the initiative to seek an internship in sports journalism. I can't deny I've been helping her find a position—it's deserved."

Holmes raises a brow. "Who did you reach out to?" She already knows, of course, which is why she's masking her disappointment. I should've gone to her first. With all her traveling, she's built this web of connections with journalists everywhere. It's her forte. "Raees?"

"Yes?"

"Who?"

I clench my jaw. "Anne Williams."

At the mention of the name, Holmes groans.

The rivalry between her and Anne Williams dates back decades, to the late seventies when they were locked in a fierce academic competition. Not that Holmes didn't have her share of rivals, but Anne, in particular, was the pebble in her shoe that never quite went away. Now, Anne stands as a veritable titan in sports journalism, a legend in her own right.

"Anne Williams," she repeats, dragging out the name as if tasting something bitter. She leans back, crossing her arms, and I can feel her recalibrating. "If Mrs. Williams doesn't reply within the next three days, send me your email outlining Miss Arian's achievements and her interest in sports journalism. I've got a few contacts in that particular field. I'm sure we can find something suitable for her. Sounds good?"

"Absolutely. I know I'm overdue in expressing my gratitude, but thank you once again for everything you've done for me, Professor." I extend both hands to shake hers. "I'd also love for you to meet Zinneerah now that you're back. She's a fantastic listener."

"I'm sure she would." With a decisive shake, Professor Holmes turns to leave but suddenly stops, spinning back around. "Bring her as your plus-one to Professor Wei's retirement party next month. I'll send you the details."

"I'll check with her first."

Holmes gives me a once-over. "No playing favorites, Professor Shaan."

I flash a smile. "Ditto, Professor Holmes."

Pushing a quarter into the shopping cart, I free it from its latch and wheel it toward Zinneerah, who stands by the sliding doors of the supermarket.

She's wearing loose black trousers paired with a snug long-sleeved black top that highlights her collarbones. As always, her gorgeous hair is braided into a crown on her head, and her bowed-lips are painted a warm coffee-brown.

She's so stunning.

"Do you have a list?" I ask, pushing the cart through the store entrance. Zinneerah unfolds a handwritten list, and my heart tenderizes. She took the time to write it out instead of just typing it on her Notes app. Yes, I'll always make a big deal out of every little thing my wife does. She truly is one of a kind.

We head to the vegetable and fruit section first, and I watch as she struggles to open the translucent bags. She glances at me with that adorable look, offering it. I peel it open with ease and assist her each time she needs to bag something.

I suppress a sigh when she points at the tomatoes, silently asking for my permission to buy them. First, it was the cilantro, then the mint, the peppers, and now the garlic—every time she hesitates. All I want to do is cradle her face in my hands and whisper, "My love, you can buy this entire grocery store without my permission, and I wouldn't think twice about it." Instead, I settle for: "Zinneerah, you don't need to ask me. If you want the tomatoes, just put them in the bag and toss them in the cart. You're the captain here, okay?"

She purses her lips for a moment, thinking it over, then nods.

In the international aisle, Zinneerah carefully arranges the boxes and packets of spices. Unlike me, who would just toss them in without a second thought.

Serenity settles on her face when she's in the baking section. There's even a little skip in her steps to get there as fast she can as if it's a Black Friday sale.

Holding up a box of custard powder and a cake batter mix, she gives them both a little shake. Seeing her so excited and vibrating with energy bakes my heart at a thousand degrees. I mean, look at her.

"Both," I say.

Blinks. Lots of adorable blinks.

I inch the cart forward, and she carefully places the boxes inside, glancing at me with raised lashes as if she's waiting for me to reject the idea at the last second. When I simply smile back, she turns around, her cheeks flushed pink, and starts searching for the specific baking tools she needs.

In the dairy aisle, I take a moment to grab a yogurt I love as a snack for work, checking the expiration date. "Next week? Damn—"

"Jesus Christ, lady!"

Suddenly, my attention is yanked away by the sound of something crashing to the floor.

I turn to see Zinneerah huddled down, rubbing her palms together as if she's washing them or trying to warm them, then closing them into fists. Meanwhile, a bulky man is picking himself up off the floor, covered in broken eggshells and yolk.

I rush over to Zinneerah and position myself protectively in front of her. "Is there a problem?"

"You tell me, buddy," he snaps, gesturing to his shirt now smeared with egg yolk and bits of shell. "I saw your lady struggling to grab a carton, so I stepped in to help, and she shoved me back."

My eyes narrow. "You approached her from behind?"

"She had the damn door open!" he spits back, crossing his arms like he's somehow the victim here.

"The door being open doesn't mean you sneak up on her. You could've easily walked around, maybe said 'excuse me' or offered to help without startling her. It's common sense." I glance down at Zinneerah, my voice softening as I take in her bright teary eyes, and the way her lashes are still fluttering with the shock of it. I reach out, brushing her hand. "I'll handle this. If you'd like, you can wait by the cart or stay close to me. The choice is yours."

Just then, I feel a tap on my shoulder, followed by the man's irritating voice. "You gonna reimburse me, buddy? She ruined my favorite t-shirt."

At that moment, a worker approaches, surveying the spilled eggs on the floor and the stains on the man's shirt and shoes. "Oh, no. I apologize for the inconvenience, sir."

"It's not your fault," he says, jabbing a chubby finger at my wife. "She should be the one apologizing. Hey, do you hear me, lady? I'll take that apo—"

"She's not apologizing for something that isn't her fault," I cut in, taking a careful step toward him and feeling the cracked eggs crunch beneath my shoes. He clears his throat, glaring up at me as I dig into my wallet, pulling out a fifty-dollar bill and sticking it to his t-shirt. "Are we good?"

"Yeah," he mutters. "We're good."

"Great." I turn to the employee, flashing a smile. "I'm really sorry for the commotion, Miss. Would you like me to help clean up the aisle?"

She flushes red, shaking her head. "No, it's fine. Don't worry about paying for the damage either."

"Thank you for understanding." I shoot a glare in the man's direction, then turn to my wife. "Let's go, Zinneerah."

She pinches my sweater to stop me, then turns around to face the man ogling the fifty-dollar bill in his hands. With a clap to get his attention, she signs, I'm sorry.

I take a sharp breath, nearly reaching out to hold her hands.

"Oh, shit," the man mutters, suddenly looking guilty. "I didn't realize she was deaf. I'm sorry, lady."

"She's not—"

Zinneerah shakes her head, cutting me off. She takes my arm, holding it for a moment as she steadies her breathing, then signs, *Home.*

6

Zinneerah

I sit in the middle of my walk-in closet with my guitar bag in front of me.

For the past half hour, I've been contemplating whether to unzip it.

Inside lies my first guitar, which Baba purchased for me on my tenth birthday. A customized blackwood, Martin D X-2E, with a golden crow embellished on the pickguard.

I've composed nine hundred pieces using this guitar, starting from middle school, then playing in cafés and bars, and performing a solo on the day of my graduation from SLU with a Bachelor of Music degree.

I packed it up midway through my previous relationship and forgot it ever existed afterwards.

Dua must've snuck it into the U-Haul truck when I was moving my things into Raees' house a week before our wedding. It only caught my eye then before I tucked it behind my clothes to keep it away.

I pinch the zipper and run it along the shape of the guitar bag, lifting the case, and shuddering as my mind transports into an unwarranted memory.

"No way!" I lift the cover of the guitar case, and as soon as I see the gleaming blackwood inside, my eyes start to fill with tears. "No freakin' way! Baba, you really got me this?" My gaze flicks over to my siblings; Shahzad's grinning like he knew this secret all along, and little Dua is already waddling toward my new treasure.

Before she can reach out with her sticky fingers, I gently pull the guitar out, clutching it close. Shahzad scoops Dua up just in time, plopping her onto his lap and peppering her with kisses to quite her.

"You like it?" Baba asks from his spot on the armchair, his eyes warm and twinkling. "It's the same one you spotted when we went window shopping."

"How did you know I wanted it?"

He chuckles, settling onto the floor beside me. "Meri zindagi, you might not say much, but your eyes do all the talking." I look at him, silently asking if I can play it. He smiles, nudging my shoulder. "You don't need my permission, Zinnie. You're the captain now." He glances at my siblings with a playful frown. "Was that offensive? I've never actually seen Captain Phillips."

"The only thing offensive was your shitty impersonation, Baba."

"Shut up, Shahz!" I snap.

"You shut up!"

"Enough!" Baba interrupts, giving Shahzad the "dad glare." I flash him a triumphant smile. "Apologize to your sister."

"Me? She started it!"

"And you, as the older brother, should be setting an example for your sisters. Apologize, and while you're at it, apologize to Dua for scaring her."

Dua giggles, holding her tiny hands up. "I'm not scared."

Baba winks at her, dropping the strict act for a moment. "I know, meri pyari." He's back to being stern a second later, though. "Go on. Apologize."

Shahzad sigh. "Fine. I'm sorry for raising my voice at you, Zinnie."

"Apology accepted." I lean over, and Baba plants a kiss on my cheek. Shahzad tries to dodge, but Baba catches him and smacks a kiss on his forehead anyway.

I hug the guitar close. "Can I play now?"

"Yes, yes." Baba laughs, settling back with a proud smile. "Let's hear something from our little Gilmour."

I snap the case shut, shutting away the memory along with it.

Walking out of the closet, I head straight to bed, pulling the comforter around me. Why am I still like this? Curled up, hiding from things that shouldn't have power over me anymore? I close my eyes, hoping sleep might give me an escape, but it just comes in pieces, giving way to flashes of moments I wish I could unfeel—

Three knocks on the door pull me out of my fog, and I flinch, my heart jumping into my throat.

"Zinneerah." It's Raees. "Would you like to join me for dinner?"

I feel my body ease a bit, but I just sink back into the comforter, tucking my chin down. I want to say yes, but I'm stuck. And God, I hate it. I hate that a single moment from a grocery store still has me blaming myself for how I reacted, like I'm the one who did something wrong.

She's not apologizing for something that isn't her fault.

It only happened days ago, but I can still feel the unwelcome press of that stranger's hand at my waist, his chest too close against my back. I'm tall—Abbu's genes gave me a solid 5'9"—but those eggs were stacked high and shoved way back on the shelf. Just before I could turn to ask Raees to reach them, that man closed in. When I felt his clammy grip, I acted instinctively, shoving him away, recoiling from the unwanted touch.

"Clap twice for yes, once for no," he says softly, patiently waiting.

I want to. I really do. But instead of clapping, I just lay here. Because maybe he'd be better off without a wife who freezes up over some small, stupid touch. A wife who wouldn't be like this.

Raees' footsteps fade away.

I cover myself and squeeze my eyes shut.

Dear brain, this is a safe space. Raees is a safe man. He had defended you at the grocery store. He protected you from that man. He paid for the groceries. He is going to take care of you. He is a good man. This is a safe, good space. Please, try to understand.

I slip a hand out from under my comforter, fishing for my phone and pulling it back under the covers to dial Dua on FaceTime. The camera opens and, man, do I look like a mess?

Black streaks of dried eyeliner trail down my cheek from all the ugly-crying I've been doing these past few days. And my smudged lipstick looks more like I had an intense make-out session with a bowl of melted chocolate than anything else.

Chocolate. Sweet. Raees. *Damn it.*

Dua doesn't pick up, of course. She's probably monitoring a game or out with the guys' volleyball team again.

Taking a deep breath, I close my eyes, sinking back into the quiet, and repeat my bedtime mantra.

This is your home now. This is a safe space you'll be sharing with your husband. He is a safe man. He will not hurt you. This is a safe space that belongs to you, too. This is your home now. This is a safe space you'll be sharing with your husband. He is a safe man. He will not hurt you. This is a safe space that belongs to you, too. This is your home now. This is a safe space you'll be sharing with your husband. He is a safe man. He will not hurt you. This is a safe space that belongs to you.

I wake up to the still-dark quiet of six a.m., eyes gritty but mind alert, already ticking through the steps of my routine.

Wash face. Brush teeth. Braid hair. Cotton sweater and maxi skirt. I've followed this ritual for years.

Out on the balcony, I step into the cool morning air, locking eyes with the Bells' orange cat perched on the fence between our yards. She stares at me with her green eyes. I give her a small wave; she just blinks slowly to humor me.

In the kitchen, I brew a cup of Earl Grey, breathing in the soothing scent, and start breakfast for Raees and myself.

The truth is, I'm terrified of diving into a career, of putting myself out there in a world that still feels too big and too loud. So here I am, leaning into Mama's training, determined to be the best house-wife I can be. Raees deserves that, at the very least—he waited an entire year for me to say yes, without a single complaint.

After the way he stood up for me without hesitation, I can't shake the feeling that he deserves more than I know how to give. Every little thing he does—always checking with me before even the smallest gestures, treating me like I'm something precious—it's rare, and it's something I want to spend this marriage understanding.

I start with his coffee, carefully scooping in three tablespoons of sugar even as I second-guess myself. Three's a lot, but I don't want to mess up his morning by holding back. I pour in the oat-milk creamer, debating whether to text Ramishah and ask if her little brother has always been so committed to his sweet tooth.

When the toaster dings, I spread strawberry jam over one slice and butter on the other—more generous with the butter than the jam—before pressing them together. I slice up a crisp apple, add a handful of blueberries and some mango cubes, and set them in a small bowl with his favorite spoon.

Upstairs, the shower is running.

I take a long breath, drying my hands on a dish towel before starting on his lunch. I bought all his ingredients yesterday, carefully chosen just for him since the pantry's already packed with my go-tos.

In the pan, garlic sizzles as I add the chicken breast, sprinkling paprika, pepper, salt, onion powder, and a hint of sriracha over it. The kitchen fills with the smell of spices, and I turn to the baguette slices, spreading mayo, a dab of ranch, and another small swirl of sriracha. I layer on fresh lettuce and tomato slices, then gently place the grilled chicken on top, pressing the sandwich closed.

Raees steps into the kitchen, looking almost surprised to see me already awake, his gaze sweeping over the breakfast I've set up. He's in a navy dress shirt, sleeves rolled to his elbows, glasses slightly askew as he blinks at me.

"Good morning," he murmurs, still looking a bit dazed.

I sign, *Breakfast for you.*

It takes a minute for him to process. Then, a smile. He picks up his coffee, takes a sip, and I hold my breath. "Is it selfish if I ask you to make my coffee every morning from now on?"

I shake my head with a small smile.

He raises a brow. "Are you sure?"

Yes.

His grin deepens, and he notices the sandwich I'm wrapping up in a lunchbox. "What's that?" he asks, curious.

For you, I sign.

He blinks, a bit taken aback. "For me?"

Lunch.

"For *me?*" He repeats, eyes widening as if he's been handed a priceless treasure.

I nod, closing the lid on the lunchbox and sliding it across the counter to him. *I will make lunch for you always.*

He stares at the box, and then at me, the sunrays brightening his gaze. It's adorable, really. The slight tilt of his head, the purse of his mouth. "I apologize. I didn't catch that."

I point to the lunchbox, then to myself, and give a thumbs-up.

"He chuckles, rendered speechless by the bare minimum. His hand runs down the side of his face, like he's trying to hide how much this means to him. "Well, if that's the case, I'll make you proud and savor every last crumb. Deal?"

I nod.

He glances over my shoulder. "Have you already eaten?"

I lift my Earl Grey as an answer.

"That's your breakfast?" he asks, lifting an eyebrow.

Later, I sign, trying to shrug it off.

"You'll eat . . . later?" he repeats, his brows knitting together in concern. Without a second thought, he splits his sandwich in half and offers me the larger piece. "Eat. Now. Or I'm calling in sick, and all your hard work on this incredible lunch will be for nothing." He dangles the half-sandwich in front of me.

I carefully take it without brushing his hand, and his face lights up in a way that makes my chest tingle. Like a kid, he munches his sandwich and pops a blueberry into his mouth, watching me as he chews. He even nudges the bowl of fruit toward me and pulls out the stool beside him.

I shake my head, gesturing that I prefer to stand when I eat.

"Very well." He shrugs, standing up to match me, now towering over the kitchen counter. It's small, but my heart skips at his gentle thoughtfulness, and I feel the faintest twitch of a smile.

"You can drive, yes?" he asks.

I nod.

"I'm not sure if you've had the grand tour of the garage, but there's an extra car in there. It's yours if you ever need to get out."

My hands instinctively mime steering a wheel. A car? Then I point to myself. *For me?*

His cheeks are still full from the last bite. After a quick sip of coffee, he swallows and says, "Yup. It'll always be ready if you need some fresh air. Maybe a trip to see Dua or a friend."

I don't have any friends, I sign, forgetting to slow down.

"What was that?" he asks, frowning slightly.

Ah, shit. I probably signed too fast. *Nothing.*

"No worries."

Side by side, we eat our breakfast in the soft early light.

7

Raees

My wife made me lunch.

My *wife* made *me* lunch.
Lunch.
She made me lunch.

A sandwich, something I wouldn't typically choose, but if Zinneerah made it, I know it'll be different. It's her love in every slice.
Snap!

A quick picture, and into the group chat it goes to Ramishah and my mom.

I finish swiping through my text messages and take a bite of the sandwich, savoring its flavors as I make my way towards the music building. The same building where my wife spent her student days. If I want to understand Zinneerah better without bombarding her with questions, this seems like the right place to start.

It's a quaint structure with tall, arched windows that let in the afternoon light. The bricks are weathered and layered with ivy, giving the building a sense of history of its first appearance in the 1890's. A few students pass by, some deep in conversation, others rushing with instrument cases in hand.

Inside, advertisement posters and bulletin boards detailing upcoming concerts, recitals, and music festivals line the walls of the hallway leading to the practice rooms and classrooms. Soft murmurs of students tuning instruments, and the occasional burst of laughter sounds from one of the rooms.

"There they are," I whisper, drawn to the graduation photos lining the left side of the room.

Immediately, I spot Zinneerah's gentle smile and dark eyes amongst the sea of still faces. She had bangs back then, but her makeup looks just the same.

"Can I help you?"

I step back from the photo of my wife and hastily stash the remaining half of my sandwich back into the lunch box. A short man with a grey beard and wavy, silver hair approaches me. He's dressed like me in a cashmere sweater and trousers.

"Nice to meet you. I'm Raees Shaan. I work as a professor in the journalism department." I instinctively pull out my lanyard badge, just in case he's suspicious. Even though we're in a public space.

"Professor Daniels," he greets, shaking my hand. "What brings you to our department, Professor Shaan?"

"My wife."

He blinks, looking slightly uneasy.

"She's not a student anymore!" I clarify quickly. "She used to be here when I was finishing my Ph.D." My finger singles her out in the first row among the other distinguished students. "That's her."

"*What*?" Professor Daniels exclaims, adjusting his glasses. He shifts his gaze between Zinneerah's frozen expression and my wide smile. "Zinneerah Arain is your wife?"

"Proudly," I confirm. "Did you teach her?"

"Yes," he mutters, stepping back with a distant look. "And she was exceptional. I always hoped she'd visit after graduation." He smiles faintly. "But I suppose she's been busy with her singing and songwriting?"

My heart sinks at that. I don't understand how Zinneerah lost her voice—whether it was an accident or something more traumatic that happened after she graduated. And it's not just her voice that's missing. It's like she's lost herself—the vibrant, rock-and-roll persona she always used to carry whenever I saw her.

But now she's just . . . she's *just*.

And I love her just as much, if not more. There isn't a limit to my love for her.

I clear my throat, trying to mask my curiosity. "Professor Daniels, what was it about Zinneerah that made her such a standout? She hardly mentions her university days—gets all shy when I ask."

"That's unlike her." Professor Daniels chuckles, and gives me a friendly pat on the back, steering us down the hall. "Ah, well. She was a marvel with any instrument that had strings. Guitar, sitar, even the banjo once, just for laughs. And she wasn't just playing them, she owned them." He opens his office door and waves me in, then settles behind his desk. "And her voice . . . well, she'd capture a room. Imagine Amy Winehouse, but with a sense of delicateness that could bring you to tears." His eyes soften as he remembers. "So much heart in every note."

Well, one thing's for certain, she captured me by the very first note six years ago. "I wish she'd tell me all about it."

He smiles knowingly. "Classic Zinneerah. Humble to a fault. She's probably the last one who'd ever brag, but the whole department knew how special she was. She poured her soul into everything she touched."

Pride fills my chest. "Sounds just like my Zinneerah."

Professor Daniels leans back, reaching into a drawer, and pulls out a small stack of CDs. "I figured you might like to hear some of her work." He selects a disc and slides it into his computer, turning the monitor so we can both see the screen. "This is from her sophomore showcase. Think of it as an exam, but with an audience of potential recruiters and industry contacts. It's where she really shone."

The screen flickers, and there she is—Zinneerah, stepping onto the stage from the left, acoustic guitar in hand. The audience claps, and she gives a shy smile, looking exactly like she does when she's flustered now: head a bit down, that slight tilt of her chin. She's wearing a black turtleneck, black dress pants, and the high platform boots she still owns.

She steps up to the mic. "Hello to the Saint Lawrence University music department and everyone who's joined us today. I'm Zinneerah Arain. A second-year student from Monday to Friday, and a composer every day."

I find myself leaning in, grinning at the sound of her little laugh.

She adjusts her guitar strap across her shoulder. "I'll be performing an original today," she says. "I wrote this at three in the morning on my kitchen floor . . . on my father's death anniversary. Every song I write is, in some way, for him." She glances down, clears her throat. "This one's called "House of Gold.""

As soon as her fingers sweep over the strings, the first powerful chord jolts through me, transporting me back to that night, sitting in the front row of Studio 365, watching her pour herself out on the small, circular stage. She begins to sing, and my grip tightens on the armrests, my pulse climbing.

Her voice starts soft, then builds up, the emotion swelling with each verse, the chords growing louder. Each sharp, downward strum makes the guitar jerk slightly, like she's wrestling with it, wringing every ounce of feeling out of the wood and strings. Her eyes squeeze shut as she sings, her voice catching on parts that clutch at her heart, and in turn, mine. At one point, she smiles, a bittersweet curve, as she sings about a fragment from her childhood in that "house of gold."

A hand gently touches my arm. "Are you okay?"

I startle at Professor Daniels' voice. My fingers brush against my damp cheeks as I quickly swipe at my burning eyes. "Yeah. Fine."

Not fine. Not even close. It wasn't just Zinneerah's voice or her confidence that hit me like this—it was the song. The one she wrote for her late father. A song so full of love and admiration that it made me ache for something I never had. I love my wife, but I don't think I can listen to "House of Gold" again.

"I'm glad Zinneerah is doing well," Professor Daniels says. "She worried me for a while there."

My brow furrows. "What do you mean?"

He looks past me, gathering his thoughts. "She wasn't quite herself that last year. Barely any performances, hardly any recordings I could keep. I thought maybe I'd been too nosy, or asked too many questions, but . . ." He trails off, giving me a reassuring smile. "That's all history. Just let her know I miss her."

I make a mental note of his words for later. "Of course."

"Oh, one more thing." Professor Daniels shuffles through a stack of papers and pulls out a flyer, passing it to me. "If she's available, we're looking for additional guitarists for our summer concert next month. A few alumni are joining, and I'd love for Zinneerah to be one of them."

I scan the flyer, noting the date—August 31st at the university's football field. It's a reunion event, raising funds for the music department, with performances by both current students and alumni. His contact information is there for anyone interested in participating.

"Thank you, Professor," I say, folding the flyer carefully and tucking it into my pocket. "I'll make sure she sees this."

He nods, a fond smile spreading. "It would mean a lot to hear her play again. She'll always have a place in our department."

As I rise to leave, he extends a hand, which I shake firmly. "It was really nice speaking to you, Professor."

"Take care," he says. "And give Zinneerah my best."

"I will. Thank you, again, for everything."

Heading down the hall, I pull out the flyer one more time, picturing the moment I'll hand it to her. Knowing her, she'll try to play it cool, but I'll catch the excitement in her eyes.

The thought has me smiling all the way down the hall.

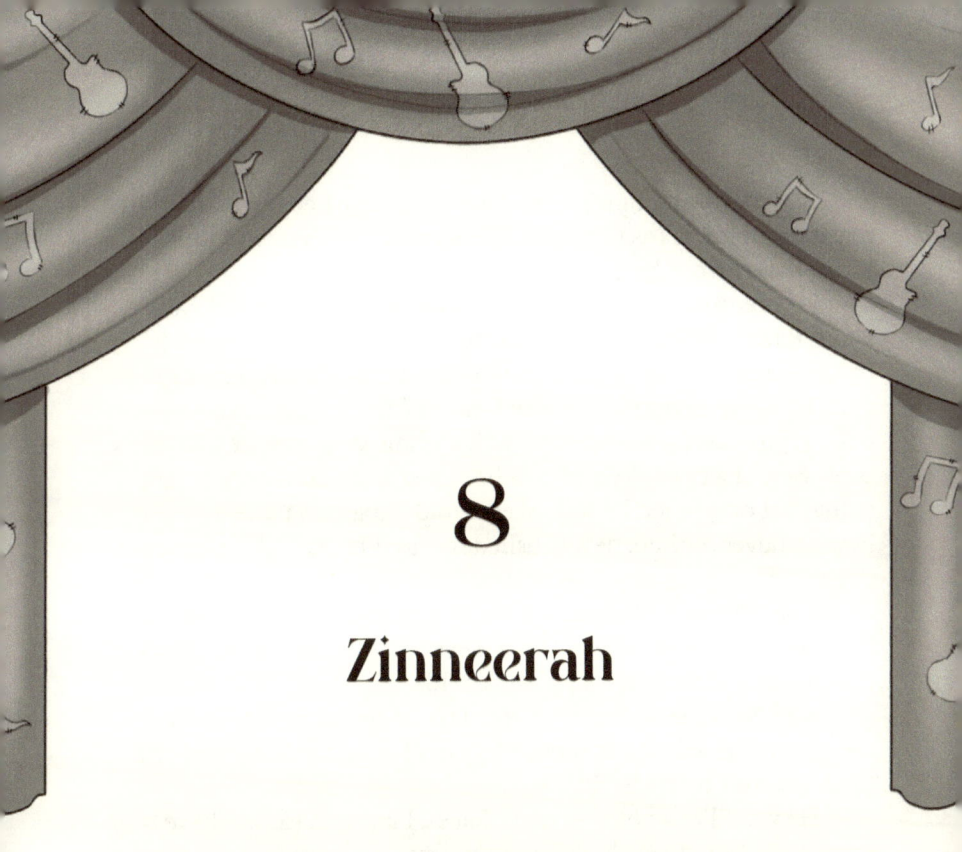

8

Zinneerah

I stand over Baba's grave, cradling a bouquet of white roses and a fresh stack of wedding photos that arrived in the mail this morning.

As soon as I tore open the envelope and saw the glossy images, I thought of him. He should be the first to see them before anyone else.

I lay the bouquet on the cool stone, nestling it close to his name carved into the granite. Then I place a single framed photo of Raees and me beside it. He stands with his arm around my shoulder, smiling. I'm beside him, doing the opposite, eyes distant, caught mid-thought. The photographer had kept bullying me to smile, but all I managed was this awkward look. Maybe Baba will find it funny.

Slowly, I sink down onto the grass, hugging my knees to my chest.

I've come here often since he passed, stealing quiet moments to share my thoughts and secrets. But with the wedding preparations, and Mama's constant presence, these visits have become harder to make room for. It's as if, by getting married, I've stepped a little further away from him.

I remember so clearly the first time I came here to tell Baba about Raees. I had pictured him sitting right across from me, his hands wrapped around mine, listening with that familiar spark in his eyes. I'd spoken confidently, like I was making my case in court—telling him how I'd made Raees wait a whole year, how he was Dua's professor, of all people, and how he talked and talked once he got going, but only when he was asked. I told Baba how patient he was, how he never pushed, never rushed me, as if he had all the time in the world.

I can almost feel myself blushing again when I described his lopsided smile, those honey-brown eyes that crinkle up into half-moons behind those flimsy glasses of his.

And Baba, he was smiling, too. I could see it in my mind as clearly as if he were right there. He knew I wasn't holding back this time, that this man was different.

He would've wanted to meet Raees, I know it. He would've been eager to sit him down, look him in the eye, and give him the classic father's speech about taking care of his eldest daughter. He would've teased me, too, warning Raees that I can be clingy, that he'd better watch his tone because Baba would come back from the dead if he ever dared to raise his voice at me. I can almost hear his laugh, that smooth, deep chuckle, and I know he would have just wanted to hold me close.

I cried that day, right here, feeling so full of love and loss all at once. I let myself imagine his strong arms around me, like they'd always been. And when I wiped my tears and looked up, he was gone, the moment slipping away grain by grain, like sand through an hourglass.

Nothing but a stone saying, Yusuf Arain: the first son, a devoted husband, and a loving father of three.

"Baba." My voice scrapes out. "I don't know what I'm doing. I don't know how to be anything. A good daughter. A sister. A wife." An unexpected breeze stirs brushes through my hair like a gentle hand.

My chin trembles as I force out more. "Sometimes, I wish you'd taken me with you. It'd be easier than this. Than feeling like I'm . . . like I'm disappointing everyone. Over and over."

It's true.

In high school, I didn't care about sports or fashion. I was the quiet one in the back row, scribbling in my lock-and-key journal, writing cringe-worthy love songs about everyone else—the soccer captain and his girlfriend who wore pink every day like it was a uniform, the chess prodigy and the goth girl sneaking smokes under the bleachers, the two rivals in English class who nearly came to blows over Shakespeare. Everyone else seemed to have these dramatic little storylines going on, and there I was, writing songs about their lives because mine just didn't have anything worth singing about.

Then I got to university and realized I wasn't even that unique. Everyone around me loved music just as much as I did—only they were better at it. Way better. I was a small fish, barely staying afloat, dragging myself through classes and assignments. Most nights I was crying into my pillow, running on no sleep, feeling so burnt out I thought I'd go up in smoke. Alone, miserable, trapped in this tiny, airless bubble I'd built around myself.

And on top of all that, I was still grieving Baba's death.

By sophomore year, I couldn't carry it all anymore. I had to let go of something. So, I unpacked the baggage, sifted through everything, kept my father's memory, and tried to start fresh.

I signed up for coffeehouse open mics to sing covers. I stopped writing sappy pop ballads and taught myself to play classic rock and indie instead. I found friends who felt like family, people who made me laugh, who saw me. I broke out of that bubble. For the first time, I started to feel like maybe I had something to offer after all.

And then, just as I finally hit my stride, just as I felt like I was getting somewhere, I lost it all.

Sniffling, I rub my eyes with the undersides of my wrists, the lace on my sleeves grazing against my skin. A small, empty laugh sputters out of me. I must look so pathetic, standing here in front of the man who once kept the fragile threads of my life stitched together, who held himself together just for us.

In the end, maybe the only thing I'm really good at is falling apart.

I look down at the wedding photo.

"I know, Baba. I know Mama loved someone else. You never said a word about it—not to me, not even to her. But Shahzad told me and Dua everything. You knew, too, right? She never loved you the way you loved her, and yet . . . every day, you tried. You fought for her, even when it was hopeless, even when she kept her heart locked away from you, from all of us. That's the kind of man you were. You gave everything, knowing there was nothing for you in return." I waver, choking on the words. "A part of her hated you for being so good. For being everything she couldn't be. Maybe she thought she didn't deserve you."

I cough from overworking my voice and take out my water bottle, gulping down the cool liquid.

Do I feel sympathy for Mama? Yes. Shahzad said she was pushed into an arranged marriage with a stranger. That wasn't her choice; it was her family's, and I can understand the bitterness that must have come with that.

But could she have tried to move on? To see Baba for who he was, to let herself care about him after everything he did for her? He promised he'd take care of her, uprooted his whole life to bring her here, to the West, away from the very family that had forced her hand. He did everything he could to give her a fresh start. She could have met him halfway.

But she didn't. She didn't even try.

She took it all out on Shahzad because he was the oldest, the easiest target. And she kept going back to the very country that ruined her life, clinging to her home like it was her only comfort, pretending we didn't even exist.

But sometimes, when I look at her sunken face, I see flashes of my childhood that I had forgotten. I *imagine* her and Baba dancing in the kitchen, or kissing when us children weren't looking, or her treating him like a human being. Treating *all* of us like we're one, big happy family.

"You don't think I'll end up like her, do you, Baba?" I run my thumb along the rough ridges of the bottle cap. "I'm trying to be different. I chose a husband with qualities that remind me of yours. That's why I said yes to him. But I can't ignore the fact that it's her blood running through me, too." Another dry cough rattles through me, and I press a hand to my chest. "I did make progress today, though. I got up early and made him breakfast and lunch. He was so happy over something so simple. He looked at me like I'd given him the world. It made me proud to be able to give him that. It made me want to set my alarm and do this every day. To be that source of comfort for him, the way you always were for us. Even if I'm a mess inside, it feels good to give him a little bit of peace."

I vow I won't be like Mama in her marriage. I won't take Raees's kindness for granted. I won't let him carry my burdens, or shoulder half of the work at home. If he keeps being the man he is, I know I'll come to love him, in time. I'll give him not just one child, but children—when I'm ready—and I'll be there for them. I'll grow old and gray beside him, and one day, we'll be buried side by side. Because he's my husband. Because I chose him, and he chose me.

Warmth springs in my chest, pooling down to my stomach, filling me with something I haven't felt in a long time. These thoughts are breathing life back into a heart I'd almost forgotten how to use.

A chime pulls me out of my thoughts. I fish my phone from my pocket, pressing down on the security notification: the front door has opened.

My lips curve up.

I stand up, dust off my bag, and gently rearrange the flowers, tucking the photo snugly between the petals.

"My husband's home now," I murmur. "I want to ask him how his day was." Oh, God. I'm only just realizing how much I want to do this simple thing. "Next time, I'll bring him with me."

I lean down, pressing a kiss to his gravestone, letting my forehead rest against the cool stone for a moment longer.

Then, with a deep breath, I turn and make my way out of the graveyard, heading home.

Raees is standing at the counter, dicing vegetables when I arrive.

He glances up, then does a double-take, and I brace myself to apologize—for slipping out without a word, for not texting him where I was, for the mess I must look with my braid half-undone and my lipstick barely there after all the nervous biting.

But he breaks into a smile that makes my thoughts scatter.

"Welcome back," he says. Not a sliver of worry in his voice. Doesn't he care that it's eight in the evening and I was out alone? Or does he just trust me that much? "I noticed you didn't take the car. How was your walk?"

I carefully approach him across the counter and type out a response on my phone: I went to see my father. I'm sorry if I was late. I'll text you next time. I didn't mean to worry you.

Raees reads it and his smile softens. "Or you could just take me with you next time," he says, "so I can pay my respects to Abbu-ji."

The first time Raees met my father was the day after I told Mama I wanted to marry him. I'd spent hours at Baba's grave that morning, turning the decision over and over in my mind, picking apart every tiny flaw I could think of, looking for some reason to back out. But nothing came. After a year of talking—well, him doing most of the talking—I was so at ease with Raees that my very soul knew he was meant to be my husband.

It was a beautiful day, sunny with a breeze, as if Baba was listening. When I told him about Raees, it felt . . . right. And then the next day, when Mama told his family about my agreement, he surprised me by asking if he could visit Baba's grave himself to get his blessing.

He showed up with a bouquet of roses and lilies, and asked if I'd mind giving him a few minutes alone. So, Dua and I stood at a distance, watching as he knelt there, talking quietly, a huge, earnest smile on his face the whole time. He didn't stop smiling, not once. He looked so genuine, so open, like he was really trying to introduce himself, to say 'I'll take care of her.'

"You don't have to apologize to me for seeing your father, Zinneerah," Raees says. "However, I would like it if you text me beforehand for safety purposes."

I should have let him know—I can only imagine how worried he might've been. I almost type out another "I'm sorry" on my phone, but instead, I delete it and send a little smiling emoji.

I catch his eye and sign, *What is that?*

Dinner for us.

My eyebrows rise in surprise. *Learn ASL?*

He taps his temple, then gestures toward me, that playful smile tugging at his lips. "For you."

I swallow hard, suddenly feeling my face flush. He turns back to the stove, oblivious, and I press my hands to my warm cheeks, trying to calm the flutter in my chest with a few quiet breaths.

"I picked something up on the way home," Raees says, heading toward his bag on the dining table. He must have gone straight into the kitchen when he came in; he's still in his work clothes.

A wave of guilt sinks my shoulders. If I'd gotten home on time, I could've made us dinner. He's probably exhausted, running on fumes, and yet he's still somehow over-the-top enthusiastic about making dinner for us.

"Here we go." Raees approaches, stopping just a few steps away. With a little flourish, he pulls something from behind his back—*a diary?* Bound in smooth black leather, with a gold lock and a tiny key dangling from it.

My fingers tremble as I take it from him, brushing my hand over its surface.

"I thought we could use it to share the things we're too afraid to say out loud," Raees says, a soft glow in his eyes. "It doesn't have to be just the sad stuff. You could tell me about a childhood memory with your father—something that's hard to talk about, maybe—and I could share some of mine." His jaw tightens. "Though I can't promise mine will be as lighthearted as yours."

Ramishah once mentioned, almost offhandedly, that their father was still alive but had become a distant figure. I'd been on the verge of telling her she should visit him before it was too late. But looking at Raees' expression now, and remembering the guarded look on his sister's face back then, it seems their relationship with him isn't like the one I shared with my father.

Not even close.

"Or, you could keep it all to yourself," he continues on. "I've been writing since I could hold a pencil. Every time I couldn't say something to my family, I'd write it instead. The good, the bad, the beautiful, the ugly—it all went onto the page. It's . . . cathartic, you know? Better than keeping it all locked inside." He gives me a small smile. "There's a reason it's called 'writing.' Everything you write is right."

I duck my head, hiding a smile as I fumble with the key, rolling its edges between my fingers before slipping it into the lock. With a soft click, the diary opens, and the scent of fresh paper wafts up. The spine creaks faintly as I turn the cover back. Just holding it makes my fingers itch to write.

I've brought all one hundred and twelve of my diaries—journals spanning every corner of my life, from childhood scribbles to adult confessions. But I haven't written in one since . . . well, since the incident. Like Raees said, I've kept it all locked inside and sealed tight. Maybe pouring it out onto a page, like I used to, can help me find a way forward. Help me become someone new.

And again, like Raees said, I don't have to write about sad instances. I can jot down random ideas, sketch doodles, scribble bits of song lyrics, even note recipes. Maybe this diary can become a way to tell him all the things I struggle to say out loud.

I want to share this diary with my husband.

I don't want to be like my mother, who could have used words to express her anger but instead let her palms do the talking. It's going to take time before I can fully open up to Raees, to sit across from him and speak everything that's hidden in me.

But for now, I'll start small. I'll use the tools he's given me.

Pen? I sign.

"Pen?"

I nod.

He tilts his head thoughtfully, then holds up a finger before reaching into his bag. A moment later, he returns with a black fountain pen, holding it out to me like an offering.

I take it with a small thanks, and flip open the cover of the diary, landing on the first blank page—the one that reads 'This diary belongs to:'. I pause for a moment, then slowly write in the space below: *Zinneerah and Raees.*

When I look up, he's already watching me. My heart skips, stalling in mid-beat. His lips are slightly parted, his dark brows drawn together, and there's a flicker in his left eye.

What's wrong? I sign, my fingers hesitant.

Raees inhales, then shakes his head, pressing his lips into a reassuring smile. "Nothing. Just . . . I'll finish up dinner, and call you down when it's ready."

Help? I offer.

"I'm almost done, anyway." He turns back to the cutting board, resuming his careful dicing of fresh mint.

I clutch the edges of my—our—diary close to my chest. Just as I'm about to leave, he glances over his shoulder.

"Oh, and the lunch you packed for me?" he adds. "Absolutely perfect." His eyes light up with their usual childlike gleam. "Thank you for waking up so early to do that."

You don't have to thank me.

He blinks.

Shoot. I signed too fast.

"Apologies, Mrs. Shaan," he says teasingly, "but I don't take orders on this one." The title catches me off-guard, and I have to bite the inside of my cheek to keep from grinning too wide.

Mrs. Shaan. That's who I am now. Not Zinneerah Arain, but Zinneerah Shaan. It's still new enough that it feels like a small miracle.

Zinneerah Shaan. I roll it around, tasting three tablespoons of sugar in my mouth.

It has a nice ring to it.

THIS DIARY BELONGS TO:

Zinneerah and Raees

9

Raees

After dinner, Zinneerah volunteers to wash the dishes.

I pick up a towel and stand beside her to dry, happy for any excuse to steal a few extra minutes with my wife.

Her blouse sleeves are rolled up to her elbows, exposing smooth, caramel-brown skin that catch the light as she moves. Her slender fingers methodically glide over plates and pans, orchestrating the utensils like instruments. A few stray wisps of hair have escaped her braid, clinging to her flushed cheeks and the damp curve of her neck. She's really working up a sweat over these dishes.

It's kind of adorable.

I feel a swell of happiness, thinking about the diary. After my meeting with Professor Daniels, I'd stopped by a bookstore and picked it up, imagining two possible futures—either it would be something for us to share, or it would be hers alone. I never expected her to want to share it.

I damn near cried when she wrote our names inside the front cover of the diary.

Zinneerah and Raees.

Us.

We.

A light poke on my arm brings me back.

Zinneerah is watching me with those wide, dark eyes of hers, holding out two plates fresh from the sink, waiting for me to dry them.

"I apologize." I quickly take the plates, my mind still looping around, caught up in everything that reminds me of her.

Nothing out of the ordinary.

For dessert, I indulge in two brownies and a strong coffee, while she nibbles on oatmeal cookies, sipping her chamomile tea.

My eyes glance at my bag, where the flier Professor Daniels gave me lies folded. I'd been waiting until after dinner to bring it up. She devoured her plate of aloo and curry rice in minutes, even going back for seconds. Knowing she enjoys my cooking has made my entire week.

I reach into my bag, pull out the flier, and smooth the creases before setting it on the table. She watches me in silence. "The music department was handing these out today," I say.

Zinneerah's gaze drops to the paper. The only sign of movement is the quick flick of her tongue as she wipes a crumb from the corner of her downturned lips.

"I had the pleasure of meeting Professor Daniels today."

The moment I say it, I see her shift, her eyes lifting to mine with that startled look that always makes me question who put it there. She tries to hide it, but I know her too well—I can practically feel her heartbeat quicken.

"He spoke of you," I continue. "He said you were one of his most exceptional students. That he'd love it if you visited him sometime soon." The CD's still safe in my backpack. But after her visit to her father's grave today, the last thing I want is to reopen wounds that are barely beginning to scab over.

Instead, I hold out the flier he asked me to give her.

Zinneerah doesn't take it. Her gaze drops, lashes lowering, and she curls her hands around her mug, knuckles pale against the ceramic. She closes her eyes, and something in me pricks to see her this way, her spirit folding in on itself.

She thinks she's let him down, somehow. That she's let them all down. And for what? Because she's no longer the girl who once stood on stage like she belonged there, drinking in applause with that bold smile that made me fall in love with her a little more each time?

Going back to the music department now, I know what it would mean for her. All those memories she left behind, all those dreams—she'd have to look them in the eye, and I think she's terrified of what she'd feel. And maybe, deep down, she's scared of what she wouldn't feel.

But how long will she let this fear have power over her? How long will she let it keep her from fighting for herself?

If she agrees to volunteer for the summer concert, she can just play the guitar. She doesn't need her voice to do that, and I know she'd be brilliant. I've seen her pluck the strings so many times, fingers moving like they were born for it. God, she's a force. She may not believe it, but I've witnessed it, and nothing could ever change that.

One day, maybe, I'll find the courage to tell her just how much her music has meant to me. How, six years ago, her playing was the only thing that kept me going.

I wasn't a stalker, for God's sake—I didn't even approach her. I just . . . couldn't stay away. I went to her café nights, sat in the back, drunk on every note. Maybe I checked her Facebook once or twice. She was in a relationship then, so I kept my distance, just watching her from across a crowded room.

I doubt she remembers the one time we actually spoke. If she did, she would've recognized me when I showed up at her door, ring in hand.

But that doesn't matter now. She's my wife, my entire world. And someday, I'll tell her the whole story. I'll tell our children, too, how I fell hopelessly in love with their mother long before she ever knew my name.

Whoever says love at first sight doesn't exist has clearly never met her.

It's real.

It's terrifyingly, undeniably real.

And she's right here, sitting across from me, staring at that flier like it's a divine prophecy.

I clear my throat, lifting my coffee to my lips. "Take your time to decide," I say. The coffee is toasty and smooth, just the way she makes it. Somehow, she gets the balance perfect—just enough cream to minus the bitterness, with loads of sweetness. I don't know how she does it, but I'd drink a thousand cups if it meant sitting here with her a little longer.

She folds the flier, sets it aside, and reaches for the last biscuit. Then she stands up and signs, *Goodnight.*

Wait. What? No. She's leaving? Now? I glance at my watch. *Eleven.* She's usually in bed by now. I'm so used to sitting here with her, watching her eyes flicker with thoughts she rarely says out loud, that I lost track of time completely.

I nod, swallowing my disappointment. "Goodnight, Zinneerah."

She gives me this tiny, almost guilty smile, then turns and heads upstairs, her tea in hand. I watch her until she's out of sight, until the sound of her footsteps fade, and I'm left staring at the oatmeal cookie crumbs on the table.

Suddenly, I'm right back to that first conversation we had six years ago.

"Marty! Are you serious? Out of oatmeal cookies again?" An irritated voice cuts through the noise. "You swore you'd have them ready this time, you dick!"

I nearly spit out my coffee as Zinneerah Arain sidles up right next to me at the bar, close enough that I catch a faint trace of her perfume—something sweet, with a hint of spice. The place is packed, mostly because of her. She's the reason we're all here.

"Calm down, superstar!" Martin yells back from the kitchen window, grinning like he's heard this a million times. "Delivery got held up. They'll be here tomorrow, I promise. Next batch is on the house!"

She rolls her eyes, then turns them on me with a look that's half dramatic sigh, half mischievous smile. "Can you believe this guy?"

I just manage to nod, barely holding it together, because she's talking to me. I open my mouth to say something, but she's already spun back to Martin.

"Fine! Then at least make me a chocolate shake, extra whipped cream. And I'm timing you!"

Martin laughs, throwing her a mock salute. "Coming right up, your highness!"

Zinneerah leans over the counter, drumming her fingers, her gaze sliding around the room, catching the glow of fairy lights, the laughter from nearby tables, the easy confidence of her friends who seem to belong here as naturally as breathing. She's incandescent, and I can't take my eyes off her— like she's drawing every bit of light in the room to her—"You got a staring problem, buddy?"

I freeze, caught like a deer in headlights.

Dammit.

I've always tried to blend into the background—hard to do at my height, especially here where everyone else is a student, and at least a head shorter. But somehow, she's got me rooted in place, completely at her mercy.

She raises an eyebrow, her fingers snapping in front of my face. "Hello? Earth to tall, dark, and awkward. You alive in there?"

I clear my throat, flustered, and take a scalding gulp of coffee to cover up my embarrassment. "I, uh . . . I apologize. I didn't mean to stare at you."

She gives a little shrug, then grins, this effortless, devastating grin that seems to crack the whole world open. "Nah, you're good. I'm used to it." She bats her eyelashes at me in exaggerated flirtation, clearly teasing. "Hard to be this charming, you know?"

Zinneerah breaks into laughter, loud and shameless, and it hits me like a shockwave. Man, I feel ridiculous, sitting here like some tongue-tied kid while she's having the time of her life. She notices my expression and gasps, clapping a hand over her mouth.

Her grin widens as she watches me squirm. "Oh, my god," she says, dark eyes dancing with delight. "You're actually blushing."

"I'm not blushing."

"Oh, you totally are. Look at you." And then, before I can react, she reaches over and pinches my cheek, pulling at it like she's a Desi Aunty who's known me forever. *"Cute and in denial. Dangerous combo."*

I'm so caught off guard I don't even move. Is she drunk? High? Or just like this? I've heard she's outgoing, always the center of every room she walks into, but this is something else.

She lets go, but her touch leaves a tingle. *"So, are you a student or what?"* she asks.

I clear my throat, struggling to pull myself together. *"Y-Yes, I—I mean, no, actually. I was a student last year, but—but I'm a professor now. Started a few months ago."*

"Why are you stuttering?"

"I'm not—I'm not stuttering," I say, stumbling over the words. *"I just—"*

"Am I making you nervous or something?"

Yes. God, yes. But I just stand there, because admitting that would be too much, and lying feels impossible.

"Hmm." Zinneerah bites her bottom lip, and I catch her giving me this lazy, shameless once-over, head to toe, like she's deciding what to do with me. *"Aren't you a little too young to be a professor?"* Is she flirting with me? Because I think she's flirting with me. *"Not that I mind, though."* She reaches up and ruffles the hair at the back of my head. *"In fact, you're really working the whole 'hot young professor' thing. Totally checking off a box on my fantasy list right now."*

I swear my brain short-circuits. I can't remember the last time I felt this off-balance. Disarmed. My throat is dry, and any attempt at a clever response is lost to the sheer force of her presence. I'm just staring at her, probably looking like an idiot, but I can't help it.

She chuckles, low and throaty, and leans in even closer, her lips brushing my ear. *"What's the matter, Professor? Got a little thing for your students?"* Her voice is a wicked rasp, like she's daring me to react. *"Don't worry, it can be our little secret."*

My heart is hammering in my throat. She's so close, too close, and the way she bites her bottom lip sends heat flooding through me. Those dark, siren eyes hold mine, and I swear she knows exactly what she's doing.

Zinneerah pulls back just a little, enough to look me in the eye, and traces a finger down my chest. *"You know, I'm just messing with you, right?"* And *then, as if to make things even worse—better—she reaches up and brushes her thumb across my bottom lip, just for a second. "Unless you're into it."*

God help me, I am. I really fucking am.

"Little tip, Professor." Her hand finds my back, rubbing up and down in a way that should make me flinch, or pull away. But instead, it only draws me in deeper, steadying me and undoing me all at once. "Next time, maybe don't give a girl those fuck-me eyes if you're not planning to do anything about it."

I can feel my face turning redder than ever. I try to come up with something to say, something that won't make me sound like a nervous wreck, but all I manage is a quiet, "I didn't mean to."

"Yeah?" Her fingers drift up, brushing along my jawline, and I swear I'm about to melt right there on the spot. "You look like you'd pass out if I kissed you right now."

I'm scrambling for anything to say, something clever that might keep her here, but my mind is blank. Before I can get a single word out, the barista sets her drink down in front of her.

"See you around, Professor." She winks, lifting her glass in a mock toast, then disappears into the crowd, leaving me sitting there, still trying to catch my breath.

The lecture hall is silent, save for the occasional rustle as my students work through their quizzes.

Moderators stroll up and down the aisles, ready to answer any questions, while I lean against my desk, arms crossed, scanning the room for any suspicious behavior.

A few students glance up and, upon meeting my gaze, quickly look away, nervously chewing on the ends of their pens.

Do I really make them *that* anxious?

I wet my lower lip and continue my sweep, locking eyes with a young man near the back.

I give him a small smile.

His eyes widen as though I've caught him cheating—though he definitely wasn't—and he visibly shrinks in his seat.

What on earth?

I frown and turn back to my desk. "Fifteen minutes left, everyone."

The shuffling grows louder as students finish up, filing down the aisle to drop their quizzes on my desk.

They mumble goodbyes without meeting my eyes.

Enough is enough.

I pull out my phone and open RateMyProfessor, a habit I've developed ever since Dua casually mentioned it a week before my engagement to Zinneerah.

Now, I check it obsessively. Not just my own ratings, but everyone else's in our department, too.

Holmes has a strong 4.7: praised for engaging lectures, professional warmth, and fair grading.

Me, on the other hand? I'm sitting at a 3.2.

My "friendliness" score is a brutal 1.2, and my "difficulty" is maxed out at 5.0. Quality? Also, a 5.0, which, I suppose, means I'm good at teaching but terrible at everything else.

A student tosses her quiz onto the stack with a frustrated sigh.

I arch an eyebrow. "Everything all right, Sarah?"

"Well, considering half my grade depends on a missing comma, I'd say just peachy, Professor." She hitches her backpack up and storms out without waiting for a response.

Next in line is Dua, the only one who's smiled at me all day. She leans in and whispers, "You're doing great, you know."

Relief settles over me. Somewhat. "Thanks, Dua. See you tomorrow."

"Yes, Professor." She gives a casual two-finger salute before heading out, trailing behind a pair of glowering classmates.

When the last students have filtered out and the moderators finish their final sweep, I sink back at my desk, scrolling through the stack of reviews waiting for me.

RAEES SHAAN
3.2/5 (Overall Quality Based on 800 ratings)

MM01:
QUALITY: 5.0 / DIFFICULTY 5.0

He's super clear about the syllabus and actually explains assignments in a way that makes sense. His slides are solid, too. But JFC, his grading is brutal. Like, have a heart, Professor.

MM01:
QUALITY: 5.0 / DIFFICULTY 5.0

I'm usually fine with blunt feedback, but Shaan takes it up to a whole new level. The man shoves an entire f*cking bottle of bitter pills down your throat. I legit cried for hours after seeing my midterm grade. If he wasn't actually a good teacher, I'd have noped out of his class so fast.

MM01:
QUALITY: 1.0 / DIFFICULTY 5.0

Yeah, he sucks lol.
(hot as hell tho)

MM01:
QUALITY: 5.0 / DIFFICULTY 3.0

Yes, he's a hard-ass, but that's actually a good thing. Shaan is preparing us for those moments when we're not sitting in a meeting room, panicking while some editor tears our work apart. We're adults now, and he's not going to coddle us just to have the industry crush us later. Thanks to him, I'm now a successful journalist at Elle. P.S. Check his top drawer—he keeps sugar cookies in there.

I tug at my top drawer, and instead of sugar cookies, it's Zinneerah's baked cinnamon and molasses cookies.

"You look like you just got assigned extra office hours."

I jump, not expecting to see Professor Holmes leaning in the doorway of my lecture hall. "Oh. It's nothing, I'm just . . . yeah."

"Just 'yeah'?" She raises an eyebrow, unconvinced. "Why haven't you responded to Professor Wei's retirement party group chat?" She strolls over. "Trouble at home? Marriage on the rocks?"

"God, no." I laugh, but it quickly fades as last night's events rush back, followed by that *RateMyProfessor* nonsense. I hesitate, then ask, "Do you . . . think I'm a bad professor?"

Professor Holmes tilts her head, studying me. "Do *you* think you're a bad professor?"

"That's why I'm asking you."

She chuckles softly, picking up a stack of quiz papers from my desk and straightening them. "Why does my opinion matter so much?"

I sigh and flip my phone around, showing her the screen. "It's this."

Professor Holmes lowers her reading glasses, squinting at the screen as she scrolls through my mountain of reviews. She snorts, reading one out loud. "'He's got a sweater for every occasion.'"

I sigh, stretching out my legs and fiddling with my wedding ring. "Well, that's one of the three nice ones out of, like, a thousand." I shake my head. "Makes me wonder if my 'realistic' teaching style is doing more harm than good to their—"

"Egos?"

"—mental health."

Professor Holmes snorts again and flips my phone face-down on the table. "Honey, if you're worried about their mental health, wait until they graduate and get tossed out of this hellhole into an even bigger, smarter, and more ruthless one that profits off mental health struggles."

She's right.

Because she's Professor Nicola Holmes, and I'm . . . well, I'm the guy who has a sweater for every occasion.

"I made a student cry last week over her midterm grade," I mutter, my nails digging into the armrests. "I just wish they understood my job isn't to spoon feed them. The industry will shred them alive. There's no future for them if they keep churning out these half-baked, copy-pasted articles."

"Oh, I feel ya', kiddo," Holmes says, nodding sagely and gazing into the middle distance. "Reminds me of this student I had once—Pete. Kid had dreams of being a big-shot freelance photographer. He joined up with the sleaziest little rag in the city just to get his foot in the door. His aunt was severely sick around the time he graduated, so he did what any enterprising young photographer would do."

I squint at her, sensing there's a punchline coming. "And that was?"

She grins, eyes glinting. "Cooked up a whole story about being the city's hero. He sold his boss these grainy photos of a masked vigilante in a discount Halloween costume. You should've seen it— those pictures were plastered across every front page. Or, well, you would've seen it, but this all went down before you were even born."

My mouth falls open a little. Why does this all sound weirdly familiar? I don't even watch movies. Only documentaries on aquatic mammals, and the occasional TLC show, thanks to my sister's lifelong obsession with *Say Yes To The Dress*.

Holme's grin just stretches. "Anyway, Pete's boss absolutely hated this so-called hero running around the city. But, hey, those photos got Pete the recognition he needed. I was hard on that kid, sure, but his editor? Toughest son of a gun in the business. Still, I remember Pete telling me later how grateful he was for all those life lessons I drilled into him." She leans back, looking pleased with herself. "I told him you don't have to write an article to tell a story. Photography's a medium of storytelling, too."

Yeah, I'm ninety-nine percent sure she just told me the origin story of Spiderman.

Nevertheless, I let her spin her yarn anyway. "That's incredible, Professor. You've completely convinced me that teachers are the real superheroes."

She beams, flicking a finger dramatically through the air. "Exactly! They might see you as the enemy now, but just wait. One day, you'll be the hero they never knew they needed." Then, Holmes rolls her eyes and swipes my phone out of my hand. "And stop reading this trash if you care about *your* mental health. Honestly, Professor Shaan, you're too smart for that. Half these reviews don't even have proper punctuation. Or basic grammar." She clicks her tongue in disgust. "Future journalists, my ass."

I sigh. "Thank you, Professor."

She responds with an exaggerated bow. "You're very welcome, Professor." She turns to leave, tossing over her shoulder, "And reply to the group chat, please. I refuse to be the sole architect of these decorations."

With a resigned sigh, I check my phone and pull up Messenger, scrolling through the chat.

My thumb stops.

Jenna Carlson added Saira Nadeem to the group.

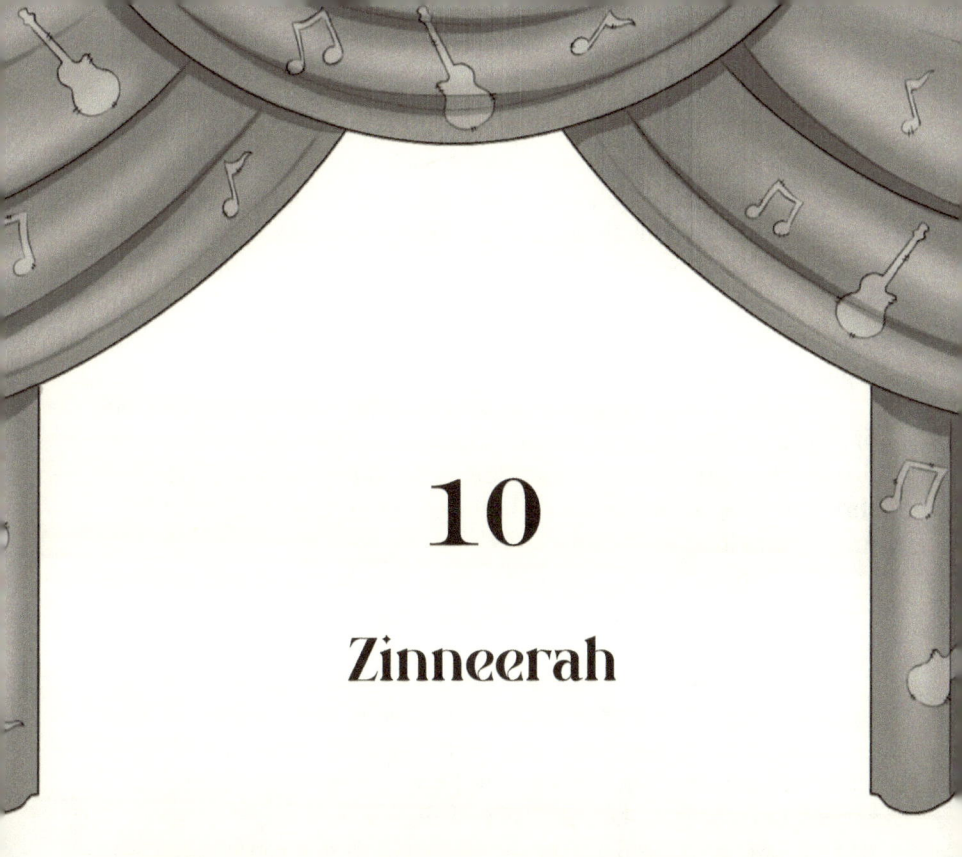

10

Zinneerah

My teeth worry at my bottom lip as I stare at the blank email draft, fingers hovering over the keyboard.

What am I even supposed to say to Professor Daniels? I feel like I owe him a thousand-word apology just for not visiting. After Baba, he was the one who always had my back, who pushed me to keep chasing my dreams, aiming for the stars—no, higher. *The celestial level, Zinneerah*, he used to say, like it was just within my reach if I kept stretching.

I can still picture him, that slightly exasperated look in his eyes as he pressed play on another one of my recordings, the two of us hunched over the playback as he encouraged me to pick apart every mistake. He went out of his way for me more than anyone else. He reached out to performance troupes, trying to get me a spot as a guitarist. Even emailed record labels to try to get our band signed.

Our band. God, I almost forgot how much I loved that chapter of my life. An all-female lineup, and we were good. *Extremely* good. I was lead singer and guitarist, Alex on bass, and Ophelia on drums. We called ourselves The Cryptics. If Pink Floyd had a lovechild with The Cranberries, that would've been us—dark, gritty, a little romantic around the edges.

The band name didn't mean anything. Just a random collection of words we slapped together one night when Ophelia and Alex were drunk on cheap beer, and I on wilder ideas. If anyone asked, I'd shrug, maybe throw them a wink, and let them read whatever they wanted into it.

Truth is, there was nothing to read. We—Alex, Ophelia, and I— weren't exactly ones for hidden depths. We wore our mayhem like gold medals.

I was the "fun" one, I guess. The one who could get a whole bar singing along by the end of karaoke night. Alex was more of a wild beast. She'd climb on tables, draw every eye in the room. She'd hit on whoever struck her fancy, take them home if she felt like it, then show up to rehearsal the next day wearing some stranger's ring or a pair of sunglasses she'd lifted from her night shift at some motel. And then there was Ophelia. Rational, slow-moving, always half-lost in a haze of discounted bourbon and whatever she could smoke. She was our landing strip, or maybe our warning light. Hard to say which.

In a way, maybe the band name was ironic. People would see us, and have questions.

Especially him.

They're bad for you, Neerah. You're too smart to hang around with people like that, Neerah. Why don't you just write your songs with me, Neerah?

My fingers curl into tight fists on instinct. A high-pitched ringing settles into my left ear, drowning out his voice in my head. It's like the ghost of him still lives there, waiting to crawl into the stillness, plaguing the empty caves where my thoughts should be. It's been years, and somehow, he's still there, choking out the sound of my own conscience. I don't even remember what my voice sounds like anymore. Just his.

I grab my headphones, fingers trembling a little, and hit play on *Don't Fear the Reaper* by Blue Öyster Cult, cranking up the volume.

Professor Daniels doesn't deserve an email.

No, I need to go see him, look him in the eyes, and just wrap him in a long hug. Let him feel my apology, as if it could transfer from my skin into his. He'll have questions, of course. And I'll do my best to answer. But really, all I want to talk about is music. And the summer concert.

I open my desk drawer and pull out the flier, smoothing its creases with my palms.

When Raees handed it to me last night, I froze.

The summer concert. *My* summer concert. I used to run that thing, back when I was at S.L.U., back when I was on fire. It was my stage, my spotlight—a chance to play my heart out in front of label managers and production scouts. I used to walk off that stage with a fistful of business cards, promises and possibilities pressed into my palm. And the devil I'd danced with tossed most of them out.

If I do this, if I sign up as a guitarist again, I'm going to have to face down this ridiculous fear of mine. The fear of even touching that instrument.

God, I've tried so many times to take it out of the bag, to just strum it like I used to. But every time I lift it; it feels like holding . . . I don't know, a stranger. My body remembers—the rhythms pulsing under my skin, my brain still tuned to every chord progression—but the moment my fingers brush those rusty strings, something inside me threatens to snap.

But that doesn't mean I shouldn't try.

Strings can always be replaced; I know that better than anyone. I've swapped them out dozens of times, all in the name of getting that perfect sound. It's just a little patience, and the payoff is worth it. Picking up the guitar again, it would be like honoring everyone who believed in me, everyone who pushed me to where I am. Especially Baba.

I glance at the clock. It's 3:30 p.m., and Raees' last lecture ends at five. If I leave now, I could catch Professor Daniels in his office.

I tuck the flier and a few other essentials into my bag, slinging it over my shoulder as I head downstairs.

By the door, I spot the car keys sitting in the little ceramic cup. I pluck them out, letting them dangle from my fingers.

When I step outside and see the car he picked for me, I actually have to bite back a laugh.

A cream-colored Volkswagen Beetle.

My dream car, sitting right in front of me. Why didn't I check the garage on my first day here?

I press the unlock button, and the cheerful little beep of the car welcoming me sends a giddy thrill down my spine.

When was the last time I felt this excited about anything? For something as simple as a car? *Your dream car, Zinnie.*

I slide into the driver's seat, and the scent of citrus and mint from the air freshener washes over me. My fingers trace the curve of the steering wheel, pausing over the horn, then settling around the leather-wrapped grip. The dashboard is a soft, cream color to match the outside, with a perfectly retro dial in the center that almost makes me feel like I've time-traveled back to a sunnier decade.

I close my eyes for a quick second, sending up a little prayer. It's been a while since I was behind the wheel, and the idea is nerve-wracking after the accident.

But then I turn the key, and the engine purrs to life alongside my smile. "Oh, I could definitely get used to this."

The campus is packed—too many people, too many cars, and not a parking space in sight.

I finally settle for the plaza down the road, the one with all the little restaurants, and, of course, Tapioca Time.

I haven't been here in ages. The girls and I used to come after every open mic night, spilling in at the end of the evening, laughing too loud and ordering one last round of drinks until they practically had to kick us out.

As soon as I step inside, the bell above the door chimes, and the warm, sugary scent of milk tea and grilled cheese wraps around me.

I glance around, taking in the groups of students huddled at tables, some hunched over laptops, others absorbed in board games from the shop's collection. There, on a shelf by the window, is the old Ludo board. I remember teaching the girls how to play.

I bite my lip and get in line, pulling out my phone to distract myself from the nostalgia that's creeping in. Ever since Raees handed me that flier, The Cryptics is all I've been able to think about. The girls were my world once, and if I take up Professor Daniels' offer, will it mean finally seeing them again?

I drove all the way here, though. I told myself I wouldn't come back to these places. And yet, here I am, pining for the past. If I can do this, if I can walk in here and breathe the same air I used to swear off, maybe I can reach out to the girls, too.

With a shaky exhale, I tap into the search bar and type: Alex Watanabe.

My lips twitch upward as the search results load a cascade of images, articles, and videos—all of her. It's been a couple of years since I last checked up on her. Back then, she was just starting out, releasing singles on streaming platforms, pushing her name out there like any inspiring new artist.

But here we are.

Alex is on fire. Millions of streams on every song, like it's nothing. Her whole brand now feels like some kind of neon-cyberpunk fever dream. And apparently, she's on tour. Selling out clubs, lounges, even full-blown concert halls.

And her last stop? Toronto. Our hometown.

In two weeks, she'll be here.

My tongue darts out to lick my lips as I stare at the concert date, half in disbelief. Tickets are still available. I could be there. I could actually—

"Hey, there! What can I get for you today?"

The voice snaps me out of my thoughts, and I blink up at the barista. I fumble with my phone, tapping out my order before I lose my nerve. Large taro milk tea with tapioca for me, warm milk tea for

Professor Daniels. She punches it in, I pay, and then I step aside, clutching my phone.

Two weeks. Alex will be here in two weeks.

The path to campus winds through the plaza, cutting across the metro tracks that slice the square in two. The plaza feels like a stage, a wide-open space where everyone's watching, or maybe that's just me, nerves crackling in my veins. Past it, campus unfolds—a widespread medley of ancient, ivy-clad walls and modern glass buildings.

Now I'm here, standing outside the music building like I'm a freshman again.

My heart's pounding, trying to make itself heard over the chatter of students spilling out of the glass doors, violin and cello cases slung over their shoulders. I catch someone's eye and manage a polite smile.

I step inside, and a wave of anxiety takes over, prickling my skin with sweat. Every nerve in my body is screaming, "Turn around, just leave!" but I've made it this far. And I have to do this. I know the way to Professor Daniels' office by heart, and my feet carry me there on their own.

I stop in front of his door, taking a large gulp of breath, and knock.

It swings open so fast it startles me. "For God's sake. Book your student hours—" His voice cuts off, eyes widening as he takes me in. He inhales sharply, and I do the same, mirroring him. "Zinneerah?"

"Professor," I whisper.

He presses a hand over his mouth, and I see the shock settle into his blue eyes as he takes in . . . everything.

Back then, I was all edgy and colorful—maroon-dyed hair, nose ring, tight jeans, neon crop tops under a leather jacket, and Alex's endless chains around my neck. I wasn't afraid to be seen.

Now I'm barely there. Black skirts that skim my bony hips, long-sleeved sweaters hiding everything beneath, my hair dyed back to its natural black. There's barely a hint left of the girl he knew, except maybe the kajal swept along my waterline, my cat-eye sharp and precise. He used to ask me to show him how to do it for his wife.

"Come in," he breathes, shifting aside to let me pass.

I step through the doorway, and his office is exactly as it's been for years. Nothing's changed. The walls are still sky-blue, shelves sagging under the weight of countless old music theory books, each one crammed in without any regard for order. Music sheets and assignment papers cover every available surface, scattered around the table. There's a faint smell of coffee, ink, and dust that settles on things long-loved.

"For you." I hand him the drink, smiling as he takes it with a nod of thanks, his eyes lighting up as soon as he tastes it.

"This is exactly what I needed."

A tiny bud of satisfaction blooms in my chest. It's good to be remembered for the small things, even after everything else.

But then, he's eyeing my own cup, and that delight starts to fade. "You shouldn't be drinking something cold," he says, pointing at my mug with a frown. "You don't want to swell your vocal cords."

I press my lips together as I lower myself into the seat opposite him.

He picks up on the sudden shift, leaning forward with that attentive look he gets when he knows he's missed something important.

"Can't talk for too long," I whisper, voice cracking, "I'll keep it short."

He blinks, and in that tiny pause, the worry in his expression deepens. "Zinneerah," he says carefully, "you're scaring me. What's wrong? Where have you been?"

I take in a deep breath.

You can do this.

And then, slowly, the words begin to spill out.

I tell him the story, piece by piece—the disaster that followed graduation, the sudden fracture of my friendships with Alex and Ophelia, the devastating loss of my voice, the endless months in and out of sterile hospital walls, the countless therapy sessions. And then, finally, my wedding with Raees, the chapter of healing that came after all the damage.

He holds his breath. Frowns here and there. Tiny reactions that make me want to look away, to give him space to feel whatever it is he's feeling as he hears my confession.

But I don't. I can't. I'm frozen, clutching my cold drink, forcing myself to take slow gulps, letting the chill settle in my throat.

Then, he dabs at his eyes with a crumpled tissue, sniffles, and finally smiles. Somehow, that makes it worse, seeing him affected, knowing that my pain has reached him. That it's real enough, powerful enough, to make someone else feel.

"Zinneerah," he says, rolling the tissue between his fingers. He lifts his head to look at me, and his smile stretches. "I'm really glad you're here. And I don't just mean here in my office, talking to me. I mean here. You are here. You made it here. And I know you'll keep making it out there."

I drop my gaze, unable to keep looking at him, and trace my fingers over my throat, a protective reflex. There's so much I want to say, but the words are locked up, sealed behind the scar tissue of all I've been through.

"Don't let that bring you down," he states. "You may have lost your voice, but you didn't lose your spirit." He holds up his fingers, counting off slowly, one by one. "You didn't lose your talent. You didn't lose your skills. And you most certainly didn't lose your will to push through the pain."

My breath catches as tears slip silently down my cheeks. It's not the first time I've cried over this, but right now, it feels like some part of me is being stitched back together caringly.

Professor Daniels opens his hand, and without really thinking about it, I place mine there. His hands close around mine; warm, calloused fingertips from all those years of plucking and practicing.

He looks at me, a mellow smile in his oceanic eyes. "Zinneerah, you've always been a daughter to me. You're brave. You're remarkable. You walk into a room, and everyone knows who you are, without you even saying a word. We all see it. We're nothing but proud of you. And that . . . is never going to change because of your disability. Not for one second." He lifts our hands, and nods toward mine, like it has its own little heartbeat. "This? This is still yours. And I'd bet it's itching to play, isn't it?"

I swallow. "I'm scared."

Then a cough breaks free, catching me off guard, and I fumble for my drink, taking a quick, desperate sip to clear the itch away. That's enough talking. I think I've met my speaking quota for the next week.

"Being scared doesn't make you weak, Zinneerah. It makes you human," he whispers. "Fear—real fear—that's what makes you dig your heels in. That's what gets people moving. Because nobody wants to feel small or shaky doing the thing they love most. Not when it's the one thing that usually makes them feel untouchable."

I looked down at our hands. His wisdom prickles a part of me that still remembers how it feels to play without a care in the world, to be the kid with a guitar who thought she could take on anything.

"Tonight," he goes on, giving me instructions I better not ignore, "I want you to go stand in front of the mirror. And I want you to really look. Look until you figure out what's making you shake like this. Hold your guitar while you do it—don't even think about leaving it out of this. Then, when you're ready, just strum one chord. Your favorite one." He gives my hands a reassuring squeeze. "Can you do that for me?"

My chest heaves, and I can barely choke out a nod as the tears spill over. I feel foolish, crying my eyes out like the time I was fifteen and snapped my low E-string right before my high-school talent show.

But Professor Daniels just watches, his own face a little damp. And then he steps around the desk, coming close. "Would it be all right if I hugged you?"

I can't get any words out, so I just stand up on trembling legs, wrapping my arms around his waist. His arms go around me, one hand moving over my back in slow, careful circles, the other cradling the back of my head, holding me together. And I cling to him, burying my face in his shoulder, sobbing hysterically.

"You're safe now, Zinneerah." His voice is a thread of sound. "You've got a whole team of people backing you up. I'm just one player in the orchestra, but I'd say your husband's definitely the first chair."

I pull back, sniffling as he hands me a tissue. I dab at my nose, trying to keep some dignity, though at this point, it's probably a lost cause. He bites his lips together, shoulders shaking with a laugh he's trying to stifle.

"What?" I mumble, instantly suspicious.

He gives me a crooked grin. "It's . . . well, your makeup."

I pull out my phone and flip the camera. Smudged eyeliner and dark streaks under my eyes. "Oh, jeez." I look like I just crawled out of a cave. Or maybe like a raccoon who's been through a tough breakup.

Professor Daniels chuckles outright, giving me a little pat on the back. "Tell you what, I've got an idea. Why don't you go splash some water on your face, and then we'll head over to the auditorium? Take a little walk down memory lane."

"What do you have in mind?"

"You'll see."

After I've splashed some cold water on my face and tried to pull myself together, we head into the empty auditorium.

It's quiet as a tomb in here, but someone's left their mark—a piano pushed off to the far left, a guitar leaning against it like an old friend, and a drum set lurking in the back with a couple of stray chairs scattered around. Whoever was here before us must've just packed up and gone.

Professor grabs a chair and drags it across the stage with a scrape that echoes through the room, then settles himself on the piano bench.

"All right," he says. "We'll take it slow. Step by step." He nods toward the department's provided guitar. "Why don't you pick it up? Just lay it across your lap. Get used to the feel of it again."

My hands feel shaky as I reach for it, fingers hovering for a second before they actually make contact.

"Take a deep breath," he whispers.

I try to push down the lump that's crawling up my throat, and grip the neck of the guitar.

But that's as far as I get. I just . . . hold it.

It sits there on my lap like it's got teeth, or might turn on me any second. The guitar was an extension of me—it knew my hands better than I did. Now, it feels like I'm sitting across from an old friend I haven't seen in years, and neither of us knows what to say.

"Good job." Professor gives me a light pat on the back. I must look like an idiot. "So, what song should we play?"

I just shrug. My mind's blank.

He lets out a thoughtful breath, crossing his arms as he leans back, his eyes going a little unfocused. Then, a slow grin starts to spread. I can see the gears turning, that lightbulb flickering to life. He cracks his knuckles, slides his fingers over the keys, and says, "All right. Don't laugh. But I'm dedicating this one to my star student."

He starts playing, and it takes me a second to catch on.

But then the melody clicks, and I recognize it—"Hey Jude."

Is he serious? A smile sneaks onto my face, big and goofy. I probably look like I've swallowed the sun, but he's too busy bobbing his head to notice, foot tapping the pedal.

The tears start prickling before I even realize, and I have to blink hard, trying not to turn into a blubbering mess. My grip on the guitar loosens, and I slowly ease it up, settling it in my lap where it belongs.

Professor Daniels suddenly bursts into song, not holding back in the slightest. "'For well you know that it's a fool who plays it cool by making his world a little colder.'" He's belting it out, loud and proud, and I laugh, startled, as he leans into the "na-na-nas" like he's on stage at Wembley instead of a university auditorium.

My fingers instinctively find their way into the opening chords for the second verse, muscle memory kicking in before I even think about it. I fish out my old, chipped guitar pick from my pocket—the same one I've kept since I was a kid—and hold it ready above the E-string.

Professor Daniels catches my eye, his head nodding in time with the beat. One, two, three, four.

I start strumming.

A shiver runs down my spine.

But my hands keep moving, and once I'm playing, really playing, the song has taken over.

Professor Daniels' obnoxious singing is so loud, it drowns out every single doubt rattling around in my brain. I can't hear a single one of those little voices telling me I can't, that I shouldn't. They're gone, blasted to smithereens, and I'm—God, am I crying?

Yes. Yes, I am.

But it's not the ugly, scared kind of crying. No, these tears are electric, like I've been hit with a lightning bolt of something euphoric and lustral, something I thought I'd buried a long time ago.

Because I, Zinneerah Shaan, just played the fucking guitar after five years.

11

Raees

I lean against my Audi, twirling my keys around my fingers,
wondering if puncturing my own jugular would hurt less than getting
through the rest of today.

Morbid thought, yes, but that's the headspace I'm in, staring
blankly at the gravel in the faculty parking lot. Everything's been a
mess since last night—no sleep, no peace, just this endless loop of
worry grinding away in the back of my head.

By the time the sun came up, I was practicing in the bathroom
mirror, trying to nail down some kind of polite, non-confrontational
greeting that wouldn't sound insulting.

Breakfast with my wife helped. Just sitting there with her in the
early quiet crushed some of the boulders on my shoulders. But the
minute I stepped back on campus, it was like that tension slithered

right back in, knotting itself up in my neck, my back, growing tighter with every tick of the clock during my lecture.

"Raees!"

I shut my eyes for a second, bracing myself, then look up.

Saira strides out of the faculty building and down the walkway, her thin scarf fluttering in the July wind, loose curls bouncing as she hurries toward me.

It's a scene I knew well: Saira spotting me from across the quad, arm up, waving with that big, unguarded grin of hers. It ended with her barreling into my arms, pulling me down into some kiss that had her laughing against my lips, catching her breath when we pulled apart.

That's not how things play out anymore.

Saira's hair is still chopped short, that same dark-brown bob she's had since we were together. She's in some kind of tailored pantsuit, the color of old coffee grounds, with those thin heels she always thinks make her look "professional." And a grin plastered wide across her face. I used to think her smile was the most charming part about her, once upon a time. Now it just feels theatrical. Like she's under the spotlight, and I'm supposed to be clapping.

"Hey!" She finally slows down as she gets closer, slightly out of breath, cheeks flushed. "Sorry I'm late. Professor Wei cornered me to go over last-minute course details."

"Yeah, no worries." I push off the side of the car and move to the driver's door, not bothering with small talk. She gives me this tight smile, like she's waiting for me to say something else, but I don't.

She slides into the passenger seat, and we both pull on our seatbelts in silence. I reverse out of the lot, turning on the air conditioning as we merge onto the main road.

"How have you been?" Saira sing-songs.

I predicted she'd start with small talk, so I've got my canned responses ready to go. "Good. You?"

She shrugs, her smile fading just a touch. "Oh, you know. I'm okay."

I stay focused on the road, signaling left and merging over. There's a part of me that feels the automatic urge to say something, to pretend I care.

But I bite it back.

This woman cheated on me two weeks before our wedding. Two weeks. With a stranger. I remind myself there's zero reason to waste breath playing an empathetic ex-fiancé.

"How's married life treating you?" she asks.

At the mention of my wife, I can't help the happiness that washes over my face. Zinneerah's all soft, black eyes and quiet smiles, and the thought of her is like flipping on a light in a dark room.

Saira notices, of course. "Yeah, that glow says it all," she comments. "Congratulations, really. I'm so happy for you, Raees."

I force out a quick, "Thanks."

She tilts her head. "What's her name again? Zari? Zina?"

"Zinneerah," I say, curtly. I don't elaborate. The last thing I need is her trying to file away details about my wife.

"Zinneerah, right. Pretty name," she murmurs, looking out the window. I catch the faint scraping sound of her nails against her thumb. "What does she do?"

This isn't small talk; it's an inquisition. If anyone else asked, I'd happily tell them about Zinneerah's work, about how talented she is. But when it's your ex-fiancée, you start to guard details like they're state secrets.

"She's a baker."

"A baker?" I see her head turn toward me in my peripheral vision. "Wow. That's cool. Does she own a bakery? Café?"

"Not yet."

"Maybe Rosy Aunty can work her real estate magic and hook her up with a bakery?"

That's . . . not the worst idea. I let myself imagine it for a moment: Zinneerah's face lighting up at the sight of her own place, the smell of fresh bread and coffee filling the air. If my wife told me she wanted that, I'd make it happen. Hell, I'd hand her the keys tomorrow.

"How's your family doing?" she questions.

"They're good," I say, keeping it brief. "Yours?"

There's a pause, then, "They . . . well, they're not great. My parents split up last year."

I glance over. She's got a weak smile, fingers fidgeting in her lap. I remember enough to know she was never close with her parents— not exactly estranged, but definitely not daily visits with presents. They were always too wrapped up in their own lives to really notice they had a daughter. It was something she didn't talk about much, but it was always there, eating her up alive from the inside.

"I'm sorry to hear that," I say.

"Don't be. You know as well as I do, it was only a matter of time." She shrugs, letting out a short, humorless laugh. "Might as well rip the Band-Aid off, right?"

And that puts a pin in our conversation.

The moment we step into the party store, I mentally split the list in half, handing her the easier part, and head straight for the supplies, weaving through aisles of cheap, cheerful plastic and overpriced sentimentality. We've got maybe twenty minutes until I hit my tolerance limit.

A bouquet of shiny balloons proclaiming, "30 Years!" Another set of lettered balloons that'll spell out "Happy Retirement." I'm methodical about it, plucking each item from the shelf and dropping it into my basket without fuss.

"Raees! Look!"

I glance up from my letter balloons to find Saira grinning, a plastic tiara perched lopsidedly on her head, the kind with sparkly pink gems and a cartoonish heart in the center. She strikes a pose, like she's twelve years old and we're shopping for her birthday party instead of a retirement.

"Sleeping Beauty," she says, waggling her brows. "Leftover from their Halloween stock. Should I get it?"

I drop the "T" balloon into my basket, giving her tiara nothing more than a disinterested glance. Her basket, naturally, is almost empty—just a scattering of trinkets and other nonsense she's picked up, none of which have anything to do with the list.

"Did you get your half of the supplies?" I ask, ignoring her theatrics.

She frowns, spinning in place and pinching the ends of the tiara like it's an elegant crown. "Not the answer I was hoping for, Professor." I stay silent, returning to my list, hoping she'll take the hint. But no, she sighs dramatically. "Oh, come on, Raees. You know Aurora is my favorite princess. Lighten up a little."

I resist the urge to remind her we're here on faculty duty, not some shopping spree. "Saira, if we could focus on the task at hand, I'd be grateful. I've got twenty-five minutes left on my break."

I step past her and glance at the assortment of trinkets cluttering a display rack. A little black guitar keychain catches my eye, and I pull it free, dropping it in the basket without a second thought.

"Want to grab lunch on the way back?" she asks, barely looking at me as she tosses a plastic tiara into her own basket. She's picking through the banners with indifference. "Benny's Burritos? My treat."

I remember, in a flash, that I left my lunch sitting on the counter at home—but I have no intention of admitting it. Last thing I need is spending any more of my break with her, let alone sitting across from her at some booth, pretending I've forgotten everything that happened. "No, thank you. I've brought food."

"Your loss." Saira disappears between the shelves without another glance, leaving me alone in the stale balloon-air of the store.

We make our way through the faculty building, bags in hand.

Saira's is weighed down with knick-knacks—ceramic owls, a lavender-scented stress ball, something resembling a mini-Zen garden, the sort of things that end up forgotten in drawers.

I spent a modest five dollars on a single keychain for my wife. If there'd been more in stock, I would have bought them all.

At my office door, I twist the knob and find it . . . *unlocked*?

Zinneerah is there, perched in the chair across from my desk, her face lighting up when she sees me. She offers a little wave, and for a moment, everything's back to my regularly scheduled programming.

Saira barges in behind me, and I watch Zinneerah's smile falter, slipping away as if on cue.

"Oh?" She looks Zinneerah up and down, and lets out a short, derisive snort. "Didn't know your students had free run of your office when you're not around, Raees."

"She's not a student." I set the bags down with an unhurried calm. "She's my wife." Zinneerah's eyes, dark as polished onyx, meet mine, as I give her a reassuring smile. "What a pleasant surprise. Let me guess, Professor Holmes let you in?"

She nods. *Are you okay?*

With a small gesture, I sign back, *Bad day.*

Zinneerah tilts her head, a slight crease between her brows. *Talk? Talk.*

"Well, this is unexpected," Saira's voice cuts in. "I didn't realize you knew ASL, Raees."

Who is this? Zinneerah asks.

I give her a resigned smile, but I'm already moving toward the door. "I'm going to have lunch with my wife now," I say, holding the door open and gesturing for Saira to exit. "Thank you for accompanying me, Professor Nadeem. I hope the rest of your day is as stimulating as ever."

Saira licks her lips, straightening her posture like she's about to pose for a photo. Her gaze darts to Zinneerah, who's watching us with a confused expression. "Lovely to meet you," she says, stepping out. "We'll catch up soon, Raees."

I shut the door behind her, locking it with a quiet click. Then I turn to Zinneerah and sigh. "I apologize about that."

It's okay.

I slip off my blazer, draping it over my chair as I settle in behind my desk. "So, what brings you here?"

Her lips form the word 'Professor.'

"Right, right," I say, suppressing a smile. "One moment." I power up my computer, log in, and open a blank document, sliding the keyboard toward her. I angle the screen so we can both see. "Whenever you're ready."

She begins to type, her fingers light on the keys. I came to see Professor Daniels.

I nod, already aware of her reason but glad to hear it straight from her. "Are you going to be performing in the concert?"

Yes, she types, her eyes flicking up to mine.

A grin breaks across my face. "I'm so happy for you, Zinneerah. You're going to be fantastic. And hey, as a bonus, we'll get to see each other on campus almost every day."

She blinks, caught off guard, and I realize how that sounded. Okay, actually, that's a bonus for me.

"What I mean is, you know, we can commute together. Go to work together, come home together." I can hear myself digging deeper. "Be co-workers. Married co-workers." I can't talk in this woman's presence.

She looks at me, then starts typing something, her fingers moving fast. You think I'll be fantastic?

That's what surprised her?

"Of course!" I exclaim. "You'll be better than fantastic. In fact, 'fantastic' doesn't even cover it. Just don't doubt yourself. Not while you're practicing, and definitely not when you're up there."

She signs, *Thank you*, then types: I'll do my best not to disappoint you.

I can't help but laugh, shaking my head. "Zinneerah, you couldn't disappoint me if you tried."

Her fingers hover over the keyboard, but then they curl into little fists, knuckles whitening as she stares unfocused at the screen.

Wherever she is right now, it's not a good place. I don't know who or what put that look on her face—could be her mother, or maybe some ghost from her past still haunting her.

Whoever it is, they'd do well to keep their distance. Anyone who hurts her might as well be hurting me, and that's not something I take lightly.

It's time to change subjects. Not that it's about to be any lighter. I've been sitting on this too long, and the longer I keep quiet, the worse it'll get, creeping into the cracks of our marriage like acid seeping into the foundation.

"Zinneerah," I begin, "there's something I've been meaning to disclose to you for a week now."

She blinks, pulling away from whatever had her claws in her. A little crease forms between her brows.

"You know I was engaged before I met you," I say. She nods cautiously, trying to read between lines I haven't written yet. "It ended because my ex-fiancée . . . cheated on me." Her lips part, eyes widening in shock. But I'm not done. "With some guy at her bachelorette party." Eyebrows shoot up, hitting her hairline. "Two weeks before the wedding."

Zinneerah slumps back in her seat, crossing her arms and letting out a sharp huff, like my words are smoke and she's trying to blow them away. Can't say I blame her.

Why? she signs.

"Because," I start, running a hand through my hair, "I don't know. I really don't know. And I definitely don't want to dig it all up. I buried that part of my life for a reason—shoveled dirt over every bad decision, and every stupid habit. And I've got no interest in unearthing it just because fate, or whatever twisted higher power, thinks it's funny to throw my past in my face. I didn't ask for this. Not even close."

Zinneerah's dark brows scrunch together. *Are you okay?*

"No." I rest my eyes, then, against my better judgment, I add, "The woman you just met . . . is my ex-fiancée."

Her face goes blank.

I lean back, rubbing my temples, feeling the old story claw its way up my throat, even though I hate talking about it. But my wife deserves to know the details.

"She was a literature journalism major at North Haven University, just next door. I was here. We met at a journalism conference, hit it off, and became friends. Two months later, we were dating. During my master's program—right in the middle of finals

96

week—I proposed. She happily said yes." I let out a shaky breath, then continue. "And then one night, while I was knee-deep in midterm papers, red pen in hand, she called me up. Out of nowhere, she's slurring her words, saying she got drunk and slept with some guy. Apparently, he and his friends had crashed her bachelorette party." My hand rubs over my jaw. "And now she's replacing one of our retiring professors. Which means I'll have to sit in meetings with her, make polite small talk at faculty events, pretend everything's perfectly civil."

I nearly wrench my neck looking up as Zinneerah stands. Dark thoughts circle like vultures. *She's going to leave you. She's going to walk out of your life. She's never going to trust you*—I stop myself before I go down that road. She's still standing there, watching me, and I make myself meet her gaze, waiting for her to say something, anything, that'll let me know she's not about to walk out the door.

My wife drags her chair around my desk and connects it with mine, close enough that our knees are almost touching. She sits down, gives a firm nod, and mouths the words, "I trust you."

"I didn't know," I whisper. "I promise I didn't—"

She shakes her head, a gentle smile on her face, like she's telling me I don't need to explain. She's trying to calm me down, to make this easier. But the fear of losing her digs in, and I can't stop myself from rambling.

"I've buried everything, Zinneerah. Everything that existed before you, it's gone. There's no one else in this world for me. Just you. You and my family."

She reaches over and takes a tissue from the box on my desk, pressing it into my hand. I didn't even realize my eyes were damp until I feel the paper against my skin.

I dab at my eyes, trying to get control of myself, and then I feel her hand on my back, moving in slow circles.

"Thanks for listening," I murmur sheepishly.

She nods, glancing at me with that shy smile of hers. God, it's adorable. It makes me want to cup her face, run my thumbs along her cheeks, and kiss every last inch of that softness. And she smells incredible, like Arabian incense—smoky, rich, hypnotic. It's pulling me in, making it hard to keep my hands to myself. A siren's song.

Zinneerah drags the keyboard onto her lap and starts typing. Is it okay if I go to my friend's concert next week? She's coming to Toronto for a show. I'll take Dua with me.

Selfishly, I want to be there. I want to share every experience with her, even the little things, but I'm her husband, not her shadow. This is her chance to reconnect, to be with her friends without me hovering nearby. She deserves that. And who am I to hold my wife back from something that makes her happy?

"You don't need my permission," I say softly. She lifts her gaze, those obsidian eyes locking onto mine. I could spend hours lost in them, honestly. "Just like you didn't need my permission to surprise me on campus." I grin a little. "You're free to go wherever you want, as long as you keep me posted. Same goes for me." *Though, let's be real, I'd take you with me everywhere if I could.* "For, you know, emergency purposes."

She tilts her head, studying me, a little uncertain. The action reminds me of this sparrow I had as a kid, a tiny thing my sister and I nursed back to health after it crash-landed on our porch with a busted wing. There was this wide-eyed innocence to it, the way it tilted its head, taking everything in.

Zinneerah has that same look sometimes, like she's trying to figure out if she can trust this strange new world she's in.

"Use my card," I state. She starts typing but I force shut my computer with a smile. The flabbergasted expression on her face makes me chuckle. "I know you haven't touched that card since I gave it to you. It's still sitting on the TV stand, isn't it?"

She shakes her head, trying to hide a smile. Stubborn as ever.

I sigh, pressing a hand over my heart in mock distress. "Come on, you're killing me here."

Another head shake. *Your card.*

"No." I pull out my wallet and showing her my Visa. "*This* is my card. But the black card? That one's yours. Just promise me you'll start using it, okay?"

She hesitates, her hands lifting as if to sign something, but I reach out, gently brushing my fingers over her wrists to stop her. Her eyes flick up to mine, and I can see the guilt there, clear as day. "Please, Zinneerah?"

A defeated sigh.

"Thank you. My heart is mended once again."

She smiles, and rises from her seat, brushing invisible creases out of her skirt.

"You're leaving?" I ask, wishing for the opposite.

I make dinner tonight. She doesn't use ASL with me, not really— just these exaggerated movements, hoping I'll catch her meaning. And I always do.

What she doesn't know is that I actually know the language from studying it consistently since our first meeting. I keep telling myself I'll tell her soon, that I'll end this little charade, but not yet.

I kind of like being the only one in on the secret. For now.

"Very well," I surrender. "I'll see you tonight, then."

She nods, giving the chair a little nudge back into place, then grabs her bag and heads toward the door. But she pauses in the doorway, glancing back at me.

Cheeks flushed, her hands fly into a blur of rapid-fire signing. *Ibakebrowniesyoufeelbetterokaybye.*

Before I can respond, she's darted out the door.

I burst out laughing.

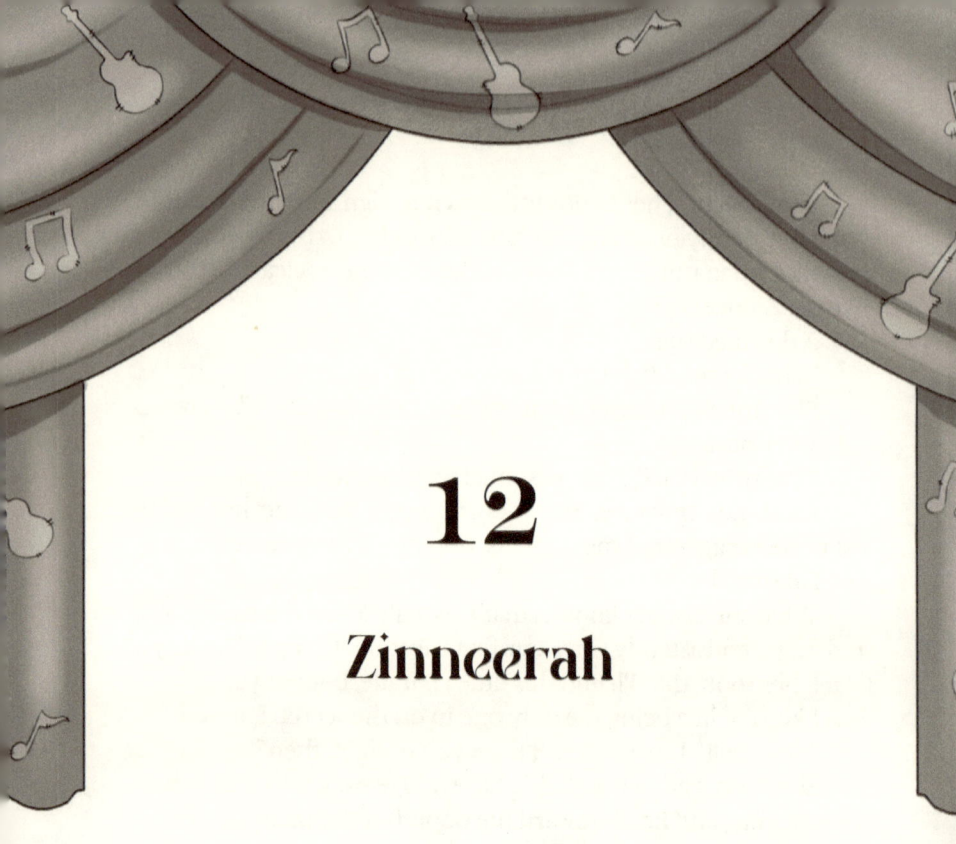

12

Zinneerah

My trembling finger hovers over the 'place order' button.

This tiny screen has me so high-strung, it's not even about the tickets anymore.

If I buy these tickets, I'm saying, "Hey, Alex, I still remember every little piece of us, and maybe you do, too. That is, if you still don't hate me for everything I've done."

Oh, fuck it.

I press it before I can talk myself out of it, and the order goes through.

Just like that, it's done. Two nosebleed tickets to Alex Watanabe's show. I stare at the QR code on my screen. Two little boxes and a tangle of lines that decide whether I'll see her again or not.

Her cocky, brash voice sneaks into my mind when she had just enough tequila to think we could actually pull it off. *We're gonna be rockstars someday, ladies. You hear me? Rock-fucking-stars. Zinister on vocals and guitar, Lia-IKEA on drums, and me, rocking the bass and backup vocals. Grammys by next year, bitches. Just you wait.*

My mouth pulls into a smile. There we were, sprawled in the open trunk of father's beat-up truck, a hand-me-down monster of a vehicle she'd fought tooth and nail to borrow. A whole week's worth of his chores just for one night out under the glittering stars, telling each other big, stupid dreams as if they were inevitable.

Alex was always the one pulling us all together; the ringleader, the planner. She'd come up with the ideas, and I'd be there, the reliable sidekick, ready to drop everything at a moment's notice. And then there was Ophelia, our little introvert project, the reluctant third musketeer we had to yank out of her apartment with promises of minimal human interaction.

And then I went and ruined it all by falling headfirst for someone I shouldn't have. I allowed that whole mess to swallow me up, and one by one, our plans just . . . vanished.

If my girls still hate me for it, I don't blame them.

My phone starts buzzing somewhere behind me, snapping me out of it. I close my laptop, roll over to the edge of my bed, and fish it out from under a tangle of blankets.

Dua's name flashes across the screen.

I swipe to answer, setting the phone on my lap. Her face fills the screen, flushed from volleyball practice, ponytail askew, sweat trickling down her temples.

"Hey, Zinnie!" she says, flashing a tired grin.

I smile back. "How was practice?"

She rolls her eyes. "Oh, you know. I'm hardly aiming for the Olympics here, but the guys needed an extra player, so I jumped in. Zayan was not happy about it, by the way. Pretty sure he spent half the game aiming spikes at Aaron's face just for asking me to play."

I laugh softly. "He really loves you."

"Tell me about it." She groans, tossing her bag onto the bench in an empty changing room and propping the phone up against the mirror. "Sometimes it's sweet; other times, it's like, please, back the fuck off." She grabs a tissue to blot the sweat off her face. "Did you actually get the tickets to Alex's thing, or did you flake?"

I nod. "You're still coming with me, right?"

"That's why I called," she says. "But, Zinnie, you know I can't promise anything. The match is in two weeks, and Coach Ryerson's got everyone running drills like it's life or death." She crumples her damp tissue and tosses it into the trash. "I do want to go. I miss Alex. And I want to be there for you, too." She's staring straight at me now. "But if I can't make it, I'll let you know, okay? I'll text you beforehand."

Great. Brilliant move on my behalf. Who buys tickets without even checking if their sister is free?

Dua's eyes narrow, reading me like a book as usual. "Stop beating yourself up." She reaches down, peeling her shirt off in one smooth motion. Underneath, she's in her black sports bra. "Just take Raees bhai with you if I can't make it. Poor guy could probably use a night out. Think of it as, I don't know, training wheels for a first date."

My throat goes dry. *First date.* I've been on plenty dates before, but I agree, it would feel like a first date with my husband. "Raees doesn't like that type of music."

"Oh?" Dua gives me a raised eyebrow while rummaging through her duffel bag. "And how exactly do you know that?" She pulls out a small towel, patting down her face and neck. "Have you two even covered the 'favorite color' conversation yet?"

My mind wanders back to those first few months with him. Months that were . . . well, quiet.

Just the two of us in my old apartment's living room, sitting ten-feet apart from each other in a wordless bubble. He'd clear his throat every so often, drum his fingers on the table, throw me these hopeful glances that I'd politely ignore. It got to the point where I actually scrawled *Please talk* on a scrap of paper, and shoved it across the table like it was a hostage negotiation.

And, oh boy, did he take me seriously.

Suddenly he was Mr. Chatty, spilling every story he could think of, like he'd been saving them up just for me.

He told me about the time a giraffe at the zoo almost chomped his hand off because he was holding the lettuce wrong. Or how he once faked an asthma attack in middle school to get out of the annual Terry Fox run. *"I respect the cause, of course, but I'd bought a Nintendo DS that same week. Priorities, you know?"* He said it with such deadpan honesty that I almost laughed out loud.

Raees tried involving me in his tales, or kept looking at me with this hopeful, open expression like he was ready to be let in. But I wasn't ready to unpack all my mess for him just yet.

So, I just listened. And he never pressed. Somehow, that silence between us turned into its own language. That's partially why I married him. He made space for me in his world without ever asking me to fill it with noise.

"Hello?" Dua jolts me back. "Zinnie?"

"Please let me know if you can make it. I can ask Raees if he wants to come, just in case. Backup plan. Sounds good?"

"Sounds gre—" She barely has time to turn around before the door swings open. "Zayan Jafri, for the last time, this is a women's changing room. You're breaking like three laws just being here!"

"And are there any women present in the room with us right now?"

And then he's in view, sweeping her into his arms, his fingers digging playfully into her waist. He leans in, probably aiming for one of those dramatic, stagey kisses he likes to pull, but he catches sight of me on the screen and pauses. His face splits into a grin. "Oh, hey, Zinneerah. How are you?"

I lift a hand in a half-hearted wave. "Fine. You?"

"Oh, you know, just trying to keep up with this one." He hooks an arm around the front of my sister's neck, pulling her close even as she squirms. She's rolling her eyes, trying to duck out from under his gentle hold, but he just presses his cheek against hers. "How's married life with Professor Shaan?"

The million-dollar question. The question everyone's been asking with too-enthusiastic eyes since the wedding. As if the answer might reveal some piece of gossip they're all dying to sink their teeth into.

I don't have anything bad to say about Raees.

Not a single scowl, not one raised brow or awkward silence. We're neutral, I guess? But in a way that feels safe. He hasn't done a single thing to make me flinch or question myself. He hasn't poked at old scars or dug up memories I'd rather leave buried. Honestly, I don't even think Raees knows how to be angry.

Even after the wedding, there's no pressure from him to take things to some undefined 'next level.' He just seems content. Unbothered. Like he's perfectly fine being the calm center while I swirl around him like a little hurricane.

I feel a tiny smile beginning at my lips before I can stop it.

"Ooh," Dua coos, giggling. "She's blushing."

"She's definitely blushing." Zayan snickers beside her, scratching the back of his head. "But still—just be careful, all right? He might be your husband, but men are . . . well, *men*. Completely unpredictable."

Dua scoffs. "Rich coming from you."

Before she can blink, Zayan swoops down, scooping her up with ease and throwing her over his shoulder like a sack of onions. His hand settles on her ass.

"Put me down, you dick, or I'm screaming bloody murder!" she snaps, her fists drumming on his back.

"Sorry to cut your girl talk short, Zinneerah," he says, picking up Dua's phone as she squirms, "but your sister's stubborn streak is really doing it for me right now."

I snort, fighting the urge to laugh.

"Zinnie, I'll call you back!" Dua shouts, voice muffled as she's carried away, still pummeling his back. "I love—" The call ends.

With a sigh, I plug my phone in to charge, fully aware I'll be getting a play-by-play update later whether I want it or not.

I'm halfway through Alex's EP when my phone pings with the security app notification.

Raees is home.

Pausing the track, I slip off my headphones and ease my door open just a crack, peeking out.

All I catch is the top of his dark waves as he bends to untie his shoes downstairs, then the familiar march of his footsteps on the stairs.

I close the door, leaning back against it. *Okay, Zinnie. You've got this. He's your husband. He'll say yes. He'll come with you.*

But my brain, as usual, doesn't listen.

What if he says no?

What if he has some perfectly valid reason—work, or fatigue, or a meeting early tomorrow?

What if he just . . . doesn't want to go? And then, what, I go by myself?

If that happens, I won't go either. It took everything I had just to drive myself to campus a few days ago; the idea of facing a concert crowd on my own feels like standing at the edge of a cliff.

I'll die.

No, stop it. This isn't a big deal. Just ask. If he's busy, fine.

I'll message Alex, maybe see if she'll have a minute to meet up privately. Not that she'll see it in time, or respond, but fingers crossed. Or I could wait outside the venue after, catch her for a quick hug before she slips away into the night.

But I don't want that. I want to be there, in the strobe lights, surrounded by people who feel the way her music makes me feel. I want to see her perform. I want the whole experience.

"Damn it," I mutter, pressing the heels of my hands into my eyes until colors bloom in the darkness.

It's fine. It's just a question. I can ask Raees. He's my husband; that's what we're supposed to do, right? Talk to each other?

Right. Okay, go.

I open the door, only to collide with him on the other side—he's right there, hand raised, about to knock.

We both freeze for a moment, our chests nearly brushing. I take a step back, and he mirrors me, tucking his hands behind his back in that polite, old-fashioned way he has.

"I apologize," he murmurs, eyes flicking down. "I was just coming to see if you'd eaten anything."

I shake my head. *I will make dinner.*

His brow furrows slightly as he processes my words. He's always so careful about reading me. That's why I make sure I mouth them while I sign. But he's a quick-learner. "No, it's fine. We could get takeout instead. Are you craving anything?"

Craving? What am I craving? Why is it always about what I want? Why doesn't he ever ask me to make him something, or tell me what he's in the mood for? There's this strange imbalance in the way he defers to me, like my happiness is some fragile thing that needs to be coddled and fed, while his can just sit on the shelf, unattended. It makes me uncomfortable. I don't want him to think I'm tallying up favors or waiting for some payback. I don't do things for him so he'll do them for me. I just . . . I just want to be a good wife.

I lower my gaze to the floor and sign slowly, *What do you want to eat?*

Out of the corner of my eye, I see him let out a soft breath. For one irrational second, I think he's annoyed with me, but when I look up, I find him tapping his chin, brow furrowed in thoughtful consideration. "How about Mexican?"

Oh, God. No.

Don't get me wrong, it's not the food itself—it's great, honestly, I used to inhale it without a second thought back when I was with my ex.

But it's the years I spent swallowing mouthfuls of salsa and pretending everything was fine, sitting across from a man who smiled in public and turned monstrous in private that tarnished it.

All those dinners I tried to choke down under the scrutiny of his sunken eyes, waiting for his mood to change. Mexican restaurants were his favorite; he'd even bring home greasy takeout bags when he wanted to smooth things over, like an olive branch I was supposed to be grateful for. I'd sit there with an upset stomach, eating because if I didn't, he'd notice. If I didn't smile, he'd notice.

I know it's ridiculous. I know I'm safe now. And I've got bigger things to untangle than my stupid aversion to a plate of enchiladas. But try telling that to my pulse as it starts to pound, or the stones gathering at the base of my throat.

Raees is waiting for an answer, smiling a little, looking so damn hopeful. He has no idea. And I hate this. I hate that I can't be normal and say "Sure, Mexican sounds great!" without feeling like my whole body is about to shut down.

For him, I tell myself. I press my lips into what I hope is a smile and sign, *Okay.*

His handsome face lights up, and he starts scrolling through his phone, rattling off something about how amazing this place is, how he's been going there for years. He turns the screen to show me the menu, all proud and cheerful.

My heart dives off a cliff.

No.

No, no, no. It can't be.

But there it is, right in front of me.

The same logo, the same green-and-gold color scheme, the same fucking restaurant.

My stomach clenches so hard I feel nauseous.

It's his place. The place he always insisted on. The place we went to that Friday night on my 22nd birthday at half past ten.

The details are burned into my brain.

He sent me in to order one shrimp taco, five chicken empanadas, an orange Crush, extra guac and chips. The total was thirty-fifty. I paid in cash, felt the crumple of bills in my hand, left a tip even though I was running low on money that week. I was always the one who paid.

I got back to the red Nissan, climbed in with the food, and buckled up. Radiohead was playing. God, how I *hate* Radiohead. I told him that, under my breath, and he just smirked, turning it up louder. The car stank of marijuana, of him, of everything that made my skin crawl. And when I tried to just sit quietly, to make myself invisible like I always did, he told me to feed him. Like I was some kind of servant. *"Come on, Neerah, I'm driving."*

The bag was warm on my lap, rain slashing down, loud enough to drown out my own breathing. He leaned over the steering wheel, one hand holding his joint, the other reaching out, impatient. *"Feed me,"* he slurred, eyes glassy with the weed and whatever else he's on.

I'd learned to read his threats like a weather forecast. And that night, the storm had already arrived. *"Feed me!"*

"Just focus on the road, okay? We can eat when we get back to your place."

But that's not good enough. It was never good enough.

"Take it off."

"Take what off?"

"Your seatbelt, Neerah. Take your fucking seatbelt off."

"Dame—"

"Take it off!"

I knew better than to argue when he sounded like that. *"There. It's off."*

He reached over and grabbed the belt, pulling it toward him, stretching it across the console, his focus split between me and the road.

"Dame, what are you doing—?"

"Shut the fuck up." He looped the seat belt around my throat.

Once.

Twice.

The coarse fabric bit into my skin.

"Dame, please—augh!" My voice came out strangled as I clawed at the belt, fingers scrabbling against it, trying to loosen it, but he just tightened his grip until every breath was a battle.

He yanked my head forward by the belt, then twisted his fingers into my hair, wrenching me so hard that my skull felt like it was splitting apart.

I barely had time to gasp before my forehead slammed into the dashboard with a sickening crack. Pain exploded as my seat belt cut into my throat. He pulled me back and shoved me forward again.

And again.

And again.

Something hot and metallic had filled the back of my throat, dripping down my chin.

Blood.

There was so much blood.

It was everywhere, coating my tongue, making me choke as I struggled to breathe, to think, to make it stop. The belt around my throat carved deeper, cutting off what little air I had left. My lungs burned, my vision swam, and all I could hear was the relentless pounding of my own heartbeat.

The music was blasting, bass thrumming against my ribcage, swallowing his words—but I could still hear them, each one shot like a bullet.

"Bitch."

"Ungrateful slut."

"Fucking whore."

The car lurched, the wheels skidded on the slick road, but he didn't stop. He didn't let go. He was so consumed by his rage that he didn't even notice the world spinning out of control around us.

CRASH!

I take a deep breath, pressing my fingers to my throat, feeling the skin there itch and burn, as if the belt is still leashing me. The air feels congested, like I'm breathing through wet cotton, and every time I swallow, it hurts. It burns.

My bones ache, a marrow-deep ache that remembers every bruise and fracture. My temples pound in time with my heartbeat. *Thud, thud, thud.* My forehead throbs with phantom pain, and my nose prickles, numb from the memory of breaking.

Black spots drift across my vision, tiny bursts of darkness that swell and blur everything around me.

I stagger backward, the world tilting, my legs folding until I'm on the ground, clutching the carpet, trying to find something solid. But nothing feels real. The sounds around me are muffled. Warped. I'm underwater again, trying to end my life in the bathtub.

There's a voice calling my name.

Is it him?

Or is it Shahzad?

Dua?

But I see flashes of hospital lights too bright, the smell of antiseptic. My siblings' pale, shocked faces as they stare at me lying there, twisted in casts, my neck immobilized, broken blood vessels in my eyes, my legs wrapped tight. The doctor's voice: *We did the best we could to preserve her vocal cords.*

I curl my hand around my throat.

No cast. There's no cast. But there was. There was. The scar tissue tightens, and I feel that awful constriction, like I'm suffocating all over again.

They should've done more.

They should've left me to die.

They should've brought my voice.

"*Zinneerah!*"

A voice slices through the fog, tethering me back to reality, but only just.

I look up, blinking hard, my vision still struggling to clear.

My heart seizes when I see a pair of honey-brown eyes staring down at me.

Raees. It's Raees.

My husband, Raees.

That's true. I have a husband now.

Raees is my husband.

I'm not Zinneerah Arain anymore.

I'm Zinneerah Shaan.

The thought shatters something in me, and before I know it, I'm crying.

Big, wracking sobs that I can't stop, like my body is purging something it's been holding onto for too long.

Dear brain, this is a safe space. Raees is a safe man. He had defended you at the grocery store. He protected you from that man. He paid for the groceries. He is going to take care of you. He is a good man. This is your home now. This is a safe space you'll be sharing with your husband. He is a safe man. He will not hurt you. This is a safe space that belongs to you, too. This is your home now. This is a safe space you'll be sharing with your husband. He is a safe man. He will not hurt you. This is a safe space that belongs to you, too. This is your home now. This is a safe space you'll be sharing with your husband. He is a safe man. He will not hurt you. This is a safe space that belongs to—

Something soft brushes my cheek, and I feel a tiny sting in my eyes as I blink myself awake.

Raees' face comes into focus.

His brows are knit in concentration, mouth pressed into a serious line. He's being so careful, dabbing at my cheeks with the corner of his sleeve, his fingers light as a feather as they tuck a stray strand of hair behind my ear. I didn't even realize I'd cried this much.

God, how did I let myself get to this point? Again.

A hiccup shudders through me, and I bite my lip to stifle it, but it only makes my throat ache worse.

Raees doesn't say anything. He doesn't ask questions or poke for answers. He just stands up, strides over to my desk, and grabs my water bottle. I should be grateful—most people would've been asking if I was okay by now, if I wanted to talk about it. But he doesn't. He just unscrews the cap with a little pop, and kneels back down, holding it out for me.

I reach for it, my hands still trembling, and take a long, desperate sip, letting the cool water soothe the rawness in my throat. He watches me quietly, never once looking away.

"How about sushi?" Raees whispers.

I blink at him, surprised, and he gives me this adorable, lopsided smile as he reaches out, brushing a thumb against my chin to catch a stray drop of water. It's such a simple gesture, such a gentle gesture, and it makes me want to curl up and hide at the same time.

I turn my face away, swallowing the guilt that's rising in my throat.

I don't deserve this. I don't deserve him. Sitting here, offering me water, and soft smiles, pretending I'm not a walking disaster. He should be with someone who doesn't crumble at the slightest mention of food, who doesn't need to be pieced back together over and over again.

I thought I'd buried this—this *needy*, broken part of me. I thought I'd learned how to keep it all locked up, safe and sound, where it couldn't hurt anyone. Or make anyone feel obligated to take care of me.

I wipe at my own cheeks, taking over the job he started. Then, I stand, pulling my arms tight around myself so I don't fall apart. My fist presses against my chest in a slow, absent circle.

Sorry.

Raees dips his head, trying to catch my downcast eyes, and when I finally glance up, he's doesn't drop that gorgeous smile of his. "Please don't ever apologize to me."

It's strange hearing that. He's looking at me like he won't budge until he's sure I understand.

My lips press together, and I manage a small nod. It seems to satisfy him, but my hand is still curled tight against my chest.

He glances at his watch, then back at me with a spark in his eyes. "Actually, I think I feel like cooking tonight. But only if you'll bake with me," he says, running a hand through his hair in a way that makes my stomach flip. "I was hoping for chocolate chip cookies. The soft, gooey kind. What do you say?"

I rub the last dampness from my eyes with the back of my wrists and nod. Of course I'll make him cookies. I'll make him a hundred cookies if it will make up for being such a mess today, for ruining our take-out plans.

It'll be a welcoming distraction.

He smiles like I've just given him the best news he's heard all day. "I mean it, Zinneerah. No more apologizing. I'm serious about this. Do you understand?"

I manage a nod.

He's like the sun coming out from behind clouds, so sudden and bright that it throws me off balance. "Why don't you take a few minutes? Whenever you're ready, I'll be downstairs."

With one final smile, he exits my room.

13

Raees

I'm lucky I haven't taken off a finger by now.

The knife's moving faster than rationality, and that's saying something.

But nothing compares to the noise in my head. All I hear, over and over, is her—the gasping breaths, the thud of her body hitting the floor, her voice hoarse and broken, nails scraping at her own throat like she could claw her trachea right out.

I chop faster, knuckles pale around the handle.

It's just spinach, but I'm tearing into it like it committed some heinous crime against my wife. My mind's a loop of questions I can't answer.

What the hell happened to her? Where's the woman who looked at me with that wicked glint, the one who pulled me close just to mess with me, to make me forget everything but her? *Where is she?*

The blade slips from my hand, clattering onto the counter, and I'm gripping the edge, fingers digging into the wood so hard it creaks. It takes everything I have not to punch straight through it.

Who hurt my wife and how the fuck do I kill them?

At least now I know. It wasn't some illness that stole her voice—it was *someone*. Someone hurt her, tore something out of her that I don't know if I can ever get back for her. And I swear, when I find out who did this, they're going to wish they'd never been born.

I hear her footsteps whisper on the wood. I could pick the sound out of a crowd blindfolded. It's how she moves through the world, like she's trying not to disturb anything, or anyone.

I paint on a smile that probably looks about as genuine as a plastic mask. But it's the best I can manage, and maybe she'll believe it. Like putting a Band-Aid on a bullet wound, but what else can I do?

Zinneerah steps into the kitchen, wrapped in an oversized sweater, with pajama pants dragging slightly, and her hair braided up in a crown that makes her look like some kind of divine entity who wandered into my life by mistake.

"Feeling better?" I ask.

She nods. *Thank you.*

"Nothing to thank me for," I say, trying to keep it light as I pick up the knife again. "Pasta sauce is almost done. Just gotta throw everything together. Give me half an hour?"

Another nod, another quiet thanks. Always so polite. It doesn't matter how many times I tell her, she'll never listen.

She points at the mixer on the counter. *Bake?*

"I wouldn't want anything else." I grab the mixer and set it up in front of her, close enough so I can keep an eye on her while I finish chopping. Not that I need to watch her every second. I like to know she's there, in my orbit, where I can reach her.

Zinneerah slips her apron off the hook inside the pantry door, the faded grey one she always uses, and starts to tie it on. Her hands are shaking, though, and she keeps fumbling the strings, a little huff of frustration escaping her lips.

I put the knife down and walk over. "May I?"

She doesn't look at me, just nods and turns, offering her back.

I take the strings and secure them in a bow. "Too tight?"

She shakes her head, and gives me a thumbs-up. I step back, letting her get to work in her own little corner of the kitchen.

Around nine, I'm plating dinner—pasta rolled just right, a bit of garnish, crispy garlic bread on the side. Zinneerah is across the room, wiping her forehead with the back of her hand as she slides a tray of cookies into the oven. She stands rooted, admiring them through the glass.

"Dinner's ready," I say.

She doesn't look up. Her smile fades, her gaze goes distant, wandering somewhere else entirely. She does this sometimes—one minute she's here, the next, miles away in her own head. It's like watching a wave pull back from the shore, leaving her empty-eyed and far away.

I used to do the same thing, back when I was younger. Back when I broke off my engagement. Spending years retreating into my mind, searching for some kind of peace in there. I get it.

But I want Zinneerah to find peace with me.

I step up beside her, give a little wave in her line of sight.

Her dark eyes refocus, and she languidly blinks up at me.

"Dinner," I say again. "Would you like to eat at the table, or the island?"

You pick.

Neither option feels quite right. At the table, we'd sit too far apart, just two people stranded on opposite ends of polished wood. But at the island, we'd be elbow-to-elbow, cramped in a way that feels too close for tonight.

"How about outside?" I suggest, nodding toward the back patio.

Zinneerah's eyes glimmer. She could use some fresh air after everything that happened, and maybe I could, too. Clear our heads a bit.

We gather our plates, glasses of water, and head out. The patio's quiet, the round table waiting under its big blue umbrella, two chairs across from each other.

I help her sit first, then take the seat across from her. Her gaze turns to the pool, where the last of the evening light shimmers in soft aquamarine hues.

I wait until she takes her first bite, watching her face, and hoping I didn't overdo it on the seasoning. "Your verdict?"

She chews, a smile spreading slowly. God, I love that smile—eyes squinting into dark crescents, cheeks rounding up, even that tiny dimple that appears on her chin when she's genuinely happy.

I love it, she signs, *you cook great.*

"Thank you, thank you." I give a little bow, grinning as I finally dig in myself.

Yeah, I nailed it.

Every time I cook for her, it feels like a small victory. I started learning my way around a kitchen after I found out her older brother was an inspiring chef. I figured she was used to good food, and wouldn't want anything less. So, I took lessons, begged Ammi-ji for her best recipes, and filled a whole binder with stuff I thought she'd like.

There was maybe a fifty-fifty chance she actually wanted to marry me. Meanwhile, I was in this at a hundred percent. Always will be.

"Excited for the concert this weekend?" I ask.

Zinneerah freezes, her fork hovering mid-bite.

Shit. What the hell did I do now?

She frowns, sets her fork down, and looks at me with that apologetic expression. Her fingers fidget, curling and uncurling.

No, no, no. What did I do? Did I say something wrong? Why isn't she smiling anymore? Maybe she's not going anymore?

Do you—She wrings out her hands then tries again. *Go with me?*

Oh.

I let out a sigh of relief. She's fine. I didn't say anything stupid. "Of course. I'd love to go. Is Dua coming with us?"

I don't know. Busy.

"Got it." I can feel myself grinning like an idiot, probably way too much, like a kid who just unwrapped exactly what he wanted. "Either way, I'm excited. I haven't been to a concert since . . . well, it's been sometime."

Zinneerah smiles in response, and takes out her phone, typing out on her Notes app: Are you sure you're not busy? I don't want to pull you away from work.

"Don't worry about it. I don't work weekends, and I already finished grading everything." That's a lie. I've got a mountain of work waiting for me tonight. I'll be pulling an all-nighter just to clear my plate so we can have the next few days free. But it's worth it.

Our first date together as a married couple. The thought sends a shiver of excitement through me, and I shove a big forkful of food in my mouth to keep it from showing too much.

Zinneerah taps the back of my hand, bringing me out of my thoughts. She's holding her phone out, screen turned toward me.

There's a paragraph typed up.

What happened upstairs, I need you to know it wasn't you. It wasn't anything you did. It was the past clawing its way up again, grabbing me by the throat when I thought I'd buried it for good. Small things that shouldn't have any power over me anymore. But they still do. I spent two years in doctors' offices and therapists' chairs, trying to strip that power away. Learning how to breathe through it, how to stand tall and stay present.

And I'm better, I am. I thought I was stronger than this. But sometimes, without warning, it's like I'm right back there, drowning in things I can't explain, not even to you. You deserve better than the silence I give you when it gets like that. You deserve more than me locking it all up inside, pretending I'm fine. I should've let you in. I wanted to let you in. But instead, I shut down, and I see the hurt in your eyes, and it's like looking into a mirror.

I'm sorry, Raees. More than you'll ever know.

I glance up at her when her phone screen goes dark. She flicks her eyes away, looking deeply apologetic. "Zinneerah, you don't have to apologize to me when you're not feeling well. I want us to communicate, always, one hundred percent. But if something's really bothering you, so much that you can't talk about it, I want you to just take a breath, get some rest, and tell me when you're ready. Even if it's an hour later, or a week."

She presses her lips together, her gaze still down, hands folded tightly in her lap. All I want to do is lift her chin and kiss her forehead, where she keeps her storms locked away.

"Hey," I say, picking up her fork and offering it to her. "Do you, by chance, have any strong opinions on candles?"

She takes the fork from me with shaky fingers, looking guarded, but a little amused. A good sign.

"So, imagine this," I continue, settling into my chair like I'm about to give an important lecture. "Teenage me, my mom, and Ramishah in Bath and Body Works. They're on a mission, right? Drowning in lotions, testing every perfume on those little paper sticks. Meanwhile, I'm off in my own little world, sniffing every candle on the shelves like some sort of fragrance connoisseur." I see her lips twitch, so I press on. "And then, I find it. This candle— campfire something—that smells exactly like my dad. And I don't mean, 'Oh, a reminder,' I mean, dead ringer. Like my dad had somehow been distilled into wax."

Her eyes widen a bit.

I continue. "Suddenly, I'm hit with this tidal wave of, I don't know emotions? Nostalgia? Teenage angst? Anyway, I completely lose it. Right there in the middle of the store."

She raises an eyebrow. *You?*

"Oh, yeah," I say, leaning back with a grin. "In front of everyone. Moms, grandmas, my entire high school girl population, breathing like I'm trying to pass a lung capacity test."

Her brows arched to their limit, meeting her hairline. I've missed those reactions. There was a time when she was so expressive, all wide eyes and open laughter, stumbling over her own feet laughing, gasping for breath with that full-on, wide-eyed grin.

"It was a rough time," I mutter. "My father was a relentless smoker, practically an ambassador for Marlboro. One pack a day, maybe more. He always carried that unmistakable scent of stale tobacco, like it came stitched into his clothes. We didn't . . . well, let's just say he and I were never close." I wave a hand in the air, warding off an invisible cloud of smoke. "So, to this day, whenever I catch even a whiff of cigarette smoke, something inside me freezes up, as though I'm a kid again."

Zinneerah bites her bottom lip, her gaze dropping down to my hand over my heart. Then she looks away, brushing a stray tear from the corner of her eye.

Oh, no.

Did I overshare? I definitely overshared. She was just coming down from a panic attack, and now she looks even more worried. I didn't mean to upset her. I only want to let her know she isn't alone.

She has me. She'll always have me.

Zinneerah huffs out a wobbly little smile and wipes the leftover tears from her cheeks. *I get sad fast*, she signs.

I breathe out, relieved. *Me, too*, I think. "But Zinneerah?"

She lifts her head, eyes curious.

"You don't have to be sad alone," I say. "You're my wife. If you're going to be sad, then I'm coming with you. We'll tackle it together, one baby step at a time. We've got, what, another fifty or hundred years to figure this out? No rush. We can afford to sit in our feelings a little."

Zinneerah's face softens. She reaches over, picks up an extra slice of garlic bread from her plate, and places it on mine.

"That's yours—"

What is mine is yours, she signs.

I reel in a deep breath through my nose and pinch my lips into a discreet smile, biting the inside of my cheek. My wife has me acting like a lovesick school-boy around her.

Clearing my throat, I mentally scramble for a safe topic before I accidentally blurt out an "I love you" and throw off the whole mood. "So, any idea on what we're supposed to wear to this concert?"

Zinneerah tilts her head, giving it that thoughtful side-to-side wobble. She starts reaching for her phone, and I jump in before she gets too distracted to eat.

"Don't worry about it," I say, holding up my hands like I'm calming a skittish animal. "We can iron out the details after dinner—cookies, coffee, and tea. I don't want your food to get cold on account of my rambling."

Zinneerah smiles and places her phone face-down, lifting her fingers instead. *You want to know my favourite candle?*

My wife wants to talk to me about her favorite candle? This feels like some kind of reward. I'm basking in it.

I give her a grand, sweeping gesture. "The stage is all yours."

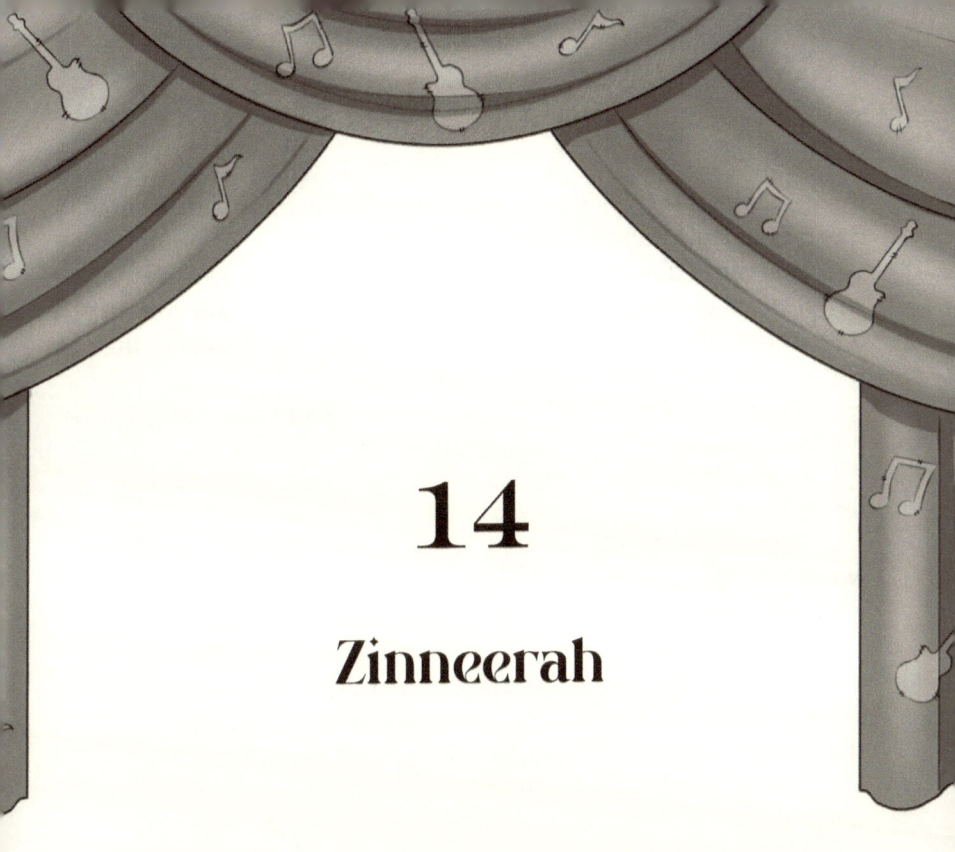

14

Zinneerah

My husband cannot stop moaning.

I can't even look at him. I'm staring down at my own cookie, trying to nibble politely, but his sounds are making it impossible to concentrate. Heat rises up my neck, spreading over my cheeks as if I'm being baked at 300 deg-Raees.

He doesn't have a clue what he's doing to me.

"This is the best thing I've ever eaten in my whole entire life," he says, eyes half-lidded, reaching for yet another cookie. His fifth. He's barely finished swallowing before he groans again, and then he mutters, "Fuck," under his breath.

Oh, that word. *That* word in *that* voice.

I press my lips together, trying to stifle a laugh—or maybe just a gasp—and clutch my mug a little tighter. It shouldn't affect me like this. They're just cookies. But the sound of him enjoying them is doing all kinds of ridiculous things to me. My mind is in the gutter, my stomach's flipping like a gymnast, and all I can think about is how much I suddenly want to kiss the crumbs off his lips.

Honestly, I didn't even know he knew how to curse. He's always so put-together, like he's stepped straight out of one of those Regency dramas Dua binge-watches every other weekend. The kind of man who'd tip his hat and bow if he wore one.

Raees' hand hovers over the plate, reaching for what would be his sixth cookie.

I slide it closer to me, just out of his reach, and he looks at me, scandalized.

"I wasn't finished, Zinneerah," he complains, sounding for all the world like a petulant child.

I shake my head, feigning disapproval. *Very sweet.*

He stares at me, deadpan, then slumps against the counter, sulking as he nurses his coffee. The theatrics don't stop—casting little sideways glances at me, practically begging for sympathy, his shoulders rising and falling with the longest sighs.

I take a sip of my chamomile tea, letting the warm liquid cover my grin.

He's so stubborn about his sweets. Just yesterday, he tried to sneak an extra brownie into his lunch after I'd packed it, thinking I wouldn't notice. Caught him red-handed with the container lid half-open and a guilty look on his face.

"No one in my family has diabetes," he grumbles, swirling the coffee in his mug. "Just so you're aware."

Oh, great. Now I feel guilty. I'm so used to his bright smiles and endless chatter that seeing him wear a long face, with those sad-puppy eyes, and that tragic little frown, tugs at my heartstrings.

I reach for a cookie, break it in half, and wordlessly offer him the bigger piece.

Raees' face lights up like a thousand Christmas trees. He snatches it eagerly, and as he takes it from me, our fingers brush. I don't think he even notices—he's too busy frolicking in the sugar high, melting against the counter as he chews, eyes closed, over the moon.

"I want you to bake for me for the rest of our lives," he murmurs.

That look of pure contentment makes my heart spin and whizz. This kitchen is finally mine. A place where I can sink into a recipe, cover my hands in flour, lose myself in measuring and stirring and creating.

Baking is like, I don't know, meditation with a purpose. I get to calm down, focus, and then at the end of it, there's this little offering I can give to someone else. A piece of myself that they can actually enjoy, even if it's just a few bites. And when it makes someone happy—especially him—it's like a little rush of joy that's all mine.

Maybe that's silly. But he's always been my favorite taste-tester, and the way he looks at me after he eats something I made? It's hard not to feel a little flustered.

I unlock my phone and pull up a Pinterest board I made for Alex's concert next weekend—specifically, for what I might wear. I'd been curating ideas for weeks now, adding in a few looks that caught my eye.

Ever since that conversation with Dua, though, I'd thrown in a few more masculine styles. Not that I was picking out clothes for anyone, exactly, but now I've gone ahead and extended the invitation to Raees. He always looks so formal—cashmere sweaters, dress pants, everything neatly pressed. Handsome, really, but this concert is more about obscure, alternative, edginess. In his case, jeans.

I pat the stool next to me, awakening him from his chocolate ecstasy.

Raees dusts off his hands and joins me, bringing that woodsy scent of sandalwood with him. I have to resist the urge to lean closer.

Opening my notes app, I type: Do you have clothes like this? Then I switch back to Pinterest and hand him my phone, letting him scroll through the outfits I'd saved.

Raees quietly studies each pin with that analytical concentration of his, pausing every so often to adjust his glasses or take a sip of his coffee.

My heart is pounding a little too hard, and I'm not entirely sure why. It's just clothes. Bunch of organized ideas. But something about this moment feels intimate.

Finally, he looks up, locking eyes with me.

I feel my face heat up, and before I can stop myself, I look up at the ceiling, pretending I'm just checking for dust, or I don't even know what.

"I do have casual clothes," he says, sounding uncertain, as if the concept of 'casual' is foreign territory. "But putting together a proper outfit . . . that might be a struggle. Unless, of course, you'd like to help me?"

He smiles, and I lose my train of thought entirely. His golden-brown eyes crinkle at the corners, and there's this tiny smudge of chocolate on his upper lip.

Without thinking, I tap my own lips.

Raees' eyes land on my mouth, and his eyes go wide. Both eyebrows shoot up high. His lips part in this little "oh" of surprise, and he stares at me like I just grew a second head.

I tap my mouth again, trying to signal chocolate, because honestly, it's driving me crazy.

"Are you . . . are you sure?" he whispers, voice a little shaky.

I tilt my head, wondering what on earth he's talking about. *Yes*, I sign.

I tap my lips again, resisting the urge to just reach over and wipe it off myself.

He lets out a breath, rubbing his palms on his sweatpants like he's bracing himself for something monumental. "Wow. Okay. I didn't think this would happen so soon."

What is he muttering about?

Raees glances around the kitchen, eyes darting over the counters like he's looking for a clue. Then, as if making some grand decision, he clears his throat and meets my eyes. "How should I do it?"

We're out of tissue paper, and I used up the last of the kitchen towel.

Oh, for heaven's sake.

I give up on subtlety and point from his mouth to my own, then stick my tongue out and gesture like I'm licking something off my lips.

To my relief, he gets the hint—kind of. He licks his lips, and the smudge of chocolate vanishes. I give him a thumbs-up and a smile.

Raees chuckles, then, without warning, raises both hands, framing my face in his palms.

What is he doing?

He leans in close, lips hovering a breath away from mine.

I push back, alarmed, and press my hands to his lips before he can get any closer.

Raees stops, blinking in surprise. "Hmm?" he mumbles against my fingers.

I quickly sign: *Chocolate. Your lips.*

The realization slowly settles within him. His mouth forms a small 'o' that he breathes out through.

Oh.

Oh, he was going to *kiss* me.

He was going to kiss *me*?

Why would he—wait. Oh, God. I'm an idiot. Of course he was going to kiss me. And instead of just wiping the stupid chocolate from his lips, I had to make a whole production out of it.

Raees drops his face into his hands, and all I want to do is disappear. Bury myself under the floorboards. Become one with the furniture. I'd be less mortified as a coffee table.

I want to die.

I want to die.

I want to die.

Should I kiss him to make him feel better? Maybe a quick one on the cheek. Or his forehead, even. But I don't know if I have the nerve to actually do it. Still, the guilt is gnawing at me. I'll be up all-night replaying this if I don't do something.

He looks up, and there's this shy, lopsided smile on his face, his cheeks flushed. I press my lips together, fighting back a grin of my own, trying to keep some semblance of composure.

Then he lets out this soft snort that tumbles into laughter, like fresh strawberry jam spreading over warm toast. It ripples through the room, slipping under my skin, making my heart trip over itself.

I go along with it, trying to forget the sensation of how his big, warm hands had cradled my face. We're close enough that our foreheads almost touch as we dissolve into laughter, letting the absurdity of it all spill out.

"Let's just pretend that never happened," he says, grinning through his chuckles.

Easier said than done on my end, but I nod anyway.

He takes a long sip of his coffee, his gaze pointedly averted. "Should we, uh, do the outfit thing now?"

Tomorrow?

"Of course." He takes my empty tea mug and stacks it on top of his own. With a tiny smile, he slips off the stool. "Goodnight."

Wait. That was abrupt. And where's my "Goodnight, Zinneerah"?

My fingers curl into fists, knuckles pressing white. This is on me. I must've totally embarrassed him. I mean, maybe I wasn't technically leaning in for a kiss, but to the untrained eye, it probably looked like I was giving him some kind of green light.

Smooth. Really smooth.

I bite my lip, sliding off the stool with half-formed apologies simmering on my tongue—*Don't ever apologize to me, Zinneerah.*

Damn it, Raees.

Instead, I reach for a cookie from the plate, my steps cautious as I cross the room and tap his arm.

He turns, eyebrows raised. "Yes—?"

Without giving myself time to second-guess, I press the cookie to his lips.

His mouth opens instinctively, teeth sinking into the soft dough, eyes widening in surprise.

Before I can think, I break off the end still dangling and pop it into my own mouth.

That's . . . almost a kiss.

Heat blooms in my cheeks, and I look away, chewing quickly before he can see just how red I've turned.

And because fleeing is clearly my go-to strategy now, I turn on my heel and hightail it out of the kitchen.

In the morning, I'm up early, moving around the kitchen as I put together Raees' lunch.

I slip an extra cookie into the bag, a small peace offering for last night's fiasco. Cookies don't solve awkward almost-kisses, but it's worth a shot.

I make his coffee, finishing my own tea while scrambling eggs and toasting bread. His toast gets butter and a thick layer of strawberry jam, just the way he likes it. Mine stays plain, as usual. I set his plate down at just the right angle, switch on his favorite news channel, and smooth out the newspaper that was delivered today, laying it perfectly beside his coffee mug.

Usually, I'd just start eating on my own, before he stumbles in, half-asleep, somewhere in the middle of my breakfast.

But today, I hover by the counter with my mug, waiting. I woke up wanting to share this morning with him—maybe out of guilt from last night, I don't know.

Tossing and turning in bed, I kept rewinding the tape, my fingers pressing over his soft mouth, stopping him just inches from a sweet kiss. I was the one who panicked, but now I can't seem to shake the feel of his hand on my cheek, the way my heart galloped when he leaned in, almost . . . almost.

The almost-kiss. It sticks to my thoughts like honey. *Honey.* Raees' eyes are the color of honey.

I take a sip of tea, only to find it's gone tepid. Maybe I should switch to iced-tea.

"Good morning!" Raees' bright baritone bounces off the walls, jolting me out of my thoughts. I look up to find him grinning at the counter where I've set out his breakfast, coffee just the way he likes it, and the news quietly playing on the TV. "You know, I say this every time, but thank you. I'll keep saying it until you're sick of hearing it."

I give him a little shrug, but I can't quite hide my smile.

He pushes his stool back, choosing to stand and eat across from me at the island, close enough that I can smell the faint scent of his cologne mingling with the coffee.

I bite my lip, eyeing the TV behind him. If he sat where I am, he could watch it easily. I don't really mind switching, but how do I say that without sounding ridiculous?

I tap the counter. *Stand here, please.*

He blinks at me, a forkful of eggs halfway to his mouth. "You want to switch?"

I nod sheepishly.

"Why?" He looks genuinely curious, his eyebrows knitting together in that adorable way that always trips me up.

I glance at the TV, then back to him, tilting my head toward his eyes, hoping he'll connect the dots. It's like a charades game, but I think he's finally catching on.

He studies me, the corner of his mouth curling up in that lopsided grin that always makes my heart stumble a little. "You're a sweetheart, you know that?" he murmurs to himself.

Yeah, I don't think he meant to say that out loud.

And suddenly, I'm feeling a little too hot, a little too happy, and trying very hard not to let it show.

Raees doesn't so much as blink after calling me a 'sweetheart'. Instead, he just opens the newspaper like he hasn't just melted half the bones in my body with one casual little 'sweetheart.' Just sitting there glowing like some kind of domestic god.

I stand there with my plate in my hand. The only reason I was stationed across the island in the first place was because I figured he'd prefer it that way. Less chance of annoying him, right? Less chance of him getting irritated if I breathed wrong. Or chewed too loud. You know, just the usual anxieties I still carry around like a purse.

It's silly. I know that. But old habits are hard to kill.

I finally slide onto the stool next to him, trying to keep my movements unobtrusive. I reach for my toast, but then hesitate, my stomach twisting a little.

I glance at Raees out of the corner of my eye. His toast is all soft and mushy, soaked with butter and jam, so it doesn't make a sound when he bites into it. But mine? It's perfectly crisp, just how I like it. It's going to make a crunch. A loud crunch. And suddenly that feels like an insurmountable problem.

The line between his brows deepens a little as he focuses, totally absorbed by an article. He doesn't look annoyed, or like he's bracing himself for the horrors of the impending crunching noises. But still, I hesitate, holding my toast like it's some kind of ticking bomb.

Get a grip, Zinnie. It's just toast. Normal people don't panic over toast.

I take the tiniest nibble possible, barely cracking through the crust. My shoulders tense, bracing for . . . what, exactly? I don't even know.

Raees' gaze flicks to me mid-bite. I freeze, cheeks flaming, but he just gives me that delightful smile. "Good?"

I nod, trying to look like I haven't just been caught red-handed doing my best squirrel impression. But I can feel a little smile drawing at my lips. I can't remember the last time someone looked at me like that over something as simple as toast.

I take another bite, a real one this time, and let the crunch ring out, fighting the urge to flinch. Raees doesn't react, or shift away or give me a disgusted, withering look I used to get every time I dared to exist too loudly. He just keeps reading, dipping his toast into his coffee like an old uncle, occasionally murmuring to himself about an article.

Raees just makes everything I was told I do wrong, right.

And the funny thing is, the longer I sit here, the easier it gets. I even pick up my tea, slurping it a little as I sip. Every little sound, every tiny act of defiance against those old rules, feels like untying a knot in my chest.

I sneak another glance at him, half-expecting him to scoff or roll his eyes. But he just keeps eating, relaxed and smiling, close enough that I could lean my head on his shoulder if I were brave enough.

It's such a small thing, probably nothing to him, but to me, it feels like someone quietly handing me back a part of myself.

"So, will you be joining me on campus today?" Raees asks.

I shake my head, and sign, *Monday.*

He folds the newspaper before he even finishes reading it, setting it aside. His full attention shifts to me, which immediately sends my pulse into some embarrassing overdrive. I frown, pointing at the paper. "I'd rather hear about your day than worry about the world's."

I bite the inside of my cheek, trying to keep my smile in check as I turn my attention back to my plate.

Scooping up the last of my eggs, I dump them onto one piece of toast and press the other slice on top, making myself a quick little breakfast sandwich. It's nothing fancy, but it'll save me from having to take tiny, bite-sized forkfuls like I'm auditioning for a dinner etiquette video.

"That's smart," Raees whispers, and before I know it, he's following my lead, smashing his eggs onto his strawberry jam toast and folding it together. My grimace must betray me as he adds, "Don't judge me." He raises his masterpiece proudly. "It's called innovation."

I try so hard not to laugh, but a little snort escapes anyway. Innovation, my ass. His taste buds don't know the meaning of boundaries.

Still, I pick up my sandwich and play along.

"Cheers," he says, tapping his sandwich against mine with an impish smile before taking a massive bite.

I watch him as he chews, picking at the crumbs that inevitably land on his sweater. He looks more than satisfied by committing the crime of pairing scrambled eggs with strawberry jam.

I take a bite, a much bigger one this time to challenge him.

One of his hazel eyes narrow at me. His lips twitch, his jaw sets, and I know exactly what's coming.

He takes another bite, even bigger than mine, and it's so comically exaggerated that I can't stop the laugh that bursts out of me. I put a hand over my mouth, my shoulders shaking with it, because he looks like a chipmunk who ate all his rations before hibernation.

Raees chokes.

Like, *actually* chokes.

He punches his chest with his fist, coughing violently.

The sandwich hits the plate with a thud as I scramble to grab a glass of water, my chair scraping against the floor in my haste.

His shoulders are jerking as his face turns a shade too close to red for my comfort.

My heart spikes, adrenaline flooding in as I rush to his side, shoving the glass into his hands. He takes it gratefully, chugging it down in big gulps while I rub circles on his back, murmuring silent prayers that I don't have to explain to someone how my husband managed to choke himself on scrambled eggs.

When he finally gets a proper breath in, I grab a tissue and hold it out to him. *Are you okay?*

Raees presses his fist to his mouth, his voice hoarse as he finally croaks, "I thought I was going to die." He lets out a weak chuckle, like this whole situation is just a minor inconvenience instead of a near-death experience.

He thought he was going to die? Well, I thought I was going to have to learn how to resuscitate a grown man using YouTube and panic alone.

I swat his arm—not hard, just enough to get my point across—and drag one of the stools over for him to sit on.

My hands are already flying before I can stop myself. *You work today. I don't want you to throw-up or call sick because of a stomach ache.*

Raees, still coughing a little, nods like a chastised schoolboy. "I know," he rasps. "I'm sorry. I'll be more mindful next time."

And that's when it hits me.

I freeze, blinking at him, my hands hanging awkwardly mid-air. He . . . understood that? All of it?

My brain stumbles over itself, trying to replay the last thirty seconds. I'd been signing like my life depended on it—fast, frantic, forming words that were definitely outside the realm of the basic ASL.

I look at my hands, then at him, then back at my hands again, because clearly one of us has some explaining to do.

Somewhere in the background, my phone chimes with a text notification.

I leave side for a second to check. It's almost like I can sense when my little sister's about to cancel on me.

Doo-Doo: sorry, zinnie. i'm gonna have to cancel our concert date. coach wants to take the boys on a retreat and i'm being forced to join as their manager. ilysm and i'm so sorry. (but totes not sorry abt this being ur first date with raees bhai hehehe)

I let out a long sigh through my nose, and tap out a quick reply: a thumbs-up emoji and a heart. That's all she's getting from me right now.

Sliding my phone back onto the counter, I turn just as Raees finishes the last sip of his coffee and subtle coughing.

"I'm going to head out now," he says, clearing his throat. He picks up the mug and carries it to the sink, rinsing it out. When he walks back past me, he lets his hand trail over my back—a quick rub, like it's something he's always done.

And oh, I don't hate it. I don't think I can hate it. Ever.

"Once I'm back," he adds, grabbing his lunch from the counter, "we can pick out our outfits for the concert tomorrow. Sounds good?"

I look up at him and smile, feeling all sorts of things I probably shouldn't feel about someone who just called me a sweetheart over eggs, then proceeded to choke on said eggs and still somehow make himself look even more attractive.

Have a great day, I sign.

"You, too, Zinneerah," he replies, his baritone back to its normal buttery smoothness.

And then, just like that, he's gone—newspaper tucked under his arm, lunch in hand, leaving behind the faintest trace of expensive cologne and something . . . him.

I glance down at my hands, rubbing my palms together like they're suddenly interesting, eyebrows arching sky-high. "Is he secretly fluent in ASL?"

July 12th

Aside from black, what's your favourite color?

Maroon. You?

Green is my favorite color, and honestly, I don't think it's just about how it looks. Yes, it's beautiful, but it's also alive, you know? It's everywhere in nature: the grass under your feet, the leaves on trees, the moss clinging to rocks after it rains. Green feels like hope. Like growth.

That's a lovely way to put it. I understand now why we have so many plants around the house.

Why do you like the color maroon?

I like to think it suits me. Especially in the form of lipstick.

Yes, I agree.

Oh. Thank you. Green suits you, too.

Thank you.

You're welcome.

Thank you.

You already said that, Raees.

I did. Lots of gratitude to give.

I know :)

15

Raees

"Jesus, looks like we've got a thunderstorm rolling in."

Professor Holmes breezes into the faculty lounge, holding her empty coffee mug.

"Not room for worries here, Nicola. I've got myself a bike poncho." Professor Harris pops his head up from behind the fridge, grinning. He's got this weird enthusiasm for things that no one else cares about, like bike ponchos or solar-powered calculators. "Waterproof and windproof, baby."

Holmes gives me a 'help me' look. It's the universal faculty signal for *I can't interact with this man today*. She even throws in a bonus eye-roll.

I'm parked on the couch, laptop balanced precariously on my knees, trying to make progress on my lecture slides for next week.

Usually, I'd be in my office, but it is currently out of commission thanks to a leaky roof that turned into a full-blown waterfall.

Maintenance is working on it, but by the looks of things, I wouldn't be surprised if they've just installed a kiddie pool and called it a day.

So, here I am, stuck in the lounge. My choices are limited to this:

1. Listen to my colleagues argue about rain gear, tardy students, and how Dean Martin allegedly tried to fight Professor Paldoni over a game of UNO. He got a little too into the spirit of competition, lost a round, and went full animalistic mode. And by "animalistic mode," I mean he threatened to fight the head of the engineering department over an accidental draw-four card. They were both intoxicated, obviously.
2. I've got no other choice.

"So, what's everybody doing this weekend?" Professor Olsen asks, snapping a hair tie off her wrist, and pulling her fiery red hair into a ponytail.

"I'm taking the family fishing," Professor Carlson pipes up. "We booked this cozy albeit costly little cottage at Newfound Lake. It's supposed to be the spot for trout."

"Fishing?" Professor Benedict scoffs, barely looking up from his crossword puzzle. "I'm going clubbing."

The room falls silent. For context: he's seventy-five.

"You're—wait." Olsen blinks. "You? Clubbing?"

"Yes. Clubs still exist. Don't act like I'm a fossil." Benedict shoots her a flat look.

Holmes, quietly stirring her coffee, says, "Maybe he means book clubs."

Laughter erupts around the room, except for Benedict, who grumbles something inaudible but definitely not polite.

"I'm hosting a dinner party," Saira cuts in. She's perched at her usual table, surrounded by a spread of papers, highlighters, and coffee cups. "My best girlfriends from college are visiting, so I'm making coq au vin. Very fancy."

"Coq au vin?" Carlson repeats, testing out the words like he's never heard French in his life. "What is that? Chicken in wine?"

"Exactly. It's very elegant."

"Wine and chicken," Olsen says, shrugging. "Sounds like a good weekend to me."

They all laugh again, except for Holmes, who's been leaning against the counter, sipping her coffee and silently judging the lot of them. She raises an eyebrow and nods in my direction. "And what about you, kid? Big weekend plans with the missus?"

As if I'd indulge any of them. "Not sure yet," I say with a shrug, eyes back on my screen. I'm hoping that's vague enough to deter follow-ups, but with this faculty? Fat chance.

"Oh, come on!" Olsen gasps, clutching her necklace. "You have to have a plan. Weekly dates are mandatory, Professor Shaan! Movies and dinner?"

"Camping?" Carlson chimes in, unhelpfully, while poking at his salad.

"Romantic bike ride?" Harrison tosses out, as if I even own a bike.

"Clubbing?" Benedict. There's always a Benedict. "Get drunk, dance it out. You know, rekindle the magic."

"Jesus, Paul." Holmes smacks him on the back of his head. "Not everybody lives their life in a nightclub."

"What?" he protests, rubbing his head. "I'm just saying—"

"Yeah, no. Stop saying." Holmes cuts him off with her no-nonsense professor glare. "What Raees and his wife do on the weekends is none of our business anymore."

Benedict throws up his hands in mock surrender while the rest of them chuckle. Holmes is clearly the staff-room general, and her soldiers take the hint, retreating back to their grading and schedules.

Everyone except Saira. Who catches my eye with a wave.

Ever since that shopping trip last week, she's been . . . extra friendly. She drops by my office now, asking about my day or a specific topic from her course plan she's unsurely very sure about. After lectures, she's out in the hallway, laughing with a couple of my students about pop music and TV shows, blending right in like she's always been part of their circle.

She's there in the small moments, too—handing me sugar packets when I'm making coffee, grabbing an extra cream-cheese bagel for me even though I've already eaten (which, for what it's worth, I used to skip entirely when we were together).

I know what she's doing. I can see it for what it is. She's smoothing things over, trying to mend whatever's left after the way we ended. She wants to be . . . normal again. To be the person I wave at across campus, chat about the weather with, or exchange polite smiles when we cross paths.

But for me, every little act feels rehearsed, soaked in guilt she's trying to shake off but has trouble doing so.

This—her stopping by, the little gestures—this is her way of apologizing without saying it outright. Her way of making peace for the way she sabotaged our engagement.

I don't have the energy to entertain it. She's a colleague now. Just a colleague. That's all.

Professor Holmes sinks into the couch beside me, letting out a sigh. "Okay, listen," she begins, "have you thought about taking your wife on a date this weekend? Or is that still on your 'maybe someday' to-do list?"

I glance at her. "What makes you think I haven't?"

She lets out a snort. "Oh, please. You talk about your wife like she's the second coming of Christ and you're her most loyal disciple."

Fair point.

She glances down at her phone, scrolling through what looks like an endless string of student emails. "Also, I met her last week when she came to drop off your lunch. Delightful woman, by the way. Shy as hell though. She reminds me of a baby bird—like she'd probably apologize if someone stepped on her foot. But sweet. Sweet is good." She waves her hand like she's done with the compliments. "You need to take her out. Because, from where I'm sitting, you two have nothing in common other than your mutual ability to sit silently in a room and not freak each other out. Which, okay, endearing, but not enough to build a marriage on, kid. Go on a date before she figures out there are other people out there who know how to use their words."

She shakes her head, muttering something that sounds suspiciously like "young people" as she goes back to scrolling through her phone.

What Holmes doesn't know, and neither does Zinneerah, for that matter, is that I've already got plans.

Well, ideas. A list, really. Places I want to take my wife. Foods I want us to try together. Sceneries I want us to experience—be it cobblestone streets in Turkey, beaches in Thailand, or a drive through the Rockies.

But for now, I have to think small. Baby steps. I'm not about to spring international travel on her when I haven't even tested the waters locally.

Maybe dinner and a movie is the way to go. Something simple but thoughtful. I can cook without veering into over-the-top territory. And then we can watch a horror movie in our home theater. The kind of date where clinging to her arm is not only acceptable but expected.

The best part? We wouldn't even have to leave the house. No reservations, no awkward small talk with waiters, no crowds. Just us.

Now all I need to do is wrestle down the anxiety about asking her out.

"We're going to her friend's concert tomorrow night," I say.

Holmes raises an eyebrow over her coffee mug. "Anyone I've ever heard of?"

I snort. "Not a chance."

Her eyes narrow immediately. "Are you calling me old?"

"What? No, of course not," I rebuke quickly, although there is a nugget of truth to it. "I just mean her music is more popular with a specific demographic of people who like alternative stuff."

"So," she says, dragging the word out for maximum effect, "you're calling me old."

"I'm not winning this, am I?"

"Nope," she replies, taking an annoyingly triumphant sip of her coffee. "Anyway, is this your first date together, or do you just like torturing yourself with bad music?"

I nod, ignoring the jab. "It's not exactly what I pictured for our first date, but it makes her happy, so I'm happy."

Holmes leans back on the couch and studies me for a second, her usual snark softening just a bit. "It's kind of nice seeing you like this. When you first told me about her years ago, I thought you'd finally lost it. You were out here acting like a character from a bad Tom Cruise rom-com, building castles in the sky—"

"Gee, thanks."

"—but," she continues, "I like that you still talk about her the same way you did back then. That's rare, and honestly, a little delusional. But in a good way."

My lips curve up.

Back then, the first people I told about Zinneerah were my mom, Ramishah, and, for some reason, Holmes. My sister got most of the scoop, though. I'd call her every time I went to the café to watch Zinneerah perform. I still remember the first time she actually spoke to me—I had to excuse myself to the bathroom mid-conversation just so I could call Ramishah, stumbling over every detail like my life depended on it. She laughed at me for hours.

"Delusional" was pretty much my middle name back then.

Look who's laughing now, ladies.

"Everything good with you and Professor Nadeem?" Holmes questions.

My eyes flick to Saira in the corner of the room, where she's suddenly very interested in pretending to write in her notebook.

"Why wouldn't it be?" I force myself to look back at Holmes. Big mistake. She's watching me with the kind of scrutiny that could crack concrete. Impossible task. I never told her about Saira, thank God.

She paints a picture of casual disinterest. "Oh, no reason. Just that since you two got back from running errands for Wei's retirement party, she's been staring at you like a hyena sizing up its next meal. But then again, every single woman on this campus does. You'd think you're the last man on Earth the way they act. And I know you hate being stared at. Makes your introvert soul want to crawl into a bunker or whatever."

"Ignorance is bliss," I deadpan, fiddling with the alignment of my slides on the laptop. "And as for Professor Nadeem, everything's fine."

"I'll take your word for it." Holmes rises from her seat with a stretch. This conversation has somehow been as taxing for her as it has been for me. She glances at me, one brow raised. "But hey, if something isn't fine, go talk to your wife about it. I don't have the bandwidth to play therapist for you—or anyone, really."

"That's already the plan."

Holmes lets out a short laugh, shaking her head as she heads toward the door. "Smart man," she calls over her shoulder before stepping out.

The staff room falls quiet again, save for the clicking of heels against the hallway tile.

Except those clicks? They're not retreating. They're getting louder. And just as I start to look up, Saira slides into the seat Holmes just vacated, like she's been waiting for her cue.

I don't turn to face her, fingers tapping briskly on my keyboard as I finalize the lecture slides. "Yes, Professor?"

"Oh, for God's sake, Raees. Drop the formalities, will you?"

That earns her a sharp look. "Yes, Professor Nadeem?"

Her smile falters, slipping into a pout. "Fine. Have it your way. I was just wondering if you had time to review my presentation notes tomorrow. We could meet at—"

"I have plans with my wife."

She doesn't budge. "Where are you guys going?"

"Somewhere," I say, dismissively, correcting a typo before pasting an image onto the slide.

"Raees, we can't just ignore this," she murmurs. "We need to talk about how this is going to work."

"There's nothing to talk about," I reply, still typing, though the words are starting to blur.

"This," she says, gesturing discreetly between us. "This needs to be talked about. I needed this job. Do you know how long I've been jumping between freelance gigs, trying to get something stable? North Haven didn't have anything open, so Saint Lawrence was my shot, a real opportunity. I couldn't say no—even if it meant seeing you again. Talking to you again. If I'd known you were—"

"Married?" I finish for her, finally giving her my undivided attention. "Tell me, how exactly does my marital status impact your career? Or your decision to work here? Enlighten me."

Her lips part, but nothing comes out.

"That's what I thought," I whisper. "Let me make this clear: what's past is past. I've moved forward. Built something better, something whole. I would strongly recommend you do the same. And while we're at it, let's set a rule. Don't bring this up again. Not privately. Not publicly. Not ever."

Her face hardens, her eyes trying to read something written on the surface. I think she's about to snap back, but then her jaw tightens, and a brittle smile appears on her lips. "You sounded a lot like your father just now."

My body locks up.

Completely.

Not a single muscle cooperates.

My legs, my arms, even my breathing—it's all stuck, frozen.

She stands, says nothing more, and leaves the room.

You sounded a lot like your father just now.

The words hit me like a metallic bat to the chest, and my head starts to spin. Of all the things she could've said, that is the one she chose?

I've always disliked Saira—resented her, even—but this crosses a line I didn't know existed.

What part of my confession sounded like my father's? Him? That man? That selfish, destructive man who blew up my family and walked away like it was nothing? The man who abused my mother again and again, and never even pretended to care about the wreckage he left behind?

He didn't just ruin his marriage; he ruined us. All of us.

And I've spent years—years—trying to be better than him.

No, more than that: trying to be nothing like him.

I've done everything in my power to be the kind of man who would never cause that kind of pain. It took months of honest conversations with myself just to decide I could risk marriage at all. Months of convincing myself that I wasn't going to be the same pathetic excuse for a husband that he was.

When Saira said 'yes' . . . God, it felt like proof. Proof that she didn't see him in me. Proof that I'd finally separated myself from his shadow. That she didn't believe I was doomed to follow in his footsteps. And for one damn year, I let myself believe it, too.

Only for it to be shattered.

Sure, I could've approached Zinneerah back then. I could've asked her out, dated her, made her my girlfriend—hell, I could've even married her. But I didn't. I didn't because I wasn't ready. I didn't because I knew how much work I still had to do on myself, and I couldn't drag her into the mess of who I was. I couldn't let myself hurt her.

So, I bided my time. Patiently. I worked on myself. I went to therapy. I did everything I could to become the kind of man who could actually love someone without breaking them in the process. And I thought—no, I believed—that patience, that hard work, was worth something.

I don't know what happened to Zinneerah. I don't know why she disappeared from performing, or who stole her voice. All I know is that everything I did—the waiting, the healing—was supposed to prepare me for the day I finally met her again.

But now . . . now all I can hear is Saira's voice.

You sounded a lot like your father just now.

I clear my throat, shut my laptop with more force than I mean to, and instantly regret it.

"Everything all right, Raees?" I hear someone ask. "You look a little pale."

I think I might pass out. God, I feel faint. What is happening?

Grabbing my stuff, I leave the staff room and repeat the mantra that appears every time my anger slowly makes its way to the surface.

I do not sound like my father. I do not act like my father. I will not be my father.

I do not sound like my father. I do not act like my father. I will not be my father.

I do not sound like my father. I do not act like my father. I will not be my father.

I repeat it again and again as I stride down the hall, my vision tunneling in a way that makes the fluorescent lights feel harsher.

My fingers fumble with the lock on my office door, but I get it open. A sharp chemical odor from the roof repairs hits me, making my head spin.

I slam the door shut behind me and throw the lock.

And then my legs give out.

I'm on the floor before I know it, sitting with my back to the door, my knees bent awkwardly, and my breaths coming too fast.

Way too fast.

I'm gulping air through my mouth like I'm trying to chase it down, but my lungs feel like they're collapsing instead.

He's here.

No, no, he's not here.

But it feels like he is, like his shadow is somehow stretching into this tiny office, filling the space with him.

That silhouette. The raised hand. The sickening snap of skin meeting skin. The force of it so hard it almost feels like I'm back there, on the floor of our living room, nimble and powerless, my face stinging, my body convulsing.

"Stop," I whisper hoarsely. "It's not real. It's not real."

But my brain doesn't care. My hands, shaking so violently now they barely feel like mine, flutter uselessly to my chest, clawing at it like I can somehow pry the pain away.

I look down at them, and clench them into fists so tight my nails dig into my palms. The urge to punch something—to punch through something—flares white-hot, but I fight it.

In. Out. In. Out.

Slow it down.

Slow.

It.

Down.

I curl forward instinctively, knees drawn to my chest, my body folding in on itself to protect me.

The world around me is blurry. I can't tell if I'm crying or if it's just the sweat dripping down my face.

And then come the sounds again. I swear I hear him shouting. I swear I hear the slap again.

Why can I still hear it?

My hands move from my temples to my ears, clamping down.

I rock back and forth against the door, pressing harder and harder to block him out.

I do not sound like my father. I do not act like my father. I will not be my father. I do not sound like my father. I do not act like my father. I will not be my father. I do not sound like my father. I do not act like my father. I will not be my father. I do not sound like my father. I do not act like my father. I will not be my father.

I take my glasses off and swipe at my face with the back of my hand, pressing my lips together hard enough that they hurt.

My body is on fire, my muscles twitching with leftover adrenaline, but the worst of it begins to pass.

The constriction in my chest loosens by degrees.

My hearing comes back first, the ringing in my ears fading until I can hear my ragged breaths.

Then the dizziness ebbs.

I don't know how long I stay on the floor, slumped against the door, legs stretched out like a used puppet that's been dropped.

My hands are shaking less now, but they're ice cold, and my skin feels clammy. I rub my right thumb over my left palm, back and forth, back and forth, trying to force some life back into them.

Bit by bit, the room stops spinning.

My burning eyes flick up to the clock on the wall. It's half-past five. I should've been home half an hour ago.

But I can't. Not like this. Not near Zinneerah.

Not with this . . . whatever this is still sweltering under my skin.

You sounded a lot like your fa—

I press my hands to my ears, rubbing them numb, so I can erase her voice by force.

It doesn't work.

I need water. I dig through my bag and grab my bottle, but then my hand brushes something else—something that stops me.

The CD. The one Professor Daniels gave me. The one with Zinneerah's song for her father.

I stare at it for a moment.

Using the door handle for leverage, I force myself back onto my feet and stumble over to my desk. My computer hums to life when I press the button.

Sliding the disc into the PC's tray, I pull my AirPods from my pocket, connect them, and press play.

And then, finally, I let myself breathe.

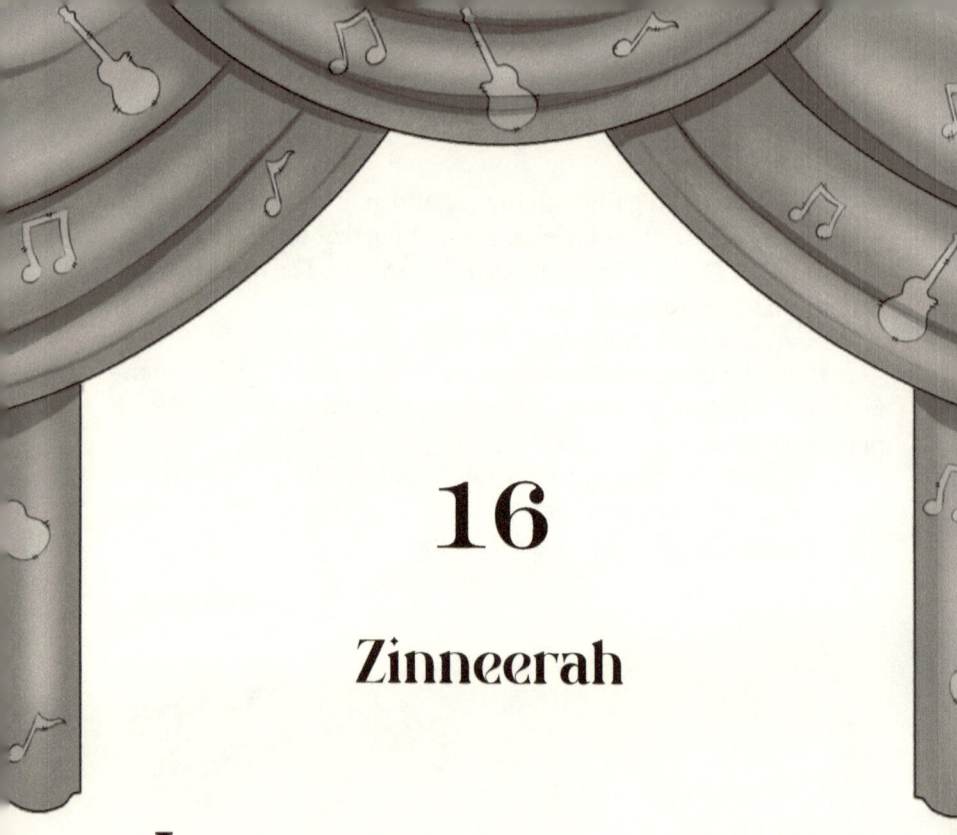

16

Zinneerah

It's seven in the evening.

Raees was supposed to be home by five.

I keep telling myself he's probably caught up finishing some last-minute grading or polishing up a presentation so he can enjoy the concert tomorrow without any loose ends.

That makes sense, right? Logical, reasonable, believable. And yet, my mind *isn't* staying logical or reasonable, let alone believable.

His ex-fiancée works with him, after all.

I hate how easily my thoughts get away from me. How quickly they spiral into the worst places. I mean, it's not like they are working together on purpose—they're just stuck in the same department.

Still, it's hard to keep the what-ifs at bay. *What if she stayed late too? What if they're still there, alone?*

I shake my head.

Stop.

146

This is ridiculous. I *know* it's ridiculous. But I've been sitting here for two hours, staring at a dead TV screen, and my brain is having a field day.

I've imagined everything from him being buried in a mountain of paperwork to . . . well, things I don't want to say even in the privacy of my own head.

I've opened his contact a dozen times, ready to text him. Just something simple: *"Still at the office?"* or *"Everything okay?"* But every time, I close it.

I don't want to be that person. Clingy, or suspicious. And anyway, he's probably just, what, in a meeting? Stuck in Toronto's horrifying traffic? He could've bumped into a friend. There are a million reasons he might be late, none of which have anything to do with her.

I let out a breath, slump back into the couch, and hug a cushion tightly to my chest. My fingers twist absentmindedly in the fabric as his words make home in my head again: *I've buried everything, Zinneerah. Everything that existed before you, it's gone. There's no one else in this world for me. Just you. You and my family.*

He was so earnest when he said it. So sure. I believe him, I really do, with everything I have. My whole heart, my whole soul.

So, if he's late tonight, that doesn't mean anything, right? It doesn't mean he's . . . *No.* It just means he's busy. Busy with—

The sound of the front door jolts me out of my thoughts.

I shoot up from the couch, my heart racing as I quickly walk toward the front alcove, smoothing my hair and trying to wipe the anxiety from my face.

Raees is bent over, slipping off his shoes. His hair is messy, his dress shirt wrinkled and untucked, the sweater he'd been wearing earlier now folded over his arm. His face isn't the one I imagined seeing—there's no reassuring smile, no lightness. Instead, there's guilt. Exhaustion.

And just like that, my stomach twists.

When he turns to face me, his eyebrows lift, startled to see me standing there.

I take another look at him, my gaze tracing over his disheveled appearance. Someone definitely ran their fingers through his hair— *or maybe it was him.* He never comes home with his sweater off. *But we just entered July; maybe he got too warm.* Even his glasses are smudged, and he's always cleaning them, fussing over the tiniest streak because he can't stand blurry vision. *Maybe he forgot this time?*

His assurance bulldozes through my skull. *I've buried everything, Zinneerah. I promise, everything that existed has long since extinguished. There is no one in this world for me anymore except for you and my family.*

I raise my hand to sign something, anything, but my thoughts won't connect. Everything inside me feels fractured, split into jagged pieces I can't fit together.

"I apologize for being late," he says quietly.

I take the safest path forward. *Are you okay?*

"No," he answers, with a smile that doesn't reach his eyes.

Dread pools my heart. *Why?*

He clears his throat, adjusting the strap of his bag. "Today was one of those days that reminded me why being a professor isn't exactly a walk in the park." His hand rests on my shoulder. "How was your day?"

Relief floods me so fast I almost feel lightheaded. Work stress. Just work stress. Of course, that still matters, but at least it's not infidelity.

Fine, I sign.

"That's good." The warmth of his hand vanishes as he walks toward the kitchen. "What should I make for dinner?"

His question pulls me out of my thoughts. I follow him into the kitchen, shaking my head. *I cook.*

"Why? I always cook."

Tired, I insist. *Shower. Sleep. I cook.*

"Zinneerah—"

No.

He pauses, pushing his glasses up the bridge of his nose, and then smiles faintly. "Let me know if you need any help."

I watch him as he disappears up the stairs. A moment later, I hear his door click shut.

My fingers grip the fabric of my shirt, twisting it tightly between my hands.

Why does my chest ache when I see him like this—his shoulders slumped, his face drawn with a sadness he's trying so hard to hide?

What happened today? Was it something on campus? A student, maybe? Dua once told me that Raees has a reputation for being unshakable in his role. Even so, his students and colleagues all respect him deeply. They'd never cross him.

Unless it *was* her.

I can still remember the day he told me about her. The way his voice was balancing on a tightrope, like he was forcing himself to continue without crashing. His hands were so still, resting in his lap, but his eyes . . . there was *fear*. Fear that I'd leave just because of the weight her name carried in his past. It broke something in me to see him that way. He didn't deserve it then, and he doesn't deserve it now.

I wonder if he feels guilty about her. I wonder if she still has that kind of power over him. I hope not. *I hope not.*

If anyone should feel guilty, it's me.

He doesn't know. He doesn't know about my past. He doesn't know why I sometimes sit in silence, even when I want to speak. Why I can't stand the brush of a stranger's hand, why I tense up, why I pull away without meaning to. He doesn't know why I think, deep down, that I'm not built for this—for marriage, for love, for the kind of life he deserves.

And yet, he chose me.

How is it fair? He doesn't know the whole truth. He doesn't know the parts of me I keep hidden away in the dark. I don't know if I'll ever have the strength to show them to him, and still, he accepted me. Somehow, he sees something in me I can't see in myself.

And here I am, standing here, seeing him like this, with that look on his face . . . it's unbearable. His sadness sometimes mirrors my own, and I hate it. I hate it because I've been there. I've lived in that space of guilt and shame and blame. I know how consuming it can be. And I don't want that for him. Not ever.

I want to protect him from it. From her. From whatever or whoever is making him feel like this. He's so much more than the things he's endured, and it kills me to think of anyone treating him like he's less than the man he is. He doesn't deserve to feel this way because of someone who couldn't love him the way he deserved to be loved.

There is no one in this world for me anymore except for you and my family.

"Me, too, Raees," I mumble. "Me, too."

Closer to nine, I make my way upstairs to call Raees for dinner.

His door is slightly ajar, spilling a sliver of golden light onto the hallway floorboards. I didn't realize he liked sleeping with his door open. Then again, how would I? I'm always in bed long before him. How he manages to be both a night owl and an early bird is something I'll never understand.

I knock softly, three times. Then wait.

No answer.

I knock again, a little louder this time. Still nothing.

I don't push the door open, but I lean closer, trying to catch a glimpse through the narrow gap, wondering if he's awake with his earphones in.

Instead, I see him slumped at his desk. Asleep.

His soft sandy skin glows under the lamplight, his ink-black hair messily falling into his face. One side of his head rests against his folded arms, and his white t-shirt stretched taut across his shoulders. That's when I catch myself staring.

I step back, biting my lip, and almost close the door before pausing at the last second.

In my room, I grab the extra blanket I brought from home and return, hesitating just outside his door. Should I go inside or just let him be?

But the way he's hunched over like that, out cold in some uncomfortable dream at his desk, makes me think of when I used to study for finals in high school. I always fell asleep the same way, head over my notes, body protesting against my late-night ambition. And more often than not, I'd wake up with a blanket draped over my shoulders, or Baba would carry me to bed.

I can't carry Raees. But I can leave him the next best thing.

So, I step inside.

His room is minimalist, awash in soft shades of cream and green. A tall snake plant stands quietly in the corner, while a collection of succulents lines the windowsill where the blinds are gathered. On the left wall, a bookshelf stretches from one end to the other, crammed with textbooks and novels.

Beside his bed, there's a table stacked with even more books, a framed photo of his mother and sister, and . . . *a Switch?*

I bite back a laugh. My husband's a gamer. Good to know.

Blanket unfolded, I shake it out before gently draping it over his back. His shoulders shift slightly under the fabric, his skin prickling with goosebumps. He snores softly, his lips parted and his long lashes shadowing his cheeks.

Carefully, I organize the papers scattered on his desk and pick up his empty coffee mug. It's such a small thing, but it feels oddly intimate—tidying his space while he sleeps, making sure he's comfortable.

Once I'm satisfied, I turn to leave—

"Zinneerah."

My heart leaps, and I stop mid-step. I glance over my shoulder, finding him stirring.

Raees stretches, groaning softly as his arms extend over his head before relaxing back into his chair. The blanket slips off him in the process, pooling around his waist.

I sigh quietly and walk back, pulling it back up to his shoulders.

This time, his eyes flutter open, hazy with sleep.

I take a step back, clutching the mug in my hands, unsure of what to do with the way his gaze softens when it lands on me.

My mouth opens to say something, anything, but instead I wave.

He blinks away the remnants of sleep, looking down at the blanket now tucked snugly around him. Slowly, he runs a hand through his damp hair, pushing it back from his face. "I didn't even realize I fell asleep."

Dinner, I sign.

"Oh, right." He rises to his *very* full height, and folds the blanket neatly over the back of his chair. It doesn't escape me that it's my blanket, but I decide not to point it out. I just let it stay there. "What are we eating?" He takes the mug from my hands, then opens the door for me.

I pull out my phone to type the answer: Chicken-cheese bread and curry rice. If you don't like it, I can order—

He places his hand on my screen before I can finish typing. "I'd be stupid not to like what you cook."

And just like that, I'm blushing again. Every time. His words always get to me.

We head downstairs, and Raees pauses at the bottom step, taking a deep breath through his nose. He grins as if he's caught a whiff of something lifechanging.

"I can taste the air," he says, stepping into the kitchen with an awestruck expression. His eyes land on the chicken-cheese bread sitting on foil, golden and gooey, waiting. "Zinneerah, this looks absolutely incredible." He moves toward the rice on the counter. Lifting the lid, he lets out a low whistle as the steam curls around his face. "I didn't know you were secretly a chef, too?"

You are too kind.

"You deserve it." He turns back to me with a lopsided grin. "You always do."

Be still, organ inside my chest.

He grabs two plates, holding one out to me. I scoop a modest portion, careful not to let him see how flustered I am.

He piles his plate high and grabs me a spoon before settling across from me at the table. "Let's see if it tastes just as good as it looks."

The cheese stretches as he pulls a bite away, and I watch every micro-movement of his face like I'm trying to read his mind. Then, he takes a spoonful of the rice, chewing slowly, his eyes narrowing slightly.

I sigh. *Bad.*

He swallows and leans forward, looking me dead in the eyes. "The only bad thing—"

No.

"—is you doubting yourself."

I look at him in surprise. *Good?*

"Zinneerah, it's *phenomenal*." He takes another bite of bread, letting the cheese pull between his fingers. "Seriously. This? Magical."

My ego is well-fed. Cooking has never been my arena—that's Shahzad's territory. I've always been the baker, the one who knows her way around a sweet glaze or a savory pie crust.

This dinner is a memory. Baba used to make it on rushed evenings, and I was his little sous chef, perched at his side, stirring and taste-testing.

Raees sets his spoon down and leans back in his chair. "After dinner, would you please do me the honor of picking out what to wear for the concert tomorrow?"

I nod, signing a quick: *Sure.*

"Perfect." He glances toward the patio doors. "Should we eat outside again?"

I glance toward the patio. I love this little tradition we've fallen into. Dinner in the summer breeze, the pool glittering in the twilight. Talking about everything and nothing.

It's simple.

It's ours.

And I wouldn't change it for the world.

Once I've washed my face, brushed my teeth, and slipped into my nightgown, I grab my phone and wander into Raees' room. His door is already wide open, and he catches sight of me before I even get the chance to ask if I can come in.

A small mountain of clothes is spread across his bed. He gestures toward them, a little sheepish. "Okay, so based on the pictures you showed me earlier, I think I've got something close to what you had in mind."

I take one look. Not even close.

The "something" turns out to be a line-up of polos (three black, one white) and a pair of trousers that look more suited for a corporate boardroom than what we're going for.

His shoulders sag. "I got it all wrong, didn't I?"

I glance up at him with a small, helpless smile.

He huffs out a quiet laugh, placing his hands on his hips. "Good thing I have you here with me, then." He steps aside, gesturing toward his walk-in closet. "Maybe you'll spot something I missed?"

I hesitate, unsure if it's okay to just dive in.

"Go on. It's all yours. I'll just . . ." He trails off, making his way to the edge of the bed where he plops down, sprawling comfortably. "I'll sit here and watch you work your magic."

I smile back, stepping into his closet, and I'm instantly surrounded by his signature woodsy scent of sandalwood. It's so undeniably him.

It all makes sense now, seeing the neat row of colognes arranged like trophies on the shelf. Below that, a perfectly curated collection of watches. And beneath that, shoes, polished and gleaming, every pair unmistakably Italian leather.

The closet itself is a palette of neutrals and monochromes. Sweaters in cashmere, wool, and cotton hang in tidy rows. Stacks of folded trousers, and somewhere in those drawers, I'm guessing, are his boxers.

I glance back at Raees. He's watching me with that lopsided grin tugging at the corners of his mouth.

When our eyes meet, he drops his gaze to the floor, but the smile stays. Seeing him like this feels like a victory. Especially after the gloominess he walked into the house with earlier.

I sift through his dress shirts, searching for something casual, but they're all far too formal. My fingers brush past starched collars and crisp fabrics until I find a plain white t-shirt tucked away—a gym shirt, of all things. *It'll do.*

I pull it down along with a navy-blue sweater. Moving to the folded trousers, I skim over the fabrics until I feel the rough denim texture.

A pair of loose, dark-blue jeans.

Perfect.

Satisfied, I carry the clothes out to his bed and lay them neatly on the silk sheets. If I ever got the chance to sleep on these, I'd be out cold in minutes.

Raees gives a thoughtful hum, then picks up the clothes. "Let me try it on." He vanishes into the closet, closing the door behind him.

While he's changing, I start folding the mess he made of his perfectly arranged wardrobe. As I'm smoothing the last shirt into a neat square, his phone buzzes on the nightstand. My eyes flick to the screen.

A Messenger notification.

From Saira.

Saira.

His ex-fiancée.

Of course, it's her. Because who else would have the audacity to pop up right now? What does she want, anyway? Closure? Redemption? A second chance? I scoff quietly to myself. Exes never know when to stay in the past where they belong.

The closet door opens, and I barely manage to school my expression before Raees sees me.

"What do we think?" His voice snaps me out of my thoughts, and I quickly lick my lips, trying to act like I wasn't just staring at his phone.

He's standing there, spinning on one foot like some kind of runway model. The collar of his white tee peeks out from under his sweater, and the hem shows just a little, too. I don't know why it's hitting me this way, but something about seeing him in jeans makes my stomach flip.

I grip the sides of my gown tighter, and give a thumbs-up.

"Thank you." He flashes that devastating smile of his, pushing up his sleeves. Oh, God, his forearms. Toned. Veiny. Dusted with hair. "Maybe you should just pick out all my clothes from now on."

I nod. My nails are about to rip straight through this gown.

"Are you okay?" Raees asks, stepping closer, bending slightly to catch my eyes with his. He tilts his head. "Your face is all red—"

I shuffle to the side, wringing my hands like they're trying to escape my body. He's so handsome, I can't even hold his gaze for longer than two seconds. And let's not forget the truth: he's my *husband*. If this isn't peak absurdity, I don't know what is.

"What are you wearing?" He adjusts the collar of the white tee underneath his sweater in front of his closet mirror.

Doesn't matter.

He catches that slip through his reflection. "I want it to matter, Zinneerah." Then he turns, and my brain short-circuits. I look away like the coward I am. "Besides, it's only fair. Don't you think?"

I want to answer. I really do. But my attention is fixed on his phone, sitting on the dresser. The notification's still glowing faintly. What does his ex-fiancée need at eleven at night? If he's blocked her number, she must be using an app to message him.

I should just ask.

"On second thought," he says, yanking off his sweater in one swift motion. The hem of his t-shirt rides up with it, flashing me a view of his torso that looks like it was sculpted by a Renaissance artist having a particularly good day. But it's the happy trail that sends me into vertigo. "Let's keep it a surprise."

My hand flies to my cheek, which is now hotter than the weather outside. *Get a grip, Zinneerah. You've seen shirtless men before.*

Yes, but this is different.

This is my *husband's* body.

And even if it was just the quickest glimpse, it might as well have been a perfectly aimed arrow straight to my chest. How am I supposed to act normal after that? Like I didn't already know he was built like a Greek statue?

Apparently, knowing and seeing are two very different things.

"Zinneerah?"

I drag my thoughts out of the gutter, kicking and screaming, and force myself to meet his eyes. *Ignore the biceps. Ignore the thick, perfect biceps.* God, what is wrong with me? Are these hormones? Am I about to get my period? Probably. I'm already three days late, so that tracks.

Goodnight, I sign with all the grace of a drowning fish.

"Wait, hey—"

156

Nope. I'm out. Retreating away from his room, his smile, his scent that's both earthy and masculine.

I speed-walk to my own room and fling myself onto the bed, face-first into my pillows like they might smother my shame.

Being attracted to my own husband has officially proven to be dangerous territory.

No, scratch that.

This is an active war zone.

17

Raees

An hour remains before the concert, and I'm standing in front of the mirror, giving myself the kind of pep talk I'd give a student who's about to blow their big story by overthinking it.

Tonight, I cannot screw this up. Not for her.

This is Zinneerah's night. She's finally getting to see her old friend perform, something she's been looking forward to for some time. And I get the honor of being at her side.

I'm not even sure how I'm still breathing.

If I'm honest, I've been half-convinced all day that last night wasn't real. She'd come into my bedroom after I'd worked myself to post panic-attack exhaustion, draped her blanket—the one with the colorful wildflowers—over me, and straightened the papers on my desk. When I woke up and saw it, I thought I'd imagined the whole thing. But no.

She's real.

She's very real.

And she's mine.

My wife. My sweet, beautiful wife.

I give myself one last look, spritz the cologne, and step out of the bedroom.

It's time.

My sister's been lighting up my phone ever since I gave her the full play-by-play. I stayed up late running my mouth to her, ignoring Saira's half-hearted apology texts as they rolled in. Around two, I finally crashed with Zinneerah's blanket still in my arms.

Ram: Make sure you hold her hand! The clubhouse gets packed. I went there for a Cranberries reunion once, and it was like sardines in a tin can.

I rub my bottom lip as I shuffle into the kitchen, dropping into one of the stools at the counter.

Me: What if she doesn't want to? You know how she is with physical touch.

Ram: Safety > physical touch. Don't overthink it, Cronkite. Just ask her.

I suppose there *is* no harm in asking her.

Ram: I know you hate crowds, so carve out a little breathing room for yourself, okay? Don't be shy about it. Shove some people if you have to. :p

Me: You're thirty-nine, Ramishah. Why are you sending emojis?

Ram: They're called emoticons, you over-educated clown. How do you teach media literacy without knowing the difference between an emoji and an emoticon?

Me: My lesson plans are for adults, not middle schoolers. I'm not exactly doing a PowerPoint on AOL chatroom culture.

Light footsteps hit the stairs. I glance toward the hall as her familiar silhouette appears in the periphery.

Me: Gotta go. Wife's here.

I slip my phone into my pocket, press my palm against my lips to check my breath, then brush a few strands of hair back into place using the oven door's reflection.

Zinneerah steps into the living room, and I nearly tip off my stool.

God help me, this woman.

This *woman*.

My woman.

She is strikingly, magnificently beautiful in a way that borders on otherworldly.

Her knee-long hair falls loose and parted cleanly down the middle; a cascade of dark silk that moves with the kind of eloquence you can't replicate. She's wearing a black, long-sleeved top that slips off her shoulders, revealing the delicate structure of her collarbones, like branches in frost. The fabric molds to her figure just enough to hint at the curve of her small waist. A dark-red satin skirt, high-waisted and flowing, catches the light as it moves around her.

Her eyes are lined with kajal—dark, smoky strokes, while maroon lipstick shapes her lips into something I can only describe as perfection.

Then she has the audacity to sign, *I look okay?*

The question is absurd. *She* is absurd, in the most extraordinary sense. If I could, I'd marry her again every single day, in every single thing she chooses to wear.

"Yes," I whisper, "you look stunning, Zinneerah." I try to say more, but the words tangle in my chest when she gives me a shy, beautiful smile. "You *are* stunning."

She reaches up, tucking a strand of hair behind her ear, and as she does, the line of piercings along its curve comes into view.

I can't stop looking at her. It's overwhelming, really. This surreal, humbling realization that she's my wife. That she chose *me*.

What have I done to deserve her? I don't know. I don't believe in past lives, but if such things exist, I must have been a saint, a hero, or something equally improbable. Because in this life, somehow, I have her.

She taps my shoulder. *Go?*

I lick my lips, nerves catching in my throat. "Yeah. Let's go."

Zinneerah strides past me, her hair swaying as she moves. Her eyes catch mine mid-step, and there's that crinkle at the corners when she smiles.

Flawless.

By the time she's at the front door, I realize I've been standing still too long, a hand pressed to my chest to keep my heart from jumping out.

When I catch up to her by the front door, she's already battling her shoes. Her purse is sliding off her arm, her hair keeps falling into her face, and she's muttering silently to herself under her breath. She's a mess—*my* mess—and I don't think I've ever loved her more.

"Sit down, please," I say, already reaching for her. "I'll do it."

She looks up, surprised. *It's okay.*

"Sit. Please."

She hesitates like she always does, but then brushes her skirt under her, and lowers herself onto the edge of the settee.

I pick up her flats and kneel down. She lifts her skirt just a bit, enough for me to see her ankle, and my mouth goes dry.

My hand wraps around her foot—small, soft—and I just sit there for a second. Or a minute. I don't know. She doesn't say anything or pull away.

I slide the shoe on, trying not to make this more than it is. But it is more, isn't it? It has to be, because I can feel the heat crawling up the back of my neck, and I'm not even halfway done.

Her other foot's already there, waiting. I take it, my fingers brushing her calf. It's nothing—*it's everything*. The second shoe goes on, but my hand stays. I don't know why.

My thumb presses against the edge of her ankle, and I don't move it. Her fingers curl in her lap, gripping her skirt, and I look up. She's looking down at me, her lips barely apart, like she's about to say something but doesn't. I brush her skirt down, fingers skimming the fabric.

I seriously can't move. She's not moving either.

Standing feels like breaking a spell. I grab my shoes and shove them on, not bothering to tie them properly because apparently functioning like a normal human being is off the table today.

After I lock the door, she heads straight for the car. Her hand goes to the door handle, but no. Not happening. I reach it first, and pull it open for her.

Zinneerah looks at my smile, and then her gaze drops. She climbs into the seat without saying a word, her hands smoothing the hem of her skirt.

She gets shy when I do things like this. She always has. I love it. I love her.

I close the door gently, and take her in through the window, the way she sits with her hands folded in her lap, her head turned slightly toward the windshield. She'll never know what she does to me, how she owns every piece of me without even trying. If she did, she'd probably laugh, and I'd deserve it.

But God above, I'm hers either way.

"Are you excited to see Alex?" I ask, once I'm settled in the driver's seat.

She signs, *Nervous*.

"That's understandable." My right-hand rests on the gear shift, the left steering the wheel. "It's always a little strange seeing someone after so much time has passed. But you know what? It'll be fine. Even if it feels awkward at first, those kinds of friendships have a way of picking up right where you left off." I smile, but she's staring at the dashboard, her brows pulled together like she's bracing for something. "Hey?"

She lifts her gaze to meet mine.

"You'll be fine," I assure softly. "It's pretty much impossible for someone to make you a villain in their life." My hands tighten on the wheel as I ease us into the flow of traffic. "You're certainly a hero in mine."

Zinneerah continues staring at me, like she's trying to decide whether to believe me. Then she looks away, her focus drifting back to the dashboard.

The drive to the clubhouse is supposed to be fifteen minutes, but with downtown traffic, it stretches to thirty. By the time we pull into the lot, the sun's sinking low, brushing the tops of the buildings with gold.

I pay at the machine, the ticket popping out with a mechanical click. Sliding it under the windshield wiper, I ease the car into a spot between two sedans that look like they haven't moved in weeks.

Zinneerah's hand goes to the door handle again, but I beat her to it, locking it with a quick flick. She pauses, confused, and looks at me. I step out without a word, coming around to her side to do what she's about to learn is my job.

"Got everything?" I ask, standing there, holding the door wide.

She glances back inside the car, scanning the seat, the floor. A quick double-check. Then, a thumbs-up.

"Good," I say, wiping my hand on the front of my jeans, the fabric coarse against my palm. "Before we head in, I've got a question."

Her brows lift.

I clear my throat. "Ramishah said it can get pretty packed in there. Wall-to-wall people. So, with that being said . . . would you like to hold my hand? It's just to keep us together, and make sure you're safe—"

She grabs my hand.

Soft. Softer than I expected. Her fingers are slender but long, almost the same length as mine. I catch myself thinking how easy it would be to kiss each fingertip, but I rein it in. *Not the time.*

We start walking, and instead of taking the lead, I keep pace with her—side by side. The clubhouse looms ahead, a hum of bass spilling out the door as a line of people shuffle forward, handing IDs to the bouncer.

Her fingers squeeze mine, pulling my focus back to her. She mouths a single word: "Wallet."

"Phone, too?" I ask, arching a brow.

She nods.

I fish both out of my pocket and hand them to her without question. She tucks them into her purse, zips it shut, and takes my hand again like she never let go in the first place.

We move forward together, weaving through the line.

Holy hell, it is packed in here. The air inside is congested with heat and sound, bodies pressed together in clusters.

I instinctively pull Zinneerah closer, and lean down to murmur near her ear. "Stay close to me."

I'd forgotten how people move in spaces like this—fish in a current, bodies flowing, colliding, squeezing past without a second thought. Two guys about my height cut through ahead of me like they've done this a hundred times.

Meanwhile, I'm trailing behind, trying not to catch an elbow to the ribs.

The crowd is a surprisingly decent ratio of men to women, most of them at least a decade younger than me. They're dressed to the nines in early 2000s throwback fashion—rhinestones glinting around their eyes, glitter smeared across lips, pink bows perched on heads.

We make a beeline for the first door.

"I'm guessing there's no seating plan?" I ask. "Not sure why I thought this might resemble a lecture hall."

Zinneerah doesn't answer. She's laser-focused, blissfully unaware of my commentary, her attention charged by the electricity of the crowd. Looks like now's the perfect time to drop the ASL card.

I squeeze her hand, then release it just long enough to sign: *We talk this way. Where are the seats?*

The shock hits its mark.

A grin pulls at the corner of my mouth as I sign, *Surprise.*

Her mouth parts wider before twisting into an upside-down grin. *Why didn't you tell me?*

I don't get the chance to sign a reply before a shoulder slams into mine, hard enough to jolt me forward. "Zinneerah? Zinn—"

Her hand clamps around mine, like catching a falling coffee mug mid-air. When I glance down, her eyes are already on me, brows pulling together in concern.

164

"I'm fine," I tell her, brushing it off as I slide an arm protectively around her shoulders.

She points toward the stairs, the ones leading up to the balcony, roped off and guarded by a bouncer. I nod, letting her take the lead as we snake our way over. My eyes stay sharp, scanning for anyone else careless enough to barrel through me again.

At the rope, she pulls out her ID, and hands me my wallet. We show our tickets together. The bouncer gives us a once-over before stepping aside and unhooking the velvet rope.

Once we're up there, Zinneerah finds a spot by the railing. There're several people up here with drinks in their hands, leaning over and watching the crowd below.

Good seat, I sign.

I hate crowds, she signs back holding the railing to lean forward, her gaze chasing the glow of the ceiling lights, and the bodies below.

I tap her shoulder, pulling her focus back. *My card?*

She blinks, surprised again. Then frowns. *You sign? Why not tell me?*

My lips pull into a smile. *Stupid, I know.* My hands falter slightly. *Still learning. Afraid I'd mess up.*

Her eyes soften in the blue neon lights. *How did you learn?*

A textbook. I buy last year. After our first meeting. Learning for you.

A shy smile touches my wife's lips. *I forgive you.*

I lean closer to her ear. "Didn't know you were mad to start with," I say, the scent of Arabian incense catching me. "But I apologize anyway."

She steps aside, her eyes darting to the stage. Her hands move without looking at me. *No apologize.*

The lights dim, and the place erupts.

Not just loud. A bone-rattling, skull-vibrating loud. The kind of loud that's primal, like the sound of a million people howling at the moon. Behind us, a tidal wave of bodies press into the railing. Their faces flushed, movements mindless, like zombies clawing at a wall they'll never scale.

I move quickly, stepping in close behind Zinneerah before someone knocks her off balance and takes her spot. My hands find the railing instinctively, boxing her in—not too tight, just enough to make sure no one tries anything. She doesn't notice. Her eyes are glued to the stage, to the flickering spotlights chasing one another through the haze of the smoke machines.

The band trickles out one by one, and every new body onstage pushes the decibel level higher.

Of course, I did my homework on The Femme Fatality. Indie underground-rock, that's their niche. They've been clawing their way up the food chain, moving from dingy basements and makeshift dive stages to clubs, even the occasional opera house. A real darling story I can use as an example in my lectures.

The music starts without Alex. No fanfare, no introduction. Just Natalia, the drummer, crashing into her kit. The bassist, Alyssa, plucking and strumming. Over on the left, Crista's buried in her fortress of keyboards, hands flying across the keys, and summoning a storm of cheers.

Then it appears. The voice. A voice that rips through the earthquake like a bolt of silver lightning:

"TORONTOOOOO!"

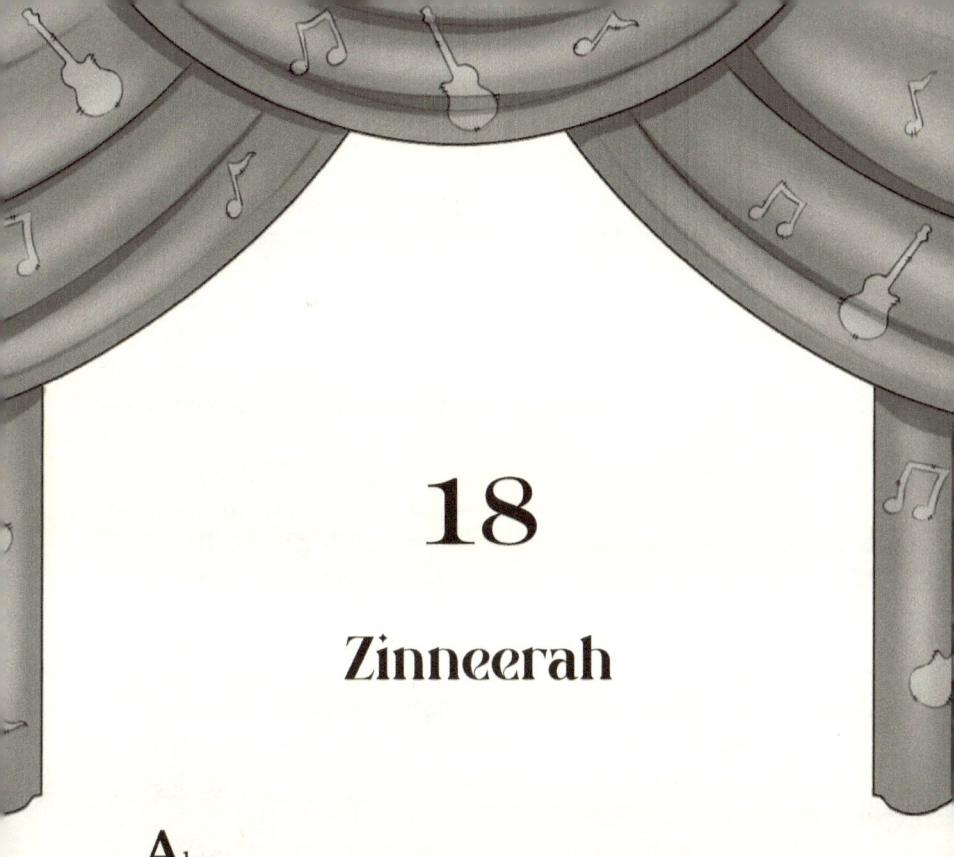

18

Zinneerah

Alex.

It's her.

Alexandra Watanabe, backlit by spotlights like some punk-rock goddess descending from the heavens. She steps out from the shadows, hot-pink guitar slung low. The same guitar Ophelia and I had saved up to purchase for her nineteenth birthday. She'd kissed our cheeks, and dashed out of her dorm, showing it off to everyone on campus.

And now, here she is.

Alex.

My Alex.

She holds the neck of the guitar with one hand, and the other pulls her mic closer, her laughter spilling out into the crowd as if she can't believe they're cheering for her. But I can. How could they not?

I lean over the railing, staring down at her, soaking in the sight of her under the lights she was always meant to own.

She's wearing a floral dress—bright and busy, like a garden spilled across her—and baggy jeans slouched underneath, the kind of pairing only Alex could make look cool. Her pixie cut is bleached the color of moonlight, with soft pink streaks framing her face. A patchwork of tattoos cover her bare arms like walking time capsules.

I recognize a few from when we were twenty and invincible, but the newer ones are strangers to me, stories she wrote after we stopped being us.

And when she sings . . . oh, when she *sings*, it's like nothing's changed. She still plants one foot forward like the music might bowl her over if she doesn't, and her lips are practically glued to the microphone. *You're making out with the microphone, Alex*, I'd tease her after every show.

The crowd screams her lyrics back at her, louder than the amps. Boys and girls press together, some crying glittery tears, their cheeks streaked with eyeliner and sweat. Black ribbons wrap around their wrists or necks like small rebellions. Some hold their phones high, recording every moment to hold onto later, while others just lose themselves in the moment. There's so much life down there, so much love, so much reckless abandon, and all of it exists because of her. Alexandra Watanabe's magic, her alchemy, turning heartbreak and anger and defiance into something beautiful.

I force myself to look away from her, from them, but all I see is the shattered relic of who I used to be. I used to be part of this. Part of her and Ophelia. Now I'm just . . . here.

What would I even say to her?

Hey, Alex, it's me. Your dumbass best friend who fell apart and never put herself back together. Yeah, hi. Surprise! I'm still a mess.

No. That's not fair. Not to her. Not to me.

I glance back down, and she's still singing like she created this universe, her head tipped back, her eyes half-closed. She's beautiful in the way hurricanes are beautiful—breathtaking and unstoppable and capable of ripping you to shreds if you get too close.

I'm so proud of her I could scream. I'm so jealous I could die.

And somewhere in between all of that, I'm just a girl who misses her best friend.

Alex finishes her first song with a hard strum, letting the note pulse and fade into the crowd. She steps closer to the mic, brushing her hair back with a quick flick of her hand.

"Well, hello, Toronto!" she says, her rasp carrying easily over the cheers. She lifts one hand, waving to everyone like she knows each one of us by name. "Man, I missed this place. I missed you." She points out at the crowd, and I could swear a dozen people just fainted on the spot. "You don't even know. I've been touring in the States for two months now, and not a single, good cup of coffee. And you know your girl doesn't support Starbucks, so." She puts her hands up in surrender, and everyone cheers in agreement. "They have Timmies there, but it's not the same. Don't argue with me, I'm right. The donuts taste like cardboard, and guys, the coffee's just depression in a cup."

The crowd howls, and I laugh quietly into my hand, shaking my head. She always did have this uncanny ability to make you feel like she was speaking just to you, even in a room full of hundreds.

Next to me, Raees' deep laugh rumbles in my ear. I glance up and realize just how close he's standing. Close enough that his arm brushes mine every time I shift, close enough that I can feel the heat of his chest at my back.

And then the thought slams into me: *How is she going to react when you tell her you're married now?* I can already picture the look on her face. She'll probably snort-laugh, roll her eyes, and say something like, "Who the hell gets married? What is this, the 1800s?"

"Anyway," Alex continues, waving the bottle of water in her hand, "I gotta say, it feels weird being home. It's like everything's the same, but I'm not, you know? Like, there's this new organic grocery store where my favorite bar used to be, and all I can think is, 'What am I supposed to write sad songs about now? A Whole Foods?'"

The audience laughs again. *My little comedian.*

"No, but seriously. This city . . . this city raised me. It broke me, too, but it also put me back together. A lot of my songs come from this place. Some of them I wrote with my best friends, drinking Nestea on rooftops, and thinking we'd never grow up. And some of them . . ." She pauses, and the room stands with bated breath. "Some of them I wrote alone, on my bathroom floor, with tequila in one hand and a notebook in the other, wondering how the hell I ended up there."

I press my fingers into the railing, hard enough that it might leave imprints on the metal.

"Songwriting has always been my way of making sense of my feelings. It's like—I can take the messiest, most complicated emotions and turn them into something clear. Something true. There were times—*so* many times—when I couldn't say the things I needed to say to someone's face. But I could write them down. Put them in a song." She pauses, her lips curving into a wistful smile. "And now, hearing all of you sing those words back to me? It feels like time folding in on itself. Like I'm reaching back to the girl I used to be. The one crying on her bedroom floor, her mascara smudged and her heart broken, and telling her, 'Hey, you're not alone. You never were.'"

"Alex," I whisper, chin quivering.

She tilts her head, brushing her hair out of her face as her fingers find the C-major chord. "We've all had moments when we lost something we thought we'd never get back, haven't we? But maybe . . . maybe those moments led us here tonight. To this room. To each other. And I don't know about you, but that feels like magic to me. Tonight feels right. You, Toronto, feel right."

A single drumbeat rumbles beneath us, and Alex glances back at her drummer, her grin transforming into something feral. "*Let's fucking do this!*" she shouts.

And just like that, the music explodes again.

Strobe lights slice through the crowd, and her bandmates launch themselves into the first song like they've been waiting their whole lives for this. Everyone in the crowd moves as one, losing their minds, their voices, their sense of space.

And I'm part of it, too. I jump and let go.

She moves through the setlist, pouring her heart out into every one of these songs. I'm mouthing the words to the ones I remember, the ones the three of us wrote together, scribbled into spiral notebooks in her dorm room. The newer ones I had to memorize—

well, let's just say I've had her album on repeat on Spotify so many times that Dua texted me to ask if Alex was paying me royalties.

And I can't stop smiling. Because I remember the version of her who dreamed about this, who begged me and Ophelia to start a band even though I had rejection anxiety. The version of her who knew this could happen someday. And here she is, living it, owning it, turning every wound she ever bared into a song that makes this whole room feel alive.

I'm just here to witness it, to cheer for her, to love her the way she deserves to be loved. Which, honestly, feels like the easiest thing in the world right now. Because tonight, Alex isn't just my best friend.

She's the damn sun. And we're all just orbiting around her.

Her pale face is flushed, a bloom of life on porcelain, and her pearly-whites are out in full glory, biting down on her bottom lip as she laughs between verses, her emotions shifting like quicksilver.

One moment, she's snarling through a breakup rock song that makes the walls shake, belting out, "*I was too big for such a little dick!*" with a wink that sends the crowd into hysterics. The next, she's leaning forward, her voice soft and raspy, touching hands with the girls at the front who are melting into puddles at her feet.

I'm melting, too.

No, I'm swooning.

The tears start falling somewhere between the bridge of her song about slashing her ex's tires and the chorus about sleeping with his mother instead—her melodies all venom and shameless victories. She tosses her head back and screams the last line like, carving it into the universe, and the crowd roars. My face is already wet, streaked with eyeliner and mascara, and I keep wiping at it, but the tears won't stop.

Fuck it. Let them fall.

Because that's my best friend. That's my best friend. I don't think my heart has ever felt this full, this proud, this *alive*. She's up there, shining like a goddamn comet, and I'd be damned if I didn't cry over it.

The whole room is with me. Everyone in the clubhouse is screaming her name, singing her words, loving her the way she deserves to be loved. And she deserves all of it—every cheer, every hand reaching for hers, every voice screaming her lyrics into the night.

It's funny, actually. Alex never thought she was capable of being loved. Not by anyone, not by Ophelia and me, not by this room full of strangers, not by herself.

Her parents? Hell no. Her little sister Sloane? As close as they were, God knows where she is now. Relationships? As if. She kept them at arm's length, too afraid to let anyone close, and too terrified they'd up and run the second they saw her real self.

But her real self is the person I came to love so fiercely. I sometimes think she burns through me, leaving me singed in the best way possible.

My wildfire.

I wouldn't have had the guts to be any version of myself in university if it weren't for Alex. I mean, I wasn't exactly invisible before her, but I was someone who let the world move around her instead of through her. And then she arrived—this five-foot tornado of opinions and winged eyeliner—trying to pick up a cello and play it like a guitar because some classical major told her Nirvana was "sonically offensive to the soul."

I didn't even know her yet, but I was done for. Who does that? Who has that kind of fearless, glorious audacity? Alex Watanabe, that's who.

I was drawn to her like a moth to a flame—or, more accurately, like a moth to a girl actively trying to piss off her music theory TA.

She didn't just crack me out of my shell; she obliterated it. Yanked me out like she was pulling a sword from a stone, except the sword was me and the stone was all my insecurities. She tore through every doubtful thought I had, every whisper that said, 'You're not enough,' and drowned them out with her sheer Alex-ness.

I didn't know someone so small could carry so many lives inside her. And somehow, she shared them all with me.

"Are you all right?" Raees' soft voice cuts through my thoughts.

I realize I'm practically convulsing, racked with sobs so hard I can barely breathe, eyes squeezed shut, shoulders shaking like a tambourine.

But these tears aren't sad.

Oh, no. Not when it comes to Alex. With Alex, even the messiest, most broken parts of life feel like they were meant to be that way.

Raees' hand finds my back, gently rubbing the nape of my neck in soothing circles. He doesn't say anything else as I pull myself together.

It's not until Alex is down to her last song of the night that I manage to catch my breath.

The strobes are replaced with a single golden spotlight that pools around her like a halo. It's just her and her acoustic guitar now, perched on a stool in the middle of the stage. Her bandmates are gone, having taken their final sweaty bow before retreating to the greenroom.

Alex adjusts the mic stand, and tilts her guitar forward, fingers curling lightly around the neck. "As much as I love this part of the night," she says, "I also hate it. Like, *really* hate it." She pauses, smiling over the crowd, her fingers brushing idly along the neck of her guitar. "I don't like walking away after the final song. It's like, I don't know, ripping a Band-Aid off or something. I just want to stay here forever and give all of you a big fucking hug." She wraps her arms around herself, squeezing tight and swaying a little, wiggling her shoulders like she's hugging the entire room. "So, hopefully, we're not too sad, huh? Let's not do the sad thing."

More cheers and clapping, and whistling like they'd never let her leave.

"How about you guys up there?" Alex leans to the left, squinting dramatically toward the balcony as if she's trying to pick out faces. "We good up there? Still alive?"

Another round of applause roars down from the balcony.

"Good. I can't have anyone dying on me tonight. It'd kill the vibe, and you. Mostly you," she jokes, shifting to my side of the crowd. "And how about over here—" Her words catch mid-air as she freezes.

Her smile drops, and her eyes go wide, almost cartoonishly so.

She leans forward, bracing her hand against her guitar as if she's not quite sure she's seeing what she thinks she's seeing.

Then, suddenly, she's on the move.

She drags her stool closer to the right end of the stage, and clambers up on it to get a better look. With one hand shielding her eyes from the glare of the lights, she peers into the crowd, her gaze zeroing in on me.

"Zinneerah?" For the first time, her voice cracks on the single syllable. "Zinnie, is that you?"

My words stick somewhere behind the lump that's been growing in my throat since the first song. But I nod. Slowly at first, and then with more force, raising my hands in a feeble wave.

Alex stares, frozen for a long second, and then, "*Holy* shit." She pulls her guitar over her back, leans as far forward as her stool will allow, and shields her eyes again as if she needs to make sure she's not imagining me.

Raees' hand tightens around my waist as I lean further over the railing, both of my arms waving frantically now like some kind of deranged, crying semaphore.

"No way," Alex breathes, shaking her head in disbelief, her voice suddenly a lot less rockstar and a lot more my-best-friend-is-alive? "No. *Fucking*. Way." Her hand flies to her mouth as she laughs, high-pitched and incredulous. I don't blame her if she thinks she is seeing my ghost instead.

The crowd is cheering, but I don't hear it. The world narrows to just her and me—the sound of her voice, the way her eyes are locked on mine like no time has passed at all. Like we're back in her dorm, her floor littered with notebooks and dreams too big for three scared girls to believe in.

I turn to Raees. *Tell her to sing. Please.*

He clears his throat like a dutiful messenger. "My wife's asking you to sing!"

"*Wife?*" Alex shrieks, and the sharp feedback from her microphone slices through the room, making a few people wince. She doesn't even flinch. Just points a dramatic, accusatory finger in my direction. "You're a *wife* now?"

I can't stop laughing through my tears.

Alex, however, is on a roll. "You're a wife," she repeats, and she scoffs loudly, planting one hand on her hip. "When? How? And why the hell weren't Fifi and I there, you little shit?"

The crowd bursts into laughter, and so does Alex, shaking her head like she can't believe me.

With a final exaggerated sigh, she hops back onto her stool, swipes her guitar back into position, and leans into the mic again. "Change of plan, everyone. I'm gonna sing a song I wrote with my best friend Zinneerah—yes, that Zinneerah, the *wife* up there—back when we were sleep-deprived students swimming in OSAP debt."

The crowd cheers again, the energy tweaking from curiosity to full-blown excitement, and I disintegrate.

Alex begins plucking at the strings. She pauses for just a second, glancing up at me, and then starts to sing.

The first few notes wrap around me like a warm blanket, and I close my eyes, transported instantly to the night of Ophelia's birthday party.

The air smells like frosting and melted candle wax, and my stomach aches from the ungodly amount of cake I ate—the cake I baked, by the way, because I can't help but overdo things. Everyone's gone home—her cousins, her relatives, even Tía Isabella, who made her wear that ridiculous plastic tiara that's now tangled in her curls. It's just the three of us left in Ophelia's bedroom, glitter smeared on Alex's eyelids, and me re-applying my lipstick.

Alex is sitting cross-legged on the floor, cradling her electric guitar. Ophelia's tapping out a rhythm against the floorboards with her drumstick, the *thwack-thwack-thwack* keeping us all in time. I've got my acoustic guitar balanced on my lap, the strings cutting into my fingers. The melody is coming together now, the lyrics bouncing between Alex and me, a back-and-forth game we can't stop playing.

"Wait," Alex interrupts. "What if we flip the chorus? Like—" She hums the tune, switching a line mid-air, her hands never stopping their dance across the strings.

"Yes!" I shout. "Do that. Exactly that. That's it."

Her phone is sitting in the middle of the circle, recording everything—our voices, our laughter, the way Ophelia groans when she loses the rhythm for a second.

The song is about how, when the three of us hit ninety, birthday parties would still be a thing. Sharing ice cream cups wouldn't be remotely bacterial—at least, not enough to kill us at that point. Blindfolded makeup sessions would still be hilarious, even with shaky hands and sagging skin, though Ophelia and I always argued that Alex would age like fine wine thanks to her East Asian genes while the rest of us turned into expired yogurt.

But mostly, it was a song about being nineteen. About how, fifty years down the line, we'd sit back and cackle over Alex's decision to get her ex-girlfriend's hickey tattooed on her neck (yes, really), Ophelia's short-lived, but deeply committed furry cosplay phase, and dear, misguided me almost trying to pierce my own nipples with a safety pin because I couldn't afford an appointment.

We'd titled the song "To You."

No explanation necessary. It just . . . made sense.

The final note fades, and I lose it. I'm crying so hard I'm pretty sure my face is ninety-five percent mascara at this point. Alex isn't much better. She's standing on stage, her bottom lip jutting out in an exaggerated pout, tears streaming down her face as she throws her arms up dramatically, looking right at me. The gesture is loud and clear: *Where the fuck did you go, Zinnie?*

I laugh through the tears, my chest heaving, and make a talking motion with my hand, pointing my thumb over my shoulder like I'll explain later.

Alex nods, swiping at her own eyes with the sleeve of her jacket. Then she turns back to the crowd, giving one final bow with her whole heart. She blows kisses, grazes hands with fans in the front row, and flashes that signature Alex grin where her pierced tongue pokes out from the side. She throws a few more kisses as she disappears backstage, bouncing as she goes.

Exhaling, I release the death grip I've had on the railing and press my palms flat against the cool metal. My chest is light, my face is sticky, but my heart? My heart feels like it's floating somewhere near the ceiling.

"That was incredible," Raees says from behind me. He gently takes my hand, and tugs me toward the corner where some space has opened up as the balcony crowd filters downstairs. "Alex is . . . wow. She's a terrific performer."

I nod, still catching my breath.

He smiles at me, tilting his head. "Did you enjoy it?"

I lift my hands to my cheeks, gesturing dramatically at the black streaks running down them, and let out a hoarse laugh.

"Not to worry." Like the absurdly prepared person he is, Raees pulls a packet of tissues from his back pocket with a little flourish. "I figured you'd shed a few tears seeing your best friend perform, so I came ready."

My chin wobbles at the thoughtfulness of it, and I quickly press my lips together to stop myself from crying more. I take a tissue from him with a shaky hand, dabbing under my eyes and along my cheeks. *Still scary?*

"You never were." Then, holding up another tissue, he adds, "May I?"

I nod, placing the now-wrecked tissue back in his hand.

Raees raises my chin with the lightest touch, his fingers brushing under my jaw as he starts dabbing carefully at the corners of my eyes. The tissue glides softly along my cheek, and the noise of the concert, the crowd, even my own heartbeat, fades away. That's just Raees' magic. Gentle magic.

I blink up at him, a little awestruck, the concert high still pulsing faintly in my veins. He doesn't rush, or flinch, or seem to notice that I'm staring at him like he's just handed me the moon.

"Thank you for inviting me," Raees says, meeting my gaze briefly before focusing back on the task at hand. This time, I don't look away. "Seeing you tonight—jumping, laughing, crying-laughing—it's something I won't forget." He finishes dabbing at my cheek and sweeps the tissue down to my chin in one smooth motion, folding it neatly in his hand. "Your happiness is contagious."

God, he's such a smooth talker.

Normally, I'd shrink up from the embarrassment, cringing like I'd just walked into a glass door in front of a crowd. But with Raees, it's different. When it's his voice, like a hum of an old song, I feel calmer. Looser. Deep in my bones, I know he'd never use his words to hurt me.

"Come here." He takes my hand and guides me closer to him. A group of friends pool behind us, their voices blending into the background noise. His fingers slip through mine, intertwining like they've always belonged there. His thumb brushes lightly across my knuckles, back and forth, absentmindedly.

My chest tingles, a shiver running up my spine. When I glance up, I catch him looking anywhere but at me—over the heads of the crowd, down at the confetti-strewn floor, and then up at the stage lights glowing overhead.

Finally, his gaze lowers to meet mine, and when he smiles, it's like the whole room turns into a field full of life. His golden-brown eyes crinkle at the corners, the kind of smile that's earned from laughing too much. His high cheekbones sharpen with it, his jawline defined in the harsh colors, a dust of gray at his temples making him look even more impossibly perfect.

I drop my gaze to the floor. I feel like some common pauper staring up at Adonis, wondering what the hell I did to be standing here holding the hand of someone made of stardust and good intentions.

When people see us together, I wonder what they're thinking. Are they marveling at how gorgeous he is, or are they trying to figure out why a man so magnetic, so put-together, is with someone like me? Someone dreary. Someone gray.

Do his co-workers wonder the same thing? Or do they even know I exist? Has he ever shown them our wedding pictures? Does he mention me with that big, beautiful smile, or does my name stay tucked behind his teeth?

And then there's his ex-fiancée. If she's still texting him, clearly, I'm not much of a topic of conversation. Why would I be? He's not obliged to parade me around. He hasn't suggested hosting a dinner party to introduce me to his friends—not that I'd know what to say to them anyway.

Does he even *have* friends? Does he have anyone like Alex and Ophelia?

God, I know nothing about my husband's social life.

Raees gives my hand a squeeze. "Let's go downstairs."

I let him take the lead as we begin descending the steps. When my bag slips down to the crook of my elbow, he stops to fix it on my shoulder, his touch as careful as ever.

I release his hand for a moment. My eyes catch a scrap of pink confetti on the floor, and I reach down to grab it, tucking it carefully into my purse.

"Zinneerah?"

I turn my head toward the voice. A woman in a sleek black suit is descending the stairs from the side, heading straight for us.

"Hi!" she chirps, extending a hand. "I'm Bianca. Alex's touring manager."

I shake her hand quickly, my heart pounding harder now.

Raees follows suit, introducing himself as my husband.

"Well," Bianca says, glancing between us, "Alex is waiting for you in her dressing room. She asked me to come get you. Unless . . ." She hesitates, looking at Raees. "Unless you both have somewhere to be?"

I shake my head so fast I'm surprised it doesn't snap off my shoulders.

Bianca chuckles. "Lost your voice from all the singing, huh?" She gives me a quick wink. "Been there, done that."

I look up at Raees. *Would you like to come?*

He gives me a small, assuring grin. *Stand outside the room.*

"Oh, my god," Bianca suddenly blurts, her face falling into a cringe. "I'm so sorry! That was such an ignorant thing to say. I didn't mean—"

"It's fine," Raees interrupts, clearing his throat. "We'd like to see Alex now, if that's all right."

"Yes, of course!" she says, clearly relieved, snapping back into professional mode. "This way." She begins walking, her black heels clicking against the floor.

We follow, my hands twisting together as I mentally rehearse what I'll say when I see Alex. I'll hug her. For an hour. At least. Then I'll catch her up on everything—half-speaking, half-typing on my phone, like I did with Professor Daniels. I'll apologize a thousand times for shutting her and Ophelia out, even though I know Alex won't let me.

But I have to. I have to explain to her why I vanished. I have to tell her that shutting her out was the only way to keep her safe. If I hadn't, I would've dragged her into my hell, and I couldn't have lived with myself if she got hurt.

Bianca halts in front of a red door and knocks lightly. "Al—"

The door flies open before she can finish her sentence.

Alex stands there, barefoot, her eyeliner smudged and her hair sticking up at odd angles, like she'd run her hands through it too many times.

Her eyes lock onto mine immediately, and her mouth falls open.

She doesn't say anything at first, just stares like I'm some fever dream she's about to wake up from. And then, "Oh, God," she breathes. "You're actually real."

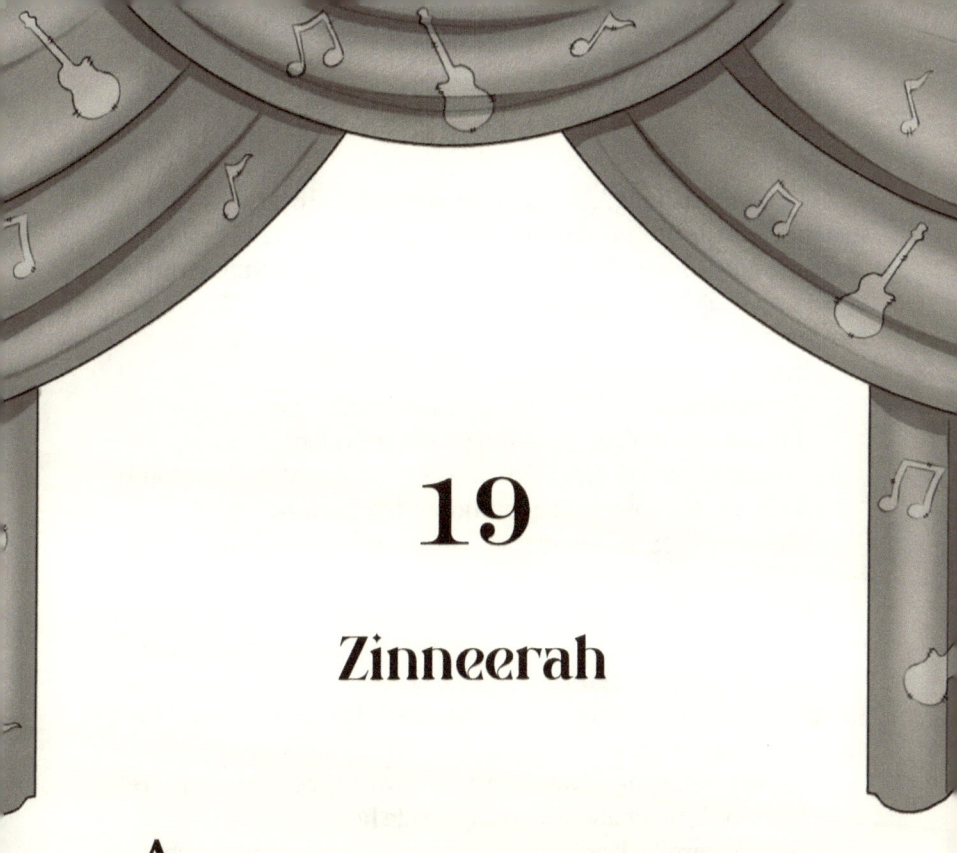

19

Zinneerah

Alex stumbles toward me like she's forgotten how to walk, her arms outstretched, her face already crumpling.

I meet her halfway, throwing my arms around her neck.

Neither of us lets go.

The door clicks shut behind us, but it feels like the whole world has closed in, leaving just me and Alex.

Her sobs break against my bare shoulder. Mine fall just as freely, staining the faded white of her band tour tee.

"Alex," I choke out through the lump in my throat.

"Zinnie!" she cries, high-pitched and cracking. Then she jerks back suddenly, holding me at arm's length. Her hands tremble as they cup my face, her thumbs brushing away my tears. Her eyes widen as they roam over me, to memorize me all over again. "Oh, my god. I missed this stupid, sexy face of yours so much."

I let out a laugh, but it dies the moment she pulls me back into her arms. "Talk. Please."

"Oh, we're talking," Alex says between her leftover sobs. She snatches a tissue box off the vanity, shoving it toward me before grabbing one for herself. She dabs at my face, and I do the same for hers—two broken halves trying to clean each other up. "Where the fuck have you been, Zinnie?"

"Hell," I whisper.

She freezes, the tissue halfway to her cheek. "Zin . . ."

"I mean it." I look down at my hands, trembling in my lap. "I can't . . . sing anymore, Alex." The words taste like ash in my mouth. "Car accident. My voice is like this now. Permanently."

The tissue box slips from her hands and hits the floor with a hollow thud.

Her glassy, brown eyes lock on mine. Before I can brace myself, her hands shoot up to cradle my face, shaking as she brushes her thumbs along my cheekbones. Her touch lands softly at my throat, where my perfect voice once lived, where the faded scars are. "He did this to you," she whispers.

I nod, swallowing against the knot in my throat. "Much more."

The words detonate something inside her.

She staggers back as if she's been struck, her hands clenched into fists. "Fuck!" Her hair tangles in her fingers as she grabs at it, pacing the small room like a caged animal. "Fuck, Zinnie! He better not still be walking free. Tell me he's not."

"Prison." I force out the answer. "Shahzad and Azeer helped."

Her pacing slows, but her anger doesn't abate. She turns, her face blotchy with tears. "Your voice, Zinnie," she murmurs, and sinks down onto the couch, burying her face in her hands. When she looks up again, her tears flow freely. "Your voice was everything to you."

My breath catches. I move to sit beside her, my hands fidgeting before I reach for hers. "It's okay," I whisper. "I use ASL now. I'm still learning, but it works."

Alex gives me a wobbly smile. "You're so strong. You always have been. You just . . . figure things out, no matter what."

I smile faintly and lean into her touch, letting my cheek rest against her palm. "I don't know if I feel strong anymore, but I want to tell you everything." I dig into my bag, my fingers brushing over random odds and ends before I pull out my phone. Unlocking the screen, I scroll to the Notes app, hesitating for just a second. "I wrote it all down. The good, the bad, everything."

Alex takes my phone hesitantly. "Fuck. Okay."

I sit beside her as she begins to read.

Occasionally, I reach out, tucking a strand of her hair behind her ear or squeezing her hand when she starts shaking too much. Her tears keep falling, and soon enough, mine join hers. Quick glances. Tight hugs. Choked apologies.

When she's done reading, she hands the phone back to me, her knuckles white from gripping it too hard. "I'm going to kill him," she grits out. "I mean it, Zinneerah. I'll end that fucker."

I shake my head. "It's over. He got what he deserved—" I start racking out coughs.

She grabs a bottle of water and presses it to my lips before I can protest. The cool liquid soothes the soreness in my throat. Her thumb brushes the corner of my mouth, wiping away a stray drop.

"Did they give him life?" she asks quietly. "Or just some bullshit bail to get out?"

I lower the bottle and look at her. "Latter. Two hundred thousand."

Her expression twists into rage, disgust, despair. "Are you fucking kidding me?" she snaps, her arms crossing tightly over her chest. "Two hundred thousand? For what? So he can go back to destroying someone else's life when he makes bail?" She laughs bitterly, shaking her head as her leg bounces restlessly. "God, the system is such trash. A man can tear his girlfriend apart—mentally, physically—and he still gets a second chance. What about you? Where's your second chance?"

"I'm working on it," I mumble, glancing down at my hands. "Every day."

"Well, I hope that bastard rots in prison. For the rest of his pathetic excuse for a life." Her voice breaks at the end, and before I can say anything, she pulls me into another hug. This one lasts longer than the others, both of us holding on like the world's ending.

My temples pound from discussing my ex-boyfriend so I quickly change subjects. "How's Ophelia?"

Alex gasps, smacking her forehead. "Ophelia! Jesus, I almost forgot. She's hooking up with some hotshot lawyer. Jack or Jake—something like that. Honestly, they change weekly."

That makes me laugh. "Is she happy?"

"Well, she's currently in St. Lucia with him."

"And her job?"

Alex exhales, slumping against the couch. "She's a single mom working at a Food Basics."

My eyes pop open. "*Mom?* Since when?"

She stares at me like I've sprouted a second head. "Wait, aren't you on Facebook?"

I shake my head. "He made me delete it, and I never went back."

Alex's face softens. She scoots closer, already pulling out her phone. "God, Zinnie." Her fingers tap against the screen as she searches. Then she turns the phone toward me, a collection of photos lighting up the display. "Here. Meet Juliette. She just turned eight last week. Isn't she a doll?"

I take the phone, staring at the photos. A bright-eyed girl grins back at me in each one, with curls so yellow and wild they practically bounce off the screen. The kind of kid who'd say 'hello' to everyone in a grocery store.

"She's beautiful," I murmur.

"You'll love her. She's so much like you were . . . well, before everything." Her voice drops on the last part, but she recovers quickly. "But I know my rockstar is still in there somewhere." Alex's finger pokes my chest. "She just needs her best friends to root her out."

I chuckle, and lean my forehead against her shoulder. "Think we could visit her?"

Alex's reaction is immediate. "Fuck yeah, we're gonna visit her!" She launches herself at me, arms enveloping me whole. "As soon as she's back. And since I'm done touring, we'll get the whole gang together. Maybe we'll even make some music again—if you're up for it." She nudges me with her elbow. "What do you say?"

I nod, tucking a strand of hair behind my ear. "Summer festival. Professor Daniels asked me to play."

Alex freezes mid-reach for her water bottle, her jaw dropping. "*No. Freaking. Way.* Daddy Daniels?"

My face twists in immediate protest. "Ew, don't call him that."

"What? It fits!" She grins wickedly. "You know I've got a thing for older men, and women. Something about all that emotional intelligence . . ." Her eyes twinkle. "And let's not lie to ourselves, Zinnie. Daniels is hot. He's like Patrick Swayze and young James Dean had a baby. A very distinguished baby."

"He's in his mid-seventies."

She shrugs. "I have no notes. Just taste."

Before I can even try to argue, she shifts gears, her eyes narrowing as she taps my wedding ring with a perfectly manicured nail. "Speaking of daddies." Her voice dips into a purr. "You gonna tell me more about the big, manly man you're married to? Or do I have to bribe it out of you?" She pinches my cheek. "And why the hell were Ophelia and I not invited to the wedding?"

"Mama," I say flatly.

Alex throws her head back with a groan. "Makes sense," she mutters, sinking back into her chair like she's mourning a great injustice. Which is fair. Not having your best-friends at your one and only wedding is a crime.

"Raees," I say. "His name."

Her head snaps up. "Reece? Baby, that's a white man's name."

A hoarse laugh bubbles out of me. "No, silly. Rah-ees."

She rolls her '*Raah*' dramatically, dragging out his name as she shimmies her shoulders. "More like *Rawr*-ees." She curls her fingers into mock claws and winks. "Tell me this man's not boring. What does he do?"

"Journalism professor. At S.L.U."

Alex moans, her head lolling back like she's just tasted the world's finest wine. "Goddamn, Zinnie. You married a literature nerd. I bet he's whispering Shakespeare in your ear during sex. 'Shall I compare thee to a summer's day?'" She fans herself. "'Thou art more lovely and more—'"

"Alex."

But she's already knee-deep in the fantasy. "Does he wear those sexy tweed sweaters with the elbow patches? Oh, God. Tell me he adjusts his glasses right before he lays you down on a pile of freshly graded essays. Just tosses his red pen aside and says, 'Baby, the only A-plus you're getting with me is this D.'"

"Stop it, God!" I'm laughing so hard my stomach hurts, but Alex is on a roll.

"And while we're on the topic of A-pluses." Her eyes narrow to slits. "Be honest. Have you role-played as his student yet?" Her lashes flutter as she slips into her next role, sitting primly and folding her hands like a Victorian debutante. "'Oh, Professor *Rrrr*ah-ees, the only thing I want you to teach me is how to be your good girl.'"

"Alexandra!" I'm trying to smother my laugh as she grins and trails her hands sensually down her torso like some burlesque performer. "You're ridiculous. Stop it. He's outside."

"So? Juicy details. Now."

My cheeks burn, and I shake my head quickly. "There are no details."

"Zinnie. Don't tell me—"

"Uncomfortable." I look down, fumbling for words. "At the moment."

Alex's jaw drops. "Girl, he's your husband. What's he waiting for, a calendar invite? An RSVP? Does he need a PowerPoint presentation? 'Reasons Why It's Time to Fuck.'"

"It's not like that—"

"Then what's he doing?" She throws her hands up. "Reading you bedtime stories? Quoting Hemingway over tea? I swear to God, if you tell me you've been playing Scrabble instead of—"

"We'll do . . . *it* . . . at some point."

She grins, satisfied. "Last I checked, you swore you'd never marry. You were all 'marriage is a capitalist scam' and 'I'll never need a man.' And now you're out here married to Clark fucking Kent. I don't know if I'm jealous of him or you." Her hand darts out, tickling me under my chin like I'm a baby. "If you ever need a third—"

I clap my hand over her mouth. "No."

She peels my hand off her face. "Fine, fine. But just so you know, I'd do it for free. You're welcome."

I groan. "You're impossible."

Alex shrugs and slings her arm around my neck. "But for real, babe," she whispers. "You don't have to rush anything if you're uncomfortable. Let your body and mind adjust. You've been through a lot. This is just the fresh, slow pace of change, and there's no deadline, okay?"

I answer her by wrapping my arms around her waist.

She responds immediately, tucking my head under her chin and pulling me down with her as she reclines back into the cushions. "I'm not letting you go," she murmurs, her fingers absentmindedly combing through my hair.

A small smile creeps across my lips. "Me, too."

"And I mean it," she adds sharply. "Your husband better be prepared for weekly visits from me and Fifi. Actually, scratch that. He should just clear out the guest room permanently. We're crashing whenever we want."

I snuggle closer, smiling into her side. "Festival?"

"Of course!" she says, waving her hand like it's a given. "Plus, I miss Daniels. Is he still serving 'silver fox realness,' or what?"

I lift my left hand, wiggling my wedding ring in response.

She snaps her fingers. "Right, my bad. Forgot you had your own personal fox now. Guess I'm stuck drooling over academia's finest alone."

"You?" I ask, tilting my head curiously.

"Nah." She stretches out her legs, her sneakers knocking against the coffee table as she gives a languid shrug. "Tour's kept me busy, you know? And let's be real, I'm not exactly the dating-and-relationships type. People come and go, but my music? She's loyal. Never breaks my heart, never ghosts me, never eats the leftovers in the fridge with my name on it. Guess you could say I'm married to it."

I lift my head from her chest. "Happy?"

"Very." Her smile spreads slowly, wide enough to flash the tiny diamond gem embedded in her left canine—a little sparkle of her personality literally shining through.

"Good." I grin and reach up to squish her cheeks together like she's a mischievous toddler. "That's all I want."

Alex, of course, doesn't let it slide. She immediately squishes my cheeks in return. "Ditto."

We both burst into laughter.

She tucks my hair behind my ear again, slower this time, like she's trying to put every strand exactly where it belongs. "Zinneerah," she says quietly, the humor in her voice fading into something earnest, "if the pain comes back to you in flashes, or in your sleep, or even just while you're brushing your teeth, I want you to text me. Right away. I don't care if it's 3 a.m. or during an episode of *Yellowstone*. I'll show up."

Tears prick the back of my eyes, and right as I open my mouth to counter, she cuts me off with a pointed finger. "And don't even start with the whole 'it's not your fault' thing. I'm your best friend. My job is to insert myself into your life, whether you want me there or not." She tilts her head, the corners of her mouth twitching. "I'm like that weird mole you can't get rid of—always there, a little inappropriate, probably a little concerning, but ultimately harmless. Okay?"

That draws a shaky laugh out of me. "Alex . . ."

"I mean it," she says. "I want to make up for not fighting harder for you. I didn't push hard enough when I should have. I let you slip away when I knew something was wrong."

"No," I whisper. "He would have hurt you. Badly."

Tears blur my vision, and I duck my head to hide them, but Alex isn't having it. She tilts my chin up with two fingers, forcing me to look at her.

"I don't care what he would've done to me, Zinnie. I would've gone through hell for you. *Hell.* I'm stubborn as shit, remember? The same girl who went head-to-head with a campus cop for giving me a parking ticket is not someone who just gives up. Please don't shut me out again. Not even if you think you don't have another choice."

Her lips press gently to my forehead, and I crumble, the tears breaking free. I don't even try to stop them.

CRAZY LITTLE THING CALLED LOVE

"I'm here now," she murmurs against my skin. "Ophelia's here, too. We're not going anywhere. And together?" She pulls back, her hands sliding up to hold me by the shoulders. "We're gonna make new memories. Kickass ones. The kind that makes the bad stuff look like a boring rerun you don't even remember watching."

A half-sob, half-laugh escapes me, and she grins, brushing a tear off my cheek with her thumb.

"You think I'm kidding, but, baby, I'm dead serious." She starts counting down on her fingers. "We're talking road trips with zero planning. We're talking breaking into a country club pool at night. We're talking matching tattoos, probably astrology or some sentimental shit." Then, her face softens again, her fingers squeezing my shoulders. "I love you, Zinnie. So freakin' much. For whoever you are now, whoever you were, and whoever you're gonna be next. And there isn't a single goddamn thing I'd change about you. You got that? Not one." She leans her forehead onto mine. "I love, love, love you. Like, stalker-level love, but in a healthy way. The kind where I'll stand outside your window with a boombox if you ignore my texts for more than a day."

I'm laughing and crying at the same time now, the tears streaming freely as she cups my cheeks with both hands. "I love you, too."

"Don't cry," she says, even as her own voice cracks and fresh tears spill down her cheeks. She swipes at them uselessly with the back of her hand, sniffling. "Shit. Now I'm crying. Thanks a lot."

That only makes us laugh harder—wet, hiccup chuckles that dissolve into more sniffles.

"I missed you so much," I whisper.

"Me, too." She cleans the tears off my left eye with her thumb and gives me a watery smile. "So, did you like the last song?"

"Loved."

She just stares at me, scanning my face like she's memorizing the new details since we last saw each other.

Then, without warning, she leans in and plants a quick kiss on my cheek before yanking me into a hug so tight it feels like she's trying to fuse us together. "I'm so glad you're here, Zinneerah."

"Not leaving."

"Good. Neither am I. Never."

"Ever."

She pulls away just enough to look at me, her face still damp but shining with a grin. "All right, let's get you together, babe." She grabs the water bottle off the table and presses it into my hands, then tosses the tissue box onto my lap. "Drink and dab, because right now you're giving Kendall Roy mid-crisis. And unless you're about to rap 'L to the OG,' we're not doing this today."

I let out a surprised laugh, dabbing at my face with a tissue. "You're so stupid."

"And you love me."

We sit back down together, exchanging numbers. Hers changed because of some cyberstalker situation—"Which, by the way, just means I'm, like, *actually* famous," she says—and mine changed because of him. She doesn't comment on it, just gives my knee a reassuring squeeze that says everything I need to hear.

My fingers twist around the water bottle cap, and I look back at her. "Alex?"

"Yes, babe?"

I take a deep breath. "Do you want to meet Raees?

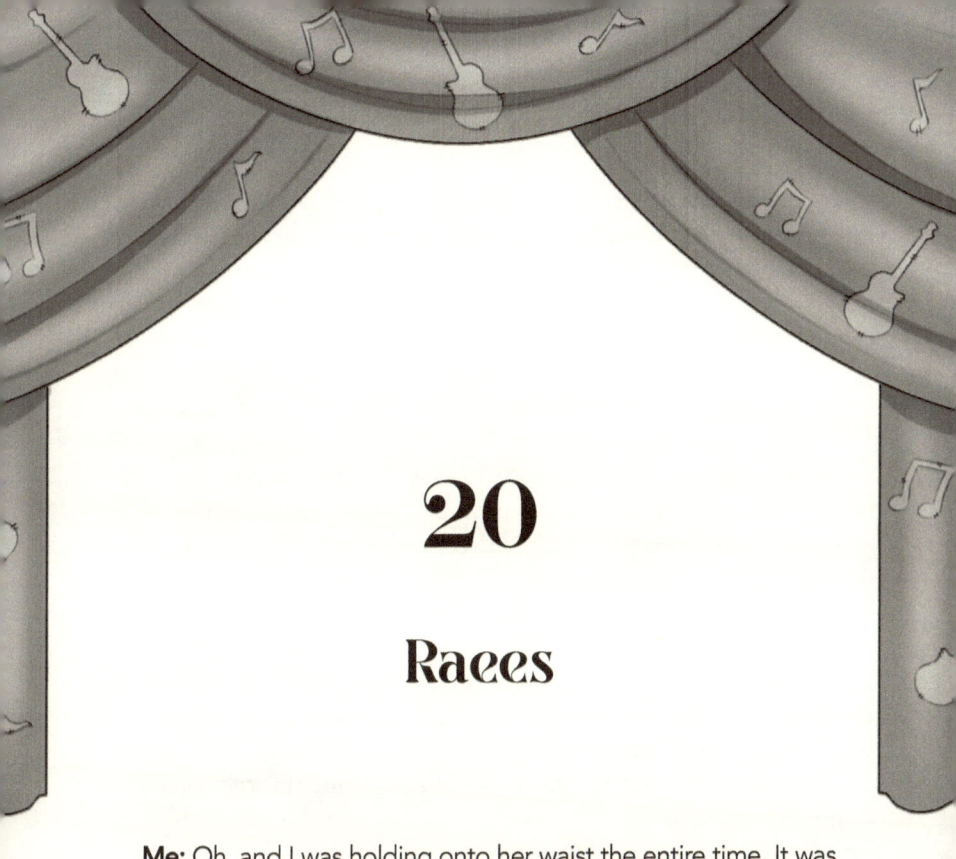

20

Races

Me: Oh, and I was holding onto her waist the entire time. It was the best feeling in the world. I thought I might actually die of excitement.

Ramishah: Please make a friend and text them instead.

Me: One more thing. She looked so cute picking up the confetti. I swear, I wanted to take a thousand pictures of her. Just her jumping around, smiling like that. Holy shit. I love my wife.

Ramishah: I should hope so.

Me: I want to marry her a thousand times over.

Ramishah: Goodnight, Rumi.

It's embarrassing, really. All I can do is replay Zinneerah's face in my head: her wide, giddy smile while she reached for the tiny scraps of colorful confetti.

The last time I saw her like that—so carefree, so utterly her—was the night she performed with her band. She'd jumped around the stage with her guitar slung over her shoulder, the crowd shouting every lyric back at her. She owned that moment, every second of it. And she hadn't stopped smiling the entire time. That same perfect, pearly smile. God, I could live a hundred lifetimes and never get enough of it.

I shudder, suddenly overwhelmed.

It's terrifying, isn't it? Loving someone this much? It feels too big for one body to hold. Sometimes I scare myself, thinking about it—the lengths I'd go to keep her safe, to make her happy. She's been the center of my world for six years now. Every waking thought revolves around her, and every goodnight dream ends with her. She makes me better, just by existing.

Loving her is . . . Loving her is self-care.

The dressing room door creaks open, and there she is. My Zinneerah. Her eyes are red-rimmed, but she's wiped away most of the evidence. The eyeliner is gone, and her lipstick has faded into something softer. Even like this, she's striking.

Those dark eyes meet mine, and for a second, I forget what I was doing. "Everything okay?"

Yes. You?

"Never been better."

Her gaze drops, and she nods toward the room behind her. *Meet A-L-E-X?*

"I'd love to."

She shifts to the side, giving me space to walk in. The dressing room smells faintly of hairspray and something candy-ish—probably Alex's perfume.

Speaking of, she's shorter than I expected, standing by the couch with arms crossed, her eyes fixed on me like I'm an uninvited guest. She doesn't smile. Instead, she sticks out a hand, all business. "Professor Raees."

"Raees works." I take her hand, giving it a firm shake. "Congratulations on finishing your tour, Alex. Zinneerah and I had a wonderful time tonight. You're a hell of a performer."

Her lips curve into a smirk as she bends into a bow. "Thank you, thank you." She plops down onto the couch. "Go on. Sit down."

I pick a chair diagonal to her. Zinneerah sits next to me, close enough that our knees brush.

Alex doesn't waste time. "So," she says, leaning back her elbows. "When's the second wedding? You know, the one where Ophelia and I are the only guests?"

I blink. "Ophelia?"

Zinneerah doesn't hesitate, signing, *Our other friend.*

"Oh," I say, nodding slowly. "Well, I don't think another wedding is in the cards, but we'd love to have you both over for dinner sometime. You're always welcome to stay over."

Alex puts a hand to her chest, mock-affected. "That is, like, so sweet. I was planning on showing up either way. With or without your permission."

I chuckle. "I'm glad you two have reconnected. Watching my wife jump around tonight was a sight for sore eyes." Zinneerah immediately looks down, cheeks coloring as I aim a soft smile at her. "Maybe I should book Alex for a weekly residency if it means seeing that again."

"For her? Dude, I'd do a whole world tour," Alex quips, winking. "And you know what's wild? Half the songs I performed tonight, Zinnie was there when I wrote them. She even helped me finish the last one."

"Really?" I raise my brows, playing at surprise. The truth is, I've always suspected Zinneerah's old university days involved more creativity than she lets on. Knowing her knack for words, and her tendency to downplay her own brilliance, I wouldn't be shocked if she's sitting on a vault of songs no one's ever heard.

"She's the best songwriter I know. Better than most pros, honestly," Alex continues. "She's got a special connection with words. The kind of lyrics that make you feel like you're living in an old, blurry home video. Once, I cried in the middle of editing a song she helped me with. I'm talking fat, soul-crushing tears."

Zinneerah shakes her head quickly, her face now fully flushed.

"Oh, it's true." Alex leans forward, locking eyes with her like she's challenging her to deny it. "Now that you're married, though, you're out of excuses. You have to start writing love songs. Big, swoony ones. Give John Legend a run for his money."

I can feel my own face warming at that, but Alex just smirks, clearly pleased with herself.

If Zinneerah wrote a song for me—*about* me—I'd listen to it on a loop until the end of time. I'd burn it onto a CD, get her to autograph it, and keep it in a fireproof safe. I'd brag to everyone, especially her perpetually grouchy brother, about how I'm her muse. My wife's muse. A man whose last creative endeavor was playing a one-man game of tic-tac-toe in the margins of a tax form.

"So, Raees," Alex says, popping a chip in her mouth from a nearby bowl. "How'd you convince Zinnie to marry you? I'm sure it wasn't just, like, an impulsive brunch decision."

"Oh." I try to keep my focus on Alex instead of the breathtakingly shy woman I somehow managed to marry. "Well, we'd known each other for about a year before getting engaged. I don't know exactly what convinced her to say yes, but for me . . ." I smile when Zinneerah's gaze flickers up at me. "For me, it was instant. There wasn't any convincing needed. I'd like to think she liked the sound of my endless rambling."

"Ooh," Alex coos. "Love a man who's both charming and a podcast. You know, back in the day, Zinnie used to ramble, too. She once went to see three horror films in a row in the dingiest theater in the city because Ophelia and I chickened out. And when we finally met up, she spent hours explaining every single plot twist, and the IMDb trivia about which actors have kids and which don't."

You like scary movies, Zinneerah signs in my direction.

I despise horror movies, but for my wife—"Oh, absolutely," I lie, with the confidence of a man stepping into quicksand. "I love horror movies. One of my all-time favorite genres."

"Yeah?" Alex smiles, swinging one leg over the other. "What's your favorite?"

I lick my lips, casting a glance at my wife, who's watching me like I've just promised to recite *War and Peace* from memory. I fumble for a title—any title—and latch onto the last one Ramishah forced me to watch. "Uh, I love the one with the train. And the zombies. Korean zombies . . ."

Zinneerah claps her hands together, her face lighting up as she points at herself and nods. *I love that movie. The ending was sad.*

Sad? I barely remember it. I spent most of the runtime hiding behind my hands like a five-year-old in a haunted house. The ending was just blurry shapes and muffled sobs—mostly Ramishah's. Which, by the way, was a brutal betrayal of my expectations. She was supposed to be the tough one. "Yes. It was quite gut-wrenching."

"How sweet," Alex says, propping her chin in her palms. She bats her lashes at both of us and tilts her head. "You two are just painfully adorable, you know that?" She narrows her eyes and tilts her head, studying me. "Now that I get a closer look at you, Raees, I swear I've seen you somewhere before."

"Oh?" I say, feigning an air of polite curiosity. "Maybe. I was also a student when you two were. Close to graduating, actually—"

"Did you visit Studio 365 often?" Alex asks, cutting me off.

Panic prickles at the back of my neck. This isn't a good sign. She's sharp. "Hmm?" I laugh nervously and rub my palms together like I'm cold. "No, I—I don't think so. What's that?"

Alex looks all too pleased with herself. "It's a coffee shop," she says, her gray eyes breaking me down molecule by molecule. "Zinnie, Ophelia, and I used to perform there all the time. Open mic nights, acoustic sets, that kind of thing. I swear I've seen you sitting at one of the tables. How else would you feel so familiar?"

Oh, she knows. She definitely knows.

The realization drops into my stomach like a bowling ball. Of course, Alex would remember. I could've sworn I'd been subtle, sitting in the back with my notebook, pretending to work while Zinneerah's voice turned my spine into melted wax.

Apparently not.

"Is that so?" I mutter, smiling just enough to appear unbothered, though my palms are clammy and I'm certain she's enjoying this way too much. "Maybe I did. I don't recall. Those years are a bit of a blur."

"Are they?" she repeats, her grin resembling the Cheshire Cat. Then, sighing, she surrenders with a slap of her hands against her lap.

"Oh, well. The past doesn't really matter now that you've got a future to build together, huh?"

I exhale through my nose, trying to keep my relief subtle. Zinneerah is staring at Alex, puzzled, like she doesn't understand what just passed between us.

Bless her.

The whole I-was-secretly-obsessed-with-you-for-six-years-before-I-finally-said-hi thing isn't exactly a topic I've planned to discuss with her in detail. Yet.

"I'm glad you both found each other," Alex says. Zinneerah and I both snap our heads up, startled. Her eyes crinkle at the corners when she smiles. "I've always wanted nothing but the best of the best for Zinnie. She deserves it. And even though it's been, what, six minutes of us talking? I can already tell you're the one for her." She brushes a strand of her silver-dyed bangs out of her face with a flick of her fingers. "I'm not great with sentimental stuff—kind of allergic to it, actually—but just . . . don't ever drop her hand, Raees. That's all I'll say."

On cue, my left hand seeks out Zinneerah's right one.

I thread my fingers through hers, offering a small squeeze. She startles at first, her movements going still, but then she lifts her gaze to meet mine. Her eyes, usually so dark they're almost black, catch the light, revealing a soft cocoa-brown hue. I never quite know what she's thinking behind them, and it drives me insane. A good insane. The kind where I'll spend my whole life trying to figure her out and never once regret it.

I wink.

Zinneerah blinks at me, rapid and restless, like her body doesn't know how to respond to the gesture.

And then, like a gong sounding at the worst possible moment, Alex springs to her feet. "Well, lovebirds. All this *Love, Actually*-ing has officially worked up my appetite. Let's grab some food before I choke on this tension, 'kay?"

Zinneerah vibrates with excitement the moment we step into One Stop Chicken Shop.

The place looks like it hasn't seen a health inspection since the invention of electricity, but judging by my wife's shining eyes, and the nostalgic grin on Alex's face, we've just walked onto a sacred ground.

"We used to come here all the time," Alex explains, catching my confusion as I take in the flickering fluorescent lights and sticky linoleum floor. "Fancy-schmancy meals weren't exactly in the budget, so it was shawarma bowls, ramen, and greasy chicken. Ain't that right?" She grabs Zinneerah's shoulders from behind and gives her a shake.

My wife looks around like she's just discovered a long-lost temple, her awe fixed on the half-faded menu above the register and the bushy-browed, middle-aged cashier texting on his phone. The chairs don't match. The tables are scarred with initials and lopsided hearts. The whole place smells like deep fryer oil and regret.

It's perfect.

Joints like these guarantee the food's going to be good. Incredible, actually. With a side of heartburn or food poisoning, if you're unlucky. But still, worth it.

Alex approaches the counter like she's the owner, rattling off an order for herself and Zinneerah without consulting either of them. Then she turns to me, propping a hand on her hip. "And you, tall king? What'll it be?"

Tall king?

I stall, glancing at Zinneerah, who's still mesmerized by the ambiance like it's Michelin-star dining. "I'll have what she's having." If there's food poisoning in my future, I'd rather it happens together. "But no tomatoes."

The two women dive into a very serious debate about who's going to pay. I stay quiet at first, watching my wife insist with big, round, pleading eyes while Alex raises a pierced eyebrow like she's ready to throw down.

It's adorable.

Zinneerah rarely gets feisty unless it's about something like this, wordlessly stubborn in the way that makes me want to scoop her up and kiss her forehead.

But my so-called tall king status wins out, nudging both of them aside as I slide my card onto the machine before either can react.

"Hey, come on!" Alex groans, throwing her hands in the air. "I was going to treat you guys as a wedding present."

Even Zinneerah pouts, crossing her arms and glancing up at me like she's planning revenge. It's the most heart-melting thing I've ever seen.

"Perhaps another time." As I'm tucking my card back into my wallet, Alex snatches my wrist, her sharp eyes zeroing in on the photo inside.

She opens her mouth to say something, her grin already forming, but I silence her with a quick shake of my head. *Don't you dare.*

"Why not?" she mouths, feigning innocence.

I shake my head again, more firmly this time, but she's already poking at my ribs with a childish giggle. "That's so old-timey of you, Professor."

So, what if I keep a picture of my wife in my wallet? It's from the solo photoshoot she did for our wedding. The files came bundled with the rest of the pictures, but this one—the one where she's smiling for the first time that evening—this one begged to be printed. Passport-sized, tucked neatly into the little leather pocket of my wallet, it's a talisman. I like to open it when I'm stressed or overwhelmed, or when everything feels too good to be real, and I need a tangible reminder that this isn't some fever dream. That she's actually mine.

When our food's ready, I grab the tray and set it down at one of the mismatched tables, brushing crumbs away with my hand. The women follow, their energy elevated as if this greasy little joint has unlocked something primal in them.

As soon as they take their first bites, the table transforms into a scene straight out of a food documentary. Alex moans dramatically, throwing kisses toward the chef behind the counter, who looks singularly unimpressed but probably gets this reaction a lot. "Still got the best fried chicken in the city, Mohammed!" Alex declares, waving a drumstick like it's the Olympic torch. "Never change! You're an icon!"

Zinneerah, meanwhile, takes a more civilized approach. She bites into her burger, closes her eyes, and shakes her head like she can't believe what she's tasting—

BANG!

Her fist hits the table, a loud, decisive thump that sends Alex into peals of laughter, and takes me by surprise.

The burger's solid. Not as life-changing as it seems to be for Zinneerah, but I respect the craftsmanship. I angle my phone just so to capture the perfect shot of the slightly charred bun and the melted cheese oozing over the edges. Then I open my messaging app and send it to Ramishah, who's fast asleep halfway across the world.

Zinneerah catches my eye just as I slip my phone into my pocket. Her face is blank, her lips pressed into a tight line. My heart skips. Is she okay? Is she about to experience the first stage of food poisoning?

Everything okay? I sign.

She blinks, then shifts her gaze to Alex, who's currently mid-monologue about a musical.

Okay, that was weird. Usually, if Zinneerah spaces out, and she does space out often, she snaps back the moment I wave a hand in front of her. Nine out of ten—no, ten out of ten times, she acknowledges it with that soft, apologetic grin of hers.

Alex, on the other hand, is having no trouble finding her joy. She pats her stomach with both hands after wiping her mouth, reclining in her chair. "Oh, man. I'm slipping into a food coma." She rests her head on Zinneerah's shoulder, closing her eyes. "This is how I go. Wake me up in five days."

"Would you like us to drive you home?" I offer. Honestly, I wouldn't mind wrapping the night early, pouring my wife a cup of tea, and asking her what's going on in that quiet, beautiful mind of hers.

"Home?" Alex jerks upright, looking genuinely offended. "Buddy, the night is still young for Alex Watanabe. The girls are meeting me at a club in an hour to celebrate the last leg of the tour. You can just drop me off there." She slides her gaze between Zinneerah and I. "Unless, you two wanna join?"

I desperately want to say no. *Desperately.* Clubs are not my thing. The pounding bass, the overwhelming crowds, the spilled drinks—it's the complete opposite of how I'd like to spend my time. But Zinneerah's opinion matters more. Alex is her best friend, and I don't want to speak for her. Knowing Zinneerah, she'll probably decline, too.

Why not? Zinneerah signs, tilting her head ever so slightly.

I blink. *You want to go?*

Am I not allowed to?

Her tone, if it could be called that through her hands, lands somewhere between annoyance and exasperation. My heart sinks a little. Of course she's allowed to go. Of course she's allowed to want things, to make decisions without checking my every preference first. I know that.

Did I do something wrong? Did I say too much? My brain churns through possibilities, searching for the misstep. But I already know what to do next. I've known since I was a kid. You don't argue. You don't prod. You don't hold your ground and risk the consequences. You smile. You say: Okay. You survive.

"Okay," I say now, forcing the word out with a smile so thin it could snap in half. My pulse ticks in my neck. Compliant. It's second nature. I don't even have to think about it.

"Perfect!" Alex squeals, leaping out of her chair with the unshakable energy only she can summon after midnight. "I'm gonna hit the bathroom and freshen up." She winks and spins off toward the bathroom, leaving us alone at the table.

It's not that I don't want Zinneerah to go. It's not that I think she shouldn't have a good time with Alex. It's that clubs are . . . well, clubs. Something could go wrong. It always can.

Zinneerah hates all of that. She hates crowds, and people stumbling into her personal space. At least, that's what I've concluded.

But maybe Alex is breathing back her previous life into her. The woman I fell in love with. This is who she used to be before me—a woman who liked noise, liked recklessness, liked a little wildness. Maybe she's been to a hundred clubs, knows the scene, and can handle herself.

The sound of fingers tapping on the table draws me out of my thoughts.

I blink and glance up to see Zinneerah watching me. When I meet her gaze, she smiles. *I was joking*, she signs.

I blink, caught completely off guard. *About what?*

I hate the club.

I stare at her, confused. *You said you wanted to go.*

When I am in a better mental space. No risk right now.

Relief crashes over me like a tidal wave, though I don't let it show on my face. She was joking. Of course she was joking. My mind runs too far ahead sometimes, spiraling before I can stop it.

I'm sorry. You should celebrate with her.

Zinneerah glances at the crumpled wrappers and empty trays between us, then gestures toward them like they're the answer to everything. *We did. Time to go home. She will understand.*

"You can invite her tomorrow," I suggest.

I will see her on campus. Agreed to help with the festival. She pauses, looking thoughtful, then signs, *Is it okay to see O-P-H-E-L-I-A after?*

I nod immediately. "Make sure you text me beforehand."

Zinneerah's hands shift, her fingers preparing to say something else, but then she stops. Lowers them to her lap.

What is it? I sign, leaning forward.

She shrugs, avoiding my eyes. *Nothing. Thank you for the food.* Then, after a pause, she adds, *Alex likes you a lot.*

I lick the smug grin off my lips. "What isn't there to like?"

Her foot nudges mine under the table, and she rolls her eyes, but not before giving me a smile. It's the smallest things with her that always undo me—the twitch of her lips, the way her shoulders relax when she feels safe. Even now, in a fluorescent-lit chicken shop, she glows.

Alex arrives, sweeping back into the scene with her hair gelled into sleek perfection and eyeliner sharp enough to cut metal in half. She takes one look at Zinneerah's helpless smile and groans. "Let me guess. You're not coming?"

"She said she'll see you on campus tomorrow," I answer on my wife's behalf. "You two can practice for the summer festival then. And, after that, you're supposed to go see Ophelia."

Alex smacks her lips in mock exasperation and plops down onto the chair beside Zinneerah, swinging an arm around her shoulders. "Works for me. We'll celebrate with just you, me, and Fifi when she's back. Girls' night, no boys allowed. Plus, you'll get to meet Juliette! Speaking of, we should buy her a present . . ."

Her words trail off as the conversation veers into a territory I don't entirely follow, but I don't mind.

I lean back, resting my arms on the table, and let myself do what I love most: watching my wife.

21

Zinneerah

Raees is leaning against the counter, phone in hand, thumbs moving over his phone keyboard.

He doesn't notice me watching him. Or maybe he does and doesn't care.

I press my lips together. I need assurance. I need it to *not* be her. That it's someone else. Anyone else.

Tapping his arm, I sign, *Dinner party for your friends?*

He glances up, eyebrows knitting as he tucks his phone into his pocket. "Why?"

I set my scuffed boots by the door. *Would be nice*, I sign. *I did not see them at the wedding.*

Raees rubs his bottom lip, the kind of absentminded gesture that tells me he's stalling. Thinking. Maybe avoiding it. "I'm not great at making friends," he says.

Uninvited guilt bubbles up in my stomach. Why'd I assume he'd be this effortless, magnetic social butterfly? After Sahara and me, he's probably the third most awkward human I've ever met.

Invite family? I sign. *Your family. My family.*

"A dawat?" His voice lilts upward in surprise, but there's no judgment there.

I nod. *Mama will push me to do it soon. I want to*—I shrug, gesturing to the open air. *Get it over with.*

Raees exhales in resignation. He starts juggling his keys in one hand, the metallic clinking. "Okay," he says, nodding. "We'll host it early in the afternoon. That way, everyone's out by six."

Six o'clock. Perfect. *I can survive that.*

His smile brightens as he moves to lock the door behind us. He pops the trunk, and I hoist my guitar case into the back. Then, like always, he opens the passenger door for me before settling into the driver's seat.

I sign as soon as he's buckled in. *Can I invite my friends?*

"Of course," he replies. "You don't have to ask for my permission, Zinneerah."

Habit. I am—

"Nope," he cuts in before I can apologize. His lopsided grin shoots through my chest, making me clutch the belt tighter than I always do. "You know, Alina told me when her and Azeer hosted a dawat, they ordered takeout and pretended they cooked it."

The memory makes me suppress a laugh. Of course, they did that. I don't know whether to be horrified or impressed they got away with it.

I shake my head and quickly sign, *I am surprised they are still married.*

Raees throws his head back and laughs infectiously. One hand stays on the steering wheel, the other gripping the gear shift like it's a lifeline, even though we're in an automatic. That's how Baba used to drive. It's how I drive, too.

"But we'll cook," he says with a wink. "I'll cook. You can bake."

The light turns red and we coast to a stop. I can feel his attention on me now, fully. *Call my brother. Ask for recipes.*

Raees' smile fades just a little.

I know the look all too well.

Shahzad is five years younger than Raees, but if I didn't know better, I'd think the gap was a lot wider. Shahzad's towering height and those daunting tattoos, are enough to make even the bravest hesitate. And, well, the death stares on our wedding day didn't exactly help.

But with Nyla there to smooth things over, I'm sure the dinner won't end in a brawl. I'd put money on it.

"I'll . . . see," is all he offers before the light changes to green.

Once we park on campus, Raees and I go our separate ways.

I veer toward the winding path that leads away from the English department, my boots crunching against the familiar gravel. The music building rises ahead, a destination I've walked to so many times it feels like a song my body knows by heart.

"Zinnie!" Alex is outside Professor Daniels' office, waving her arms like an inflatable tube man outside a car dealership.

I jog over, and we meet halfway in a quick hug.

"How do I look?" she asks, fanning her black jean-jacket bedazzled with pins and chains.

I gasp, widening my eyes and staring over her shoulder. "Professor."

"*Where*?" Her head snaps around so fast it's a wonder she doesn't give herself whiplash. I double over, laughing so hard my ribs ache. "Not funny."

"He's married," I whisper between giggles.

She snorts, fluffing her pixie cut like she's about to walk into a runway show. "Never stopped me before."

As a married woman myself, I choose the high road: selective deafness.

"Why don't we hit one of the music rooms while he finishes his morning lecture?" she asks. "Get some practice in?"

I nod enthusiastically.

She skips ahead, tugging me along as she points out every chip in the wall ("That one looks like Mufasa's profile if you squint"), the weird stain on the ceiling ("Tell me that's not the perfect outline of a human ass?"), and her personal favorite: speculating on Professor Daniels' cologne. "Cedarwood and George Clooney," she states, sniffing the air like a bloodhound.

By the time we reach the music rooms, I'm exhausted from laughter. This is why I keep her around.

The music building is quiet this early in the morning, with most rooms still empty. By afternoon, though, it'll be a completely different stage—every corner filled with students cramming for their spring-term exams.

I can still remember those days, spending hours with my guitar until my fingers felt like they were made of stone. Ophelia, ever the mom of the group, would shove my hands into bowls of ice water, and then slather them with organic coconut oil like I was some kind of indie rock star in rehab.

"Is Ophelia back yet?" I ask, pulling the zipper of my guitar bag while Alex unloads her things by the piano. She is one of those annoying prodigies who can pick up any instrument and play it like she's been practicing her whole life.

"She lands around four." Alex stretches her arms overhead. "We'll wrap this up an hour early, head out, and grab Juliette a gift. Maybe even get our favorite gold-digger something, too."

"Mean."

"Please, she thrives on it. If I don't call her a gold-digger at least once a week, she thinks I'm mad at her."

I'm relieved that Alex and Ophelia stuck together, even after I pulled myself away. They could've let it all dissolve when I left, but they didn't.

The three of us were always a unit, but it never felt like anyone was competing for space. Whenever we split off into duos, it didn't spark jealousy or insecurity—it just gave us time to miss the third. And we always did. We'd spend hours talking about how much we needed her there, until one of us finally snapped and showed up at her place. Sometimes we'd drag her out of bed; sometimes we'd just climb in with her and refuse to leave. Those mornings always ended the same way—three heads pressed into the same pillow until we all fell asleep from laughter.

"It'll be fine," Alex says, catching whatever look is on my face. "She never blamed you. Neither did I. You're our best friend, our sister, our soulmate. We're in this together." She winks at me and spins back toward the piano, her fingers immediately finding their place on the keys.

One corner of my lips twitches up. My fingers trace the smooth curve of my guitar as the familiar smell of the music room surrounds me—old wood, sheet music, and Alex's citrus shampoo.

She starts ah-ah-ah-ing, warming up her vocals with over-the-top theatrical scales. "Ahem. Okay. Here's the plan." Alex whips around to face me again. "We throw a concert."

"But the event?"

"Dude. Daniels will survive. Him and his little music minions can do their fancy orchestra thing for the event, and we'll help—obviously. But after that? Nighttime rolls around, and boom. Small concert. Encore set. Original songs only. Hell, I'll even bring in my girls, toss in a couple of our viral shit just to keep things spicy."

It's hard to argue against her overwhelming confidence.

Professor Daniels did say it is for a good cause—the money goes toward schools with underfunded arts programs, scholarships for high schoolers, and improvements to our own department.

I chew on my bottom lip. "Archives?"

Alex smirks, like she's been waiting for me to ask. She reaches into her oversized tote bag and pulls out a stack of journals—five of them, piled haphazardly but handled with care.

My breath catches as she sets them down on the piano bench.

I recognize each one instantly. Leather-bound journals, glossy spiral notebooks, even the ridiculous furry one with a golden lock. That one held the explicit lyrics we never dared sing in front of anyone but each other.

"All this time?" I whisper as Alex drags a chair over, spins it backward, and sits on it with her arms resting on the back.

She giggles, flipping through the journals like they're old photo albums. Doodles fill the margins. Words are scratched out, replaced, scratched out again. Metaphors that barely made sense when we wrote them. Writing so messy it might as well be a doctor's

207

prescription. "This is how I coped with your absence. I revisited your handwriting. Your songs. I sang them like you used to. I did it for months. Over and over and over."

My chin quivers. "Alex."

She reaches out and pinches my cheek. "You didn't walk out on me. You know that, right?"

I nod my head firmly.

"You were always here," she says, holding up the journals. "Every time I opened one of these, you were right there. I didn't feel alone with these little shits locked in my drawer."

That's it.

I drop my guitar and wrap my arms around her neck, curling into her like we're teenagers again. She lets me, her hand coming up to scratch the back of my head the way she always used to, like I'm her favorite stray cat.

We decide to sprawl out on the floor, sorting through our songs and debating which ones are concert-appropriate. Alex has opinions about everything—her opinions have opinions—but somehow, we manage to narrow it down to five. I write the setlist neatly in my notebook: three tracks from Alex's EP and two from my stash of originals.

"Melody?" I ask, glancing up.

"We'll make it now." Alex bounces to the piano. I drag a chair over next to her bench, grab my guitar, and settle it on my lap. "God, I missed the sight of that."

"Yeah?" I glance at her, half-smiling as I tune the strings.

She nods with a wistful sigh. "I really miss those days of playing in coffee shops and dive bars. Remember when your mom found out we performed at a pub during Super Bowl night?" She shivers. "Chills. Literal chills."

I groan, the memory washing over me like a migraine. "Don't remind me. One of the most traumatic experiences of my life."

The gig had been worth it at the time. Packed pub, drunk Super Bowl crowd high on touchdowns and beer. It was the kind of audience that screams for an encore and throws money at the stage like you're the second coming of Freddie Mercury. We stayed until three in the morning, playing everything from our originals to "Wonderwall"—because, apparently, no drunk white person can resist yelling along to "Wonderwall."

But of course, Mama found out. Not because I told her, but because one of Baba's cousins, who had no business being there, snapped pictures of me mid-performance and forwarded them straight to her.

The thing is, Mama couldn't care less why Ayesha was there—Baba's family had long since been relegated to "irrelevant" status in her mind. But because it was me, because it gave her the perfect excuse to lose her mind, she stayed up until five in the morning waiting for me to come home. When I finally walked through the door with Alex and Ophelia, Mama went nuclear.

She slapped me multiple times in front of my best friends. Shahzad and Baba had to pull her off before she could kill me. I ended up sleeping at Azeer's place for a week, just to avoid dying.

"Worth it, though." I snort, plucking a low E string.

"Oh, totally," Alex says, her nose scrunching up in mock disgust. "Isn't Asian parenting just chef's kiss? So nurturing."

I roll my eyes. "Cream of the crop."

"Honestly, I think my mom's entire personality would improve if she just divorced my dad." Alex taps the C key idly. "Sloane's always saying that being a great father doesn't automatically make someone a great husband."

I glance at her, curious. "How is Sloane?"

Alex frowns, her fingers gliding across the keys. "Oh, you know, living the dream. Being the younger child and therefore the family favorite, she gets all the leeway. She's at NYU now."

"No way." My jaw practically hits the floor.

"Yup," Alex says, dragging out the word and popping the 'p' like a piece of gum. "I was jealous at first. I mean, before my career took off, obviously. Did you know I got into Juilliard?"

"What?"

"Yeah." She solemnly looks at the piano keys instead of me. "I could've been composing for a Ghibli movie by now. Or, like, having brunch with Hans Zimmer, talking about how to make violins sound even more tragic. But nope. Eldest daughter duties called. Instead of moving to New York, I stayed in Toronto to help my parents do their taxes and reset the Wi-Fi password every time they forgot it."

I bite back a laugh. "Truly, your sacrifice deserves a monument. Or at least a plaque."

"Right? Like, where's my Nobel Prize for Patience and Sacrificing Dreams?" She presses a dramatic chord on the piano, letting it ring out before giving me a sidelong grin. "Don't get me wrong, I love where I am now, but sometimes I wonder, you know?"

I just nod, strumming a few quiet chords in response.

She perks up again. "Although, silver lining: I got to meet you and Fifi. And honestly, Juilliard was probably crawling with stuck-up snobs who'd sip overpriced wine and argue about Wagner at their daddy's opera parties. I don't know, rich people shit." She shrugs, completely unbothered. "I'd rather miss out on all that than miss the memories we made."

I love you, I sign.

"Fuck, yeah. Rock and roll is where the heart is." Alex throws up a "rock on" hand gesture, grinning like an idiot.

I laugh, shaking my head. "It doesn't mean rock and roll." I lift my hands and sign again, slower. "See? Pinky is 'I,' index and thumb make the 'L,' and pinky and thumb together make 'Y.'" I repeat the motions. "I. Love. Yo—"

Before I can finish, I choke on the last word, coughing hard enough to make my eyes water.

"Jesus, Zinnie." Alex is already grabbing my water bottle, unscrewing the cap. "Drink. And no more talking. Seriously, I'll learn sign language. My sister's picking it up anyway. She's been taking notes for a friend who's hard of hearing. Laura? Lily? Something like that. Whatever. I'll force her to give me a crash course."

I smile, wiping my mouth with the back of my hand.

Alex rubs my back in little circles until my breathing evens out. Then, she cups my cheek with one hand, tilting my head toward her. "Are you ready to sing through your strings, Zinnie?"

I smile at her as I lift my guitar and strum a G chord.

22

Zinneerah

I still think we should have bought the LEGO set rather than a stuffed puppy toy.

"You got LEGO money?" Alex shoots back, her eyes on the road as the speech dictation app reads my note aloud. "Because I sure don't. That's the hot attorney's problem. And let's be honest, with the way Fifi's working her magic, he's about two months away from spending Christmas with her and Juliette. He might even throw in a sibling as a bonus gift."

I blink at her, startled, then type out my next question. Are they really that serious?

"She's flying back from St. Lucia, Zinnie." Alex gives me a pointed look, one hand briefly leaving the wheel to flail around. "The only place my situationships have ever taken me is straight to Trauma Town. Population, me." She switches lanes without checking her blind-spot. "You know those t-shirts college kids have been wearing these days? The 'I Love Milfs' one?"

"No."

"Yeah, well, we could slap Fifi's face on one of those and watch it sell out in twenty minutes." With zero warning, she adds, "You know, we hooked up once."

My head jerks forward. "*What?*"

"Oh, yeah. A few months after you left," she recalls. "We ran into each other at a bar. She told me she was pregnant by some guy she met at a writer's club. Juliette was conceived in a library bathroom, of all places. Anyway, we went back to my place and had sex for two hours. Afterward, we made birthday cake pancakes. Good times." She sighs wistfully, like she's just described a trip to St. Lucia with her. "Going down on a woman? Paradise. Highly recommend it."

I narrow my eyes at her, hands quickly typing: I knew something was going on between you two.

Alex throws me a mock-offended scowl. "What, you didn't know Ophelia was tasting the rainbow? Babe, the bitch wore thrifted suspenders with a carabiner keychain hanging from the loop, and those weird frog earrings. She didn't have a single straight bone in her body." She pauses, smirking. "Okay, maybe like . . . half a bone."

I blink, trying to process, and Alex cackles, clearly enjoying herself.

Damn. If I'd known my best friends were secretly hooking up, I would've staged an intervention. Or maybe just shoved them together and told them to quit dancing around it. Their chemistry had always been obvious, but they probably didn't date for the same reason most friends don't—fear of ruining everything if it all went south.

Why didn't you guys date after I left?

"Life happened," she says simply. "I stuck around to help her through the pregnancy, but I was also putting out music at the same time. A month after Juliette was born, so was my career. Things just got busy." She glances over at me with a cheeky smile. "That's why I call Juliette my good luck charm. Everything took off after her."

If Ophelia broke up with her boy-toy, would you date her?

Alex snorts, shaking her head. "No, thanks. I'm not gonna be someone's sloppy seconds. Especially not after a man."

212

"Fair enough."

Alex remains silent, then, "It'd be nice, though." She sighs like the idea is impossible to begin with. "It's all just performance art now. Dates are just bad plays with no intermission and a way-too-expensive second act. And don't get me started on dating apps. Swipe left, swipe right—might as well swipe down and end it all."

"True words have honestly never been spoken before," I whisper.

Ophelia's apartment complex comes into view—a tall, pale orange building standing out against the shorter homes and squat, trailer-like structures nearby. It's a quiet, middle-class neighborhood, sitting somewhere between metropolitan and suburban dreams.

We park in the visitor lot, and Alex scoops up the box of donuts while I grab the stuffed puppy. As we head toward the entrance, she presses the buzzer for unit 380.

"You anxious?" she asks, glancing at me out of the corner of her eye.

I've been staring at the floor, but I manage to pinch my fingers to indicate 'a little.'

The speaker crackles to life, and a child's voice chirps through: "What's the secret password?"

Alex groans, leaning on the buzzer again. "Dickmaster."

The door clicks open immediately.

"Dickmaster?"

She shrugs. "I'm a fan of *Hazbin Hotel*."

Chuckling, we wait for the elevator, and as it creaks its way down to us, I steal a glance in the mirrors by the door. Fixing my hair and rolling back my shoulders, I clear my throat like it'll somehow get rid of the knot of nerves in my stomach.

The elevator dings, and we ride it up to the thirtieth floor. Alex doesn't bother making small talk, and honestly, I'm grateful. My mind's already racing ahead, anticipating how terribly, or beautifully, this is going to go.

When we finally reach Ophelia's door, I stop and take a deep breath through my mouth.

Alex, on the other hand, wastes no time. She abuses the doorbell, then smirks as she slaps her hand over the peephole. "Oh, by the way," she says, "Ophelia has no idea you're coming."

My stomach drops. "What?"

The door creaks open, and there she is—Ophelia, standing tall, with a mini version of herself peeking out from behind her.

Juliette, with her bed of deep-golden curls and wide hazel eyes, tilts her head at us. "Who are you?"

Ophelia's gaze lands on me, and I watch the realization bloom on her face. Her breath hitches, and then her hand flies to Juliette's shoulder. She pulls her daughter behind her, stepping out into the hallway and shutting the door.

Terrible, it is.

"Ophelia," I whisper.

She looks down the hallway, first left, then right, like someone might appear out of the shadows. "Are you alone?"

"We are," Alex says. "Can we come inside now?"

Ophelia's eyes sweep over me, searching for signs of, what, trouble? Danger? Her focus drops to my hand, to my wedding ring. "You married that fucker?"

"N-No—" I stammer.

Alex steps forward, placing herself between us like a human shield. "Back off for a second."

Ophelia's fists are clenched so hard I think she might punch a wall. "Do you have any idea what you've done, Alexandra?" she hisses. "If Damian finds out where I live—"

"He's in prison," I say quickly. "He's . . . imprisoned."

She freezes, her whole body going stiff. Her eyes narrow, searching my face like she's trying to figure out if I'm lying. "What's wrong with your voice?"

"Jesus, Fifi," Alex mutters, spinning back toward me. Her hands bracket my face. "Hey. Look at me. Remember what I told you? In my dressing room?"

I blink at her, my heart pounding. "Blame," I whisper.

She nods. "We don't. We never did."

"What's going on?" Ophelia asks, appearing at Alex's side. "When did you get married, Zinnie?"

"We can talk about it inside," Alex says, motioning toward the door.

"No. Not until I know it's safe."

"Fifi—"

"Not until I know it's safe."

I fumble for my phone, pulling it out and typing as fast as my shaking hands will allow. What did he do to you, Fifi?

Her face hardens, jaw locking as she glares at me. "Oh, you mean besides showing up here with a knife and asking me—violently, of course—to stay the hell away from you? Absolutely nothing, Zinnie. Nothing at all." The words slap me across the face, but she doesn't stop. "I need confirmation. I need proof that that psychopathic bastard is actually in prison. Right now."

I stretch out my hand to Ophelia, palm up. "Trust me?"

Ophelia's eyes flicker down to my hand. Her lips part, then close again. For a moment, I think she's going to pull away, lock me out. But then, her hand slides into mine, and I almost start sobbing from how familiar it feels again.

I guide her down to the floor with me. The carpet feels rough against my knees as I pull out my phone and hand it to her, the screen lit up with the note I wrote last night. Hours of staring at the blinking yellow line, trying to find the right words for her. I still don't know if I got them right.

Alex sits down cross-legged next to Ophelia. "You have to read it, Ophelia."

"I know," she mutters. Her fingers curl tighter around mine, squeezing like she doesn't believe I'm alive, as her other hand takes the phone.

She starts reading.

The corridor is quiet except for the hum of the heating vent and the occasional chime of the building's elevator. It feels suffocating. I can hear every rustle of fabric, every tiny shift in Alex's posture beside her. I can feel the pulse in Ophelia's hand, quick and uneven, as if her body is battling the words she's taking in.

When the screen finally goes dark, the only movement comes from her thumb, still pressed against the phone. Then, without warning, she tosses it onto Alex's lap, and I barely have time to react before she lunges forward.

Her arms wrap around me like she's trying to keep me from slipping through her fingers. One arm clamps around my waist, the other pulls me close, her hand cradling the back of my head. She squeezes so tightly I can barely breathe, but I don't care. Her curls tickle my face as I bury it in her neck, and her whole body shakes, trembling like she's been holding herself together with strings, and it's finally giving out.

"I'm so sorry," she chokes out. "I'm so fucking sorry, Zinneerah. I should've—I should've done something. I shouldn't have shut you out. I shouldn't have let you go through it alone. I—" Her voice cracks, and she pulls me tighter, like holding me close will make the guilt hurt less.

My throat burns, but I force myself to speak, rubbing slow circles on her back like I used to when we were nineteen and she'd cry about something stupid, like losing her favorite hair clip. This isn't stupid, though. This is years of pent-up guilt pouring out of her all at once.

"Don't apologize," I whisper. "I'm okay now. See?" I draw back and smile as best as I can. "My siblings helped. Therapy helped. And you helped, Fifi. You and Alex . . . even when you didn't know it."

But her head shakes fiercely, her blonde curls swishing against my face. She's not letting herself off the hook that easily. She doesn't know how to. "I thought I lost you forever." Her hands come up, framing my face as her forehead leans against mine. When her eyes open and lock on mine, they're glassy with tears. "I thought . . . I thought I lost you."

I sniffle, holding onto her wrists gently. "Never."

"I was so scared, Zinnie," she whimpers. "For you. For Alex. For me. Why didn't you call us?"

I close my eyes, pressing my forehead back against hers. "I was scared. For you, too."

Her shoulders quake as she pulls me close again, and I let her. I let her hold me as though she's trying to glue back all the pieces of me that shattered. And then Alex, predictably, worms her way into the hug. Her arms wrap around both of us, squishing us together like she's the missing piece that's been waiting to slide into place. "Get off. Let me have my moment with her."

"Nope." Alex's voice is all smug certainty. "We're a package deal."

A small laugh escapes Ophelia. She lets one arm slip from my waist and slings it around Alex, dragging her in without a second thought. The three of us collapse into this messy, awkward pile— limbs everywhere, no sense of space, like we're nineteen again, cramming into Ophelia's twin bed and pretending the world didn't exist outside of us.

For the first time in forever, I don't feel like I'm holding everything up on my own.

The door creaks open, and standing there is Juliette, staring at our sentimental, sappy pile. She tilts her head at me, studying me. "You're the lady from Mom's school pictures."

Ophelia, still holding onto the last shreds of her composure, brushes herself off as she helps me stand. "Julie, this is your Tía Zinneerah," she says, smoothing the dust off my skirt. "She's been my best friend since university."

Juliette blinks at me. "Why am I meeting her now?"

Ophelia freezes for half a second, her brain clearly scrambling for an answer before she recovers, her voice dipping into the kind of overly sweet tone moms use when they're lying through their teeth. "Because she just got back from a trip."

Juliette crosses her arms. "Oh. Where'd you go?" Her delivery is flat, uninterested. "Was it Europe? I keep asking Mom to take me there, but she says she's too broke."

Ophelia's mouth drops open, her head swiveling to Alex. "When did I—"

Alex, already grinning, scratches her neck and looks away. "Kids hear things. It's wild. Anyway, I'm hungry." She barges into Ophelia's apartment. "Come on. We have to discuss Zinneerah's husband."

"Oh?" Ophelia arches a brow and turns to me, her lips tugging into a smirk despite the redness in her eyes.

Before I can answer, Juliette slides her small hand into mine, giving me a toothy smile. "I'll give you a tour."

I nod and follow her inside.

The living room is a mismatch of soft, inviting furniture, covered in throws that don't quite match but somehow work anyway. The walls are a soft beige, but covered in pops of life: photos of Juliette, scribbly kid-art in mismatched frames, and a massive bookshelf bursting with everything from children's picture books to thriller novels. There's a sweet smell of coffee and vanilla candles, blending with the earthiness of the dozens—no, *hundreds*—of potted plants scattered around the space.

"Do you want anything to drink?" Juliette asks as she skips toward the kitchen, opening a cabinet. "I always make coffee for Mom when she's running late to see her rich boyfriend."

Alex barks out a laugh.

"For fuck's sake." Ophelia groans, dragging a hand down her face as she follows us in. "Julie, honey, why don't you take a donut and this puppy toy thing"—she scoops the stuffed animal off the counter—"and go play on the balcony while I have a grown-up discussion?"

Taking the items from her mother's hands, she slips out the sliding glass door onto the balcony, disappearing into the jungle of potted plants like a tiny explorer in a greenhouse.

The second she's out of earshot, I turn to Ophelia, raising a brow. "Motherhood?"

Ophelia lets out a long sigh as she collapses onto the couch. "Don't even get me started." She stretches her legs out, crossing them at the ankles and throwing her feet onto the coffee table. "It's draining. It's loud. It's exhausting. But . . ." Her voice softens, and she glances at the balcony. "When she smiles like that, or says something ridiculous, it kind of makes up for it. I guess. I'm just glad it wasn't a boy."

"Dodged a bullet," Alex says.

"I want a baby, too," I mumble.

Alex sucks in a sharp breath through her teeth, dragging it out for maximum effect. "Ooooh, yeah, see, the thing is, you're gonna wanna kiss your husband first before skipping to baby-making. Little life hack for you."

My face heats up instantly.

Ophelia waves a hand. "Speaking of, can I see his picture already? I've been waiting for, like, years over here."

I pull out my phone and open my camera roll, scrolling until I find the folder labeled Wedding Pics. It takes a second of scrolling past blurry reception shots and candids of people mid-bite before I find a decent one of me and Raees.

Her eyes widen the second she sees the first photo. She blinks, then pinches the screen to zoom in on his face. "*That's* your husband?" Her voice pitches up. Her face flushes. Ophelia rarely blushes, which only makes it funnier. "Holy shit. Is that gray hair?" She blinks again, as if to double-check. "How old is he? Does he, like, have a retirement plan already? A yacht? A library?"

I hold up three on my left hand and five on my right.

"Thirty-five? Zinneerah, you married a whole man. Like, a *real* grown man. Is he one of those guys who orders black coffee and talks about how 'kids these days don't understand hard work'? Because I swear to God, Zin—"

"No," I cut her off, rolling my eyes. "He drinks coffee with way too much sugar, and teaches media journalism at S.L.U."

"Damn," Ophelia whispers.

Then, in perfect sync, both she and Alex say, "He's hot, though."

Ophelia continues. "Is it weird that I want to see him in regency attire?"

My eyes widen at the logical fantasy. "You mean, like, a cravat and tailcoat?"

She nods. "Preferably with an air of tortured longing."

Alex claps her hands together, pointing at me like she's had an epiphany. "Loose tunic. Breeches. Wind blowing through his hair. He's walking through a field of daisies or riding a black stallion toward the sunset—" She cuts herself off when both Ophelia and I stare at her. Her expression doesn't falter for a second. She just shrugs. "Don't lie. You're both thinking about it, too."

And, well, she's not wrong. I glance back at the picture of him on my phone. He's standing tall beside me, that soft, lopsided smile on his lips, his hands clasped neatly behind his back even though the photographer all but begged him to wrap an arm around my waist.

Alex leans in closer, studying the image with intense focus. "I mean, it's like young Hugh Jackman and Theo James had a genetically blessed love child."

"Agreed," I admit quietly, still staring at the picture.

My cheeks are already burning, but Ophelia, of course, doubles down. She zooms in on his face like she's investigating a crime scene. "Mm-hmm. He's got the whole brooding romantic lead thing going for him. If we were in *Bridgerton* or something, half the women in the ballroom would be faking fainting spells just to get his attention."

I laugh, but the words hit closer to home than I want to admit. It's true. Everywhere we go, women stare at him. The kind of stares that make me want to smooth down my hair or check my reflection just to make sure I don't look like a complete mess next to him. And sometimes, just sometimes, it eats at me.

"Time to glorify our girl," Alex says suddenly, snapping me out of my thoughts. She zooms in on me in the picture. "Raees is attractive and all, but Jesus Christ, Zinnie. Look at you." She puckers her lips and blows exaggerated kisses at the screen.

"Iconic," Ophelia states, but instead of joining Alex's theatrics, she squishes my cheek between her fingers and presses a quick kiss to it. "If Penélope Cruz dies, you could easily replace her. You're, like, too pretty."

I bury my face in my knees, my cheeks burning so hot from being showered by their compliments. "Lawyer," I say, trying to change the subject. "Pictures. Show me."

Ophelia groans like I've asked her to carry a boulder up a mountain, dragging her phone off the table. She swipes through her gallery lazily, finally handing it to me. "His name's Jason," she mutters. "Doesn't he kind of look like Tom Hardy? If Tom Hardy got eight hours of sleep and drank green juice."

"Why do you have a celebrity reference for every person you see?" Alex pipes up.

"You know I have a thing for movies," Ophelia says flatly, tucking her hair behind her ear. "It's a full-body experience. I watch, I analyze, I Google the cast. It's called being cultured, Alex."

I swipe through the photos without comment, starting with their St. Lucia trip. Jason is, admittedly, attractive in that cover-model, toothpaste-commercial kind of way—sandy skin, perfectly cropped brown hair, ocean-blue eyes. He's got one of those smiles that's engineered to charm grandmas and bouncers alike. And, of course, muscles so defined you could probably shred cheese on them. Ophelia, naturally, has her hand on said abs in every couple's shot.

But my attention shifts. The variety of bikinis Ophelia wears is distracting—some knitted and barely holding on, others sleek one-pieces that make her look like she's walking out of a Bond movie. She's stunning. Curvy hips, a tiny waist, and breasts that, well . . . let's just say they could solve world problems if people used them as pillows.

"Beautiful," I whisper under my breath.

Alex gulps loudly next to me. She doesn't even try to hide it before grabbing the phone from me with a swipe. "Let me see."

"Alexandra," Ophelia starts, sitting up straighter.

"Relax, I'm not judging your little green-juice Tom Hardy." She scrolls, squinting at the photos. "Okay, he's got abs. Noted. Next. Oh, more abs. And more abs, shocker. Does this man own a shirt? Or do you just confiscate them?" She swipes again.

"Wait, no—" Ophelia suddenly leans forward, a hand darting out. Too late.

A video starts playing. The camera angle is shaky, but it's clear enough: Ophelia's back, her Orion constellation tattoo front and center, her curls tangled around a hand that's definitely not hers. The bed is moving in ways that make the context painfully obvious.

Ophelia snatches the phone back so fast it's like it burned Alex's hand, shoving it under her thigh as though that'll erase what we just saw.

The room goes dead silent.

I'm too stunned to speak.

Alex, of course, is the first to recover. "Well, then." She clears her throat. "Let's all collectively agree to pretend we didn't just see Ophelia getting backshots."

"Fuck off, Alexandra!" Ophelia growls, hurling a pillow to shut up Alex's laugh. Her eyes catch mine, narrowing when she sees me staring. "You got something to say, Artemis?"

I snort. "Looked fun."

Alex shoots to her feet like a firecracker, holding the pillow aloft as she starts thrusting wildly against it, moaning in a voice so over-the-top it could probably summon a noise complaint. "'Oh, Jason! Pound me like one of your courtroom gavels!'"

"Oh, fuck you!" Ophelia is already on her feet, wrapping one arm around Alex's neck and yanking her into a chokehold. It's laughable, really, because Ophelia is taller, brawnier, and could probably snap Alex in two if she wanted to. "Say it again. I dare you!"

I can't stop laughing as I pull out my phone, hitting record just in time to catch Ophelia grabbing an indoor slipper and chasing Alex across the room.

Juliette appears suddenly, sliding the balcony door shut behind her. She looks frazzled, her hair a little windblown, but that confused "I've been out of the loop for five minutes and everything's gone to shit" expression on her face is priceless.

"What is going on?" she demands, her hands on her hips.

Alex darts behind Juliette, crouching low and clinging to her body. "Your mother is attempting to kill me with your chanclas."

Ophelia brandishes the slipper and points it at Juliette like it's Exhibit A. "Move aside, sweet child of mine. Justice must be served."

Alex pops her head out from behind Juliette. "Do you hear this? Threats! Threats against the innocent!"

I'm still recording, tears in my eyes from laughing too hard, when my phone suddenly buzzes in my hand. A low battery notification flashes across the screen, and my recording cuts off. I toss the phone into my bag, wiping at my face.

"All right, enough," I say, clapping my hands once to get their attention. "Music."

Ophelia glares at Alex, slipper still in hand, her eyes narrowing like she's debating whether to end her right here. When Alex retreats to the couch, squeaking like a startled hamster, Ophelia feigns a punch at her shoulder, making her flinch.

Juliette, ever the little diplomat, takes the opportunity to scoot over and sit beside me, her small hand patting my leg. She tilts her head and gestures for me to lean down. I oblige, curious. "You're so pretty," she whispers like it's a secret just for me. "I love your hair."

My cheeks bloom pink. "Thank you. So are you. And I love your curls. They're gorgeous."

She beams at me. "Thank you! My mom brushes them for me."

"That's so sweet." I smile softly. "My dad used to do my hair when I was little. He'd—"

"Hey, hey, hey!" Alex suddenly materializes from the other side of the room. She grabs Juliette around the waist and hoists her onto her lap, plopping back down onto the couch. "Don't even think about stealing my Best Tía award, Zinnie."

"At least this Tía doesn't hump other people's pillows like a dog in heat," Ophelia cuts in dryly, slinging an arm across the front of my shoulders as she leans back.

"Music," I drag the word out with all the exasperation I can muster. Their bickering feels like it could last forever if I let it.

"Oh, right." Ophelia finally focuses, snapping her fingers. "My drum set is locked in storage. You know I can't practice on those trash cans the department calls drum kits."

Alex launches herself off the couch like a firework, startling Juliette, who immediately scrambles onto her back, her arms wrapped tightly around Alex's neck. "We need take-out dumplings, a bottle of discounted rosé for moi, and then we're cracking open the journals and getting down to business."

Ophelia and I burst out laughing, clutching each other as Alex takes off again, zig-zagging through the room while Juliette cheers her on. The sight feels like someone's pressed play on a long-lost scene from a movie I thought had ended.

The Cryptics are back in business.

23

Raees

"She thinks I have no friends," I say, stabbing a piece of broccoli.

Ramishah doesn't even look up from juggling a cherry tomato and Amina, who's wriggling in her lap like a worm. "Well, you're having dinner with your sister on FaceTime, so yeah, I'm with her on this one." She pops the tomato into her mouth and chews. "Harry! Are the vegetables done?"

"Almost!" Harry's muffled voice floats in from the background.

I roll my eyes and nudge the steamed carrots around my plate. "Why would she think that?"

"Where is she, anyway?"

"Out. With her . . . friends."

That gets her attention. Ramishah snorts so loudly that even Amina pauses her squirming to stare up at her mom. "Oh, my god. She has friends, and *you* don't? That's rich."

I glare at her through the screen. "Just say you don't want to have a virtual dinner with me."

"I don't want to have a virtual dinner with you, Chotu."

224

I frown. "You weren't supposed to actually say it."

Her expression softens for a fraction of a second—just long enough to make me think she's about to apologize or something— but that's just wishful thinking. "Fine. Let's talk about your lack of companionship. Want me to introduce you to some of my friends?"

"Absolutely not. Your friends are . . ." I trail off, searching for a nicer way to say "suck-ups with too much time on their hands." Instead, I settle on, "They're a bit too verbose for me. I don't think I'd be able to keep up with their, uh, profound insights."

"Verbose?" Ramishah repeats, stabbing a cherry tomato with her fork so aggressively that I flinch. She squints at me, and for a second, I swear I see Abbu's glare reflected in her face. It's unsettling. "Well, if you can't keep up with my *verbose* friends, why not mingle with her friends instead?"

I groan. "Alexandra is eccentric. Half her references during our first conversation went right over my head."

Ramishah shrugs with zero sympathy. "That's what you get for marrying someone eight years younger than you."

"Unlike me." Harry suddenly pops his head into the frame like some kind of glittery jack-in-the-box. His shaggy curls are pulled back with Amina's butterfly clips, and he's got a streak of blue glitter eyeshadow across one eye. "Mimi and I were playing dress-up this morning."

Ramishah barely blinks at his appearance. "We're only a year apart, Harry. Don't make me feel ancient." She shoves his face out of the frame with a single hand, but he just scoots into the chair beside her like an oversized Labrador, plopping Amina on his lap and handing her baby carrot sticks. "Do you really think making friends will impress your wife?"

"I don't know," I admit, rubbing the back of my neck. "I think she's sick of me always being at home or something. Why else would she bring up hosting a dinner party?"

"Or maybe because she's being nice? Think about it. Your quiet, introverted wife suggests throwing a dinner party for your nonexistent friends—"

"Thanks."

"—where she's willingly volunteering for social interaction—*on your behalf*—because she wants her tall, clingy, tragically antisocial husband to be happy."

"Cute," Harry chimes in, wiping some drool off Amina's chin. "You should just hire some friends. You know, like those actors who pretend to be your family at weddings?"

"If he's desperate enough to sink that low," Ramishah says, smirking.

"Just a suggestion."

"Here's a suggestion." She grabs a baby carrot from Amina's stash and shoves it into Harry's mouth. He chews obediently.

"I'm starting to think my niece would offer better advice," I say, leaning closer to the screen and flashing Amina my best, most winning smile. "Isn't that right, sweetheart?"

Amina giggles, her tiny fists batting at the air like she's already defending me. Finally, an ally.

"Wait a minute," Ramishah says, pointing a cherry tomato at me. "That's not a totally shitty idea coming from you. Did I hear a brain cell firing, or was that just an accident?"

"I'm one offense away from ending this call."

She ignores me, already steamrolling ahead with her grand plan. "You can make some friends at Amina's second birthday party this weekend. If you're still coming, that is?"

"How could I not?" I scoff, resting an elbow on the table. "Believe it or not, I love my niece more than I love her mother."

"More for me," Harry says, only to be met with her palm shoved between their faces like an invisible "Do Not Enter" sign.

"Not here, Kitten Whiskers," she says, attempting to glare at him before refocusing on me.

My head jerks back. "I'm sorry, but did you just call Harry—"

"The birthday party is perfect," she cuts in. "Everyone attending is married or dating, so there won't be any hot moms or dads hitting on you. Tragic, I know, but that means you and Zinneerah can grow your sad little social circle together. By the end of the month, you'll be hosting dinner parties left and right."

I blink. "Dinner parties?"

"Yeah, you know, those things adults do when they have more than one friend?"

"I know what dinner parties are, Rami. I'm just—I'm trying to avoid those, and so is my wife. Our social batteries drain on the same wavelength."

"Ugh, you two were made for each other. The most boring couple alive." She groans, throwing her head back like she's physically in pain. "Just do as I tell you to do. It's not rocket science."

I set my fork down. "Fine. I'll make some friends at Amina's birthday party. Then, once I'm drowning in my new social life, we won't have to do these virtual dinners anymore."

Her eyes narrow into dangerous slits. "Are you giving me attitude?"

"Not at all," I grumble as I glance away from the screen. Growing up, Ramishah's tantrums were legendary. There's no way I'm falling into that trap tonight.

"Good." She shifts in her chair and changes the subject. "How's everything at work? Are you doing all right?"

"Yes," I lie. Because the truth is, I haven't told her about my panic attack the other day, or Saira's offhand comment that cracked me open like a dropped egg.

The last thing I need is for Ramishah to go berserk on her, digging through social media accounts until she uncovers some old tweet Saira made in 2011 that could get her fired. My sister is 'Cancel Culture' personified (I've used her instances during lectures), and I've seen her in action. She's a human hurricane when she gets worked up, and I'd rather not stand in the path.

"You know I don't do the whole 'gentle and supportive' thing," Ramishah continues, tossing Amina's baby bottle to Harry like it's a football, "but I'm here, okay? If you need me to ruin someone's life, just say the word. First name, last name, LinkedIn profile—I'm on it."

"Thanks, but I'm pretty sure shouting at my colleagues isn't part of the company's conflict-resolution policy," I say, dragging my fork across the remains of my sad, soggy vegetables.

"Don't knock it till you try—"

"I *said*," I grit out, "I'm fine."

Ramishah licks her lips, then gives an exasperated glance at Harry. Her eyes flutter shut, rubbing at her forehead, as if I'm her biggest headache of the day. "Abbu wasn't too great at making friends either."

I scoff. "That's because he punched his colleague and threatened to kill his children at a realtor award ceremony."

Harry's head jerks up, and he quickly covers Amina's tiny ears.

"I know," Ramishah says softly. "I know how he is, but still. We should check up on him. He's trying to move back into the city. Three years clean."

My fork clatters to the plate. "You're a witness to my reasoning, Ramishah. The last thing I need is to give my abuser a bouquet of tulips and pat him on the back for being sober." She opens her mouth, but I hold up a hand, silencing her. "You can visit him on my behalf if you really want to, but for God's sake, do not talk about me, or my wife. Is that clear?"

Ramishah swallows hard. For once, she doesn't fight back with a smartass comment defending Abbu's so-called "path to redemption." She knows better than to push me on this topic.

She was his favorite child, after all—or she liked to think she was. The prodigy. The one who actually wanted his approval. The reason she went into medicine wasn't because of some noble dream to save lives. No, it was because Abbu told her she'd never be good enough to be a nurse, let alone a dermatologist. She'd been hell-bent on proving him wrong ever since. Desperate for his attention. Desperate to be the exception to his scorn. Meanwhile, I'd been desperate to escape him altogether.

He didn't want a son who cried reading *The Little Prince* or stayed up late writing articles about his neighbours. He wanted someone he could mold into a mirror image of himself. He wanted a real estate prodigy, someone who'd inherit his sharp suits, sharper temper, and cutthroat morals. What he got instead was me, and he was hell-bent on breaking me into the man he thought I should be.

Harry clears his throat. "Isn't it late for Zinneerah to come home?" he asks, glancing down at his watch.

I check mine. It's already past nine, and I haven't heard a single word from her. She hasn't texted me. Not when she left for Ophelia's house. Not after I got home and sent her a couple of follow-ups. No delivered messages. No notifications. Nothing.

I don't even have her friends' contact information, which is a stupid mistake on my end.

Shit.

Why the hell am I sitting here, wasting time arguing about Abbu, when I should be checking in on my wife?

"I'll call you back," I say, already grabbing my phone and ending the call before either of them can get a word in.

I dial Zinneerah's number.

Voicemail. Again.

My thumb hesitates before sending a text: Are you on your way home? Have you eaten? Are you safe? The questions are simple, practical, and, if I'm honest, masking my real concern.

Zinneerah is capable, more than capable, but I can't help worrying. Being back with her old college friends, swept up in nostalgia, might lead her to decisions made on impulse rather than reason. And I've yet to meet Ophelia.

The floor feels cold beneath my feet as I shuffle into the kitchen. I wash my dinner plate, then inhale three cookies afterward.

I drop onto the couch and let out a defeated breath. "I have friends," I tell the empty room. "There's Professor Holmes. A colleague I can actually hold a conversation with. That counts as a friend."

Speaking of colleagues.

I reach for my phone, scrolling back to Saira's last text while Zinneerah was helping me pick out something presentable for the concert. I barely skimmed it at the time, unwilling to open that door.

Saira: Raees, I want to apologize for what I said. I know bringing up your father is a sensitive topic. It was an ignorant mistake made in the heat of the moment. Let's put the past behind us and move forward as co-workers :)

I stare at her words longer than I care to admit, then hold down the message and tap the thumbs-up emoji. A perfunctory response. Petty, perhaps, but anything more would feel like entertaining her.

The phone slips from my hand onto the carpet with a muted thud. I lean back, hook an arm over my eyes, and will myself to sleep.

A sudden chill jolts me awake.

My eyes flutter open, disoriented, to find Zinneerah standing over me, her silhouette softly outlined by the golden glow of the living room lamp. She's tucking a blanket around me, her hands careful to wake me.

"Hey," I murmur, my voice rough with sleep. "You're back."

Zinneerah offers me a small smile, though her eyes seem to hold unease. *I'm sorry I'm late.*

The blanket slides down to my lap as I sit up slowly, disappointment gnawing at my chest despite my efforts to push it down. "It's okay. I just wish you would've texted me. My calls kept going to voicemail. I didn't know if you were safe."

She sits beside me, folding herself neatly into the corner of the couch, but her body remains taut. Her hands rise again, but this time, her fingers fidget mid-sign. *I know. I should have texted. I'm sorry.*

"Zinneerah," I begin, reaching out to gently take her hand, but instead, I cup my kneecap. "I understand that we're still getting to know each other. But communication is important to me, especially when it comes to things like this." I motion towards the clock on the wall, its hands ticking away. "It's half-past midnight. Do you understand how dangerous the city is at this time?"

Her frown deepens. My heart aches to see her like this, but I have to voice my concerns as her husband. It is out of care. Out of love.

"I know you can take care of yourself," I continue, "but knowing you're out there, alone, it worries me. Just a simple text, letting me know you're okay, would have eased my mind."

Her hands start moving frantically. *Not alone. With the girls. No going out. Stay in O-P-H-E-L-I-A apartment. Phone died. I forgot to plug in. I promise. Not go anywhere. I have a video—*

I take her hands in mine. "I trust you."

She shakes her head.

"Hey. Look at me," I whisper, tilting her chin upwards until her gaze meets mine. "I trust you. You don't have to prove anything to me. Nothing. I trust you completely."

There's a moment of hesitation, a brief pause as she searches my eyes for any hint of doubt. And then, slowly, almost imperceptibly, the knots in her shoulders ease, the frantic flutter of her lashes reducing to slow blinks.

I smile and release her hands. "How'd you get home?"

A-L-E-X.

"That's sweet of her." I lean back, resting my arm on the back of the couch. "Did you have fun today? Was Ophelia happy to see you?"

She nods, still resembling a wilted flower. *Are you disappointed? I am sorry.*

I sigh, raking a hand through my hair as I glance at the clock again. I've got an early morning lecture that I need a sufficient amount of sleep for. "Zinneerah, I'm not disappointed that you came home late. I'm . . . Well, I am disappointed because you didn't even bother to let me know when you left the campus like I asked. That's all."

Her eyes widen with guilt. Shit. Was that too much? Should I have just let it go? I meant to say it—it's important—but now she's looking at me like I've scolded her, and that's not what I wanted.

Before I can speak again, her hands rise in a rush. *You are right. My mistake. What can I do to make it up to you?*

"Nothing, Zinneerah. You don't owe me anything. I only ask you to be mindful next time." I lean my head low to capture her eyes. "Is that all right?"

Her lips curve up and I take a mental breath of relief. *Thank you for understanding. I trust you.*

"I would cry if it was otherwise."

We fall into a silence that stretches for what feels like a century. Her eyes hold mine, and the lamp light catches the curve of her cheekbone, painting her features with an ethereal glow.

Eat dinner? she asks, her hands moving gently, like she's speaking in a whisper.

"I did," I say, just as softly. "You?"

Zinneerah opens her mouth as if to speak, but the lips I was shamelessly staring with heavy lids tuck back in. *Take out. Not good.* She tilts her head and smiles. *I like your cooking.*

I'm going to loop the sight of this picturesque woman for the rest of the week. "Good," I say, matching her smile. "That was my evil plan all along."

Mastermind, she signs slowly.

She has no idea. None. But one day, she will. One day, I'll tell her how long I waited for her. How I never thought she'd look at me the way she does now. How fate, against all odds, handed me her heart and trusted me not to break it.

Sleep, she signs.

And that's that.

I stand up and fold the blanket over the couch's armrest. Zinneerah remains seated, fiddling with the ends of her sleeve. She's still overthinking our conversation. It's hurting me. I shouldn't have used the word 'disappointed.' God knows how many times she's heard it.

But how else could I explain how I felt? What I said was fair to both of us. She's my wife. My comfort. My responsibility to protect and love. If anything were to happen to her, I wouldn't be able to live with myself. Expressing disappointment wasn't scolding her—it was honesty.

So why does it feel like I hurt her?

At times like this, I wish I had my father's guidance. But the truth is, I wasn't raised with a blueprint for this kind of love. He never taught me how to handle moments like these, only how to break things.

You sounded a lot like your father just now.

That damned thought slashes through me.

I grit my teeth. If I had the power to rip that memory out of my head, I would. But it's stuck to me like a blood-sucking leech.

I exhale slowly, forcing my jaw to unclench, and crouch down until I'm at eye level with Zinneerah.

She blinks in surprise. *What's wrong?*

"I'm sorry if I hurt you in any way," I say, cradling her left hand. "Please, don't think about it too much. I just want you to get a good night's rest. Tomorrow morning, we'll make breakfast together. We can eat by the pool, then drive to campus for work. Afterward, we should buy a gift for Amina's birthday, and pick up groceries for the dinner party." My anxiety travels down my throat. "Does that sound like a plan? If there's anything else you want to do, just tell me. I'll take you wherever you want to go."

She squeezes my hand, her right one coming to rest gently on top of mine. Her smile blooms, perfect, pearly-whites on full display.

Her happiness stops time, and for a moment, it feels like the entire universe bends to her. It always does, doesn't it? The way she can fill a room without even trying, without even knowing. I don't think she realizes how rare that is—how rare *she* is.

That smile. God, it breaks me. It's soft, shy, but it shines. It's her. And it's mine, for now.

I want to kiss her. Everywhere. Her flushed cheeks, her pointy nose, the corners of her lips where that smile lives, that tiny space between her eyebrows when she's thinking too hard. I want to feel her breath hitch against my skin, to hold her in my arms and whisper every thought I've ever had about her—how brilliant she is, how much she means to me, how much I need her in my life. I want her to know, to *really* know, that she's safe here. That I would ruin myself for her without hesitation. That I already have.

It terrifies me, how far I'd go for her. I'd burn bridges, scorch the earth, move heaven and hell if it meant I could keep her like this. I want to find whoever extinguished the fire in her heart, the person who made her doubt herself, who made her anxious before showing her joy. I want to destroy them. I want to wipe their fingerprints off her soul, to undo whatever damage they left behind.

But I can't. And that kills me.

233

But I'll fix it. I'll make her whole again, if she'll let me. Not that she's broken—God, not at all. She's not fragile. She's not weak. She's stronger than I'll ever be, and that's the part that humbles me. That's the part that makes me want to give her the world. I want her to know she doesn't have to be strong with me. She doesn't have to carry it all alone.

And every time she's in my view—every single time—I have to stop myself from saying it. *I love you.* The words are right there, sitting on the edge of my tongue, begging to be set free. They're a truth I've swallowed so many times I'm surprised I haven't choked on them.

Because I do. I love her. So much it feels unbearable some days. No, every day.

I can't say it. Not yet. Not until I know she's ready to hear it. I don't want to scare her or push her. I don't want her to think I'm trying to take something from her, or that I expect anything in return.

So, I hold it in. I wait. Patiently. Painfully. Counting the moments until I can say it out loud. Until I can tell her, not once, not twice, but every chance I get, until she believes it. Until it's part of her, like it's already part of me.

For now, I release her hand and stand, pulling her up with me. "We'll make breakfast together. Okay?"

Okay, she signs, a little dazed.

I start walking backwards, pointing at her. "Don't wake up before me."

I won't, she signs.

"I trust you."

Her face softens. *I trust you.*

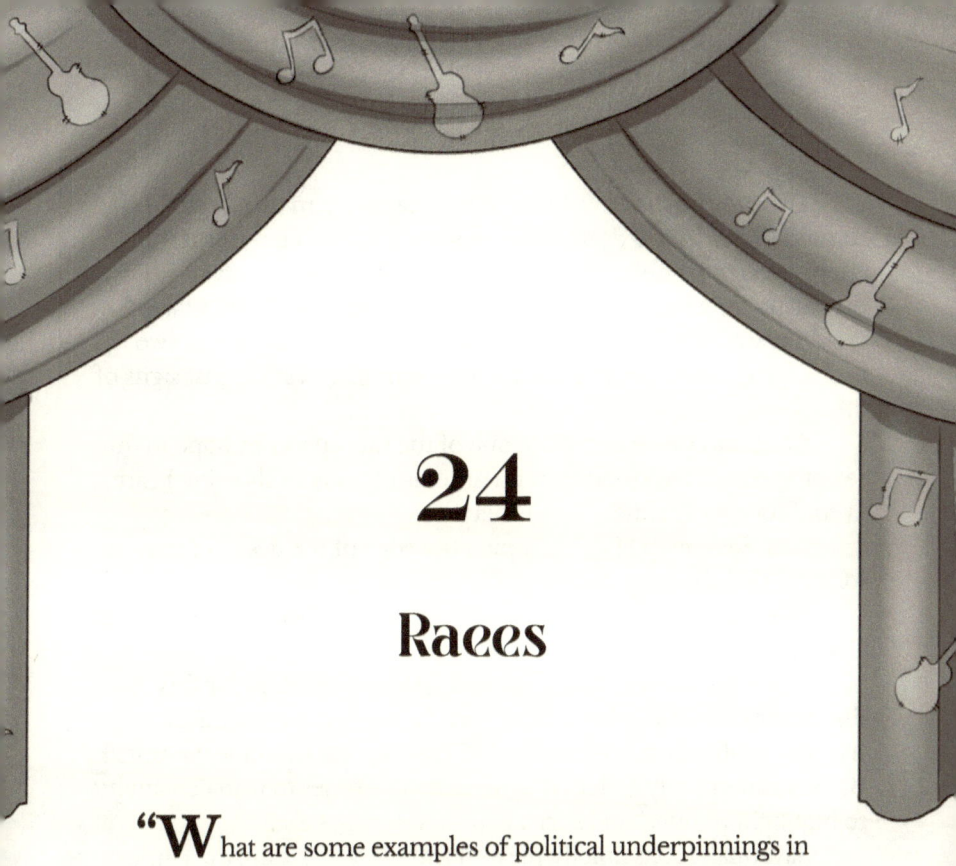

24

Raees

"What are some examples of political underpinnings in digital communication?"

Ninety-seven students sit before me, but you'd think I was addressing a collection of particularly unresponsive houseplants.

I lean back against my desk, arms crossed, letting the silence marinate.

Most stare back at me with eyes dulled by exhaustion or disinterest. A couple of students are still typing furiously, even though I've made it abundantly clear this is a discussion, not a transcription. Maybe they're chronicling my lecture for posterity. Or maybe they're emailing their mothers to ask if the laundry money came through yet. I certainly did that when I was in their shoes.

Dua, meanwhile, is in a near-horizontal slouch, eyes half-closed. She's usually one of the sharper ones, but I can guess what's got her in a coma—still no word on that prized internship she's been obsessing over. A shame, really, because she's one of the few who can actually keep up when she's awake.

Time to prod them a little. "Final exams are in two weeks," I remind them. "And I don't mean to sound harsh, but if this is the energy you're planning to bring into the exam, then I'd start preparing for a long conversation with the registrar about retakes."

A few of them shift uncomfortably in their seats. One or two exchange glances. Good. I don't need a standing ovation, just signs of life.

Savannah raises her hand, one of the rare sparks of hope in this sea of apathy. Memorizing their names is my way of showing I care, even if RateMyProfessor says otherwise.

"Yes, Savannah," I say, gripping the edge of the desk as I lean forward slightly.

"Well, uh . . ." She hesitates, twirling her pen between her fingers. "Banksy?"

I lift a brow. Predictable. Banksy is the poster child for this discussion—a go-to answer I've heard far too many times. Still, friendly professor mode engaged. "That's a great example, Savannah. Banksy is definitely a pivotal figure when it comes to using creativity to highlight political and social issues. Now, what else?"

Savannah looks quietly pleased with herself, sitting up a little straighter. Small wins.

Jeremiah raises his hand. "I mean, there's a lot of musicians," he says. "Like, Pink Floyd, for example. Their song "Another Brick in the Wall" was basically a big 'fuck you' to the education system. Shit was so hard it had the Royal Family's knickers in a twist."

Laughter ripples across the room, and I can't help the smile tugging at the corner of my mouth. At least they're awake now.

"Another great example," I reply, raising a finger to temper the mood. "For the record, I won't be accepting any expletives or the word 'knickers' on the exam."

Jeremiah leans back, grinning. "What about 'underwear?'"

"'Panties?'" someone chimes in.

"'Undergarments?'" Jeremiah counters.

"'Boxers?'" another voice adds.

"'Bush and tush protector?'"

The room erupts. Even I sink my head and laugh under my breath. Jeremiah grins like a man who's just won the lottery.

"You know what?" I say, gesturing vaguely at him. "I'll allow one synonym on the exam. One. Choose wisely."

"Let's go!" Jeremiah exclaims, slapping hands with Marcus sitting next to him. "Bonus points for making you laugh?"

"Now that's crossing the line. Who else wants to take a stab at this?"

Erica hesitates before lifting her hand. I can't recall hearing her voice all semester. "If we're discussing bands that made a political stance," she starts, her words coming out like she's testing the water, "I can name one. "Bonzo Goes to Bitburg" by the Ramones. The band wrote it when Ronald Reagan visited a German war cemetery. The 'Bonzo' in the title refers to a movie Reagan starred in during his acting days—*Bedtime for Bonzo*." She shrugs. "I only know this because my dad's a huge Ramones fan."

I give her a small smile. "That's a very insightful example, Erica."

Before the gears of conversation have a chance to grind to a halt again, Michael shoots his hand up. "Queen?"

There's a ripple of murmurs across the room—Queen, now that gets their attention. But then, predictably, Michael falters.

"Elaborate," I encourage, weaving my marker between my fingers.

He lowers his hand slowly, squirming from his own lack of follow-through. "Well, I don't really know. Weren't they, like, super woke back in the day?"

"Eh!" Dua's buzzer sound cuts through the awkwardness like a referee on a bad call. "Actually, Freddie Mercury didn't want to involve himself in political songwriting. He just wanted to write songs without causing debates. Of course, some songs can be interpreted politically—like "I Want to Break Free" or "Bohemian Rhapsody," especially the singles that came out during his battle with AIDS—but that's the beauty of music. The meaning is up to the listener."

Michael scowls. "What the suck-up said."

Dua holds up her middle-finger.

I pinch the bridge of my nose, fighting the urge to sigh audibly. "Michael, since you clearly brought Queen into this with absolutely no ammunition, I'm going to suggest you stick to bands you actually know something about next time." I pause, glancing at Dua. "And Dua, please limit your rebuttals to actual words. Gestures are for traffic arguments, not the classroom." And I'll definitely be informing Zinneerah about this.

"You know, Professor Shaan," Dua drawls, "my older sister loves Queen." She grins sinisterly, her eyes daring me. "Do you have a favorite Queen song?"

I stare at her with a warning smile.

But it wears off when I recall the night in the coffee shop where Saira and I had a conversation about her infidelity. The only thing that kept me from breaking the glass on our table was Zinneerah's singing. "I'm a little sentimental, so I'll have to go with "Who Wants to Live Forever.""

Dua quirks up a shoulder, clearly satisfied with whatever subtle test she'd been putting me through.

""Bohemian Rhapsody" is the shit," Jeremiah pipes up. He's leaned back in his seat, legs stretched out like he's in his living room. "Did you see the movie, Professor?"

"Yes." I don't elaborate, though the truth is I saw it the night it came out. I'd hoped—foolishly, I admit—that I might run into Zinneerah at the theater, but no such luck. So, I watched it again. And again. The first time out of curiosity, the next three because, well, it's Queen.

Before Jeremiah can drag us further down the cinematic rabbit hole, I steer the conversation back on course. "What other mediums can we think of that have served as platforms for political or cultural commentary?"

Several arms shoot up, and the spark of engagement I've been chasing all morning flickers to life.

I take a deep breath, letting myself enjoy the moment. Friendly professor's actually working. And also, because I made pancakes with my wife this morning.

"All right." I straighten up from my desk. "Let's start with Andrea."

During group discussions, I leave my desk and take a slow walk up the aisles. It's not something I usually do, but today feels different. The students are deep in conversation, tossing ideas back and forth with an energy I haven't seen in a while.

I pause by one group, leaning slightly to catch what they're saying. They're arguing over the role of corporate sponsorship in modern protest movements, voices overlapping as they counter each other's points. I nod, impressed—*not bad.*

The next group is quieter but focused. They're mapping out the evolution of grassroots journalism, linking it to the rise of digital platforms. Someone mentions Substack newsletters, another adds something about online influencers, and before I know it, they're debating the ethics of monetizing advocacy.

It's strange, really. My approach to teaching wasn't always this reflective. Early in my career, I'd walk into a room full of first-years like a drill sergeant, expecting sharp answers and polished essays from a crowd that had barely figured out how to format a Word document. I was impatient back then, relentless.

First-years and second-years are different. They're still figuring out how the world works, what they want, who they are. They stumble over their words, make half-formed arguments, and forget deadlines because they overslept or got distracted by the university partying lifestyle.

I used to find that infuriating. Now, I find it oddly endearing. They're not just future journalists—they're kids with messy lives, learning how to walk the tightrope of responsibility for the first time.

I've been there. I don't know how I survived my twenties without completely combusting. If someone had held me to the same standard I held these students to, I probably would've dropped out, run off to some forgotten corner of the world.

But Zinneerah . . . she's softened those edges. She's shown me that patience isn't complacency, it's care. Towards her, towards myself, and, if I stretch that definition far enough, towards my students.

With her, I can't charge ahead with the same reckless efficiency I used to.

Love, real love, isn't about checking off milestones or earning gold stars. It's about waiting for the other person to catch up, about learning how to be still when the moment calls for it. I can't expect my students to be perfect overnight. I can't expect my wife to meet me halfway when she's still working through her own emotions. And that's fine. Because we'll get there together.

I hold back a smile, but the vision unfolds anyway. Children with her eyes, her smile, pieces of her woven into the fabric of our lives. A bigger house, or wherever she feels most at home. A backyard with an orchid tree stretching toward the sky. A garden I'd plant just for her, surrounded with the colors and scents she loves. Maybe a cat, maybe a dog, something small to make the house feel fuller.

Happiness suits me.

Zinneerah suits me.

I wait outside the music department, phone in hand, firing off a barrage of texts to Ramishah. Mostly nonsense—how I made chocolate chip pancakes this morning, and how Zinneerah insisted on her strawberries being sliced, not served whole.

My sister finally reads them.

Ram: IF I HEAR ONE MORE DING FROM MY PHONE, I'M TURNING YOU INTO A PANCAKE. LEAVE ME ALONE SO I CAN FINISH WORKING ON A SERUM FOR THESE 11-YEAR-OLD SEPHORA GIRLS TO SPEND THEIR PARENTS' MONEY ON. >:((((

I frown, thumbs hesitating over the screen.

Me: Sorry. I don't know who else to talk to.

The typing bubbles appear. Then vanish. Then come back. She's probably feeling guilty for snapping at me. And fair enough, I deserve it. But the truth is, I really don't have anyone else to text. Ammi-ji would pick up, sure, but she prefers calls over messages. And unlike

Ramishah, she'd be patient about it, softly chiding me to stop narrating every grin Zinneerah blesses me with.

Ramishah leaves me on read.

I sigh, tucking my phone into my coat pocket. I'm mid-brood when someone tugs the back of my jacket, startling me.

I turn, and there she is.

My lovely wife.

She clutches the straps of her guitar bag, her dark, smoky eyes framed by her open hair. Today, she's dressed in a frilly green blouse and black skirt, unlike her usual black-on-black style. She's so achingly beautiful, like a melody you'll never hear the same way t

"Professor!" Alex bounces down the building's steps, her energy levels always high as she loops her arm through Zinneerah's. "How's it going?"

"Good," I say. "Yourself?"

"Fantastic!"

Another woman steps up beside Zinneerah—short blonde curls, tan skin dusted with freckles. She pulls her round sunglasses up to her forehead and gives me a once-over. "Hmm."

What's that supposed to mean?

"This is Ophelia," Alex says, gesturing.

I offer my hand. "Raees. Zinneerah's husband."

Ophelia shakes it briefly, her grip firm. "Huh. Wouldn't have predicted this at all." She pushes her shades back down. "Zinnie usually goes for the edgier types." She tilts her head, still inspecting me like I'm an artifact under glass. "You look like you wandered out of *Dead Poets Society*."

Zinneerah elbows her sharply. Alex snickers.

"I'll take that as a compliment," I reply, smirking.

"It is," Ophelia says, deadpan. "Just making sure—you're taking good care of Zinnie, right?"

I glance at Zinneerah, cocking an eyebrow. "Think I'll let Zinnie answer that one."

Her cheeks flush, lips twitching with a shy smile. She nods five times in succession.

Alex drapes her arm across Zinneerah's shoulder with a grin. "So, Professor—"

"Raees."

"Right. Know any hot poets on campus?"

"Can't say that I do," I reply, veering the conversation elsewhere. "How was practice?"

"Productive," Ophelia answers, stuffing her hands into her jean pockets. "It's been a while since the three of us were in that room together, but it felt like no time had passed."

Zinneerah squints into the sunlight, smiling, her bronze skin illuminated. My heart thrums in my ears, and I grip the strap of my bag a little tighter.

"You should come by sometime," Alex suggests. "Do you play an instrument?"

My fingers dance across invisible piano keys. "But not very good."

Zinneerah blinks, her lips parting slightly. *Really?*

"I took lessons in high school . . ." My words falter, nearly revealing more than I want to. I clear my throat and try again. "It was just a hobby—something to keep me busy. I haven't played in years. I'm probably rusty."

Ophelia's eyebrows lift. "Well, if Alex ever takes a sick day, you're welcome to join us."

"Not gonna happen," Alex says, crossing her arms.

I chuckle. "I appreciate the offer, but I'd rather listen to your magic than risk ruining it." My gaze lands on Zinneerah. "Speaking of which, I've yet to hear you play."

Her eyes drop immediately to the ground.

Alex steps in, and grabs Zinneerah's face, squishing her cheeks together and puppeteering her mouth. "'Oh, yes, my sweet husband.'" She pitches her voice higher in a theatrical mockery of Zinneerah's voice. "'I'd love nothing more than to serenade you with my musical genius!'"

"Stop," Zinneerah mouths, brushing Alex's hands off her face.

I press a fist to my lips, stifling my laughter. "It's good to know my wife keeps such a lively company. If you two are free, you're welcome to come over for dinner sometime. As long as Alex brings her jokes to the table."

Alex clutches her shirt and widens her eyes. "Professor," she says in a whisper, "I'd be honored to clown in your humble abode."

Zinneerah chuckles softly, looking up at me for a split second before averting her eyes again.

"Zinnie mentioned you two were hosting some dinner party next week," Ophelia says. "We'll drop by. Cool if I bring my daughter?"

"Of course," I reply. "Our family's overrun with kids—she'll fit right in." Ammi-ji's relatives are the ones who always come to these gatherings, ever since most of Abbu's side stopped reaching out years ago. I'd never cared much for them anyway. "Just let Zinneerah know if there are any dietary restrictions. I'll make sure we've got something for everyone."

Alex's jaw drops. "He cooks?" She spins to Zinneerah, her hands out like she's just been hit with divine revelation.

"He does," I say before Zinneerah can respond.

"Well-deserved, Zinnie." Ophelia sighs. "You're living a life of pure luxury. A husband who cooks and plays the piano? Next thing you'll tell me is he writes poetry, too." She pats Zinneerah's back lightly before checking her phone. "Anyway, we better get moving. I've got to pick up Juliette from school."

"It was nice meeting you," I say, offering a polite nod.

Ophelia gives a two-finger salute. "Likewise. Take care."

She grabs Alex's arm and drags her off like a mother tugging their impatient child.

Alex twists her body back to face us, waving frantically. "Bye, Professor! Bye, Zinnie! Don't forget about me!" She blows a kiss in Zinneerah's direction, and my wife captures it, pressing it to her heart.

"I'm jealous," I say, earning her attention. Her head tilts toward me instantly, concern flickering in her eyes. "I mean, I'm jealous that I don't have friends like Alex or Ophelia." I laugh a little, rubbing the back of my neck. "My sister's already torn me apart over it, but watching how you all are together, made me realize I need to try harder. Be a better friend, let alone have friends."

Zinneerah steps in front of me, close enough that her presence is all I can focus on. *I'm your friend.*

Oh, no.

My heart's gone rogue again. She's my wife, for God's sake, and yet here I am, falling apart because she called herself my friend.

I'm my wife's friend.

I should say something. Anything. "You're my friend, too," I somehow manage to say. "You've always been my friend." Too much. That's too much. Backpedal. Fast. "I mean—since we've known each other. For a year. Right? That's how long we've been friends." My voice cracks slightly, and I want to kick myself. What am I even saying? Never mind that it's been six and a half years of me quietly losing my mind over her. But, yes. A year. Let's go with that. "So, I assume we've been friends since then. Right?"

Her eyes soften. *You have been my friend since you told me about the pirate ship ride.*

I told her that embarrassing story in the third week of our weekly Friday engagement meetings. "You still . . . remember that?"

Of course, she signs so matter-of-fact about it, like she can't believe I'd even ask. *I remember every story. It was the best I could do for you.*

"Oh."

My chest physically hurts. I need to sit down. I need to think. I need to sift through my brain for more childhood stories, more memories, more anything I can offer her. Anything to make up for the fact that all I've done is talk about myself.

"I'm sorry. All I did was go on and on without even thinking you might've wanted to share something, too."

She shakes her head. *Don't worry. I didn't*, she signs. Then her fingers hang suspended in the air, as if she's considering whether to go on. Her gaze drifts to the side for a moment before settling back on me. *I like your voice.*

It feels like my heart's about to give out on the spot. Right here. Right on campus. They're going to find me collapsed in the middle of this conversation, because how the hell am I supposed to survive hearing that from her? Never in my life have I been so profoundly grateful to have been born, to have grown up, to have somehow stumbled my way through all the twists and turns that led me to this moment—to her. My wife. My friend. And she likes listening to me.

I'm useless. My voice? Gone. My thoughts? Evacuating.

Somehow, I pull myself together just enough to sign, *Thank you.*

I want to tell her that I love her voice, too, but she doesn't know that I used to sit in the back of the café during open mic nights, trying to be inconspicuous while she serenaded everyone.

Her voice used to make my heart stop. Now, it's the way she looks at me.

And if I'm being honest with myself, I've fallen in love with her silence just as much.

She tilts her head, one brow arching teasingly. *Where's my compliment?*

I stammer, my brain scrambling to keep up. I didn't expect her to ask that. Why didn't I expect her to ask that? God, I'm an idiot.

Of course, I should've been ready with something clever or sweet or, hell, at least coherent. That's what normal people do. That's what husbands do. But no, here I am, blinking like a deer in headlights

Zinneerah dips her head, breathy laughter spilling out behind the curve of her palm. My brain stops functioning again. She glances up at me, her eyes crinkling, and I know she sees exactly how frazzled I am.

Kidding, she signs. *I was the funny one in the trio. A-L-E-X is waking up the clown inside again. I'm sorry if I made you uncomfortable.*

"No!" I blurt out loud. She blinks at me, and I try to recover. "I mean—yes! Yes, that's great. The, uh . . . the being funny part. I'm glad. Really glad." I know I'm making this worse, but I can't stop. "I was just—uh—processing your compliment. That's all. Thinking about how I, too, like your voice. Your words. Especially the ones that poke fun at me."

Kill me. Just end it now.

She blinks at me again, and then—God, help me—she licks her bottom lip, holding back another laugh, before her gaze flicks down to the pavement.

I'm hopeless. "Uh, so." I gesture toward the parking lot like an awkward tour guide. "Shall we?"

She steps in beside me without a word, her pace matching mine, and I can feel her warmth brush against my arm. And that smile of hers? It doesn't fade. Not even for a second.

I glance down at her out of the corner of my eye, and it hits me, like it always does, like it always will, I'm the reason for that smile. *Me.* I'm the one who put it there.

And I'll spend the rest of my life to keep it there.

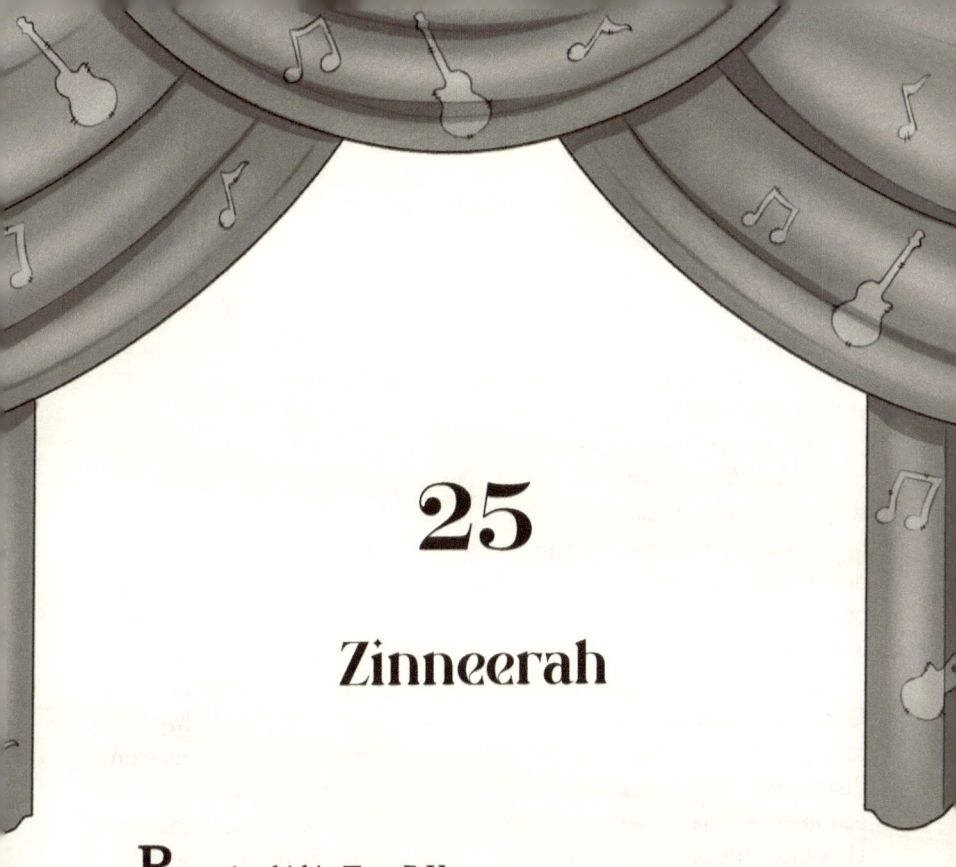

25

Zinneerah

Raees is a kid in Toys R Us.

A six-foot-five, broad-shouldered, grown-man-shaped child.

We drove half an hour to find the perfect birthday gift for his baby niece, but I can already feel it in my bones: we're not leaving with a stuffed animal or teething rings. Nope. On a scale of LEGO Death Star to Pokémon, we're leaving with whatever shiny, nostalgia-laden treasure catches his eye.

"Whoa! No way they have this!" His voice ricochets off the shelves like a pinball as he disappears into another aisle.

I sigh, but it's not the exasperated kind of sigh. It's the kind that sneaks out when you're trying really hard not to laugh. With a smile tugging at the corner of my mouth, I follow him. Sure enough, he's cradling a plastic box like it's some sort of ancient artifact.

I raise an eyebrow and cross my arms, which is basically shorthand for: *What is it?*

He takes that as his cue to go full infomercial mode. "A ten-inch Optimus Prime figurine that transforms into his truck mode. And—this is the best part—it comes with a remote so you can drive him around. If you press this red button, he automatically shifts back into the figurine." He stops to inhale, finally, and I swear he's a second away from ripping the package open. "Isn't that the coolest thing you've ever seen?"

He is. For being a handsome geek.

I thought you read books, I sign, narrowing my eyes in mock suspicion. *Not play with toys.*

"No, you're right," he murmurs, unspooling a memory he doesn't revisit often. "Ramishah had Barbies and Polly Pockets. I had one Dragon Ball Z figurine. Ammi-ji snuck it into the house for my tenth birthday. She hid it under my pillow like it was some kind of contraband." He chuckles, but it's brittle. His hand hovers over the Optimus Prime box again before he puts it back, reluctant. "My father . . . he didn't believe in these sorts of things. He said they were distractions, and just a waste of time. He wanted me to focus on school—no 'make-believe.' No playing around. Just work, work, work." He sighs, stepping back and staring at the figurine like it's a piece of his childhood that's still out of reach. "That's just how it was for me."

What a pathetic excuse for a father.

It's clear from the way Raees' shoulders hunch that he's already hearing it in his head, whether I say it or not.

Speaking of my father-in-law, I don't actually know much about where he is now. "In rehabilitation" was the phrase Rosy Aunty had vaguely used.

Why is he there? How long is he staying? No one's ever volunteered that information, and I've never asked. Not because I don't care—well, okay, maybe a *little* because I don't care—but mostly because Raees doesn't seem interested in visiting him.

And honestly? I'm not about to push the idea. There's a fine line between healing and reopening wounds, and I think Raees understands that line better than most.

"We should get Amina's birthday present before I get carried away and spend all our savings," he says suddenly, snapping out of nostalgia. He gives me a sheepish smile as he steps out of the aisle. *Our* savings, he said. Like we're a little team with a shared piggy bank. It's adorable. "Are you coming?"

I take my phone out of my pocket and hold it up to my ear, my fingers flicking through the air. *D-U-A*.

He reads the name I spell and nods, his grin returning to his eyes. "Okay. I'll be in the toddler section."

Once he's gone, I turn back to the shelf. The glossy plastic packaging shines under the lights. The price tag catches my eye, too. A hundred dollars before tax.

Damn.

It's fine. I've got enough in my account, thanks to Baba. When he passed, he left behind large sums to me and my siblings. It's strange having access to it. Sometimes I feel guilty spending it considering how hard he worked to save up for our family.

Right now, though, I don't feel anything except certainty. Raees deserves this. Not because he needs it, but because he doesn't expect it. He doesn't even let himself want it fully. And that's exactly why he should have it. I know Baba would approve.

I grab the figurine off the shelf and tuck it under my arm, glancing around the aisle to make sure he isn't gonna pop out of another aisle.

All clear.

I head for the checkout line, quickening my steps. "Gift wrap?" I ask the worker behind the counter, tapping my card on the payment pad. "I'll come back. To pick it up. Later."

"Sure thing!" she chirps, taking the box over to the wrapping section. I nod and step away, relief unfurling in my chest.

One secret purchase secured.

I make my way to the toddler section, weaving through bright colored aisles until I find Raees.

He's standing in front of a wall of toys, holding up two options like he's solving a life-or-death puzzle. In one hand, he's got a bag of bath toys shaped like cartoon animals. In the other, a LeapFrog notebook with buttons and flashing lights.

"One of these will last her a lifetime," he says, shaking the toys for emphasis, "and the other will definitely break in the next few weeks."

I tilt my head and signs, *I agree. Bath toys are common. Lots of people will probably get her those.* I point again at the notebook, signing, *Add some clothes? If you want.*

He nods, immediately sold on the idea. "You're a genius." He sets the bath toys back on the shelf, the package looking comically small in his hand.

It's only now, as he reaches for the notebook, that I really notice his hands. They're large, and so soft, with long, yet thick fingers, the nails smooth and almond-shaped. Not bitten to the quick, but clean and well-kept. They're the kind of hands that belong to a piano player, or an artist. Hands that create, that craft, that hold mine protectively.

"What's wrong?" Raees asks, his voice cutting through my thoughts.

I blink, startled, and quickly shake my head. But the motion is a little too vigorous, and I send myself spinning into a momentary dizzy spell.

Raees chuckles softly. "Let's go pick out some clothes."

I follow him deeper into the maze of racks, with explosions of pastel pinks and purples that is the baby girl clothing section. It's surprisingly busy for a weekday. Couples flip through tiny hangers side by side, some women cradling baby bumps, others with babies tucked snug in strollers. A few toddlers dart between the racks, squealing with laughter while their fathers stumble after them, reminding them to 'be careful.'

My heart softens as I spot a pair of baby shoes on display, their soles no bigger than my thumb. When Dua was born, I used to tag along with Baba for shopping trips just like this. He never cared that I picked the loudest, brightest, cheesiest clothes for her—he'd always let me choose whatever I thought looked best. I guess you could say I have some experience in this department. An expert, really.

Meticulously, I pick out a pair of sundresses in Amina's month size, a pink onesie patterned with tiny white daisies, a trio of T-shirts with cute sayings ("Daddy's Princess," "Future Scientist," and my personal favorite, "Queen's Don't Cry, They Rise and Shine"), and the tiniest pair of jeans imaginable.

Raees holds the growing stack of clothes in his hands, watching me with crinkled eyes.

What is it? I sign, tilting my head at him.

"Nothing," he mumbles, shaking his head.

Are the clothes okay? I ask, anxiously. *Would you like to pick something out?*

"Well . . ." he drawls, leaning back and pretending to think deeply. "Maybe I can pick out the shoes?"

I nod. *We've got enough clothes*, I sign, motioning toward the stack in his hands.

Raees' faint dimples make a dangerous appearance, and he strolls his jolly self off toward the shoe section.

Out of the corner of my eye, I catch movement. The mothers nearby, pushing strollers or chasing toddlers, are sneaking glances at him. Quick, darting looks that turn into full-on double-takes.

One of them hovers a moment too long, her eyes sliding up and down his six-foot-five frame like she's reading the fine print on a very attractive contract. She notices me watching her, and her cheeks flush. Quickly, she looks away, straightening her posture like she suddenly remembered her husband exists.

I bite the inside of my cheek.

Every time we're out in public, someone is ogling Raees. Women. Men. Couples. I don't blame them. He's . . . well, Raees. Broad-shouldered with the kind of swimmer's build that he's perfected in our home gym. His hair falls perfectly into place, even when he runs his fingers through it. And that lopsided smile of his never goes away. And then there's the glasses. The *glasses*.

God took His sweet, *sweet* time putting Raees together, like He paused production on the rest of humanity just to perfect my husband. And He succeeded, obviously.

It's funny, in hindsight, that one of the reasons I hesitated to marry him was because of those good looks. Not because I thought he'd be arrogant—he's the least arrogant person alive—but because I didn't think I'd suit him.

I figured people would look at us and assume I was his personal assistant or, at best, his overworked PR manager. Meanwhile, he'd be the CEO of some sleek cybersecurity company, shaking hands and closing deals while I stood in the background holding his coffee.

But here we are. Married. Quite happily.

Still, I can't help but step into his bubble when I notice a woman standing *way* too close to pop it. She's shopping with a toddler perched in the cart compartment, but her body language is noticeable. She's leaned slightly toward Raees, like gravity just couldn't resist the pull, and I can already feel my lips tightening into a firm line.

Before I can do anything, my gaze locks with the toddler, who's staring at me with blue, curious eyes. His chubby cheeks are smushed against the cart's handle, and I raise a single eyebrow at him, exaggerating it for effect. He blinks at me, confused, so I widen both my eyes and start blinking rapidly while pulling a ridiculous face.

It works. The kid giggles, his little shoulders bouncing with laughter, and I suppress a smile.

Raees turns around, frowning slightly at the cart wedged between us. Without a word, he shifts it aside with one hand, balancing the three shoeboxes he's picked out in the other. "Excuse me," he says politely, glancing at the woman who owns it.

She startles slightly, then offers a smile. "Oh, I'm sorry." Her gaze drops to the shoeboxes in his hand. "Those are great choices."

"Thank you." Raees nods. "They're for my niece. My wife and I are going to her second birthday party this weekend."

He gestures toward me when he says the word wife, and her eyes finally flick over to me, like I've suddenly appeared into existence. Her smile is the kind of polite, obligatory expression I've seen more times in my past relationship than I can count. Seriously, should I tone down the eyeliner? The dark lipstick?

"How sweet," she says, her voice overly bright. "Do you two have kids? Or are you expecting?"

"No," he replies. "Not yet."

I raise a brow, slightly caught off guard by his phrasing. *Not yet.* The way he says it is like the question of children was already answered somewhere in the future, and we're just waiting to catch up to it.

Of course I'll have kids with him. Well, a kid. One. I've always pictured just one, because raising a child is enough of a lifelong commitment without also inviting an entire soccer team into your house. I've read about husbands who stop seeing their wives the same way after they've had children—men who start looking at them as mothers instead of women. Sahara once declared that she'd rather die than have kids, mostly because she refuses to torture her body.

The woman's voice interrupts. "Would you like a boy or a girl?" She tilts her head at Raees. I'm sorry, but is she, like, conducting a personal interview or something?

Raees shrugs lightly, still smiling. "It doesn't matter."

"Well, I always wished for a boy, and ta-dah! Mason blessed me two years ago."

She turns toward her cart and pinches the toddler's cheek. He gurgles in response, clutching his stuffed animal and looking entirely uninterested in the conversation. *Me, too, Mason.*

Raees gives a polite chuckle. "He's adorable. Do you have any tips for us?"

Tips? Are we really doing this?

Apparently, we are, because she lights up like he just handed her a golden ticket to keep talking. "Prepare to lose all your sleep," she says with a nervous laugh, tucking a stray lock of hair behind her ear. Her emerald eyes glittering up at Raees a little too obviously, and I can feel the corners of my mouth tightening on reflex.

I get it. He's smiling. It has one hell of a gravitational pull.

"The qualities depend on the baby," she continues, trying to keep the conversation going. I'm trying to check out Amina's presents, *and* surprise my husband with Optimus Prime—not make small talk with a stranger who's clearly more interested in Raees than she should be. "Mason didn't like sleeping as much as I did, but now he's learning to respect his mommy's needs." She gives his cheek another pinch, cooing at him. "Honestly, though? As long as you both have each other, it'll all be smooth sailing."

Raees shifts closer to me, his hand resting lightly on the small of my back. My body leans into it instinctively. I've grown so used to these little gestures—his hand on my back, his arm around my shoulders—that they've started to feel like second nature.

"Thank you for the advice," he says with finality. *Thank you for wrapping this up, dear husband.* "We'll definitely do some research before we take that step."

The woman blinks at him, fumbling to come up with something else to say, but when her gaze drifts to me, I'm already staring at her.

My expression is blank, but I don't look away. I don't even blink.

"Well, um, nice talking to you both," she mutters, her hands tightening on the cart's handle. She gets the message, finally, and wheels away down the aisle, her cheeks pink.

Raees watches her leave, then turns to me with an easy shrug. "That was nice of her."

I shouldn't roll my eyes, but I want to. I really want to.

Once we've checked out Amina's presents and had them gift-wrapped, I wait for the right moment.

Raees steps over to a donation box by the exit, pulling out a ten-dollar bill from his wallet. The second his back is turned, I slip the Optimus Prime figurine into my bag.

He has *no* idea.

As we head to the car, Raees opens the passenger door for me. Since I can't wait until we're home to give his present, I take it out of the bag and hug it close to my chest, quickly climbing into my seat before he can ask questions.

He sets the shopping bag in the back and walks around to the driver's side, sliding in. "What's that?" he asks, his eyes flicking toward me as he buckles his seatbelt.

I pull the box from where I'd been cradling it and hold it out to him.

His brows knit together as he takes the package, staring at it as though it might combust in his hands. "Zinneerah," he says cautiously. "What is this?"

A present, I sign, smiling. *For you.*

His hands hover over the gift. "But . . ." He glances at me, then back at the neatly wrapped box sitting in his lap. "Why would you get me a present?"

Why not?

He gulps, and I watch as he runs his hand over the paper, his fingers flicking the little white bow I'd insisted the gift-wrapping worker add. "Can I open it?"

I stifle a chuckle, and nod.

He doesn't rip into it like most people would. No, Raees takes his time, carefully pulling at the edges of the wrapping paper as if it's some priceless artifact he's afraid to damage. There's something almost childlike in the way he does it. When's the last time he was on the receiving end of something so thoughtful?

When the paper falls away and the box is revealed, he freezes.

His eyes widen as he stares at the gift, blinking rapidly like the toy might be a mirage his brain conjured up just to mess with him.

"Zin . . ." My name catches in his throat. He flips the box over carefully, memorizing every detail, every word printed on the glossy surface, as if he needs proof that this is real. That this *is* his. "You bought this for me?"

It occurs to me, not for the first time, how much joy I find in giving.

I love gift giving. Always. A quality—I pause, the thought snagging on my ASL vocabulary. How do you sign "inherited"? I fumble over the memory of it, unsure. Maybe I should simplify: *A quality I share with my father.*

Raees settles the toy down, a mellow, dewy look on his face. "Zinneerah, I . . . I don't know what to say aside from thank you. Thank you so much."

He takes off his glasses and runs an arm over his eyes.

Huh?

Are you crying?

He can't see me signing because his head is bowed, so I tilt my head slightly and reach out, lowering his arm.

Oh, my god.

He is crying.

Not a downpour. Just a light drizzle.

He chuckles in disbelief. "Nothing of any concern. I've always been sensitive growing up."

Me, too.

Though the way our sensitivity manifests couldn't be more different.

Taking out my phone, I use the type and voice dictation to communicate: I used to cry over the smallest things—like when the yolk in my fried egg spilled out onto my plate. It was a betrayal of breakfast, and I couldn't handle it. I only liked egg whites back then, and I remember being absolutely annoying every time my mother made a mistake. Sometimes, I think the only reason my brother became a cook was so our mother could stop shouting at me for being so picky. He used to make me separate dinners when she cooked something I didn't like—lentils, vegetables, anything remotely healthy. He never made a fuss about it. Just quietly handed me a plate of whatever I wanted, even if it was something as ridiculous as buttered bread with ketchup.

In retrospect, none of that really makes me sensitive, does it? No, that wasn't sensitivity at all. That was just me being a brat.

There was a time when I thought my pickiness was something I could hold onto forever. In my last relationship, I started off the same way, insisting on eating only what I liked, throwing little tantrums over meals that didn't suit me. But that didn't last long. Eventually, I stopped being picky.

Not because I'd grown out of it, but because it became safer to just eat whatever I was given. Safer to stay quiet. Safer to smile through a plate of something I hated, just to avoid the sting of a broken nose.

I shove the memory aside as quickly as it appears. That's not my life anymore. That's not who I am. Not with Raees.

"Lentils suck," Raees mutters.

Agreed, I sign emphatically, adding a dramatic nod for emphasis. *Rice and chicken for the win.*

"And lamb."

I grimace. *Lamb?*

"Yes, lamb," he says, shooting me a look. "Don't hate until you've tried lamb shawarma."

Oh, that's questionable, I sign, wrinkling my nose. *No offense.*

His brow arches. "You were about to say 'disgusting,' weren't you?"

I shrug, feigning innocence. *You said it, not me.*

Raees chuckles and I pitch in with a smile. "You're unbelievable."

Thank you, I sign, sitting up a little straighter and giving him a smile. *I try.*

My eyes flick to the cup holder, where his glasses are folded neatly.

I pick them up, weighing them in my hands. The temples are a little warped, probably from him shoving them into his pocket on the way out the door or tossing them haphazardly onto the nightstand. How these glasses have survived this long is a mystery.

I stare at them, debating with myself, my heart already speeding up.

Am I really about to do this?

Then I glance over at him, at the curve of his full-lips, and the way he's still staring at me with stars in his eyes, and suddenly my hands are moving.

It's just glasses, I mentally try to talk myself down. *You've known each other for a year and a half. This isn't a big deal. You're married, for crying out loud. Married.*

My brain is fighting me, screaming something about boundaries and propriety and God knows what else, but my hands are already moving. *Be gone, narrow-minded mentality*, as if that's enough to banish the voice in my head.

I lean over, holding my breath, and slip the glasses over his nose. My fingertips brush against the bridge as I adjust the flimsy temples behind his ears.

My fingers graze the curve of his left ear, a fleeting, accidental touch that sets off a chain reaction I wasn't prepared for.

I don't know why that surprises me, but it does. It catches me so off guard that I yank my hand back like I've touched something forbidden, shoving it under my leg in one swift, clumsy motion.

I don't look at him immediately, but I feel him glance at me.

He doesn't say anything for a second.

The silence feels . . . comforting, truth be told.

But I do chance a look at him.

His cheeks are a little pink, too, though he's pretending like they're not.

He clears his throat, breaking the moment.

"So," he says, holding up the toy box and shaking it slightly, "since we're already sitting in a parking lot, we might as well take Optimus Prime for a spin."

July 30th

RAEES HATES HORROR MOVIES (stop spreading lies!)

Horror movies are practically documentaries, just with better
lighting and soundtracks.

*How exactly are horror movies like documentaries? Last
time I checked, documentaries don't involve demons
jumping out of closets.*

But they're real! Not the demons, obviously, but the fear. It's human
psychology, the way people react to impossible situations. It's like
an experiment. That's basically what you love about documentaries,
right?

*Okay, but documentaries are grounded in actual facts.
Horror movies are just . . . people making bad decisions
in creepy, victorian-esque houses. It's not the same.*

You think documentaries are all grounded in truth? Half of them
have a biased narrator trying to convince you of something. At
least horror doesn't pretend to be anything else. It's honest about
what it is.

*So you're saying horror is more honest than documentaries?
That's a stretch.*

Well, I'd rather watch Saw 3 than learn about, I don't know, the
history of forks.

*It was the history of spices, and you loved that documentary,
thank you very much.*

It's like talking to a wall. Or, rather, <u>writing</u>.

Did we just have our first arguement?

26

Raees

Professor Holmes tilts her head. "What am I looking at?"

"It's Optimus Prime. From *Transformers*." I set the toy down on my desk. "My wife and I were shopping for my niece's birthday a couple of days ago, and, well, she surprised me with this."

"She bought you . . . a toy?"

"I know." I grin. "Isn't she the sweetest woman on the planet? I'd been rambling about it when I saw it, and then *boom*—she's handing it to me, all wrapped up. Best surprise ever."

Holmes sighs, the kind that tells me she's already regretting the last sixty seconds. "Raees?"

"Yes?"

"Remind me of your age again?"

I scoff, turning to set Optimus on my bookshelf. The controller stays in my desk drawer—she doesn't need to know that much. "You wouldn't get it. When she gave it to me, it was like . . . I don't know. Like I was dreaming. Every single day with her feels that way, you know? Like she's too good to be true. Like someone like me—"

"Stop right there." Holmes's hand shoots up like a referee calling a foul. "I'm not here for the I-love-my-wife-so-much TED Talk. I came to tell you I got a response about your student's internship."

Oh. Right. Dua's internship. My mind flips tracks. "And? Good news, I hope?"

Holmes crosses her arms, leaning against the doorframe. "Katie wants a portfolio. Dua doesn't have one."

I frown. "She's got stuff. A blog. Those volleyball team interviews—"

"Stuff isn't a portfolio." Holmes cuts me off like I just said something especially stupid. "Katie's picky. Capital-P Picky. If Dua wants a shot, she needs to branch out. Cover athletes outside of campus. Start a podcast. Hell, write an op-ed about something trending. Just something that doesn't look like it was slapped together between classes."

That's disappointing but not surprising. Dua's smart, clever, insightful, the kind of student who pays attention to the details that others miss. But she's also a second-year, still working her way through electives and prerequisites, with barely any real-world experience under her belt. Her professional network begins and ends with her boyfriend.

"I'll advise her going forward," I say.

Holmes raises an eyebrow, standing and brushing imaginary lint from her skirt. "Excellent. My good deed for the week is officially checked off. I'll send you Katie's contact info—forward that to Dua. Always useful to have a big name like Miss Cunningham somewhere in your orbit. Even if she's a pain."

"Got it."

She grabs her purse from the floor and slings it over her shoulder, but pauses halfway out the door, eyeing me like she's debating whether to bother. She bothers. "Oh, by the way, Wei's retirement party is at the end of the month. You've been ghosting the group chat, in case you weren't aware."

"I've been busy."

Holmes snorts. "Of course you have. No one would ever accuse you of being over-engaged." Her gaze flicks to Optimus Prime on my shelf, but she doesn't comment. The judgment is dripping from her smirk as she turns on her heel and strides out.

Truth be told, I've been avoiding the group chat, mainly because Saira treats it like her personal playground. Every other day, there's some new poll about department socials—"Team trivia night?" "Movie marathon?" "Wine and cheese tasting?" She even made a poll about which venue had the best coffee for faculty meetings. Everyone else humors her, but I can't stomach it. Even Holmes doesn't participate, so I don't know why I'm the one catching heat for not replying.

Still, if I want to be better about networking, maybe I should start practicing what I preach. And that means facing the group chat.

I open the Messenger app on my laptop, scrolling through the digital debris. It's the usual mix: inspirational quotes about academia, unfunny memes recycled from three years ago, and an unhealthy amount of cat gifs.

At the top, there's the latest poll: the next department outing. It's a tie between bowling and a hockey game. I blink at the name of the poll's creator. Ethan Benedict. For once, it's not Saira. And, thankfully, it's not clubbing.

Still, both options sound like punishment in their own ways.

Bowling? Absolutely not. The thought alone makes my skin itch. Bowling is a gauntlet of second-hand shoes, sticky balls coated in questionable pizza grease, screaming kids, and endlessly waiting your turn while someone inevitably screws up the scoring machine. The worst kind of department outing.

Not that a hockey game would be much better. But at least I'd be seated. I wouldn't have to touch anything suspicious or stand awkwardly around a sticky plastic table. All I'd have to do is watch a bunch of overgrown men battering rams in oversized jerseys. They're basically short-tempered figure skaters with sticks, and the whole thing feels like a live-action metaphor for Canadian patriotism.

I groan, but click the hockey game option anyway. It's the lesser of two evils.

Me: When's the game so I can clear my schedule?

I sit back and wait for a reply.

Professor Carlson's the first to read it. His little "seen" notification pops up.

Nothing. No response. Of course.

"Thanks for that," I mutter.

A second later, Saira reads it. Her reply bubbles pop up immediately. *Of course.*

Professor Yaaas: Look who finally decided to join civilization.

I sigh, already regretting my decision.

Professor Yaaas: It's tonight, by the way. That's what you get for lurking in the chat like some shadowy cryptid. But don't stress—we've got an extra ticket since George from Psych bailed last minute.

"Shit." I groan, letting my forehead thunk onto the desk. "I don't want to go anymore."

My computer chimes again. I glance up and see Saira's private message. Here we go.

Saira Nadeem: I'm seriously so glad you're coming, Raees! It'll be fun, I promise. We've got great seats in the back—you can see the whole rink from there.

I stare at the screen, fingers hovering over the keyboard.

Me: Great.

Her reply bubbles pop up again fast, like she's been waiting for an opening.

Saira Nadeem: Come on. Don't sound so thrilled. You used to love sports games. Where's the old Raees?

I roll my eyes. I used to go to sports games because my fellow classmates loved them, and I was always invited. Saira just happened to be there too, back when we . . . whatever.

Me: Can I bring a plus-one?

She starts typing. Stops. Typing again.

Saira Nadeem: Seats are limited.

Me: What if I buy an extra ticket?

Saira Nadeem: Godspeed.

I click my tongue and lean back in my chair, staring at her message. Would Zinneerah even want to come? Probably not. She's got better things to do than watch me try to force myself to socialize.

I send a thumbs-up emoji, shut my laptop, and grab my bag. "This better be worth it."

As I'm locking my office door, my phone pings with a notification. It's from Zinneerah.

Love of My Life: Raees, is it okay if I invite my friends over? Ophelia's bringing Juliette too.

A small smile tugs at the corner of my mouth.

Me: Of course. I'll pick up some donuts on the way.

Before I make it to the stairs, my phone buzzes again.

Love of My Life: You don't have to do that. But if you do— because there's no stopping your kindness—please, no jelly ones.

I laugh, standing at the top of the stairwell.

Me: Understood. No jelly ones. I'll see you in a few.

Twenty minutes later, I walk out the door with two dozen boxes of fresh, still-warm donuts from Studio 365.

There's a bright chatter of a little girl, the noise of a kids' TV show, and Alex's loud laughter bouncing off the walls.

Zinneerah is pulling a tray of chocolate cupcakes from the oven when I step into the kitchen. She greets me with an ear-to-ear smile that's capable of lighting up a blackout.

Alex and Ophelia are seated at the island, their conversation coming to a halt.

"Professor!" Alex swivels around on her stool at the kitchen island, throwing her arms in the air. "Dude, this house is sick! That basement theater? Yeah, that's officially my new room. I'm moving in. Hope you and Zinnie don't mind."

Zinneerah abandons her mittens on the counter to sign, *Welcome home.*

"Thank you," I say, setting the boxes of donuts down. "And Alex, you're always welcome to stay. Both of you are."

Ophelia, who's perched beside Alex, whistles. "Julie, get over here for a second."

I glance over my shoulder as Juliette—the spitting image of her mother, down to the golden curls and those ocean-blue, big-as-the-moon eyes—jumps off the couch and pads into the kitchen. "Hi, Professor."

I look at Alex, whose grin is bordering on devilish, before turning back to Juliette. "It's nice to meet you, Juliette. You can call me Raees. Or Uncle Raees. Whatever works for you."

She stares up at me, her little hand gripping mine in a surprisingly firm handshake. Her eyes get wider, like she's just solved a mystery. "You really do look like Superman . . ."

"What?"

"It's nothing," Ophelia interjects. "We were just comparing you to Clark Kent when Zinnie showed us a picture of you."

Zinneerah can't catch a break when it comes to her friends' unfiltered comments. *She watches many movies. Compare people to actors everywhere we go.*

"She's talking shit, isn't she?" Alex asks, leaning over the kitchen island to pinch Zinneerah's cheek. My wife swats her hand away, but she's laughing.

"Uncle Raees." Juliette tugs at my hand. "Can I please have a donut?"

"Yes, of course. They're for all of you." I grab the box of strawberry-glazed and sprinkle-covered donuts off the counter and crouch down to her level. "Which one's your favorite?"

"Mmm." Juliette pauses, pointing a finger as she sing-songs her way through eenie-meenie-miney-moe. Her little arm hovers over the box for a full ten seconds before she plucks out a pink-and-blue sprinkle donut like it's a prize. "This one!"

I ruffle her curls. "Knock yourself out."

"Thank you!" She beams at me, grabs a second donut, and skips off toward the TV.

"Zinnie tells us you've got a sweet tooth, Raees," Ophelia says.

I glance at Zinneerah, who's suddenly very interested in the ceiling and is twirling a strand of her hair. What's she nervous about? The sweet tooth thing? Please. I love that she talks about me to her friends. Hell, if she's pulling out pictures of me, even better.

"Sweet *teeth*," I correct, biting back a grin. "I could put away this whole box of donuts in one sitting if I wasn't being monitored so closely by Mrs. Shaan over there." I take out a Boston Cream and hold it up like a trophy. "This is my only dessert tonight. She's keeping my glucose intake on lockdown."

It is for your own good, she signs.

"I know, I know." I shrug and take a bite of the donut, brushing past her back. "Thank you for taking care of me."

"Oh," Alex croons, leaning closer to Ophelia. "Look at that. Zinnie's blushing."

Zinneerah presses her lips together, like she's holding something back. Her eyes narrow, and for a second, I think she's going to say whatever's dancing on her tongue. Instead, she scoffs, rolls her eyes, and heads straight for the pantry.

She's blushing. She'll deny it, but I know what I saw. That blush is staying with me for days.

"How was work, Professor?" Alex asks, sliding onto one of the stools. "Didn't see you on campus today. Let me guess, hiding in your office again?"

"Marking assignments," I say, grabbing a napkin to wipe my mouth. "How was practice?"

"Daniels wants to hear us perform tomorrow afternoon," Ophelia grumbles. "Apparently, we need to incorporate an orchestra into our pieces."

"Because Daniels is never wrong," Alex adds, spinning the stool halfway around and back again. "When he speaks, it's like gospel. Honestly, I'm surprised we don't all genuflect when he walks into the room."

I glance at Zinneerah, who's suddenly hyper-focused on digging through the pantry.

"I think adding an orchestra is a great idea," I say. "It'll elevate the performance. Will I be hearing any originals this time?"

Alex doesn't answer, but Ophelia's brow arches. "Wait, you didn't tell him anything?"

Zinneerah freezes, still facing the pantry. She licks her lips, stalling, and starts fidgeting with her fingers. Guilty as hell.

"We haven't exactly had time for a proper conversation," I say for her. It's true. I've been drowning in work with exam season around the corner, and Zinneerah's been neck-deep in her music again.

Alex finally speaks up. "To answer your question: yes. We're performing two originals—one Zinneerah and I wrote together—and three pieces from my setlist with my band. You know, the one you heard at the concert." She spins again, this time in lazy, wobbly circles. "Now, thanks to Daniels, we've gotta work overtime to get the orchestra up to speed. Teach them all the chords and scales and shit."

Ophelia smacks her arm. "Language."

"Scales and *stuff*," she reiterates, holding her hands up in mock surrender.

"Either way, you'll all do fantastic. I'm looking forward to hearing the final production," I say. Alex grins and gives me a bow from her seat, nearly losing her balance in the process. "And I'd love to stay and chat, but there's a staff thing I've got to attend in a few hours."

"Oh, cool. Where are you going?"

"A hockey game," I reply, grabbing my mug from the counter. Alex's head snaps up. "Wait, *you're* going to a hockey game?"

"Yep."

"With other humans?"

"Yes, Alex. With other humans."

My wife's hand movements catch my eyes. *Amazing.* Zinneerah's eyes sparkle. *We are both hanging out with friends tonight.*

"Yeah, it's fun," I mumble, though I'm not sure who I'm trying to convince. "I don't know what time I'll be home. I'll probably try to leave early. You know how my social battery is."

Zinneerah purses her lips. *Who's going?*

I lean back against the counter, rubbing the back of my neck. "The journalism department. A couple from engineering. Some business profs. Big group. Don't worry, I'll leave a breadcrumb trail if I get lost."

She chuckles, covering her mouth with one hand. Her laugh, even without sound, is still the best part of my day. *That is good to know. I hope you have fun*, she signs. *But not too much fun.*

I let out a low laugh. "Oh, don't worry. I can guarantee a total lack of fun."

Her brows lift. *Try.*

"I will." For her, I'll give it a shot. The thought of canceling has definitely crossed my mind—God, it'd be so easy. But I can't do that. My wife's got her own plans tonight. The last thing she needs is me being a flake.

Ramishah's right, even when I don't want her to be. I need to start building my own circle. Friends who are reliable. Trustworthy. The kind of people I'd actually feel good about inviting over for a weekend barbecue. Not just acquaintances I nod at in the hallway or colleagues I tolerate over bad coffee in the breakroom.

Though, I won't lie and say I'm not nervous.

After a quick shower, I throw on a white t-shirt, a loose black sweater, and a pair of jeans (yes, I've been shamelessly taking style notes from Zinneerah's Pinterest boards lately).

Once I'm dressed, I head downstairs. Laughter blooms from the basement, the muffled sound of a movie playing in the home theater.

Rather than disturbing their peace, I shoot Zinneerah a text.

Me: Heading out now. I'll text when I get there and when I'm on my way back.

I'm halfway through tying my shoes when the basement door creaks open, and Zinneerah steps out.

"Hey," I say, straightening up. "I'm sorry, I didn't mean to pull you away from the movie."

You're fine. I've memorized W-A-L-L-E by now.

"It's a classic," I say, pulling on my jacket. "A cinematic masterpiece."

Her gaze flickers towards me. *We should watch it. Together.*

I blink. That's . . . unexpected. She blinks, too, like she's trying to take the words back but can't.

"I'd love that," I say quickly, meeting her halfway.

She chews her bottom lip. *I'm sorry. Forgot to tell you more about the concert.*

"You don't have to apologize for that, Zinneerah." I take a step closer, softening my voice. "You've got so much to look forward to, reuniting with your band, playing again, it's okay to get caught up in it."

Her eyes drop to my neck, scanning the space just past me. It's something she does when she's unsure of herself, trying to avoid being read too closely.

"Hey?"

She looks up at me, finally meeting my eyes.

"Much better," I say with a small smile.

That's all it takes. Her lips tug upward, and my entire week is made. *Enjoy the game.*

"If you tune in on TV, you might catch me dozing off," I quip.

Her shoulders rise in a small laugh. *You'll do fine. O-P-H-E-L-I-A loves hockey. We will watch the last bit.*

I wish I could bring her with me. She'd make the whole thing more bearable. But for now, all I can do is linger. "I'll see you tonight. If I'm late, don't wait up, okay? Go to sleep."

She does this thing where she waits for me if I'm past the 10 p.m. mark, hanging around the kitchen or living room like she's keeping the house awake until I get home. It makes me feel a certain kind of way, knowing she does that, but I'd rather her rest.

Goodnight.

"Goodnight, Zinneerah."

She gifts me one last smile, before disappearing back down the basement stairs.

I catch a glimpse of myself in the shoe closet mirror as I grab my keys, my reflection staring back with a goofy grin.

"She wants to watch Wall-E with me."

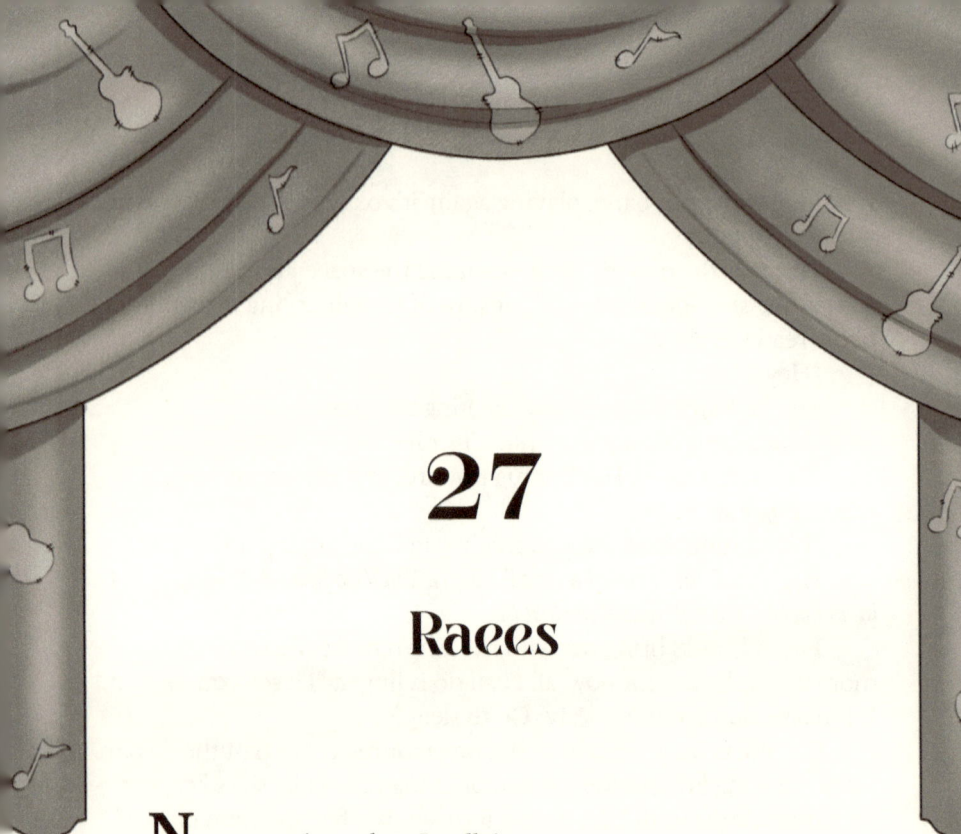

27

Races

No one notices when I walk in.

Not a single glance in my direction considering how tirelessly they've been about getting me out.

It's fine.

I didn't come here to be the life of the party. I came to try—keyword: *try*—to make some kind of social connection with these people. To feel like I belong with them outside the department, at least a little.

I weave my way through the crowd, brushing past a sea of Toronto Titan jerseys mixed with Detroit Dragons merch. Titans versus Dragons. The names alone sound like the kind of fantasy battle you'd find on the back of a paperback novel. Fitting, I guess—mythical, like their chances of beating an actual powerhouse team: The Florida Panthers. That's Ramishah and Harry's team.

Stop. Enough of that. No room for cynicism tonight.

Who knows? Maybe by the end of this, I'll walk out a hockey fan. Stranger things have happened.

I rub my fingers together as I close in on the group.

They're standing in one of those loose, impenetrable circles that's more wall than conversation.

I recognize a few faces: Giovanni Paldoni, the head of the engineering department, and a man whose laugh you can hear three offices away; Victoria Rhodes, who I think teaches thermodynamics; and Ben Nguyen, whose name I only remember because he introduced himself at a seminar by making a pun about Newton's Laws.

Giovanni is mid-story when I step up, but no one adjusts to let me in. I stick to hovering awkwardly at the edge. "—and I told her, 'Babe, I'll bring home the dough, and you can bake the pies.' You know what I mean?" The group laughs, as if Gio's delivered this punchline a hundred times. He notices me immediately given I'm the only one not laughing. "Well, look who decided to crawl out of his cave. The hermit himself!"

I force a smile. "Figured I'd take a night off," I say, nodding politely around the group.

"From the wife?" Gio slaps my arm, hard enough to make me flinch. "Congrats, by the way."

The group laughs again, and I can't tell if it's at me.

"Thanks," I mutter, stepping back slightly. My hand goes to my arm instinctively, rubbing at the spot where he hit me.

"We're glad you could make it," someone says to me. Professor Harrison. No, wait. Just Dave. He's got a splotch of mustard on his chin that catches the light every time he moves.

I open my mouth to say something, but Jenna beats me to it. She points it out with a quick laugh, and the group erupts into chuckles.

I stand there, hands shoved in my pockets, watching the conversation continue like I'm not even there. Maybe tonight isn't the night. Or maybe I'm not cut out for this kind of thing.

Find a way to make yourself part of the circle. It's just a conversation, not an interrogation.

But Gio's making it a challenge. "So, I look at the guy and say, 'You really think you're gonna out-engineer me? Good luck, buddy.' And he actually had the balls to try!"

My God, how many stories does this man have?

Jenna, standing to my left, glances at me briefly. I think it's encouragement, or maybe she's just checking if I still want to be here. Either way, it feels like an opening.

I straighten my shoulders a little and step closer, trying to look like I belong. "That's bold," I say, pitching my voice louder. "Did he actually give it a shot?"

Gio doesn't even look at me. He fires right on, like I hadn't said anything at all. "And then he brings out this duct-taped contraption, like he's MacGyver or something. I mean, come on, man."

The laughter swells again, and I feel myself deflate. I glance at Adam, but he's smiling politely at Gio, his drink cradled in one hand. I wait, thinking maybe someone will loop back to my comment. But the conversation keeps moving, leaving me behind.

Victoria shifts, turning a bit, and her elbow catches my arm—not hard, but enough to make me step back.

"Oh, sorry," I mumble, automatically.

She doesn't even notice. She's already responding to Gio, saying something about her own department's ongoing rivalry with another university. I stand there, rubbing my arm where her elbow landed, feeling more invisible by the second.

I take another breath. *Fine. Another try.*

I made sure to research in the parking lot to strike up this specific conversation. "So, uh, how about last night's game?" I say, aiming this one at Ben, who's standing a little to my right. "That save in the second period was something—"

"Hang on, hang on," Ben says, holding up a hand as he turns to Victoria. "But did you see North Haven's campus renovations? A ten-story library, people. Ten stories."

His words bulldoze right over mine, and the group shifts again, pulling closer together. I'm pushed just slightly to the outside. Not far, but enough to make it clear I'm not really in this circle.

"Okay. Cool." I take a half-step back, letting the gap widen.

Someone brushes past me from behind—a guy in a Dragons jersey holding a tray of nachos. One of his nacho chips drops onto my shoe. Without apologizing, he just walks off.

I stare at the chip for a second, half-considering leaving it there just for the metaphor. But no, that's pathetic. I nudge it off with the edge of my other shoe and stand there, hands back in my pockets, pretending I don't feel ridiculous.

"Raees!"

I groan inwardly and turn around.

Saira's coming toward me, walking fast, one hand trying to keep her purse from sliding off her shoulder.

Great. Just great. Because I made a rule tonight about not calling anyone "Professor" after hours, I'll have to extend the courtesy to her.

She stops short, eyes wide, and then, of course, cue the commentary. "Raees Shaan in jeans? Never thought I'd live to see it."

I hold her gaze, but her comparing me to my father echoes in my skull, dredging up memories of my panic attack I don't need tonight.

Not here. I shove it down. Hard. Play it cool. Stick to the rules of polite society.

"My wife dug them out of the closet."

"She's got great taste," Saira says, brushing past me. She glides over to the engineering department professors, arms wide, pulling them into hugs like she's been part of their inner circle for years.

Then again, that's Saira. She never had to work for connections the way the rest of us do. Back in the day, her friends became my friends. Thick as thieves. Loyal, at least to her. Never mind their leader was a cheater. *Dial it back, Raees.*

The group starts filing into the row of seats, exactly where Saira said we'd be. Top tier, a clear view of the action. Out of the ten seats in our designated row, we occupy seven.

I claim the aisle seat. Easy escape route if I need to cut out early. My social tolerance has limits, and tonight's already testing them.

Sliding my phone out of my pocket, I thumb a quick text to Zinneerah.

Me: At the game.

I snap a picture of the rink, the players stretching, the cool gleam of the ice under the stadium lights, and attach it.

Sent.

"Perfect seats, huh?" Saira says from my side, catching me off guard. When did she sit next to me?

I glance sideways, then lean forward slightly, scanning the row. Giovanni's parked on her other side, chatting with one of the professors. The rest of the row is filled out—professors, a couple I don't recognize, and their kid wriggling in the last seat.

Saira tucks a loose strand of hair behind her ear, already pulling the rest into a quick ponytail. "Marcus put the whole thing together, but the seats are all me." She digs around in her purse, fishing for something. "Michael Jones—his dad's an investor here. He gets comp tickets to pretty much everything. Hockey, concerts, Broadway shows. You name it, he's got it."

Her hand emerges with a small mirror and lipstick, and she pops them open like it's a ritual.

"I see," I murmur, watching the players line up for a drill.

She dabs on the lipstick, her eyes never leaving the mirror. "Remember *Hamilton*? You were fuming when it was sold out." The compact snaps shut. "Next day? Ta-dah. Tickets in your hand. That was Michael, too. A little networking works wonders."

I run my hands through my hair, letting out a slow breath as the exasperation churns beneath my ribs.

I don't even like musicals, especially not something as mind-numbing as *Hamilton*. The only reason I'd even bothered trying to score those tickets was because it had been her birthday weekend. That's it. A gesture. A thoughtful, good boyfriend move. And when she'd popped up, skipping, squealing with her own stupid tickets in hand, flapping them around like a golden prize, I'd wanted to crawl into a hole and disappear.

It wasn't just the tickets. It was everything. No matter what I did, no matter how hard I tried, it always seemed to fall short. Like I wasn't enough. If it wasn't her family or her high-powered friends filling in the gaps, it was someone else. Always someone else.

My phone buzzes in my pocket.

I pull it out, and it's like the invisible leash cinching around my throat loosens.

Love of my life: Us too.

Her reply comes with a picture: Ophelia leaning forward, laser-focused on the home theater screen, the glow of the pre-game highlights lighting her face. Juliette's curled up, half-asleep on Alex's lap, her head resting against her shoulder.

Me: The next hockey game, we're all going. I'm not taking 'no' for an answer.

The ellipsis bubbles pop up almost immediately. She's typing. Typing for a while.

Love of my life: I've been to a few at the arena. They served these chocolate pretzels in a cup that I ate. Ophelia yelled at the players like it was life or death, and Alex spent half the time trying to get herself on the kiss cam. It wasn't really about the game (except for Ophelia). It was about supporting each other's—

"Nope." Gio plucks the phone right out of my hand. "No texting while watching the Titans get their asses handed to them."

"Give me my phone back," I say as calmly as possible.

Inside, I want to plant a fist square in his smug face. The memory of Abbu flickers in my mind—him snatching Ammi-ji's phone out of my hands mid-Tetris game, not because he cared if I was playing, but because he wanted to make sure she wasn't texting someone else. That acidic knot tightens in my gut, but I shove it down.

He arches a brow. "Will you focus on the game if I do?"

"Giovanni," I say, jaw tightening, "my phone. Now."

"Give him back his phone," Saira intervenes. "The game hasn't even started yet."

His jaw tightens, then he holds my phone out like he's doing me a favor. I snatch it back, gripping it tighter than necessary. "Jesus, man," he mutters, throwing up a hand. "I was just playing."

"It's not nice," Saira adds, crossing her legs and shooting him a glare that's borderline playful rather than irritated. "What if I took your phone?"

That stupid grin returns, sliding onto his face like oil. He pulls his phone out of his pocket and offers it to her with a tilt of his head. "Just give it back with your number."

Saira snorts, shoving his face to the side with one hand like swatting a fly.

She's laughing. He's laughing. And then there's me, sitting in this godforsaken row of seats, pretending I don't notice. Pretending I'm not watching this tiny flirtation unfold.

Gio's got a wife. Kids in high school. He's married to someone who sees him as a dependable husband, not . . . this. And Saira knows that. It's not surprising that she has a way of brushing off the boundaries people cling to. It's just disappointing.

Ignoring the two, I finish reading Zinneerah's message.

Love of my life: I've been to a few at the arena. They served these chocolate pretzels in a cup that I ate. Ophelia yelled at the players like it was life or death, and Alex spent half the time trying to get herself on the kiss cam. It wasn't really about the game (except for Ophelia). It was about supporting each other's ridiculous hobbies, even if we didn't give a single shit about men chasing a puck with sticks.

I chuckle to myself, fingers dancing over the keyboard. What I wouldn't do to hear my wife curse in real time.

Me: You guys are different fonts writing the exact same story.

Saira nudges me with her elbow, pulling me back. She gestures toward the ice with a tilt of her chin, as if to say, *Focus.*

I sigh. As much as I hate to admit it, she's got a point. This is an outing I committed to, isn't it? The tickets, the seats, the awkward camaraderie—it's all part of the package. I'll talk to Zinneerah when I'm home, when my head's quieter, when it's just the two of us again.

Right now, it's hockey. And my co-workers. Some of them, anyway.

I type out one last message.

Me: I'll see you once I'm home. Enjoy your night. I'll try to enjoy mine. Maybe I'll get cotton candy. Who knows?

Thirty minutes pass in a blur.

The jumbo screens above the rink become the real show between breaks, pulling everyone's attention away from the ice.

First, it's the Kiss Cam, which is always a disaster. Two adults down the row awkwardly laugh when it lands on them, pretending they don't know each other well enough for the crowd to start chanting, "Kiss! Kiss!" Eventually, the camera moves on, sparing them the embarrassment.

Next is the Dance Cam, zooming in on a teenage boy in a hoodie who looks like he wants to sink into the ground. His mom shoves him out of his seat, and the crowd roars when he finally gives in and starts flailing his arms like an inflatable tube man to some dubstep track.

Then comes Celebrity Lookalike Cam.

"Oh, my god, Dave!" Jenna exclaims, choking on her nachos.

"What?" Dave looks up from his phone, blinking.

The screen splits, showing Dave on one side, and Alice Cooper on the other. The resemblance is uncanny—stringy black hair, a sharp jawline, even the same unhinged stare.

The crowd bursts out laughing, and Dave throws up his hands. "That's not me!"

"It is you!" Jenna says, gasping for air between laughs. "I mean, look at that hair! You're twins!"

Someone further down the row adds, "Where's your guitar, man?"

Even I crack a smile, though I feel bad for the guy. He's going to hear about this for the rest of his life.

Finally, the Mascot Showdown begins.

The Toronto Titan with his tusks stomps into the arena. The crowd goes wild as he flexes his ridiculous foam muscles and jabs his fingers toward the opposing team's bench, a challenge clear in his over-the-top movements.

Across the rink, the Detroit Dragons' mascot—a hulking red dragon with golden spots—accepts the dare, stomping onto the ice to face off.

The jumbo screen flashes "DANCE BATTLE!" and the arena erupts with cheers.

The Titan mascot starts things off, shimmying his hips and throwing in some clumsy arm waves. The Dragon counters with an aggressive floss dance, its tail wagging behind it in perfect synchronization.

"Let's fucking go, Titan!" Gio yells, pumping his fist in the air.

The Titan mascot attempts a worm but gets stuck halfway, his foam belly preventing him from finishing the move. The opposing crowd mocks him with laughter.

I just hope the man inside that costume is being paid well.

The dance-off escalates, both mascots shaking their butts and flailing their oversized limbs.

Finally, the Titan throws his arms up in exaggerated defeat, slumping dramatically onto the stairs. Our side cheers, egging him on with chants of "Titan! Titan!" while the opposing section erupts in victorious boos.

When does the actual game start?

"So, Raees," Giovanni drawls. I glance at him, already bracing myself for whatever garbage is about to tumble out of his mouth. Saira left with Marcus to grab hot dogs. I should've gone with them, and locked myself in the bathroom stall until the game started. "How's everything going with that newly-wed status of yours? Huh? You gonna introduce us to the lucky lady?"

I've learned not to give people like Giovanni anything to latch onto. If anything, Professor Holmes is the only one I confide in. But here we are. "It's going great," I say.

"Good, good." Giovanni leans forward now, like he's been waiting all night for this conversation. "You enjoying yourself?" His eyes flick toward Saira's empty seat, and I already know I don't want to hear what he's about to say. "She's been eye-fucking you since you sat down. Makes me jealous." He gives my chest a friendly smack with the back of his hand. Again. "Relax, I'm just playing with you. Married, remember?"

I take a deep breath. Count to three in my head. The last time I let my temper slip, I ended up breaking my father's nose. It took years of therapy to unlearn that instinct. But Giovanni? He's pushing it. He's really pushing it.

"That's highly inappropriate, Giovanni," I say, meeting his gaze dead-on. "I'd appreciate it if you didn't make those kinds of jokes with me."

"Why the fuck are you so uptight? Jesus Christ, Raees." Giovanni slouches lower in his seat, like I'm the one ruining his night. His feet kick up onto the empty chair in front of him, sneakers squeaking against the plastic. The chair belongs to an elderly woman who left with her grandson to grab food.

Real classy.

I narrow my eyes at him. "Can you put your feet down? There's someone sitting there."

"Yeah? Who?" He doesn't even bother looking at me, his attention glued to his phone. Probably texting someone who isn't his wife.

Before I can say anything else, Saira's voice rings out. "I'm back!" she sing-songs, squeezing past my knees to slide back into her seat. She holds a tray with two hot dogs and a pile of nachos precariously balanced in her lap.

Giovanni's entire demeanor shifts as soon as she sits down, like a dog catching sight of a steak.

He reaches over and snatches a nacho from her tray.

"Hey, that's mine!" Saira whines.

He doesn't even flinch. Just grins and grabs a second nacho, popping it into his mouth.

Saira glares at him and turns the tray away, angling it toward me instead. "Nacho?" She holds it out like a peace offering.

"I'm fine, thank you."

"You haven't eaten anything," she presses, plucking a chip coated in guacamole and holding it up like she's about to feed me. "I can hear your stomach growling from here."

"It's fine," I repeat, leaning back to put some space between me and the nacho. The last thing I need is Giovanni jumping in with some crass comment about her hand-feeding me.

Beside her, he lets out a bark of laughter. "Oh, that's gotta hurt," he says, gesturing at the screen above the rink. On it, the Kiss Cam has zeroed in on a couple. The man leans in for a kiss, but the woman slaps her hand over his mouth like she's blocking a punch. The crowd erupts with laughter and groans. "If Nina did that to me, she'd be sleeping on the couch for a month."

"I'm surprised she isn't already," Saira mutters under her breath, loud enough for both of us to hear.

I take the nacho she offered earlier and crunch into it, anything to distract myself from Giovanni's ego-fueled commentary.

God, I am hungry. Maybe I'll grab some chocolate pretzels or cotton candy, something to keep my brain occupied so I don't spiral.

Just as I stand to make my escape, a shadow looms over me.

The Toronto Titan.

He blocks the aisle with his ridiculous blue body, wagging his massive furry finger at me like I've just been caught sneaking out of class.

Before I can even process it, his oversized paw lands heavily on my shoulder, pressing me back into my seat.

What the hell is going on?

I freeze, gripping the armrests instinctively, just as Jenna exclaims, "Raees, look! You're on the screen!"

What?

I glance up at the giant screen above the rink, and my stomach plunges like I've just missed a step on a staircase.

The Kiss Cam. It's on me.

It's on me and Saira.

Fuck.

My heart slams against my ribs to escape. The arena's noise—cheers, laughs, the occasional heckle—all collapses into an incessant throb in the back of my head. The only thing I can hear are my own laboured breaths, like I've just run a hundred miles.

"Kiss, kiss, kiss!" chants the damn Titan mascot, his furry hand still clamped on my shoulder.

This isn't happening. This can't be happening.

Saira shifts beside me, and I can feel every eye in the section locked on us. My face burns, their stares pressing down harder than the mascot's hand.

"Hey, if you won't take it, I will." Giovanni's hyena laughter isn't helping the situation.

"I'm married." I'm talking to the mascot, the *mascot*, which is officially the most absurd thing I've ever done. "Find someone else."

The Titan just keeps pointing at the screen, motioning for me to stay put. His unrelenting hand pins me down, and my chest tightens. Why is he so hell-bent on me?

"Let go—" I start, my voice wobbling as I push against his arm. My breathing is too fast, my palms sweating against the armrests to the point they're slipping. My brain is screaming, *Everyone is watching! Everyone sees you!*

I'm about four seconds away from a full-blown panic attack when Saira finally leans in. "It's okay," she whispers, like she's talking to a cornered animal. "Just play along for a second."

My entire body goes stiff as she presses her lips against my cheek in what feels like slow motion, the crowd erupting into cheers and wolf-whistles.

It's over in an instant, but it feels like an eternity.

The Titan finally removes his paw from my shoulder, stepping back and raising his arms in victory, like he's the hero of the night. The crowd cheers as the camera mercifully pans to another couple, and the pressure of the arena's collective gaze finally disappears.

I shove Saira away as I stand, but my legs feel shaky, like they might buckle under me. "What is wrong with you?" The question jumps out louder than I expected. "How could you do such a thing in front of everyone?"

She has the audacity to be shocked.

Giovanni stands. "Relax, Shaan—"

"Fuck you, Giovanni!" The venomous sound cuts through the arena noise like a gunshot.

Heads turn. Conversations die mid-sentence. Phones lower. Eyes lock on me from every direction, like heat-seeking missiles.

The professors—the same people who know I'm married, the same ones who were clapping and cheering just seconds ago—are staring.

And then, one by one, they start looking away, down at their drinks, their snacks, the rink. Pretending like they weren't just watching this train wreck.

But I know they saw. They all fucking saw. And they didn't bother stopping it.

"Raees, I'm sorry," Saira says quickly. "I didn't mean—"

I don't stick around to hear the rest of that sentence.

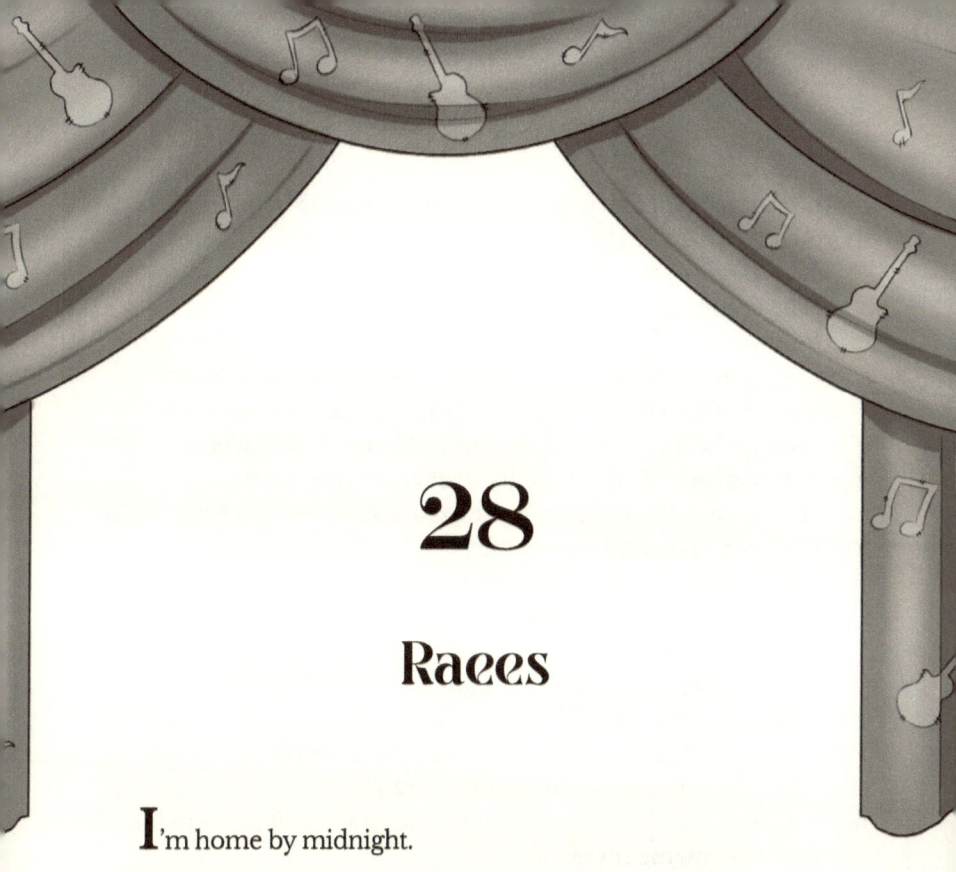

28

Races

I'm home by midnight.

The evening ended as predictably as it began: poorly.

I spent the better part of an hour driving in purposeless circles around the city before resigning myself to texting Zinneerah to say I was on my way home. She didn't reply, which likely means she's already asleep. Sensible of her since she has practice in the morning.

I, on the other hand, have classes to teach. How I'm going to summon the dignity to face a roomful of students—students who've just started to like me—after tonight's entirely valid outburst is a dilemma for future-me.

Present-me is too busy sulking in the driveway, holding a cup of chocolate pretzels for my wife that I bought after spending thirty minutes trying to calm myself down in the arena's bathroom.

I sit in the car for a few minutes, forehead pressed to the steering wheel like a penitent. My face still stings from the thirty rounds I spent scrubbing it. Soap can clean a face; it can't erase the mortification of memory. Trust me, I've tested this hypothesis thoroughly.

This is *exactly* why I hate going out.

The entire thing was doomed from the start.

Anywhere with Saira is an emotional minefield, and I have the scars to prove it. She thrives on the kind of attention that leaves everyone else ducking for cover. She's impulsive, inconsiderate, oblivious to the inner lives of anyone but herself. Even when we were together, she had this tiresome habit of answering questions on my behalf: *Oh, Raees doesn't like rollercoasters. Raees isn't really a party person. Raees only reads pretentious old classics.*

All perfectly engineered to present me as boring, aloof, and insufferable in the eyes of others.

Well, that's the answer. That's why I stopped trying.

Somewhere along the line, I convinced myself I'd become a man whose presence would add no life to a party, no thrill to an amusement park, and no debate to even the most niche of book clubs. I've spent so long in her shadow, craning my neck to stare up at her brilliance, that I've gone blind. Squinting at the light for so long, I stopped recognizing myself altogether.

Tonight was supposed to be different. Tonight, I was going to prove that I could stand on my own two feet, that I could speak to someone other than an audience of students. I wanted to make Ramishah proud; to show her I could forge a connection that wasn't built on lecture notes and office hours. I even thought, foolishly, that I might enjoy myself as per Zinneerah's request.

A laughable notion, really.

Now here I sit, glasses in hand, grinding my palms into my eyes as though I can physically press the embarrassment out of my skull.

Deep breaths, Raees. In and out.

I have no idea how I managed to drive for three hours with another panic attack rattling my bones. There were fleeting moments where the thought occurred to me: *just swerve into traffic, let it end there. Or park at the edge of some cliffside beach and stare down into the abyss below.*

Down, down, down.

I'm thirty-five, but tonight, I feel horribly close to my eighteen-year-old self.

With a sharp sniff, I reach for a tissue, wiping my eyes forcefully, then attack the streaks on my cheek like they're stains I can scrub away. The sweater, now contaminated by Giovanni's relentless smacking, has officially become collateral damage. Off it goes.

My car door creaks open, and I'm met with the symphony of crickets and the occasional Doppler whine of a car speeding toward somewhere else.

I pause outside the front door, filling my lungs with the crisp night air as though oxygen might somehow restore my composure.

With a quick swipe under the eyes, though I suspect no one is awake to notice, I step inside.

Zinneerah sits halfway up the staircase.

"Fuck!" My heart leaps in my chest before I regain myself, exhaling sharply. "Oh, my god." My hand tightens on the door handle, and I let out a strained chuckle. "Zinneerah, you scared me."

She doesn't respond. A blank canvas where I'd hoped to find some hint of what she's thinking.

Then, her fingers lift: *Come here.*

I close the door behind me, kick off my shoes, and ascend the staircase, sitting one step below her.

My legs stretch out in front of me, ankles crossed, a forced attempt at nonchalance I don't feel. "I brought you those chocolate pretzels you like. They're a bit cold now. And I also ate three. Sorry."

Zinneerah takes the cup and sets it aside, singing, *Thank you.*

"I've never sat here before. It's not bad. A bit comfortable, actually." I lean back, letting my head rest against the wall. The temptation to bang it there rises, but I resist. "I thought we agreed you wouldn't wait up for me. Why aren't you in bed?"

Just stare, stare, staring.

Finally, she tilts her head, her dark eyes softening. She raises her hand, and I catch sight of red indentations carved into her fingerprints from the grooves of her guitar strings.

When her soft hand touches my cheek, I dissolve.

What's wrong? I sign back, caught somewhere between words and the threat of breaking. *Did you see it?*

She nods.

Of course, she saw it. Of course. She'd been watching the game with her Ophelia. She had to sit at home and watch my ex-fiancée kiss my cheek, *live*, in front of hundreds of people. Thousands, maybe. By now, the clip has undoubtedly made its way online, circulating through every corner of the internet. If I end up in one of those obnoxious compilation videos, I swear to God, I'll personally walk into YouTube's headquarters and demand every last trace of that footage be erased.

But none of that matters right now.

What matters is my wife.

"Zinneerah." I squeeze my eyes shut. My knees bend, elbows sinking onto them as I rake my fingers through my hair, gripping tight enough to sting. "I didn't know she'd do that. I didn't—God, I tried to leave. To step away from it. If you saw it, if you watched—" The stones gathering in my throat cut me off.

A light tap on my knee pulls me back.

I open my foggy eyes, meeting hers. *I told you not to have too much fun*, she signs, her lips curled up in a wry, fractured smile.

"*Fun?* That's the last word I'd use," I whisper, head shaking. "It was awful. Everyone wanted something from me, but when I was there, none of them cared to see me." My hand gestures vaguely, words faltering. "I know everything about them—how many kids they have, which of their teachers traumatized them in high school, their goddamn golf handicaps."

My wedding ring catches against my knuckle as I twist it back and forth. "And maybe it's my fault," I mumble, staring at the floor. "Maybe I should've tried harder. Made more of an effort. That's what keeps playing in my head—that if I'd spoken up, if I'd just pushed through, I could've stopped freezing like some awkward idiot." I rub my hand over my face, swallowing the knot in my throat. "I wish I could take it back. Reverse everything. Stay home and watch *Wall-E* with you instead."

Zinneerah huffs a soft, pitiful chuckle. *Do not push yourself to make other people happy*, she signs. *You are perfect the way you are.*

She inches her sleeve down to cover her palm, then gently dabs at my cheeks. Her gaze doesn't waver as her hands form the next words. *A friend to all is a friend to no one. I've learned that lesson the hard way. I don't want the same for you.*

All I can give her is a smile. "Your friends are great. I appreciate when Alex lights up in my presence. It's adorable."

They only have great things to say about you. Your looks most of the time. She purses her lips. *J-U-L-I-E-T-T-E is convinced you're Superman.*

I chuckle, tipping my head back. Somehow, just looking at Zinneerah clears my head. The migraine that's been clawing at me all night loses its battle against my wife's presence.

We just . . . stare at each other. It's not like her to hold eye contact for this long. It isn't her first language, nor her second or third. A year and a half of knowing one another, and this feels like the first time she's truly letting me see her.

And she looks incredibly at home.

I plant my fist on my chest, and circle it slowly. I'm sorry.

Her hand brushes my shoulder. *Not your fault*, she signs. Then she stands, handing me the pretzels with a smile. *Sleep now.*

"Okay," I whisper. "Goodnight."

She nods, already halfway up the stairs, and I let myself stand using the banister.

But then she stops, turning just enough for me to notice.

Trepidation rises in my chest. Is she holding back her frustration? Is she about to tell me she's not okay with what happened? That she needs time, or worse—distance?

I step closer, gripping the railing. "Zinneerah."

She pauses, her shoulders rising and falling with a deep breath.

I move closer, gripping the railing, unsure of what's coming but needing her to say something.

She turns to look over shoulder, a smile on her lips.

"Raees," she says—*says*. "I trust you with my whole entire heart."

Before I can recover, she disappears upstairs, leaving me standing there like an idiot with my mouth half-open.

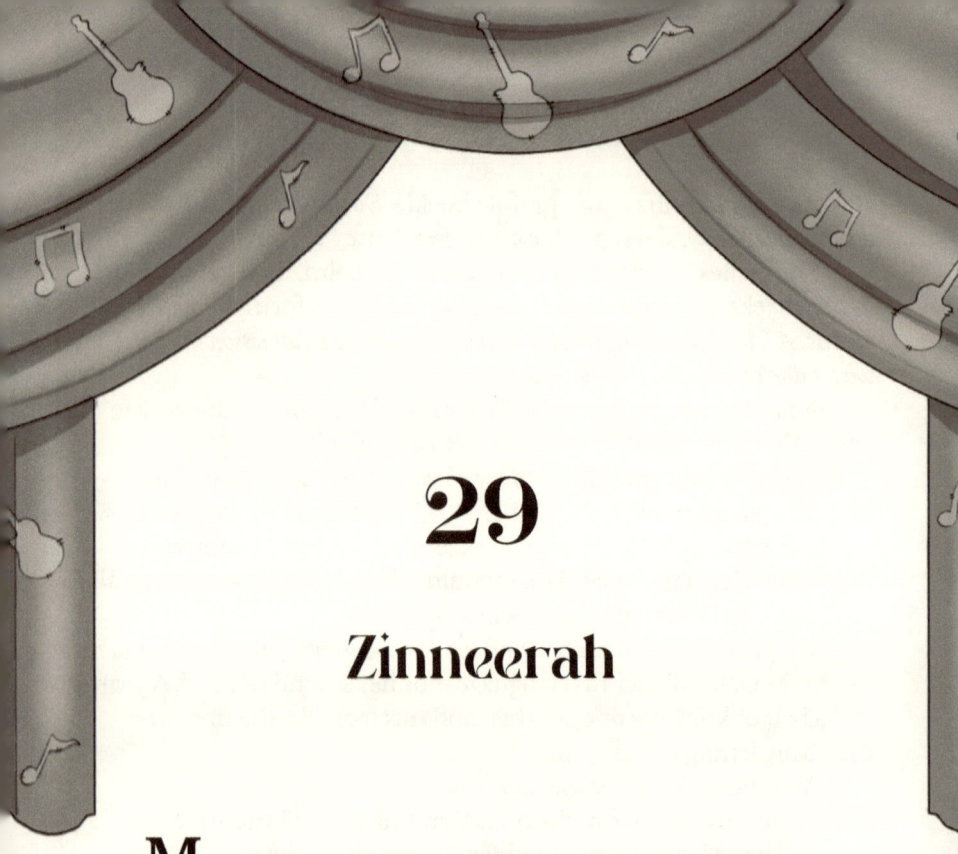

29

Zinneerah

Music filters through the practice room, looping itself between the thump of Ophelia's drumbeat and the honeyed resonance of Alex's piano. My foot bobs in time against the worn wooden floor, as I tug at the strings of my acoustic guitar, letting the notes melt between their melodies.

In the dark behind my eyelids, it's just me and Baba. He's sitting alone in the front row of an empty auditorium, his hands clasped tightly, watching me play. For him, I'd play forever. Each practice chips away at the nerves, loosening them like old strings of a leather journal.

Soon, I tell myself. Soon, I'll be able to open my eyes, meet the crowd's gaze, and finally stop living on the inside of my own head.

"Woooooh!" Alex's clap slices through my thoughts, a jolt of espresso to my daydream. She swivels on the piano bench. "That was perfection, ladies. Actual perfection. Daddy Daniels is going to *lose* his mind at the concert. He'll have no choice but to put us on the syllabus permanently."

"Please, for the love of all things holy, don't call our professor 'Daddy.'" Ophelia sticks out her tongue and jabs a drumstick toward it like she's ready to self-gag.

Alex cocks a brow, smirking. "Right, because you and knock-off Harvey Spector never role-played the whole 'lawyer and client' thing."

"That was one time!"

Alex rolls her eyes right at me. "So, did that sound fine? Or do I need to add a little more razzle-dazzle?"

"So far, so good," I say, hoisting myself up from the chair. I flip off the amplifier with a practiced flick, unplug the wire from my guitar, and start packing it up. My brow twitches at the silence behind me. "Go ahead. Spit it out."

"What the fuck happened?" Alex blurts out like a dropped vase. "It's been three days, and you haven't told us a single goddamn thing." She leans forward. "Did you guys, like, fight? Is he pissed?"

I zip my guitar bag in one smooth motion, then turn to face her. "He's just processing the fact that I can talk."

Ophelia does a *ba-dum-tsh*. "Cat's out of the bag."

"Very funny," I whisper, shooting her a look. "I can't *talk*-talk. Not yet. We haven't really . . . talked about it."

"Wait, wait, wait." Alex's hands slice through the air. "So, are you actually planning to tell him? Like, everything?"

I nod. "Soon."

"How soon?" she presses. "We're already a week into August, Zinnie. You've known him for a year and"—she counts on her fingers—"six months. A year and six months. And this is the first time you spoke to him."

The truth is, I didn't speak in front of Raees because my voice is the one thing I've never been able to face. When you grow up being told your voice is your superpower, that you'll "win hearts" and "change lives" with your singing, only to open your mouth and sound like a chain smoker who gargles gravel for fun is a little soul-crushing.

And then there's Raees, who's basically human sunshine. He's thoughtful, brilliant, a beacon of humanity. The kind of guy who makes strangers in coffee shops smile just by existing.

So, I stuck to my hands. I told myself it didn't matter—that he accepted me for who I was. But deep down, there's always been this little fear clawing at me: What if he heard me and couldn't unhear it? What if I ruined us the second I opened my mouth?

Staying silent was the only answer. And he never pushed me to speak. He never asked me to.

Until I decided two nights ago.

"You know I'm uncannily great at reading people, Zinneerah," Ophelia says. "Raees is probably the only man alive I'd say actually deserves his rights."

"Not probably, Fifi." Alex stands abruptly, her chair scraping against the floor. "He *does* deserve every right because—" She presses her lips together, biting down on her bottom one. Her fists curl at her sides.

Ophelia's gaze is as flat as a tidepool, but pinned to Alex.

"Because?" I prompt.

Alex exhales through her nose, her shoulders slumping. "Because he's great, okay?"

I sigh. "Tell me something I don't know."

Apparently done with pretending she's above melodrama, Alex drags herself over to Ophelia and flops unceremoniously onto her lap like a human-sized cat. "You're the mother of the group. Talk some sense into our child, please."

Ophelia's completely unbothered by the fact that Alex has just taken up residence on her thighs. "You need to have the conversation with Raees. He's not going to judge you for it. I know him. He'd be the biggest piece of shit to ever exist if he did."

"Wouldn't that be the plot twist of the century," Alex mutters.

"Knowing Raees?" I smile. "He'll cry."

Alex's head snaps up. "Wait. He's a crier?"

"Sensitive. Caring. Patient." Ophelia counts down on her fingers. "Probably good in other . . . sectors."

"Sextors," Alex coughs out.

"Something tickling your throat?" I ask.

"Just saying." She shrugs, clearly enjoying herself. "Instead of standing on business, maybe try bouncing on it instead."

I'm so close to sealing her lips shut with a guitar string.

Ophelia tries to reel us in. "Uni Zinnie wouldn't have touched a guy like him with a ten-foot pole—"

"Shut up, Alex," we both snap at the same time, because we already know where her brain is going, and it's nowhere helpful.

For once, Alex actually listens, her lips pressing into a tight line as she holds back what I can only assume is another borderline inappropriate comment. "Look," she says, her voice softening just a hair, "I know it's none of my business, but progress can be made. We're past baby steps now, Zinnie."

Speaking of babies. I glance at the clock and remember. "I've got Amina's birthday party," I say, hoisting my guitar bag higher onto my shoulders. "I'll update you two later."

"We're sorry," Ophelia blurts out. "If we made you uncomfortable."

I shake my head and manage a smile. "No, you're right. It's about time I told him."

Alex slides off Ophelia's lap in one fluid motion. Then, in her typical fashion, she grabs my hands and squeezes them, her grin stretching wide. "You know what this means, right?"

I tilt my head.

"Zinneerah, be honest with me." She lifts a thin brow. "Do you like him?"

Like Raees? Of course I do. He's given me no reason not to. Sensitive, caring, patient—all the things Ophelia said he was. The kind of man I thought existed only in Dua's romance books or regency movies. Especially after I swore off trusting the species altogether.

"I do."

"*No*," Alex drawls, "not that kind of like. I mean, do you have a crush on your husband? You know, all jittery, flustered, weak knees and sweaty palms, the whole 'oh, my God, he smiled at me, I'm dying thing.'"

My cheeks burn. Okay, fine. Yes. I do. A lot.

I've felt it ever since the concert.

Somewhere between the morning coffee-tea talks, his charming lopsided smile, soft touches, and childlike tendencies, I became, well, ridiculous. Like a schoolgirl clutching a diary with his name written inside a thousand times in pink glitter gel pen.

Ophelia's expression is as flat as a sheet of paper. "Someone call Nora Ephron because Zinnie is done for."

"What? No—I—" I lick my lips, suddenly parched. "I'm not—I mean . . ." How do you even argue something you can't define anymore? I'd handed the word "love" over to someone once, only to watch him twist it into something ugly. If this feeling for Raees is love, then how would I know? What if I've forgotten what it's supposed to feel like?

"As long as you're admitting you're attracted to him and genuinely like him, that's all that matters."

"Yeah, Zinnie," Alex says, fixing my hair. "I mean, shit, we love your husband, too, and we've known him for what, two weeks?"

"Yeah," Ophelia chimes in, grinning. "And I don't love many people, but Clark Kent is definitely in my top ten. I'd trust him with my drink."

"I'd trust him with my unreleased album," Alex adds. "He looks like the kind of guy who still types out W-W-W in the browser before Googling something."

He does. Oh, God, he does.

It's not something I'd consciously noticed before, but now it's all I see. I notice everything about him. The lint that clings to his sweater. The smudge on his glasses he always misses no matter how many times he cleans them. The way parsley gets stuck between his teeth when he's too distracted talking to remember to chew properly. How he taste-tests sauces with his pinky, or how he counts to three with his thumb first. The way he blinks twice—just twice—before his smile breaks through.

Well, that's interesting.

I'm not just noticing Raees. I'm *memorizing* him. I'm attracted to him. Irrevocably, catastrophically. And there's no return from here.

I knew something had shifted last night, the second his ex-fiancée kissed his cheek during the hockey Kiss Cam. A part of me wanted to tear through the television screen, grab him by the hand, and bring him home. He'd look so frightened, trying to squeeze out of the situation, like a wet puppy. It shattered me seeing him that way.

And then he came home with eyes red and swollen, a frown I can't bear to see on his face, and a cup of my favourite chocolate pretzels in his hands that he probably bought while breaking down. Right there and then I knew I was . . .

I was . . .

I . . .

Oh, my god.

I am in love with Raees Shaan.

My body jerks like I've just been struck by lightning.

"Uh, is she okay?" Ophelia's voice is somewhere far away.

My knees give out, and I plop into the chair behind me like I've forgotten how to stand.

I am in love with him.

I can't breathe.

Oh, God, I can't breathe.

"I'm in love with him . . ."

I want to murder his ex-fiancé. *Murder.* I want to carry the weight of his hurt on my back and tell him he never has to be sad and alone again. I want to pull him into my arms and press him against my chest so tightly that the broken pieces of him melt into me. I want to run my fingers through his stupidly silky hair, cup his face, and kiss him until the pain in his eyes disappears. I want to listen to him ramble for hours about whale documentaries, pretending I don't care while secretly memorizing every word.

I *need* him.

I need to feel every inch of his skin under my fingertips. I need to sleep next to him and wake up to his face, messy hair, morning breath, and all. I need to share a bathroom, bump into him while brushing my teeth, fight over the hot water in the shower and laugh about it later. I need to share everything with him.

"You're getting a call," Alex's voice cuts through the pounding in my ears. "It's Clark Kent."

I grab my phone like it's a live wire. Even the sight of his contact name sends a delicious jolt through my chest.

Why is everything kicking in now? Like the words 'love' and 'Raees' were a code that unlocked some secret compartment inside me.

I love his smile.

I love his laugh.

I love his voice.

I love baking for him.

I love feeding that ridiculous sweet tooth of his.

I love his hand on my back, my waist, my arm.

I love that he rambles, and I find myself hanging on every random tangent.

I love listening to him.

I love the crinkle between his brows when he's focused.

I love his love for newspapers, fountain pens, wristwatches, DVDs, the way he still writes in full sentences even in text messages.

I love making lunch for him.

I love his cooking.

I love the way he smells like sandalwood.

I love how hard he's trying. For himself. For his students. For me.

I love how easily he fits into my life, loving my friends without hesitation.

I love his resilience. His patience. His kindness.

Him. Him. Him.

There's no fighting it now. No escape hatch. No Plan B. No detour around this truth.

I'm completely in love with Raees Shaan.

"I hate you," I whisper to Alex, my lips curling into a shit-eating grin.

"I'm scared," Alex says, ducking behind Ophelia like a toddler. "What's wrong with it?"

There's a girl clawing her way out of the grave inside me. A familiar girl. A girl I buried years ago and promised I'd never dig up. The girl who lost her father when she needed him most. The girl who handed herself over to a man who broke her bones and left her silence where her voice used to be. The girl who froze in time because moving forward felt like death.

That girl . . . she's alive.

She's here.

And she's jumping up and down, shrieking Raees's name like it's her favorite song. *"Raees! Raees! Raees!"* Over and over, until his name sticks to the walls of my chest and reverberates in my throat, the only name I want to say.

My phone buzzes in my hands.

I read his text message.

Raees: I'm waiting outside. Take your time.

Nope. I'm leaving now.

"I gotta go," I say, launching myself out of my chair.

"Wait, Zinnie!" Alex calls.

I spin around, my grin so wide it's making my cheeks ache, and I know I probably look unhinged.

"Nothing," she says, throwing her arm around Ophelia's shoulder. "Have fun at the birthday party."

"See you Monday!" I toss back as I burst out the door.

The second I'm outside, I skip down the department building's steps.

Calm down, Zinneerah. We get it. You're in love. It's a grand reveal. Fireworks, a marching band, confetti—all very impressive. But maybe no sudden hugs, or impulsive kisses. Let's not terrify the man.

Raees spots me from across the parking lot and smiles. The kind that could knock planets out of orbit.

I pace over, trying to walk like a normal human being and not someone who just realized they're in love with their husband. I can't help it, though. I grin back, because how could I not?

"You look happy," he says. "I take it your practice went well?"

"Yes," I say, too quickly. *Get it together, Zinnie.*

Raees sucks in a sharp breath. "Yeah, I'm still reeling from the fact you can actually speak." He runs a hand through his hair. He's so adorable. Like, blindingly adorable. I'm seeing him in a whole new light. A rosy, glowing, sparkly kind of light. "But Zinneerah?"

"Yes?" *Raees, Raees, Raees.*

"I don't want you to strain your voice," he assures gently. "We're still going to continue implementing ASL, okay?"

"Yes," I say again. It's automatic. Everything he says is fine. Everything he says is golden. What is wrong with me?

His eyes crinkle behind his glasses as he smiles, and oh, I love when they do that. I love those crinkles. I want to frame them and hang them in a museum.

He motions toward his car. "Shall we go entertain a toddler?"

I nod and fall into step beside him as we head to the parking lot. My eyes flick down to his hand. Big, warm hand. I want to hold it. I want to slide my fingers between his and lock them there, like a knot that can't be undone.

But instead, I keep my arms glued to my sides and grip the strap of my guitar bag until my knuckles ache.

"Raees."

The silvery voice slices through the haze like a cold gust of wind.

My attention snaps up, and there she is: his ex-fiancée.

Goddammit. Of course she's here, leaning against his car like she has a right to it—or him.

She flicks a quick, apologetic glance at me (fake), then turns to Raees with something much deeper (performative).

"My wife and I are running late to an event." Raees doesn't even hesitate. *That's my man.* I just wish I could say it out loud. "If you don't mind, please leave—"

"I'm sorry, Raees," she interrupts, stepping forward. "For what happened. I shouldn't have done that. It was wrong, and I'm deeply ashamed of hurting you."

Hurt him? Oh, she didn't hurt him. She humiliated him. And she knows it.

She turns to me now, her face a picture of carefully constructed remorse. "I'm sorry, Zeerah."

Zeerah?

"Zinneerah," Raees clips out. "If you're going to apologize, at least get her name right."

Her lips twitch ever so slightly, a flicker of irritation, before she smooths it away with another one of her practiced smiles.

"Of course," she says. "I'm sorry, Zinneerah. I hope you can forgive me."

Forgive her? My pride scoffs at the idea. In fact, my pride would rather make an itemized list of why she's not worth forgiving. She kissed my husband's cheek on live television—*married* man, for the record—while the guy sitting next to her practically begged for her attention. She could've kissed him. She should've kissed him. But no. She aimed for Raees.

No, she purposely *chose* my husband. And I know exactly why.

My fingers tap Raees' shoulder, signing quickly. *Can we go now?*

His jaw unclenches just enough for him to speak. "Gladly." He brushes past her with a polite nod, taking just the tips of my fingers in his hand.

I don't miss how her lips tighten.

As we pass, my mind turns over her name. Was it Sarah? Sasha? Something with an "S"? Whatever. I'm not going to bother butchering it the way she butchered mine. On purpose, might I add.

If she still has feelings for my husband, I highly recommend she gets her delusions checked out before I do it for her.

Raees is silent as we walk back to the car, which is fine, because I've got plenty of thoughts to keep me company.

I sneak a glance at him. The muscles in his jaw twitch like they're fighting to escape his face. His eyes flicker to the ground, then to the car, then back again. One hand hovers near the door handle but doesn't touch it.

He's paralyzed.

I've never seen him like this. There's a quiver in his chin, just the smallest one, but enough to tell me everything.

That conniving woman. She's still got him on pins and needles.

I follow his gaze, and that's when I see it.

Hearts.

Big, stupid, cartoonish hearts drawn on the passenger window.

My husband's ex-fiancée actually drew hearts on his car window like a lovesick teenager marking her locker. Could she be more cliché? Could she try harder to leave her little fingerprints all over his life?

A deep scowl burns into my face before I can stop it.

I don't say a word.

I just pull the sleeves of my sweater over my hands and rub at the window furiously, scrubbing over the hearts until they're nothing but streaks and smudges. Let her hearts smear into oblivion. Let them rot.

When I glance back, Raees is staring at me with his brows raised in surprise.

I smile, all teeth. "I was thinking chocolate chip cookies today?"

His lashes flutter, like he's still processing the past five minutes, but then I see the shift. The knots in his shoulders undoing. The lines in his forehead smoothing.

And then, finally, *finally*, he smiles. A real smile. One that reaches his eyes. His glasses catch the light, and the crinkles I love so much settle in at the corners.

There you are, I think.

He opens the passenger door for me, still quiet, and I slide into the seat, settling my guitar bag in the back.

As he closes the door and walks around to the driver's side, I glance out the window.

The smudged hearts are still faintly there, but they don't bother me anymore.

She doesn't get to keep her hearts here.

Not in his car.

Not in his mind.

Not with me around.

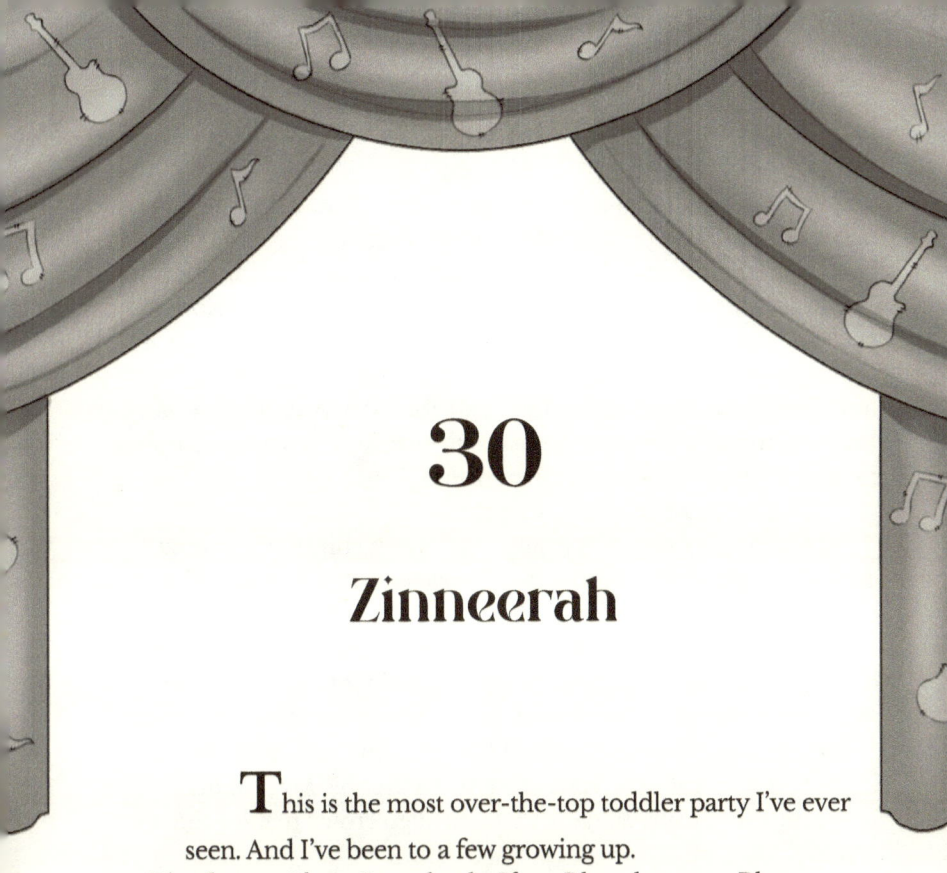

30

Zinneerah

This is the most over-the-top toddler party I've ever seen. And I've been to a few growing up.

The theme: *Bluey*. Completely *Bluey*. Bluey banners, Bluey balloons, Bluey cupcakes. I half expect the cake to start barking in an Australian accent.

I know *Bluey* because Dua adores the show. She's obsessed with the show. Actually, obsessed might be too tame a word—she cried so hard during one episode of Bluey and Jean-Luc reuniting that I started Googling if this thing was secretly a therapy program for emotionally repressed adults. Thankfully, Zayan is always on standby with hugs and tissues. Dua basically considers him her emotional support human.

"Ramishah sure knows how to throw a party," Raees mutters beside me as we stand at the entrance of the *venue*. Yes, that's right. This party isn't in an arcade or even their house. No, this is a large rented event space, and the sheer scale of the Bluey-ness makes it feel like Disney threw a tantrum and an animated Blue Heeler won.

Suddenly, our gifts feel woefully inadequate. "Though, to be fair, her parties were always pretty legendary growing up."

"Raees! Zinneerah!" My mother-in-law appears, gliding toward us with her arms outstretched. I don't have time to react before she encapsulates me in a hug. "Oh, you must forgive me for being so absent since your wedding." She pulls back just enough to study my face, then kisses my cheeks. "I've been abroad in Asia, you know. Business meetings, expansion plans, the works. I'm hoping to open a firm in Singapore soon. Isn't that thrilling?"

I nod, giving her hand a squeeze.

"Good to know you're doing well," Raees chimes in, leaning down to hug her next. "You should've called when you landed. I could've picked you up from the airport."

"Oh, don't be silly." Rosy Aunty dismisses with a wave of her hand, but not before grabbing mine and holding on. "I didn't want to disturb the lovebirds. Newlyweds need their space." Her smile softens as she turns back to me. "You and I have so much to catch up on, Zinneerah. But for now, you'll have to excuse me. My granddaughter is waiting for her special tiara, and I must go crown her as Princess Bluey."

"Ammi-ji, I need to talk to you about visiting Abbu," Raees says. I glance up at him, and the look in his eyes makes me feel like I'm eavesdropping on a conversation they're having in silence. The Shaan family doesn't talk about him. Ever. It's one of those subjects with invisible warning signs around it, the kind I've learned not to touch.

"Later," Rosy Aunty replies offhandedly. She kisses the back of my hand, winks, and flounces off toward the heart of the party.

Raees exhales, shoving one hand into his pocket as he looks down at the tiled floor.

"Well, well, well, if it isn't my favorite couple—after fifty others here."

Ramishah parts through the crowd like royalty arriving at her coronation, her shimmering sapphire gown trailing in her wake. Her glossy ombré bun is twisted high and tight, not a single strand out of place, and her twenty-four-karat gold earrings are screaming *"I can pay off your student loans!"* at the top of their gilded lungs.

Meanwhile, I'm standing here in the only blue sweater I own—it's "*Bluey* colors," okay?—and a black skirt that's seen better days. My side braid is barely holding together, because I forgot a hair elastic at home and had to take one Raees handed me from his pocket. "*I found it in the living room last week,*" he said with that charming wink of his that had me seeing stars.

Ramishah grabs my shoulders, air-kisses both my cheeks with flair. "Mwah, mwah! Gorgeous as always." Then, she immediately swivels her laser-like focus to Raees, eyes narrowing. She plucks the presents out of his hands and says in a sickly-sweet voice, "You really shouldn't have, Chotu."

Raees raises a brow. "Did you tell that to everyone?"

"Only the penniless," she fires back.

Okay, I'll admit it. That was funny.

Raees, predictably unbothered by her teasing, folds his arms. "You know pennies went out of circulation years—"

"Oh, spare me the Wikipedia entry, Professor. Seriously, how do you live with this nerd?" Ramishah loops an arm around my shoulder, steering me into the crowd.

The room is packed—young parents bouncing babies on their hips, pregnant women looking like they might pop, and not a single *single* person in sight. Thirty people, maybe more, plus what feels like a million children.

"Just so you know," she says, "these are all Amina's cousins from Harry's side. Ammi-ji doesn't have a big family, and let's be real, we've never cared about Abbu's. Most of them, at least." She tosses her head like even mentioning him is beneath her. "The rest are just her daycare friends. My baby girl's already more popular than I was at her age. Charisma like this never skips a generation."

I offer polite smiles to the couples around us, throwing small waves at the kids darting through the tables like caffeinated chipmunks. Some of them are relentlessly hounding the poor guy at the cotton candy machine, who looks like he's rethinking all his life choices.

"Where the hell is he?" Ramishah mutters. I follow her glare to find Raees wandering off, entirely absorbed in a mission to inspect the buffet table. Or more specifically, the cupcakes. "Oh, for crying out loud." She rolls her eyes so hard I almost hear them. "Raees! Get over here!"

He looks up mid-grab, now holding two blue cupcakes like a guilty child caught raiding the cookie jar. To his credit, he makes a speedy recovery, hurrying back to us with his spoils. He hands one to me, offering a quick grin. "We're gonna need this sugar boost if we're gonna survive tonight."

Ramishah scoffs, but I can see a sliver of a smile before she flips her social switch. The perfect hostess, all elegance and charm as she beckons us to follow.

"Rami should've hired you to bake," Raees murmurs, biting into his cupcake, and chewing it like it's sand rather than soft sponge.

I notice a smudge of frosting on the tip of his nose and instinctively reach out, brushing it away with my thumb. The unexpected touch makes him hum softly in surprise.

"Raees, over here!" Ramishah calls.

He snaps out of a trance, then quickly jogs after his sister.

I glance at the frosting smeared on my thumb, pause for a second, then lick it off.

Sweet, but not that sweet.

What follows is an eternity—okay, thirty minutes—of being introduced to Ramishah's many friends.

They all have one thing in common: an affinity for handing us their babies. Crying ones. I don't even pretend to play along. The moment one is thrust into my arms, I pass them straight to Raees, who manages to soothe them like some kind of baby-whisperer. He pats their backs, bounces them, and coaxes giggles out of them like a magician pulling out bunnies from his hat.

Then come the inevitable questions: *How long have you two been married? Do you have kids? What do you do for work, Zinneerah? When's the honeymoon?* And—oh, my personal favorite—*Do you have a cold, Zinneerah?*

Raees handles most of the answers like a pro: *We were engaged for about a year and got married last month. No kids yet. She's a musician.* He even flashes that off-sided grin when he gets to the honeymoon question, deflecting it with a smooth, "That's a great question. Something we'll discuss later."

For the last question, though, he hesitates and glances at me, his brow lifting just slightly. It's a silent question of his own: *Do you want me to answer this, or do you have something to say?*

Alex and Ophelia's words ring in my mind. *You're going to have to talk to him about this sooner or later.*

That conversation isn't for a room full of Ramishah's overly curious friends. That's for my husband to know.

I smile faintly and nod. "Flu season," I murmur.

"Tell me about it," one of the women—Meghan, I think—says, bouncing her squirming son on her lap. "One of my toddlers brought a cold home from daycare, and now the whole family's sick . . ."

I let the chatter fade into background noise.

My focus is entirely on Raees' thumb, which is lazily tracing small circles along my spine. It's maddeningly subtle, but I feel it everywhere—warmth spreading through my body until there's a full-blown wildfire.

I hate how easily he does this to me. I've always been hyper aware of his touch, but ever since I admitted to myself how I feel about him, it's been impossible to ignore. Even the simplest brush of his hand has my heart doing embarrassing cartwheels. I'm going to combust if he doesn't stop, and I'll probably combust if he does.

"It's almost time for my little princess to make her grand entrance!" Ramishah shakes my shoulders out of their sockets before swiping a hand across Raees' cheek. And then, like a sparkling blue tornado in heels, she flutters out of the venue.

Raees and I collapse into chairs at a nearby table.

He was right—the sugar helped a little. Three cupcakes later, I can feel the fog lifting from my brain, but it's clear we're both running on fumes. The party's barely an hour in, and my social battery is already threatening to flatline. I glance at him, and he's in a similar state, relaxed but a little detached, fingers laced over his stomach, one ankle resting casually on his knee.

"You'd think by now I'd have outgrown wishing I had Ramishah's effortless confidence, but nope. Apparently, my thirties still think that kind of magic might come in handy." He nods toward the crowd. "I don't recognize half of these faces. And I know most of her friends." His full-lips, a very faint color of blue from the frosting, press together. "It's kind of incredible, isn't it? How she charms absolutely everyone she meets. Almost annoying, if you ask me."

If we'd met back in university, Ramishah and I would've locked antlers in a competition over who could be the most spontaneous. Or maybe, in some alternate timeline, we'd have been inseparable best friends, I'd have had an embarrassing crush on Raees, and our love story would've played out in some free-will kind of way. No arranged marriage. No pressure. Just us, deciding that forever together actually sounded like a pretty good idea.

Raees tilts his head slightly, pulling my attention back to him. He pokes my forehead. "What's going on in there?"

I shake my head and smile to put him at ease. "Nothing. Just thinking how you're really good with kids."

He looks away, his focus drifting to the colorful balloons swaying gently above us. "Well, I practically raised Amina," he says. "Ramishah was deep in postpartum depression, and Harry was spread thin, trying to be there for both of them. We all knew she needed the support more."

Raees pulls out his phone, scrolling through his gallery. He angles the screen toward me, showing a picture of himself with newborn Amina fast asleep on his chest. His hair is an adorable disaster, sticking out in every possible direction, but he's grinning ear-to-ear, holding a thumbs-up.

"This was after our first all-nighter together," he says with a chuckle. The next photo is Amina on his lap at a bookstore, both of them peering at a brightly colored board book. "I took her on her first bookstore trip. She tried to eat the pages. Oh, and this one's from the aquarium. She couldn't stop staring at the jellyfish."

He presses play on a video, and there he is, wearing a baby carrier like a pro. Amina bounces on his chest, giggling and pointing as jellyfish glide across a blue-lit tank. "We're basically best friends," he says, looking smug but trying to downplay it. "Not to brag or anything."

I arch an eyebrow, fighting back a grin. "See? You do have friends."

He shrugs. "Yeah . . ."

I catch myself studying his side profile as his gaze flits around, tracking squealing kids and anyone else passing by in his line of sight. "Raees?"

Honey-brown eyes meet my darker ones. "Zinneerah?"

I open my mouth to say . . . what was I going to say exactly? "Nothing," I blurt out the lamest escape route ever.

Out of nowhere, *Air on the G String* starts playing in the background.

I know this piece. Back in university, I used to sneak into the auditorium just to listen to the classical music students rehearse. Something about it always felt like I was transported back to the 18th century.

Raees stands beside me as the venue doors swing open.

And there stands Amina.

My cheeks hurt from smiling when I see her toddle in, wearing her fluffy, baby-blue gown and glittering tiara. She's a little vision of joy, looking like a tiny queen who knows the entire room is here for her.

She pauses in the doorway, soaking up the attention of everyone watching her.

I look at Ramishah and Harry. They're grinning so wide, proud of their little star. Meanwhile, a couple of her cousins try to shuffle into her spotlight, but one look from Ramishah, and they stay glued to their spots.

Amina, unfazed, holds tightly to her parents' hands as they walk her down the aisle. Well, "walk" might be generous. She's sort of half-skipping, half-dragging them toward the three-tier cake, blue and yellow frosting sparkling under the lights.

Except she doesn't make it to the cake.

She breaks free, and those little legs move as fast as they can until she practically crashes into Raees.

"Happy birthday, sweetheart," he says, scooping her up. She throws her tiny arms around his neck and buries her face into him, giggling as he plants a kiss on her cheek.

My heart swells.

Uncle Raees beats out Bluey. That's love.

"*Raees!*" Ramishah hisses, already marching over with her arms out. "My child. Now. Please."

"Right, sorry." He hands her back to Ramishah, but not before sneaking in one last kiss on Amina's cheek.

And he doesn't stop there.

Like the good uncle he is, Raees pulls out his phone and starts filming. He doesn't miss a thing. The singing, the candles, the cake cutting. Amina's tiny hands smashing frosting into her dad's face while everyone laughs. He's locked in. Nothing and no one else exists.

And I don't know how to explain it, but it does something to me.

I tap him on the back.

"Hm?" he says without looking away from his phone.

I wait until he glances at me, and then quietly but clearly, I say, "You're going to be a great dad."

His phone slips out of his hands and clatters to the floor.

At the exact same moment, *Baby Shark* comes blasting from the speakers like a party grenade. Kids are screaming and jumping in excitement, and Raees looks at me like I've just flipped his world upside down.

"Everyone on the dance *floooooor!*" Ramishah shouts into the microphone, and like magic, every kid in the room sprints to the middle. They're jumping and flailing, half of them inventing their own choreography, while the little ones cling to their parents' hands or get twirled around in their arms.

Raees leans down, his breath warm against my ear. "Would you do me the honor of dancing to *Baby Shark* with me?"

I grin like a dork and let my hand fall into his. "Thought you'd never ask."

Suddenly, we're not at Amina's birthday party anymore. No, we're at some rowdy eighteenth-century pub, dancing on top of tables to fiddle music. He spins me out, then reels me back in, my back landing against his chest. His laugh rumbles in my ear, and I swear it makes me giddier than ever before.

We stay on the floor through all the Kidz Bop songs, not even pretending to care about how ridiculous we look. At some point, we hijack the DJ booth and take control of the playlist. Now it's our turn to call the shots: *Dancing Queen, Take On Me, Radio Ga Ga, Karma Chameleon, Footloose* (it would've been a crime not to), *Uptown Girl*. It's like an instant time machine to every feel-good anthem we've ever loved when we were children.

By the time we hit *Be My Baby*, we're all in, arms locked around each other, swaying like nobody's watching.

His eyes are on mine. My eyes are on his. And just like that, everything and everyone else disappears.

There's no DJ, no kids, no party. There's only him.

When Raees Shaan is next to me, in front of me, behind me, he's all I see. He's all I want. All I need.

All mine.

Mine, mine, mine.

By eight o'clock, the venue's cleared out because, well, kids and bedtimes. It's just us now—me, Raees, Ramishah, Harry, and the cleanup crew.

Amina's passed out cold from a day full of running, squealing, and inhaling sugar. She's draped over Raees' shoulder, her tiny body limp and completely dead to the world, drooling a damp patch into his dress shirt. Of course, the man is also balancing ten plates in his other hand like some kind of circus act. I have no idea how he does it. I have no idea how—*he*. You know?

Ramishah slides up next to me, wringing a wet cloth in her hands. "Be honest, gorgeous, how are things going with you two?"

"Good," I say, but my voice comes out hoarse from talking all evening.

She tilts her head, her lips pulling into a smirk. "The rasp is kinda sexy, not gonna lie. Makes sense why Raees was freaking out on the phone with me the other night."

I laugh under my breath. "He's adorable."

"Yeah, he really is something." She watches with pure longing, then adds, "I love that little shit to death. I'd do anything for him. I just suck at showing it."

I glance over at her. "What do you mean?"

She sighs, wiping her hands dry, then tossing the cloth into the trash. "Our dad. That's what I mean. I don't know, I think I just tried too hard to impress the guy. You know, follow his 'disciplines,' or whatever he called them. I thought maybe if I did everything perfectly, he'd stop targeting Raees and focus on me instead."

I blink, unsure of what to say.

"Wasn't the right kind of attention, though," Ramishah mutters.

"No?" I ask quietly.

"Nope," she says with a dry laugh. "It was a mess. We went through a lot of shit growing up. Emotional, physical. Especially Ammi-ji. She was doing great in real estate—better than him, actually—and it made him jealous. So, he'd take it out on her. And then Raees would step in to protect her. Every damn time."

Glass shards gather in my throat, and I glance over at Raees, now carefully positioning a stack of chairs against the wall while still holding Amina.

"It got a little better after the asshole's life exploded. He got involved with the wrong people, blew up his career, and eventually checked himself into rehab. So, you know, progress." She sounds like she's told this story before, but doesn't want to let it hurt anymore. But I feel it. Every syllable of it. I feel it like I'm absorbing it straight into my bloodstream.

Knowing the truth about Raees—the way he flinches sometimes when Alex claps his shoulder, how hard it is for him to make friends with people he's known for a good while, how hard he's trying to be a good role model for his students—it just makes me love him even more.

I mean, how does someone like him even exist? After everything he's been through, he's still out here stealing the sun's job and acting like it's no big deal.

And somehow, I don't know how, he accepts *me*. Flaws, baggage, all of it. Dua told me he didn't think twice when she showed him my picture. The man just rolled up to my doorstep the next day with a smile, a chirpy proposal, and zero doubts.

And the wildest part? I wasn't even trying. I was ready to close the door on the world, live out my days as a hermit in sweats. But then there he was, smiling like I was the only person on earth.

And then he just sat there with me. In my silence. Day after day. He didn't push, didn't pressure, didn't walk away. He just kept showing up. And somehow, somewhere in the middle of all that showing up, I'm sure I fell for him. Hard. Not because he did anything grand or dramatic, but because he talked. He talked like no one had ever told him to stop, and I was hooked from the first word. I think it happened somewhere between him confessing his fear of balloons, and the time he admitted he ate toothpaste for a month straight as a kid because it smelled like candy-cane.

The day I realized I wanted to marry Raees was also the day I yelled at Shahzad for judging him. I cried—not because I didn't want to marry him, but because I did. I wanted it so much it scared the hell out of me. What if he found out all the stuff I was hiding? What if he walked away? I thought about that a lot, so I stayed quiet until I was sure—sure that I loved him, sure that I wanted to give him a hundred babies if he'd let me.

And I do. God, I do. I love him so much. Not the kind that consumes you, but the kind that builds you, brick by brick, until you're a person you didn't think you could ever be.

"Are you going to help or not, Mrs. Shaan?"

I blink, and here he is. Right in front of me. Just swooped in and stole my heart all over again.

I take a deep breath and look at him like he's my North Star.

My hand reaches for his free one, and I squeeze it three times.

He squeezes back, just like he always does, and he doesn't even know what it means to me.

31

Raees

Saturday morning rolls around, and Ammi-ji graces us with her presence, dragging along a confectionery basket roughly the size of a small cypress tree.

Oh, and Ramishah is here, too. *Fantastic.*

In the living room, Zinneerah sits like the dutiful daughter-in-law she is, nodding and chuckling politely as Ammi-ji recounts the glorious chronicles of my childhood disasters. I don't need to hear it to know which stories she's picked. It's always the same ones: the goat incident on Eid, overdosing on Pepto, the time I got my head stuck in the banister.

Ammi-ji presses a hand to her chest. "Oh, I can't wait to see my cute little grandkids!" She reaches over to gently pinch my wife's cheeks. "I've already started baby-shopping!"

Zinneerah glances back at me with wide, panic-stricken eyes. *Is she serious?*

I sigh heavily from my post in the kitchen, where I'm slicing green peppers in what's rapidly becoming my emotional support activity. "Ammi," I say, raising my voice over the sound of her cooing, "can we maybe talk about literally anything else?"

She dismisses me with a regal wave, scooting closer to my wife and pulling up her phone to scroll through the digital hall of shame, otherwise known as my baby pictures. The ones where I'm sporting both an inexplicably chubby face and the unruliest mop of hair ever seen on a six-month-old.

Ramishah breezes into the kitchen, dropping tea mugs in the sink. "What?" she says, catching the eyebrow I raise in her direction.

"Are you going to wash those?"

"With this manicure?" She holds up her hands, wiggling her freshly painted nails like they're priceless artifacts. "You must be joking, Chotu." She hip-checks me on her way to the counter and then does . . . whatever that is with her face—eyebrows waggling, lips puckered, chin jutting toward the living room like she's trying to mime a particularly inappropriate joke.

"What's wrong with your face?"

"Fuck off." She swats my shoulder. "Don't dodge the question."

I reach for my coffee. "What question?"

She leans in close enough to invade my personal space. "Have you guys had sex yet?"

I choke on my coffee, sputtering it back into the mug. The hot splash burns my lip, and I mutter a curse, grabbing the nearest napkin to clean up. "For God's sake, Ramishah. That's not a question you ask your little brother." I dab at the dark stain spreading across my sweater.

"Grow up, Chotu. You're thirty-five, not five. And I'm pushing forty. Who else are you gonna talk to about this? Ammi?"

I pause mid-swipe, a frown already forming. "No way."

"Abbu?"

"What—? No, absolutely not."

"Exactly." She snatches the napkin from my hand with a flick of her wrist and tosses it in the trash.

"It's still weird," I grumble.

"You're weird," she shoots back, dumping what's left of my coffee into the sink with zero remorse. "Look, you don't have to be ashamed, all right? But you also don't need to let people pressure you and Zinneerah into anything you're not ready for." She pulls out the sugar jar, and pours me a fresh cup. "Also, not to be that person, but you do realize Ammi isn't getting any younger, right? And you're the apple of her eye. So, like . . ." She waves the spoon in my general direction. "Plant the seed. Make a little apple that doesn't fall from the tree."

I blink at her. "That . . . was an abomination of an analogy."

She shrugs and dumps a tablespoon of sugar into my coffee. "I don't do analogies, Raees. You know this."

"Just one spoon." I pull the mug away before she can sabotage it further.

She pauses, narrowing her eyes at me. "You used to take three."

"Used to."

"Raees."

"What?"

The corner of her mouth twitches. "Nothing."

"Ramishah, spit it out."

We lock eyes like two kids squaring up at recess, ready to toss in some playground insults. But silence stretches just long enough for both of us to break into grins.

"You've grown into such a gentleman." She reaches out, cupping my face. "I did such a good job raising you."

I brush her fake affections away before she can start patting my head like a puppy. "Why don't you do something useful for once and fill the pot with water?"

"Go to hell."

"Only if you're my tour guide."

"Shut up." Ramishah chortles as she rifles through my kitchen drawers. "Where the fuck do you keep your pans?"

"Lower cabinets." I take a sip of my coffee, watching her in bemused disbelief. "What are you trying to make?"

"The only thing I know how to make." She pulls open the fridge and pulls out an egg, holding it up like a trophy. "Scrambled. Always."

"Just don't burn down my kitchen. I need it to prepare food for the dawat later."

A groan. "How are you feeling about it?"

I roll the mug between my palms, staring into the dark liquid like it might give me answers. "I'm . . . okay. You know Ammi-ji's going to invite Tariq and Lubna Aunty. I don't know why she keeps trying to patch things up with his family. It's not like they ever gave a damn about her before."

Ramishah doesn't answer right away, cracking the egg into the bowl, dumping in some salt and pepper before whisking it with a fork. "I'll tell you why," she says, setting the pan on the stove with a metallic clang. "She's been visiting him."

I freeze, coffee mug halfway to my lips. "Visiting who?" I ask, even though I already know the dreadful answer.

"Who else?" She looks up from the stove, one hand on her hip, the other holding the whisk. "Abbu, obviously. She's been visiting him every now and then for the past few months."

"Why?"

"Because she's Ammi." Ramishah shrugs and turns back to the stove, pouring the beaten egg into the hot pan. "Apparently, they've been sorting things out. She's even helped him look for an apartment."

"An apartment?" I repeat, my voice rising. "Why the hell is she helping him find an apartment?" Before she can answer, I'm raising another question. "And where is he moving? Here?"

"She didn't say, Jesus." Her head shakes at my impatience. "But yeah, probably somewhere close. Says he wants to 'start fresh.'"

"But—"

"Look," she cuts me off. "Women—especially mothers—are empathetic creatures. It's just who they are. Men? Men don't have the range. But not Harry. He's way more empathetic than I'll ever be."

"Fine, whatever," I say, shaking my head. "She got him an apartment in the city. Now what? They're going to 'start fresh' by becoming best friends? She's going to visit him every weekend like it's some kind of therapy project? What happens when he decides to worm his way back into our lives?"

Ramishah stops scrambling.

"Raees," she says quietly. "I get it. I really do. I don't like this either. I hate that she's going out of her way to help him get back on his feet after everything he's done. We've talked about it—argued, really—and she promised me this is it. She'll get him settled in the apartment, and if he starts asking for more, she'll let me know, and I'll handle him."

My sister's the only one of us who ever stood a chance of reasoning with him. Once, when he raised his hand at her, she stood her ground. He couldn't follow through. Instead, he broke down in tears, apologized over and over, and swore he'd be better. He never cried to me, though. He made sure I never saw him like that. He didn't want me to learn those emotions. He didn't want me to think crying was ever an option. Maybe he was scared I'd use it against him.

He didn't have to worry about that. He would beat any sentimental softness right out of me.

"Are you going to visit him?" Ramishah's voice pulls me back.

"Alone," I mutter.

"You don't want to introduce Zinneerah?"

The idea leaves a bad taste in my mouth. "I don't want his hand touching my wife's. I'll tell him what he needs to know, and that's it."

She nods. "When do you want to go?"

"In the evening."

Her brows shoot up. "Like, today?"

"I just want to get it over with," I say, setting my mug down.

Ramishah frowns slightly, worrying her bottom lip. "I'll drive you," she offers.

"No, you stay here with Ammi-ji and Zinneerah."

"You sure?"

"Yes." I glance toward the living room, where Ammi is laughing wholeheartedly. Her arms are bare for once, the faded scars visible. She always tried to hide them even when I begged her not to. If someone had seen them, maybe they could've saved us. "This'll be the last time I see him."

"Me, too," Ramishah replies, shutting off the stove. After a moment, she adds, "I haven't introduced him to my family, either."

I blink, caught off guard. "Why's that?"

She shrugs, but I know her well enough to recognize the way her jaw tightens, or the way she avoids looking at me.

"He's never been proud of anything I've done. Not once." She scrapes the pan until the scrambled eggs are piled on the plate. "I used to try so hard. Joining every club, every team, just hoping he'd show up for something—a game, a recital, even one of those bullshit parent-teacher meetings." A dry, bitter laugh leaves her. "And now that I've built this little perfect world for myself? My family, my job, my life? I don't want him to see it. It's not for him. It's not because of him. This happiness is mine. Mine and mine alone." She turns to point the spatula at me. "So don't even *think* about cowering in front of a coward. You march in there with your head held high, you say what you've always wanted to say, and then you walk out with a goddamn smile."

I let her speech sink into my skin. "Can't guarantee the last part. I'm a sensitive guy."

Ramishah chuckles softly. "I never hated you for it, you know?"

My head tilts. "For crying?"

"No, doofus. All that stuff I used to say about you being the golden child? It was a one-sided competition. I was angry, sure. Angry that he poured all his attention into making you his little shadow and shut me up with Barbies, and dresses. But when you came crying into my room at night, or when I had to put ointment on your back?" Her knuckles whiten on the spatula, her next words coming out like a hiss. "I only ever wanted to *kill* him."

My eyes burn as I look at her, remembering all of it. My sister, sitting cross-legged on the bathroom floor with a first-aid kit, holding me close while I sobbed quietly; her small hands gently tending to the bruises and welts on my back; the way she never let me see her cry, even though I knew she wanted to.

The first time, I was nine—small, skinny, fearless in the way kids are when they think they can protect their mother. I didn't feel the pain of the first slap until later, when my ear rang and my cheek swelled so badly, I couldn't chew on that side for a week.

After that, it became a routine.

By the time I was thirteen, I knew how to position my body to take the brunt of the blows without breaking anything too important. My ribs were fair game, but I'd keep my face out of range; bruises there invited questions I couldn't answer.

When he was done, he'd storm out of the house.

That was when Ramishah took over, no matter how young she was. She'd sit me down in the bathroom and clean the scrapes on my arms, her small hands quick as she muttered curses under her breath. Then she'd check on Ammi-ji, helping her wash her face, combing her hair, whispering reassurances neither of us believed. She'd cook dinner, slapping together whatever we had in the fridge—dhal, rice, scrambled eggs.

Abbu had been drinking before he even came home, the smell of whiskey polluting the air as soon as he opened the door. He accused Ammi-ji of something ridiculous—talking to a male neighbor, or not folding his clothes properly, or maybe just existing in a way that annoyed him that day. I can't remember what triggered it.

But I remember the slap.

Ammi-ji crumpled like a rag doll, her head hitting the edge of the coffee table with a sickening thud.

I froze. For the first time, I didn't know what to do.

Ramishah did, though. She was fifteen, then. She grabbed Abbu's keys from where he'd left them on the counter, dragged me off the floor, and together we carried Ammi-ji to the car. She was so still, her head lolling to the side, a trickle of blood pooling at her temple. I could barely open the car door with my shaky hands.

My sister didn't say a word the whole drive. Her knuckles were pale on the steering wheel, her lips pressed into a thin line, her eyes locked on the road ahead. She had only driven once before, when a friend had let her try in an empty parking lot. But that night, she drove like her life depended on it—because it did.

Ammi-ji didn't die, thank God. She had a concussion and needed stitches, but she survived. And when we got home, Ramishah sat in the bathroom with her while I scrubbed the blood off the coffee table before Abbu woke up.

The last time I tried to fight back, I made the mistake of threatening him. I was seventeen, standing in the hallway outside their bedroom, my nails cutting into my palms. I could hear Ammi-ji crying on the other side of the door, her voice cracking as she begged him to stop. Something in me snapped.

"I'll call the police!" I shouted. *"Do you hear me, asshole? I'll call them. I'll—"*

The door flew open before I could finish. Abbu stood there, his chest heaving, and veins protruding from his neck. His eyes were wild—bloodshot, red-rimmed, the pupils dark and unfocused like he was possessed. As a child, I used to think he was every time he hit her, but even demons would refuse to possess the body of a man who abused his wife and kid.

For a second, I thought he might hit me. I almost wished he would, just to prove I wasn't scared.

The next thing I knew, his hands were around my neck, his thumbs digging into my windpipe. I clawed at his wrists, my vision blurring, my legs kicking uselessly against the floor. Ammi-ji was screaming, pulling at him, hitting him, doing everything she could to make him let go. *"Bas karo! Leave him alone! Please, Umar! He's your only son!"*

Suddenly, he released me, and I crumpled to the ground, gasping for air.

The next morning, he packed a bag, and left us for good.

That was the last time I ever saw him.

For weeks, I couldn't swallow without feeling like his hands were still on my throat. I couldn't look at my own reflection without seeing the purple marks wrapped around my neck, a grotesque necklace of weakness and humiliation. Ammi-ji tried to soothe me, pressing ice packs to the bruises, whispering reassurances I couldn't hear over the voice that kept asking, *Why didn't you fight harder? Why didn't you stop him?*

Laughter bubbles up from the living room.

Zinneerah is leaning her head on Ammi-ji's shoulder, the two of them conversing about her music. The sight is a balm to memories that still sting like fresh wounds.

"Do you mind making me some toast, Chotu?" Ramishah asks.

"Yeah, sure," I say, clearing my throat. I grab the bread from the pantry, toss two slices into the toaster, and take a long, soothing sip of my coffee.

Then my phone buzzes. Pulling it from my pocket, I sweep over a quick glance at the screen—

I choke, spitting the coffee back into the mug because the last man I ever expected to willingly text me is texting me.

Azeer: Hello, Raees. Are you free? Zinneerah isn't picking up her phone, so I was forced to text you.

Never mind.

My thumbs hover, then move fast.

Me: Of course. Is everything okay?

Azeer: I highly doubt you'd be busy.

That was uncalled for. Everyone says he's got the kind of personality you tolerate over time—if you're patient enough. I'm still not sure I am for him.

Me: What do you need?

Azeer: There's news Alina and I want to share with you and Zinnie.

The toaster pops.

"Rami, I'm stepping out with Zinneerah for a bit. Azeer needs to talk about something."

Her brow furrows. "Who?"

I blink. "My wife's cousin. You complimented his 'buttery smooth' skin or something the first time you met."

Recognition dawns on her face. "Oh, the fancy hotel guy?"

"That's the one." Walking over to Zinneerah, I catch the way her face softens when she sees me. "Sorry to pull you away. Azeer and Alina want to talk."

Her brows knit. "Is everything okay?"

"Hopefully." I turn to my mother. "I'll bring her back soon."

She waves a hand, already distracted. "Take your time. I'll find more baby pictures of you."

Lovely.

Zinneerah and I step out onto the patio and take our seats at the table. I prop my phone against the umbrella pole and hit FaceTime to call Azeer.

The screen lights up and the call connects.

Alina's face appears first, beaming, and then she holds up a white and blue stick to the camera. "I'm pregnant!" she squeals.

Zinneerah's hand flies to her mouth, her eyes wide like she's just seen a meteor crash.

"Congratulations, you two!" I break into a grin, watching Alina throw her arms around Azeer's neck, shaking him so hard I'm surprised he doesn't topple over. "When did you find out?"

"Like, literally, twenty minutes ago!" she blurts out, still grinning ear to ear. "I called my parents first, then Azeer's, then Nyla and Shahzad, and now you guys! Isn't it crazy? I mean, me? *Pregnant*? I didn't even think this could happen."

"Of course, it's possible," Azeer says, holding her around the waist. "We've talked about this since the second month of our marriage. It's time we started growing our family. Zoha's been asking for a sibling, after all."

Alina leans closer to the screen. "Zinnie, you good? You look like you just saw a ghost."

I turn to my wife, noticing the tears quietly rolling down her cheeks. Without a second thought, I pull the handkerchief from my pocket and pass it to her. She dabs at her face, her hands trembling.

"I'm so happy," Zinneerah whispers. She takes a deep breath and looks at the screen. "You've always wanted a baby."

Alina's face softens. "It took a lot to convince myself. You know, with my epilepsy and all the risks. But the process made all those doubts disappear." She shifts the phone upward, her hand instinctively resting on her stomach. Azeer sits beside her, arms folded, looking as smug as a man who's about to become a father can be. "Got a little bun in the oven now."

I smile. "Well, your baby will be as beautiful as you are, Alina. Inside and out."

Azeer tilts his head. "Just her?"

"Yes," Zinneerah and I reply in unison.

Alina bursts into laughter, while Azeer mutters, "This call is over—"

But she yanks the phone away. "You two are such honest sweethearts. If I could, I'd give you both forehead kisses right now." She leans into the camera, blowing smooches toward us.

Zinneerah gasps. "You're still coming tomorrow, yes?"

"Duh!" Alina then drops her voice a notch. "If you want an insider tip, order food from outside, transfer it into your pots and pans, and pretend you made it yourself. I can send you a list of restaurants—"

I raise a hand to interrupt. "That's very generous of you, Alina, but I'll be cooking for the dawat myself."

"We'll pack some antacids just in case." Azeer, who I hadn't noticed was busy playing Candy Crush, doesn't even look up from his phone.

Alina smacks his shoulder with the back of her hand. "Ignore him. We'll be there with *four* hungry stomachs. Zoha's so excited to see you both."

"How's she doing?" I ask.

"At a piano lesson right now," Alina says proudly.

I raise my eyebrows. "That's incredible. Is she liking it?"

"Oh, she's obsessed. Azeer got her the piano a few months back, and now we can't stop her. I swear, it's like Beethoven's ghost decided to haunt her."

"That's wonderful. I'd love to hear her play sometime," I reply. "We've got a grand piano in one of the rooms. She's welcome to use it while she's here."

"You play the piano?" Azeer asks, glancing up from his game.

"I used to," I admit. "Back in high school, I volunteered at a retirement home. One of the residents was a jazz pianist. He taught me basic chords, and how to build on them." I glance at Zinneerah, who's listening intently, a smile on her lovely lips. "Funny thing, the piano we have actually came from that same retirement home. They gifted it to me as a parting gift when I graduated."

Alina grins, shaking her head. "Of course they did. You have a way of leaving people in awe."

"Hardly," I reply, brushing off the compliment. The conversation in my head shifts naturally to her. "Oh, and Zinneerah's been playing the guitar again." The pride in my voice shines through. "She's performing on campus in a few weeks with her friends."

Azeer suddenly snatches the phone. It's frightening to see him so soft-faced. "You are?"

Zinneerah nods, her eyes locking with his. "I'm going to pursue music again," she says slowly, as if the words are still new to her. "No singing. Just guitar. Songwriting. With the girls."

"The Cryptics?"

She chuckles softly, her smile gaining confidence. "Back in business."

"Have you told Shahzad?"

Her laughter fades. "He only checks in."

"Is he coming to the dawat tomorrow?" Alina asks, her chin now perched on Azeer's shoulder. "I know Nyla's still in China and can't make it, but Shahzad's in New York. And you told him in advance, so he has no choice."

Zinneerah shrugs, her fingers brushing over each other in that way she does when she's avoiding a conversation. "We'll see."

"And Sahara?" Azeer adds, tilting his head slightly.

Another shrug.

I dredge my memory for details about Sahara Khan—Zinneerah's childhood best friend, and Azeer's adopted sister. Ammiji had mentioned Sahara recently, something about a real estate collaboration involving cottages in Europe. That's where Sahara lives now, juggling her impressive lineup of titles: realtor, Chief of Marketing at Sun Tower Hotel's European headquarters, and an investor whose business instincts rake in profits.

"I can't wait for all of us to be together!" Alina chirps. "It's going to be so much fun. Zinnie, you have to help me come up with baby names."

"I'd love to."

"And let us know if you need help with anything," she offers. "Throwing your first dawat is always daunting."

Azeer leans back and kisses her cheek. "We did excellent with ours."

"Plagiarism isn't excellent," I say, smirking at him. "But who am I to judge?"

Zinneerah rubs a soothing hand across my back. "No, we will always judge Azeer."

"I'm with her," Alina chimes in, sticking her tongue out at her husband.

He groans at the combined attack. "Yeah, no. This call has officially gone on too long."

Alina starts blowing kisses. "Bye, I love you both, and I can't wait to see—"

The call cuts out.

"You were right about what you said in the car the night of Alex's concert." I exhale hard, shaking my head. "How are those two still married?"

"And now . . . they're having a baby."

"Fire married fire. They're dangerous to a couple like us."

"Very."

We share a chuckle at that.

Her hand stays on my back, tracing slow circles over the fabric of my shirt. Then, it slips away to sign, and she turns her attention to the pool shimmering under the sunlight. *Is it for decoration?*

I glance at the pool, blinking at it like I forgot it was even there. "Now that I think about it, I haven't used it since you started waking up earlier than me."

Her gaze slides back to mine, eyes narrowing slightly with curiosity. *You swim?*

"Very well. You?"

I'm jealous. I can't swim. My siblings swim. I am too scared to try. "I thought 'Ursula' might kidnap me and steal my voice so I'd stop singing in the shower."

I throw my head back laughing, my stomach aching from the absurdity of her childhood fear. "That's . . . you know, fair enough. I used to be terrified of heights after I watched *The Lion King* as a kid. You know *the scene*. The one where Scar drops Mufasa from the cliff."

Abbu decided he'd 'man me up' or whatever, so he took me hiking once. We stopped at this cliff's edge—it looked almost exactly like the one from the movie. I swear to God, I froze. Then I looked down, and realized I'd peed my pants. Abbu yanked me back just before I could fall, then slapped me twice.

"I'm meeting him tonight," I whisper.

"Who?"

"My father."

Her brows lift. *Do you want me to come with you?*

I shake my head. "Forgive me, Zinneerah. I can't let you meet him. I'll explain everything about him once I'm back. I believe it's time you know why he isn't in my life anymore, though I'm sure you've already pieced together some of it."

She sniffles sharply, lowering her gaze to the patio floor. *Your sister told me a little.*

Ramishah would've skimmed the surface. Thankfully, she's always known where to draw the line. Zinneerah's knowledge likely ends at the edges of what's safe. Enough to understand, but not enough to hurt.

I have no interest in unpacking the worst of it tonight, not the way it fractured me as a boy. That's for later. I've got enough to deal with just seeing him again. The memories are going to come crashing in. The sound of his voice, the way my bedroom walls compressed in when he was angry, how small and cornered I felt when he looked at me like I was the problem.

It's going to wreck me. It always does. And when it's over, I'll need someone.

I'll need her. Just her. Just my wife.

Zinneerah's dark eyes lighten as the sunlight kisses her golden skin. She shifts closer and gently hooks her thumb at the corner of my mouth, tugging upward. "Much better."

I smile on cue, despite the churn in my chest. "Yeah?"

"Mm-hmm." Her hands drop as she straightens, and the softness of her touch fades as she stands, heading toward the patio doors.

But stops in the threshold, glancing back. Her hands lift again. *Let's go swimming tonight.*

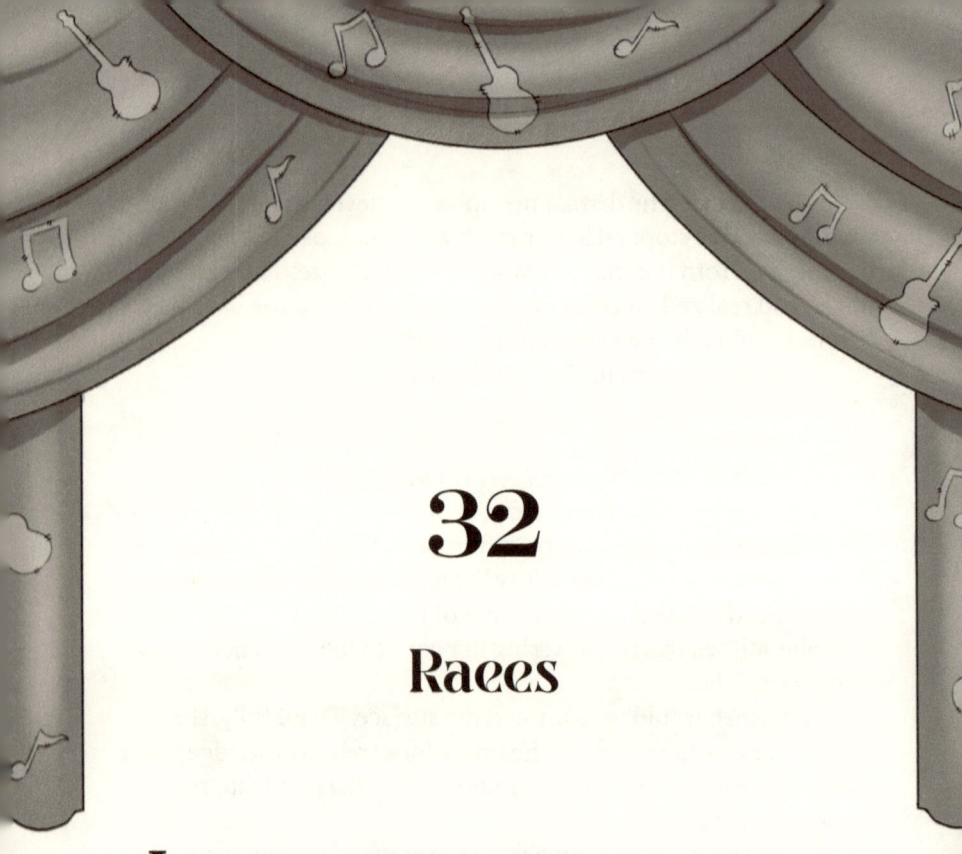

32

Raees

I stand outside Abbu's apartment door.

Eighteen years. That's how long it's been since I last saw him.

According to Ramishah, he spent a year and a half in a psychiatric hospital. Then back to the streets. Homeless shelters. Bad company. A relapse. Borrowing money from Uncle Kareem for another stint in rehab.

But this time, sobriety stuck, apparently. He's been working towards his real estate license again, climbing out of the wreckage of his life, piece by piece. My mother, soft hearted to a fault, stepped in last month when he had nowhere else to go. She refused his apology for the years of hell he put her through, but somehow, she still found him this new apartment.

A brand-new start for a man who left nothing but ash in his wake.

I lick my dry lips and raise my fist, rapping three times against the door. Each knock feels like a nail hammered in my chest.

Head high. Don't cower in front of the coward. Don't let him see the fear. Say your piece. Walk away. Don't come back. Ever.

The locks click like a gun trigger to my temple.

Sweat pools at the base of my neck, and prickles across my forehead.

My heart's a runaway train, hammering, hammering, hammering.

I still have time. I could leave. I could turn around, walk away, and let him rot in this apartment without ever knowing I came. I've lived eighteen years pretending I didn't have a father—what's another lifetime?

The door creaks open.

I stop breathing as my eyes lock onto Abbu's hollow, hazel ones.

They look smaller now, like the years carved them out and left nothing but pits in his skull. They used to burn like fire, burn through me, but now they just look . . . extinguished.

Defeated.

A part of me hates that I noticed that. A part of me hates that I care.

He stands tall in the doorway, taller than I remembered, wearing a loose t-shirt and pajama pants that cling to his narrow hips. His silver hair is combed back, still damp, as though he'd known I was coming and wanted to look presentable. But it's his body that throws me off the most. He's not the pudgy, round man I used to know. He's broader now, his shoulders square, his arms bulked, yet his presence doesn't feel bigger.

If anything, he feels smaller.

The tattoo sleeve catches my attention. A riot of ink crawling up his right arm, patterns and shapes weaving across skin. Did he go to rehab or prison?

"Raees," he says, the rasp still intact, but softer at the edges now.

I blink rapidly, trying to shun away the sting of tears threatening to spill. *Don't cry. Don't cry in front of him. He doesn't deserve your tears. You're not that boy anymore. He can't hurt you. He can't.*

But that boy is still there, trembling inside me, convinced that the man in front of me can reach out and pluck my eyes right from their sockets if I showed any weakness.

"You look . . . well," I strain out, flat and wooden.

Faint lines crease at the corners of his lips. "Come in, please." His tattooed arm gestures toward the room.

Please? My father just said 'please' to me? I can count on one hand the number of times he's ever spoken to me like I was human, and none of them involved the word 'please.'

My feet feel chained as I move past him. The apartment smells faintly of cleaning solution, a sterile attempt at starting over.

I toe off my shoes automatically. It feels strange to be doing it in his space.

"How have you been?" he asks.

I glance up, eyes sweeping across the room. The living space is cavernous but barren. There's a single couch, sagging slightly in the middle, and a battered coffee table sitting awkwardly in front of it.

"Fine," I say shortly, hands in my pants pockets. "You?"

"Very well." He drifts into the attached kitchen and opens a cupboard. "Do you want anything to drink? Water? Juice?" He pauses, glancing at the mostly empty shelves. "I still gotta go grocery shopping."

"No, thanks." My words come out clipped. "What's with the ink?"

He glances at his sleeve. "Oh, this?" His fingers graze the designs. "I've got a buddy who owns a shop in the city. Every time I felt the urge to break my sobriety, I'd get a tattoo instead." He looks up at me, and I do my best to maintain eye-contact. "There's forty-six of them. Got the last one three years ago."

Forty-six. My brain latches onto the number, repeating it like a mantra. Forty-six urges. Forty-six times he chose needles and ink over violence and poison. I don't know if I'm supposed to be impressed or horrified.

"Let's sit and talk," Abbu says. He points to the couch and lowers himself onto it like it's his throne, sinking back into the cushions.

My feet feel heavy as I cross the room, but I don't follow him to the couch. I can't. Instead, I take the armchair at an angle, putting a little buffer between us. I can feel his eyes on me as I sit, my back rigid, my arms folded tightly across my chest.

"Rosy tells me you're working in the education system." He tries to sound like we've done this a hundred times before. "Are you a teacher?"

I exhale slowly, forcing my face into neutrality. My mother is a saint, but I thank God she knows how to keep certain details to herself. She's told him the bare minimum. The city where I work. My job title, vaguely. Nothing specific. Nothing he could use.

I glance at him again—at his silver hair and his newfound calm, at the way he's leaning back, one ankle resting on his knee like he isn't sitting adjacent to a child he nearly killed—and a thought claws its way into my brain: *Has he really changed, or is this just another role he's playing?*

I don't answer his question directly. Instead, I say, "Something like that."

My vagueness doesn't bother him. He takes a deep breath, his shoulders lifting and falling. "That's nice," he says. "I thought you'd become an agent like your mother." What he means to say is 'like me,' but he's supposedly worked past his severe narcissism.

I break away from studying him. My eyes keep getting pulled to the tattoo sleeve, to the wrinkles on his face that weren't there before, to the way he tilts his head like he's assessing me.

But then his gaze drops to my hand. To the glint of silver on my ring finger. "You're married?"

"I am."

Abbu's eyebrows lift. "Who's the lucky woman?"

"I'm the lucky man."

No way am I dropping Zinneerah's name. No way. I can already picture the worst-case scenarios: him searching for her online, showing up outside our house like a specter from my past, waiting for her in the parking lot while she's grocery shopping. My pulse pounds harder at the thought, and I push it down—stuff it into the same place where I've shoved every other intrusive thought about him.

"Arranged?" he asks.

"Yes." On her end. I've been in love with my woman for six years. Six years of quiet pining, wondering if I'd ever deserve someone like her.

But he doesn't push for more details about her. No probing questions. No inappropriate jokes. Just, "Do you like it?"

The question catches me off guard. "Being married?"

He nods, leaning forward, watching me in that disarming way he always has, skinning back the layers of my skin to see what's underneath.

"I love it," I state the truth. There's no cracks in my conviction. I know he won't understand. He'd laugh if one of his friends asked him that question, cracked some brainless joke about how marriage is just a contract for mutual misery. But that's not me. Not with her. "My wife's the strongest emotion I've ever felt. She's compassionate, talented, and somehow has the ability to make my day with a single smile."

He nods slowly at each trait I list. "You don't have to explain to me how much you love her, Raees. Your eyes lit up the second I asked if you're married."

Such a simple observation, but it feels like he's reached inside me and plucked something fragile from my chest. I don't know how to respond.

His tattooed fingers lace together. "You always had so much love to give as a kid. I'm happy to know it's still there. That it's preserved in your heart, even after . . ." He trails off. "Even after everything I've done."

"You can say the word 'abuse,' Abbu."

The second the word leaves my mouth, I regret it.

My breath hitches as my muscles coil. My fists clench automatically, ready for his reaction, ready for him to swing his. The boy inside me is still, *still* bracing for impact.

But he doesn't swing. He doesn't yell. He doesn't explode like he used to.

He just sits there. His broad shoulders slumped forward, his head dipping slightly, his lips pressed into a brittle line, and a disheartened frown pulled at the corners of his mouth.

And that look . . . that look is worse than any blow.

"I'm sorry for abusing you, Raees," Abbu says softly. "I'm sorry for every cruel word, every strike against you and your mother. For eighteen years, I've been suffocating under the guilt of what I've done."

The word "sorry" feels meagre for every slammed door, every raised hand, every night I pressed a pillow over my ears to drown out the shouting.

Eighteen years.

He says it like it's a prison sentence, like we didn't all serve time alongside him.

"There's no justification for my behavior," he continues. I wouldn't be surprised if he rehearsed this. "I can't erase the scars I've left, no matter how much I wish I could. If I'm dead to you after you leave here, then I won't change your mind. I don't have the privilege of being your father anymore."

The privilege? A bitter laugh forms in my throat, but I choke it back. For so long, I thought I wanted this—some acknowledgment of the damage. And now that it's here, all I can think is: Where was this man when we needed him? Where was this version of Abbu when Ammi-ji was crying in the other room, clutching her broken wrists?

"And husband," I add quietly. "You don't have the privilege of being a husband anymore."

Abbu flinches.

He looks down, his hands folding and unfolding in his lap. "And husband." His voice cracks on the word, and for a second, I see the man Ammi-ji used to describe with a soft smile, all starry-eyed with memories I've never been able to reconcile with reality. "Despite the love I once held for your mother, I let greed consume me. I let it poison everything good within me, until there was nothing left but regret."

His gaze lowers to his bare ring finger.

"Seeing her again," he murmurs, "it was like reliving our wedding day."

I want to say something, but my tongue feels glued to the roof of my mouth.

"But you're right," he whispers. "I've forfeited any right to be a father, a husband. I won't beg for your forgiveness, Raees. You've all grown well and healthy. I'm not going to become a pesticide in your lives again."

I scoff. "'Well and healthy'?"

Abbu looks like someone crumpled him and forgot to smooth him back out.

"I suppose I owe you a recap of the past eighteen years," I mutter, adjusting myself on the chair. I'm about to bleed for the wrong human—open the wounds I patched up in therapy, and swallowed down with medication. "Remember that old stone bridge by Wilders Park? The one where the freight train passed underneath? You used to drag me there when I was barely knee-high. You said you found peace in the screeching metal. I didn't understand what you meant until much later, of course."

Abbu's head snaps up, his eyes darting to mine.

He looks like he wants to interrupt, but I push myself to follow through.

"The night you nearly strangled me, I ran for that bridge. Did you know that? Did you even notice I was gone?" My hands dig into my thighs. "I didn't stand on the bridge, though. No, I—"

Just say it. Just say it. Just say it. Just say it. Just say it.

"I laid under it," I state. "Right on the train tracks. I stayed there for . . . I don't know how long. An hour? Two? Just lying there, staring at the stars through the gaps in the beams, waiting for the rumble. For the train. For anything. And then it came." I bite down on my lip, drawing a bit of blood. "And let me tell you, when I close my eyes sometimes, I can still feel the rumble beneath me, the distant wail of the siren, and that God awful screech clawing at my ears."

Abbu stares at me, his face pale as ash. "Raees . . ."

"I finally grasped the sick comfort you found in that moment, lying there, waiting for the train to arrive. It was the realization that in the split second when flesh rips from bone, and bones splinter into nothingness, all noise fades away. No more incessant demands from your wife, no more whining children, no more suffocating pressure of climbing the corporate ladder." I mirror his posture. "Young me believed we were bonding over watching the train, but in truth, all you needed was a nudge to stay alive."

Abbu shakes his head slowly, eyes squeezing shut.

"Ammi-ji called five minutes before the train crushed me. If she hadn't, I wouldn't be sitting here, telling you a story I've told in therapy countless times," I say as I remove my glasses and fold them in the collar of my sweater. "And taking my own life didn't end there. At eighteen, I tried to cut open my wrists. At nineteen, I almost walked into oncoming traffic. At twenty, I took a hike to the trail we used to go, and pushed myself into jumping off the cliff, but I couldn't do it. You weren't there to pull me back, Abbu. There wasn't anyone to slap me after. Except myself."

Agony etches his face. He's yet to open his eyes. "Does your mother know?"

"Who do you think paid for me to become 'well and healthy'?"

He looks guilty of wording his sentence that way. "Raees, I'm sorry for everything I've put you through. I should've reached out as soon as I was out—"

"It wasn't just you, Abbu," I grit out, nails digging into the armrests. "You ruined my childhood, yes. For that, I'll never forgive you. But if you'd reached out back then? If you'd shown up when I was at my lowest? I would've killed you instead of myself. Just to find peace. That's how unstable I was. That's what *you* did to me."

My hands are sweating, but I can't let go of the armrests. If I do, I might crumble.

Don't look at him. Don't look at him. Don't look at him.

If I meet his eyes, I'll lose whatever control I have left.

"I almost hit Ramishah," I murmur. "She was just trying to help, and I almost . . ." My nails scrape against the leather, but I stop. *Don't spiral now.* "That was the moment, Abbu. That was my wake-up call. Like the universe was handing me a cue card that said, 'Get Help.'"

He sucks in a sharp breath, holding it in.

"I'd worked past the abuse, eventually, somewhat. I knew I was capable enough to put myself out there again, make better memories in university. And for a while, I did. At university, I met a girl in my program. I fell for her. I asked her out. We dated for two years before

I finally worked up the courage to propose." I let out a wry laugh, shaking my head. "And then, at her bachelorette party, she cheated on me with a stranger. The person I trusted most, the one who swore she'd always have my back, became the knife in it. And now, she works in the same faculty as me now. Every single day, I have to see her face." I shouldn't be smiling in this situation, but it's fascinating to know how much I'm unaffected by the betrayal now. "But you know what's worse, Abbu? You broke me long before she did. So, when she drilled through what little I'd managed to patch up, there was nothing left inside to kill."

His mouth parts to speak, but then it shuts again, pressing into a thin, bloodless line.

We sit like that for minutes—him staring at the pile of fast-food coupons scattered across the coffee table, me staring at his face.

What's he thinking? What's he working up to? More apologies? More carefully rehearsed, guilt-ridden words meant to make me think he's a brand-new person? Maybe some clumsy display of vulnerability, all so I'll feel sorry for him. Is that what this is leading to? Am I supposed to pull out my phone and mark a date for lunch? "Father-Son Reconciliation," penciled in between lectures?

No. Absolutely not.

I've seen this script before, and I'm not falling for it. I don't care if he cries. I don't care if he's drowning in all the regret in the world. He can't rewrite the past. He can't erase the years of shouting, hitting, blaming, breaking. That's not how this works.

"I'm selling my car," I blurt out.

Abbu blinks at me, his face blank. "Something wrong with it?"

I focus on the loose thread poking out of the armrest, twisting it around my finger until it cuts off circulation. "My ex-fiancée drew hearts on the window of the passenger seat." The thread snaps. "And my wife saw them."

He tilts his head like he's trying to translate what I just said into a language that makes sense. "You're selling your car because of that?"

When he says it like that, it sounds stupid. But that's not the point. He doesn't get it. "It made my wife upset," I explain, sitting up straighter.

Abbu squints, clearly unconvinced. "Why not just get it washed?"

"That'll be your job." My hand darts into my pocket, and before I can second-guess myself, I toss him my Audi A6's keys. The metal jingles against his palm. "It's yours now."

He stares at them, like he's holding something radioactive. "Raees, I can't accept this gift."

"It isn't a gift. It's charity."

A sigh. "Still." He holds the keys up, dangling them between his fingers. "I can't accept it."

This isn't about him. It's about getting rid of something that doesn't fit in my life anymore.

"Throw it out. Sell it for money. Put it to use. I don't care."

"Raees—"

"Is there anything else you'd like to say to me before I go?" I cut him off, standing quickly to avoid whatever protest was forming on his lips. My hands tremble as I fix the cushion I was sitting on, pressing it back into place. I don't even know why I do it. It's not like he cares about the state of his furniture.

He grips the keys. "Can I see you again?"

"No."

He looks down. "I expected that much."

What did he expect? That I'd forgive him? That we'd suddenly become father and son again, like none of this ever happened?

"I'll be taking my leave now," I say, turning away before he can say anything else.

As I head toward the door, the pantry's empty shelves catch my attention.

He's never been the kind of man to think ahead, to plan, to provide. Grocery shopping for him was like throwing a dart at a spinning wheel—you never knew what he'd return with. He'd leave for eggs and come back with a frying pan, or wooden planks for some project he'd talk about but never touch. Or boots he didn't need but somehow justified buying because they were "on sale."

And then, on occasion, a bag of candy. "For your sister," he'd say, tossing it onto the counter. Ramishah would grin and stash it in her room. Later, she'd open the bag and split the pieces with me, laying them out on the floor while we both tried to ignore the sound of his voice rising in the next room.

I shake the thought loose, and force my feet to keep moving.

"You know, all my life, I tried to conform you into becoming a man like me," Abbu says, his eyes on my shoes as I tie the laces. "I thought the world would eat you alive if I didn't toughen you up. That if I threw myself in front of the train, no one else would be able to protect your mother and sister."

I glance up at him, but he's in a staring competition with the floor, his hands hanging defeatedly at his sides.

"I was so busy trying to make you an adult," he continues, "that I forgot you were just a child. My son. My only son. My little boy."

He reaches out toward my shoulder, but I quickly stand, and step back before he can.

Slowly, his fingers curl around nothing before he lets it drop and presses it flat against his chest.

"I failed you, Raees," he whispers hoarsely. "That's a regret I live with every day, and I'll carry it until my last." His eyes are on me, glistening with tears. Actual tears. "I don't want you to blame yourself for anything that's happened. None of it was your fault. It's never been." He manages a small, trembling smile, his chin quivering. "I want you to live happily with your wife, your children, until you're gray and old. I want you to come to my funeral even for a few minutes so I can meet the woman who breathed life back into you, and my grandchildren who will proudly call you their father." I'm too numb to even realize his hand is on mine until I feel a gentle squeeze. "I'm glad you've become someone on your own terms."

Tears gather along my waterline. I don't want them to fall. I promised myself they wouldn't, but they slip free anyway, cutting warm, itchy trails down my cheeks and neck.

I blink hard, but it doesn't stop them.

Abbu wipes the corner of his eyes with a knuckle, sniffing loudly, and letting go of my hand to open the door.

I tell myself to stop thinking. *Just go. One foot in front of the other. Don't look back. Don't.*

But I can feel his eyes on me as I cross the threshold. My hand twitches, wanting to reach for his one last time. But I clench it into a fist instead. If I touch him, I'll feel the cracks—his, mine, ours—and I'll lose the nerve to leave.

The door creaks as it closes behind me.

I don't look back as I walk away.

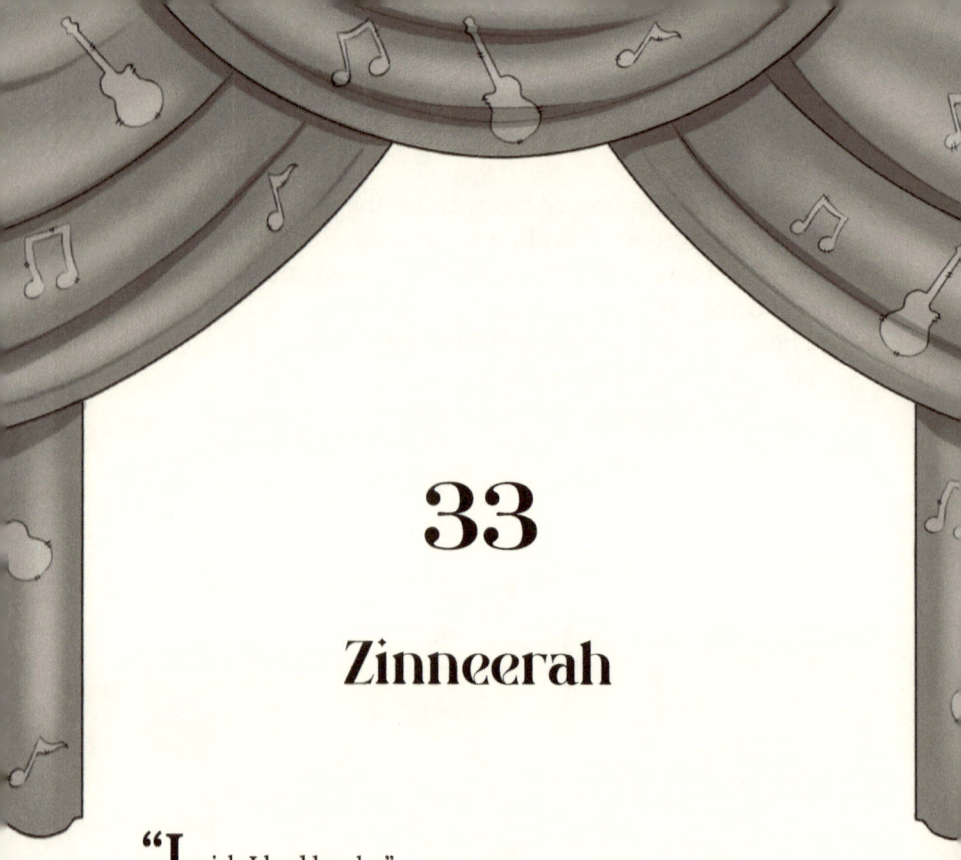

33

Zinneerah

"**I** wish I had boobs."

I sigh, tugging at the neckline of the swimsuit.

My only audience is Sahara and Dua on FaceTime, tucked in their little boxes on the screen. We've been on this call for an hour, which is 45 minutes longer than anyone should ever be forced to analyze their marriage, confront their emotional damage, and, most importantly, listen to me spiral into the abyss of self-loathing.

"I'll trade you mine," Dua says, lounging back on her bed, dangling gummy worms over her lips. "Honestly, I could do without them. Zayan loves using them as pillows, which is sweet in theory but kind of annoying in practice." She nips the head of the red worm. "My melons are not a mattress, you know?"

"Must be nice to have something people want to lie on," I mutter, turning to get a side view in the mirror. Bad idea. The mirror isn't here to help me. It's here to taunt me.

"You're perfectly fine as you are," Sahara chimes in, not even looking up from her laptop. She's been cooped up in her office all day, drafting some multi-million-dollar corporate proposal Azeer forced on her.

"Perfectly flat," I correct under my breath.

"Perfectly you," she counters.

"Maybe I should just wear, like, a bra and panties?" I offer, cringing at the thought.

"Gross," Dua says, wrinkling her nose.

"I don't see what's gross about it." Sahara finally gives me her full attention. "Though personally, I think what you're wearing now is much better. It's sophisticated. It's sleek. And I don't say this lightly: it's sexy."

If Sahara Khan, with her femme-fatale cheekbones and toned abs, thinks *I* look sexy, then maybe this black one-piece isn't the crime against humanity I thought it was.

But sexy people lounge on yachts in Italy and eat chocolate covered strawberries in slow motion. Sexy people have breezy little flings that they laugh about later over cocktails. Sexy people are not me.

"So, what's the plan? Are you and Raees bhai gonna, like, hook up in the pool or something?" Dua asks, snapping me out of my insecurities. She stretches a gummy worm between her teeth like a cat with a piece of string.

I flush so hard I can feel it in my toes. "You know, we're just gonna . . . talk."

"In the pool?"

"Your issue?"

She shrugs, grinning. "Nothing. I just think if you're looking this fine"—she gestures at the screen—"and Raees bhai will be all shirtless or whatever, you're not just gonna sit there talking about your feelings? That's some nonsense. You know, where the girl pours out her soul about her childhood trauma, and then the guy's solution is to kiss her into oblivion. Next thing you know, you're naked and emotionally compromised."

I gulp. "He isn't like that, and you know it, Dua."

"She's exaggerating," Sahara says, ever the voice of reason. "But for what it's worth, I don't think Raees is like that. From what you've told us, he seems like the type who'd rather cry with you than use your tears as a prelude to anything else. He's also sharing his feelings about his dad, right? You'll probably end up comforting each other and sobbing in each other's arms."

"Sounds on brand for them," Dua says with a shrug.

I groan, pressing the heels of my palms into my eyes. Why are they like this? Why am *I* like this?

Then, the little security notification pops up on my screen.

"Oh, my God, he's here." My voice comes out in a broken squeak. "I have to go."

Without waiting for their replies, I hang up the call, yanking a soft cotton nightgown over the swimsuit. I run my fingers through my hair, leaving it loose because I know he likes it that way.

I glance at the mirror one last time.

It's just a conversation. Just a harmless, emotionally vulnerable conversation with the man I married but still barely understand.

What could possibly go wrong?

When I step into the kitchen, Raees is at the counter, making himself coffee. The soft clink of the spoon against the mug is the only sound in the room.

I tap lightly on the doorframe. "Hey."

He turns to me, and my heart stops. His eyes are swollen, framed with red, dark circles drawn beneath them like bruises from sleepless nights. His lips are pressed in a tight frown, trembling as the seconds stretch on.

"Raees . . ." His name barely makes it past my throat. "Are you okay—?"

He breaks.

A choked sound escapes him, and his shoulders collapse under the force of it. He leans back against the counter, hands flying to his face, shielding it from me, but I can see the way his body jerks with each sob.

I can *feel* it.

Oh, God.

338

Tears prick my eyes, and before I can stop them, they're slithering down my cheeks. I take a shaky breath. "Raees."

A whirlwind of thoughts batter my mind. Did his father do this? Did he yell at him? Call him names? Refuse to see him? Hurt him, again, in some unforgivable way?

My chest burns with anger. If his father's behind this, I swear to God, I'll end his life.

But I push the rage aside and force my feet to move.

One step, then another. Slowly, carefully.

I have no idea what I'm doing.

How do you console someone who's breaking right in front of you? I think of Baba, the way he used to scoop me into his arms when I fell and scraped my knees. How Alex and Ophelia would tease me relentlessly but never once made me cry real tears. I think of my ex, how I swallowed every emotion in front of him until I forgot how to cry altogether.

Even when the sadness pressed down on me, I'd bury it deep and curl up like a fetus under my blankets.

But now . . . now the sight of my husband like this is unraveling something in me.

"Raees," I whisper again, stepping closer. My hands hover in the air, unsure, before I gently cradle his wrists and guide them down from his face. His head dips low, as if he can't bear for me to see him like this. "Did he hurt you?"

Raees shudders, and the movement splinters something deep inside me.

He shakes his head, slowly.

I press my hand over my chest and exhale a fragile breath of relief. *Thank you, God.*

"Everything . . . broke when I left." His shoulders shake, his hands pressing hard against his eyes. "He . . . he acted like—like the father I always wanted."

My heart shatters into a million pieces.

I swipe my own tears with the back of my hand, trying to collect myself. Somehow, I manage to climb onto the counter beside him, so we're closer.

I reach out and take his wrist, softly tugging him forward until he's standing between my knees, close enough that I can feel the tremor in his breathing. "Raees," I whisper. "Let me hold you. Please, just . . . let me hold you."

He lifts his head—wet cheeks, lips trembling, lashes heavy with tears that glitter like tiny stars. "Zinn . . ."

I don't wait.

I wrap my arms around his neck and pull him close, drawing him into me until his face is buried in the curve of my shoulder.

His arms come up slowly, then wrap around my waist. A ragged sob tears from his chest, and then another, and another, until his whole body is shaking in my hold. His tears soak into my skin, but I don't care.

All I care about is keeping him here. With me.

I press my fingers into his hair, stroking through the soft strands, then run my hand down his back, over and over. "I've got you," I murmur, my lips brushing the curve of his ear. "I'm right here. I'm not going anywhere."

And I don't.

I hold him as his storm rages, as the tide rises and crashes against me.

I hold him as his breathing stumbles and staggers, as his grief breaks loose.

And slowly, like waves retreating from the shore, I hold him as the storm begins to quiet, and his breaths grow slower against my neck.

"You are my healer," Raees murmurs against my skin. He draws a long breath and exhales slowly, and my eyes flutter shut. "All those times I was five seconds away from taking my own life, my conscience thought better against it. Like it knew . . . there was something, someone, waiting for me. Someone who'd make me believe in tomorrow again."

I suck in a choppy breath, tipping my head back toward the ceiling as tears prick my eyes. I try to blink them away, but they come anyway.

Raees pulls back just enough to meet my gaze, his hands coming up to hold my face. His thumbs brush the tears spilling down my cheeks, and he looks at me like I'm the cure.

"Zinneerah." My name breaks apart on his tongue. "I didn't understand the significance of existing until I met you. After everything that's happened to me, I didn't think putting myself out there was worth it anymore. That I didn't deserve to be loved the way I loved. That the fault laid within me. I believed that theory for so long, I'd started making up my own methods to prove it." A small whimper leaves him. "But I became so alone, Zinneerah."

A sob rises in my throat, and I bite down hard on my lip, drowning with him.

"You're the only good thing that's happened to me," he chokes out, and I feel it—his pain, his love, his everything—cracking me open in ways I didn't think I could be. But I'm not alone this time. We're breaking together, reshaping into something worthwhile. "I promise to you, I am never going to hurt you. I am never leaving you alone by yourself." His hands shift, tilting my face up so I'm caught in the molten glow of his golden-brown eyes. "You are my wife. Soon, you'll be the mother of our children. The woman I will be buried beside. And I am going to find you again and again and again, in every single universe we live in. It will always. Be. You."

His beautiful vow crashes over me, and I nod, over and over, my head bobbing so many times it makes me dizzy. But I can't stop. Agreeing isn't enough. I have to absorb it, imprint it into every part of me.

"Abbu said," he whispers, "that I had become someone on my own terms." His thumbs brush softly over my damp lashes, wiping away what remains of my tears. "But the truth is, Zinneerah, I wouldn't have become anyone at all if it wasn't for you. Do you hear me? I *am* because of *you*. You're the reason I'm still here. The reason I'm someone." He's searching me now, his gaze moving back and forth, desperate to catch even the faintest trace of doubt or hesitation. But there's none. There's only him. There's only us. And in this moment, I know there's nowhere else I could ever be. "Do you understand that, my love?"

NOOR SASHA

My love.

All I want to do is grab him. Grab his shirt, his collar, his entire soul, and kiss him until the world disappears. Until there's no pain, no history, no one but us. *Us, us, us.*

"I do," I say, my voice catching on a smile that trembles on my lips.

His fingers brush against the side of my neck, wiping at the dampness there.

Leaning over, I grab a couple of tissues from the box on the counter. He reaches for one, but I pull back, lifting an eyebrow. "No, I've got this."

His brows knit together in that sweet, boyish scrunch that melts my heart, but he doesn't argue. He leans back against the counter, gripping its edges, and lets me tend to him.

I start with his cheeks, blotting away the streaks of tears, then carefully dab at the corners of his eyes and the dark sweep of his lashes. His skin is warm beneath the tissue, and as I swipe gently along the column of his throat, I feel his pulse beneath my fingertips.

His gaze doesn't leave me. Not for a second. It's so intense that it makes my hands falter. Every time our eyes meet, an electric spark buzzes through me, and I have to fight to keep my composure. But then his hand moves, index finger brushing just under my eyes, catching a tear I didn't even realize had fallen. "Why were you crying?"

I glance down at the tissue in my hand, fiddling with the corner of it before answering. "Because you were."

He smiles softly. "I don't ever want to be the reason for your tears, Zinneerah." His knuckles caress my cheek, and the warmth of his touch freezes time completely. Slowly, his hand cups my face, his thumb moving back and forth in a soothing rhythm against my skin. "I'm sorry if I dumped everything on you all at once." His lips tilt in a self-deprecating smile that doesn't quite reach his eyes. "You know me. I talk too much. Always have."

I shake my head, feeling my throat hit its limit. My hands form the words in a language that feels closer to my heart. *I like listening to you*, I sign. *Not want to say the wrong thing.*

342

"You're perfect," he mutters. "As your devoted husband, I support your wrongs and rights."

A laugh bubbles up, muffled behind my palm as I press it to my mouth.

"I really like that," he says suddenly.

Like what?

"Your smile," he mumbles. "I love it, actually."

I lower the tissue still clutched in my hand, my grin growing wider, spreading until my teeth peek through. He mirrors me immediately, as though my happiness is something he can't help but reflect. "Happy?"

"And in love," Raees whispers.

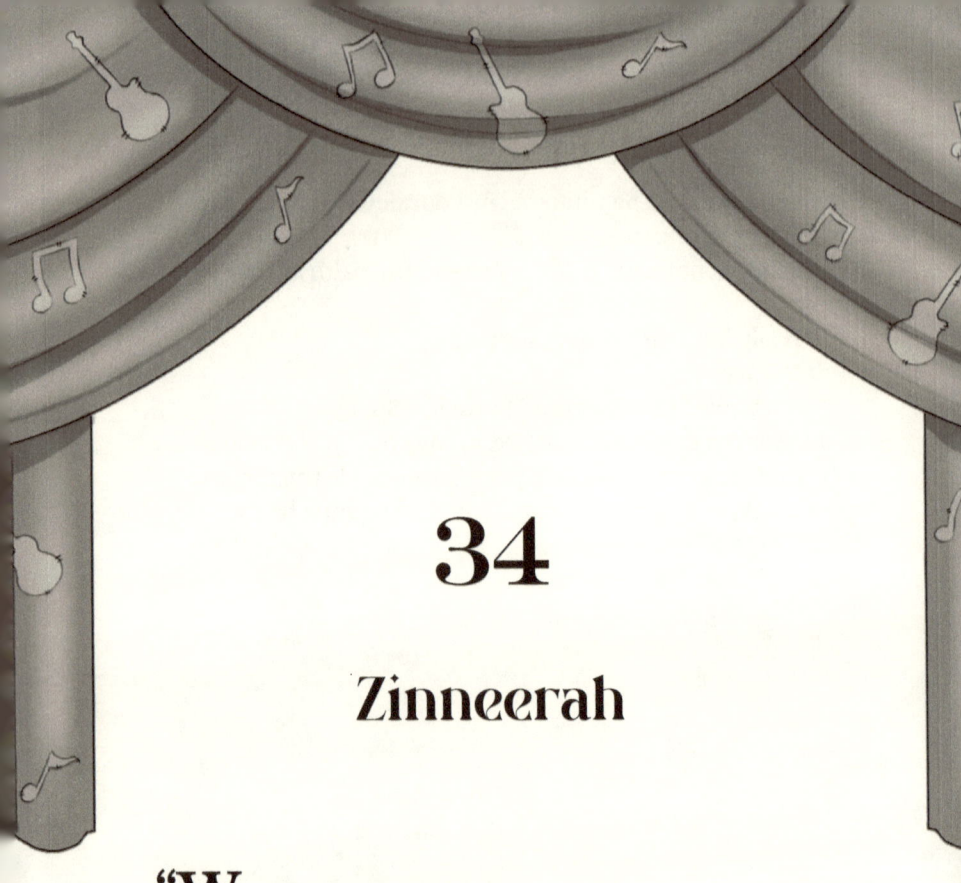

34

Zinneerah

"Wait, let me get this straight. He tells you he loves you, and your grand response is to run away? Even though you love him, too?"

I slide further down in the stiff auditorium seat, trying to disappear into the upholstery. "It's embarrassing being me."

"Well . . ." Ophelia stretches her long legs out, crossing them at the ankle. "I mean, it's not *not* embarrassing. Like, why did you run?"

"Because—" My voice cracks, and I stop. I don't even know how to explain it. How do you physically tell someone you love them without sounding completely pathetic? "Because I just . . ." My whole body feels like an untied balloon losing air. "I don't know, okay?"

"It's fine. You don't have to explain it. Maybe you're just waiting for the right moment. Us women can be like that, you know? We want it to be meaningful, special. Meanwhile, men just kind of blurt out whatever's in their heads whenever it hits them."

"Raees is romantic," I counter.

"Oh?" Her eyes are trained on the stage, where Alex and her band are halfway through some complicated piece with the orchestra. Professor Daniels stands at the conductor's podium, waving his arms like he's summoning spirits. "Okay, so what's the most romantic thing you two have done lately?"

"Romantic?"

"Well, yeah." She turns her head to look at me fully, her brow furrowed now. "You're married. You're supposed to still go on dates and stuff. It doesn't all disappear once you get a ring on your finger, right?"

I glance down at the golden band with a hexagonal diamond on my left hand, twisting it nervously. "We haven't really gone on any dates."

"Not one date? Since you got married?"

"We're both busy. It's been hard to find time."

"But wasn't Alex's concert, like, your first date?"

I shake my head quickly. "No. That doesn't count. It was more of an obligation for him."

"Obligation?" Ophelia raises a brow. "Is not doing dates a cultural thing? I mean, I don't want to sound ignorant or anything, but is it normal?"

I groan and kick the seat in front of me. "I don't know, Fifi. Can we not do this right now?"

"Okay, okay. I hear you, sister." She raises her hands in surrender, clearly enjoying how squirmy I'm getting. "But listen, if you want some help, Alex and I are totally here for you. Like, we could plan the whole thing—pick a spot, set the mood. All you'd have to do is show up, enjoy yourselves, and then, I don't know, go home and make babies or whatever married people do when the lights go out."

I give her a horrified look. "That's . . ." Well, honestly, it's not completely off base.

In fact, this whole conversation is dredging up an old memory— the one where Mama sat me down after I accepted Raees' proposal. I'd always wondered why she'd had three children with Baba, even though she couldn't stand him. And, well, I wasn't ready for the brutal honesty of her answer: *I enjoyed your father's skills.*

Even now, I cringe at the memory. I wish she'd said it differently. I sigh, shaking off the thought. "Any ideas?"

Ophelia grins and throws her arm over my shoulder, giving me a quick squeeze. "Tell me, what's your dream first date with him? Forget practicality for a second—what's the thing you've been secretly wanting to do with Raees?"

"Restaurant?" I mumble.

Her grin widens. "Classic. Okay, candlelight vibes. Romantic."

"Sushi?"

"Er, okay. Sushi, sure. Does he like sushi?"

I shrug helplessly.

"Well," she says, waving her hand, "why don't you figure out what he does like to eat? Find some common ground and work from there. Anything else?"

I tuck in my lips, thinking. "He likes sweets."

Ophelia lights up at that. "Why don't you bake something for him? Something homemade. It'll feel way more heartfelt than just buying some random box of chocolates or whatever."

That's . . . actually a great point. Raees has mentioned more than once that he's a diehard fan of my baking. "What about a dinner date at home?" I suggest, my voice warming up to the idea. "He cooks, and I bake?"

Ophelia lips curl into an approving smile. "You know what? Hell, yeah. It's cozy, low-pressure, and totally your comfort zone. You'll both love it." She leans her head against mine. "I wish I could go on a date, too."

I glance up at her. "Jason?"

"Broke it off."

"Him or you?"

"Me," she says with a little shrug. "He asked me to move in with him but leave Juliette with my aunt in New Jersey. Like, who does that? He said he wasn't 'fit to raise a kid' while he's at the height of his career. And I'm sitting there thinking, what career, dude? You're an attorney, not that fascist bastard Elon Musk."

I frown, my brow furrowing in disbelief. "He's not worth it."

"No kidding." She rolls her eyes, letting out a huff of frustration. "Should've known. He was like the Dollarama version of Harvey Specter."

That gets a laugh out of me. "You love Harvey."

"I do." She shakes her head like she can't believe her own taste in men. "Fucking love lawyers." She smacks her lips in mock disappointment before her face shifts into something sly. "You know, maybe this is a sign I should finally start dating women. Honestly, his secretary Margo is so hot. I'm talking pant-suits in every color for every occasion. And one time? She man-spread for, like, a whole minute. And all I could think was of putting my face right in bet—"

"That's lovely," I interject, cutting through her daydream. "If you're looking for a lady." I stretch my arm out slowly, gesturing toward Alex on stage.

Ophelia follows my hand with her eyes, then snorts. "*That?*"

I clear my throat, sitting up straighter and pulling out my phone like I'm about to present a well-prepared PowerPoint on why Alex is perfect.

Take a break from lawyers. Date someone who shares the same roots as you. Someone who gets you. She's been your best friend for years. She loves Juliette like her own daughter. She's successful, ambitious, completely driven. And, sure, she might not wear pantsuits, but have you seen her thighs? She's got muscles that could probably crush your head, and honestly, that sounds like a win to me.

Ophelia lets out a startled laugh, but I'm not done.

But most importantly. Alex knows you better than anyone else. She's been there for you through everything. And who knows? Maybe she likes you too.

She takes my phone, her eyes scanning over the list of points.

But her attention is caught by Alex, who's mid-song, pouring every ounce of herself into the performance, her powerful high notes carrying through the auditorium. The stage lights catch on her tattoos, the curves of her arms, the line of her jaw. She looks like some kind of ethereal rock goddess with the orchestra swelling behind her.

Ophelia's lip twitches, her fingers curling around my phone. "I don't know," she mumbles after a long pause. "We've kissed a couple of times before, hooked up maybe five times over the years. She was the reason for my bisexual awakening, sure, but that doesn't mean I should *date* her." She starts coiling one of her golden curls around her finger. "Right?"

"I only want what's best for you."

Ophelia gives a half-hearted smile, and pulls me into a hug. "Write your love story first, Zinnie," she whispers against my shoulder. "Mine can always wait."

At lunchtime, I pick up two clubhouse sandwiches from the food truck parked near Studio 365. My steps slow, almost as if my body knows what I'm about to do before I do.

A strange little flutter appears in my chest when I realize I'm heading into the coffee shop. The one I haven't set foot in since graduation.

The familiar scent of fresh espresso hits me as soon as I open the door, but everything else feels . . . a little off.

The performance corner where Marty used to host open mic nights is gone, replaced by a cold, impersonal self-checkout machine. The booths are still there, just as beaten up, the same unidentifiable stains marking the cushions like they've been frozen in time. The menu's got a few trendy summer drinks now, probably trying to keep up, and the faces behind the counter are strangers to me.

I approach the counter.

"Hi! What can I get for you today?" the barista chirps. Her name tag reads Penelope, written in looping black marker.

"Is Marty here?" I ask.

"Marty?" She pauses, tilting her head as if to jog her memory. "You mean Martin Newman?"

I nod, feeling a swell of hope.

"Oh no, I'm sorry. Martin retired a couple of years ago. Moved to Australia, actually. His younger son, Michael, took over the café." She leans in, lowering her voice. "But Michael's been trying to sell the place. Business hasn't been great."

I glance around the nearly empty shop. A couple of students sit hunched over laptops.

"Yeah," Penelope continues, following my gaze, "Starbucks opened their third bullshit location on campus, and, well, you know how it is. They've kinda eaten us alive. It's sad, really. This place used to mean something. You can see it in the old photos over there." She gestures toward a bulletin board near the far wall, cluttered with curling polaroids, each one thumbtacked. "Anyway! Can I get you anything? Our strawberry refresher's pretty good."

With my forced purchase of a strawberry refresher, I head towards the polaroid board, I drift toward the polaroid board.

Tucked between clusters of friends and couples, I find myself searching for us: The Cryptics. Alex's hair was a softer shade of blue back then, Ophelia's golden curls skimmed her neck, and I had mine scraped into a high ponytail.

We'd stick out our tongues for the camera, toss up peace signs— Alex always adding devil horns for flair—clinging to one another. The photo was from one of our first gigs at Studio 365. Anxiety wasn't our enemy in those days, it was our fuel. We gave life to that little stage, to this place, and somehow, to everyone else who walked through the door. We didn't just play music; we lit fires in people's hearts.

If only I hadn't wrecked it all by believing the promises from a man.

Then, Raees whispers, *I promise to you, I am never going to hurt you. I am never leaving you alone by yourself,* and I whisper back with, *I'll believe the moon is fake if you tell me it is because I love you.*

Tonight, after the dawat, I'm going to tell him those words aloud. *I love you.* I promise I'm going to do it.

After a brisk walk to the English building, I step inside the quiet space, and scan it.

Two winding staircases lead toward the classrooms upstairs, while the first floor stretches into corridors leading to faculty offices and study nooks. I've only been here once, back when I took an elective on Fantastical Creative Writing.

That feels like a lifetime ago.

I fish Raees' note from my pocket—folded, creased, and softened from how many times I've read it. Even Ophelia and Alex swooned over it earlier. Of course they did. Swooning over Raees is their default setting.

They love to remind me how annoyingly lucky I am.

Zinneerah, I forgot to mention my students had an exam today. I know, I'm stupid, but hey, it's fair. Last night was a tumultuous rollercoaster. I've already texted Alex to pick you up. I'm sorry again. I'll see you on campus. And, also, if I wasn't clear enough last night:

I LOVE YOU.

P.S. Sorry I had to take your car. I'll explain why later.

"Zinneerah?"

I lift my head, shoving the note back into the pocket of my bomber jacket. "Sarah."

"Saira," she corrects with a smile, walking the last few steps toward me like she's auditioning for some corporate mentorship video. She hugs a tablet and a work folder to her chest, an "Exam In Session" sign in her left hand.

"Just finished proctoring an exam," she announces, as if I asked. "Are you here to see Raees?"

I nod, keeping my expression flat. *Yeah, no shit.*

She glances at her watch. "Oh, you're right on time. He's probably in the first lecture hall upstairs—just to your right."

"Thanks."

"Of course."

I shuffle past her—

"I *am* sorry," she says, making me stop mid-stride. My jaw tightens. Here we go. "About what happened at the hockey game. I shouldn't have done that. I hope we're all good—"

"No," I reply, turning to face her. "We're not." Saira blinks, the fake smile wobbling on her lips. "I want you to practice respecting my husband's boundaries. Do not mistake his kindness for something else."

Her face morphs into a blank canvas. A weak little poker face from someone who's suddenly realizing I'm not the kind of woman you cross twice. "I thought you couldn't talk."

I let out a soft laugh. "Oh, believe me, I wish I wasn't wasting my breath on teaching you about common courtesy."

Her throat bobs as she gulps. The flush in her cheeks spreads like spilled ink, and I know I've got her exactly where I want her. Humiliated, but polite enough to swallow it.

Hopefully, she gets the memo this time. "Well, now that we've cleared the air, I'll take my leave."

I don't bother waiting for her to 'take her leave'.

I'm already moving, my boots echoing against the stairs as I climb, leaving her glued to the spot with nothing but her embarrassment to keep her company.

My fingers twitch slightly, a leftover hit of adrenaline from the confrontation, but the victorious curl of my lips makes it all worth it.

Upstairs, I find the lecture hall she mentioned, my heart beating a little faster now. I smooth my hair in the reflection of the lecture hall's glass door and take a deep breath, pulling out the sandwiches I packed from my bag.

Okay, Zinneerah. You can do this. Nothing to be embarrassed about. He's your husband. He loves you. Plus, you're going to say the words soon. No big deal.

I clear my throat and nudge the door open with my shoulder, my arms full. As I step inside and turn around, I freeze mid-motion.

A hundred pairs of eyes—blinking, squinting, bored—swivel up to me.

Dua, sitting near the front, looks like she might choke on her pen. Her eyes balloon with surprise, and she gives me a tiny wave.

One of the exam monitors clatters down the stairs toward me. "Excuse me, ma'am, you can't be—"

"It's fine," I hear Raees say. He's making his way toward me, grinning nonchalantly, as if I hadn't just burst into his exam hall like a walking spectacle.

"I'm sorry," I whisper when he reaches me, my breath still uneven. "I didn't mean to—God, I'm so sorry."

Raees chuckles softly and slides an arm around my shoulders, pulling me close. Then, in that perfect, buttery professor voice of his, he announces, "Everyone, meet my wife, Zinneerah."

A ripple of awkwardness spreads through the room. A few students manage polite murmurs of hello, others give stiff smiles, while at least a quarter are too engrossed in their exams to care.

"*And,*" he continues with a smug smile, "she and her friends will be performing at the summer festival in a few weeks. If you attend, I'll give you all a five percent boost on your final grade."

The room erupts. Cheers, gasps, outright celebrations from the back of the hall. I see one guy slap his friend on the shoulder like he's just won the lottery, while another girl exhales in obvious relief, probably calculating how many marks five percent adds to her barely-passing score.

I lean closer to him. "Raees, can you even do that?"

"My wife, my rules," he murmurs back, grinning like a schoolboy. He turns to his TAs, instructing them to keep monitoring the exam while we step outside.

The second we're out in the hallway, he glances at the door behind us. "Wait, what happened to the sign?"

I huff under my breath. *That bit*—No. No, I'm not going to call her that word again. Not again and again. Maybe she had an exam, too.

Sighing, I hold up the bag in my hands. "Sandwiches. You left early, so I couldn't pack your lunch."

"Thank you!" A twinkle lights up his eyes as he unwraps one of the sandwiches and takes a hearty bite.

Eat breakfast? I sign.

He nods mid-chew, grinning like a child. "Coffee and one of your brownies."

"Eat slower," I scold gently, picking at a stray piece of kale stuck to his sweater.

"Can't," he mumbles, eyes fluttering shut as he savors the bite. "So hungry."

I unwrap my own sandwich, taking a small nibble. "What happened to your car?"

"Gave it to Abbu."

"Really? Why?"

He pauses, fiddling with the sandwich wrapper. "He needed it more than me. Don't think I did it out of the goodness of my heart—he's the last person who deserves it. But he's trying to start over, and I figured, why not? Yesterday was the last time I'll ever see him."

I find myself taking in all of him. His openness always takes me by surprise, this willingness to share pieces of himself—even the sharpest ones—with me. Like I've been given keys to rooms no one else gets to live in. "I'm proud of you."

His laugh is as smooth as honey spread on fresh bread. "Thank you, darling."

Darling? *Darling?* My brain skids. Last night it was 'my love', and today it's 'darling'?

My cheeks light up like fireworks, the heat crawling down my neck, pooling in my chest, my legs, even my toes, *and I can't believe he called you 'darling.'*

Raees breaks the silence. "Oh, by the way, I've prepped everything for the dawat tonight. Once we're home, we just need to boil, fry, and bake."

I tuck the last bite of my sandwich back into its wrapper, feeling too flustered to trust my voice. Instead, I sign: *I saw the rice in the bowl.*

"For the pulao," he says, and then, with a solemn shake of his head: "My family isn't big on biryani."

I gasp. "Are you even allowed to say that?"

"I should cut them off, shouldn't I?"

A chuckle escapes me. *Excited?*

"To see my relatives? Hardly. But I am excited to see the nieces and nephews, and our friends. Did Shahzad and Sahara confirm?"

I sign back, *She's busy. My brother gave me a thumbs-up.*

He polishes off the last bite of his sandwich, brushing crumbs off his hands. "So, is there anything I can do to make Shahzad like me? Bring him the moon? Cure cancer? Build a hundred statues of you for him to worship?"

"The last one sounds pretty good to me."

"Gold or marble?"

I pretend to think. "Gold, obviously."

"Perfect!" He draws his phone out. "I'll call the sheikh I keep on speed dial. Statues of you, coming right up."

My eyes drift upward in a roll at his adorable nonsense. *You're perfect just as you are. If my brother can't see that, that's his problem.*

Raees is clearly not buying my pep talk wholesale, but he shrugs anyway. "I just want to make sure you're comfortable. That's all I care about."

I take his hand in mine, because I know if I don't hold on to something, I might actually dissolve from how sweet he's being. "I've got you, I've got my family, and I've got my friends. What's not to be comfortable about? Honestly, I'm golden."

His honey-brown eyes soften. "You're exquisite," he whispers. And before I can even react, or roll my eyes again, he's shoving the door to the lecture hall wide open and announcing, at full volume, *"My wife is exquisite!"*

I gasp and yank him back hard. "Raees! Are you insane? They're literally taking an exam!"

But he's already doubled over, laughing until he's almost wheezing, one hand clutched to his chest.

I cross my arms and glare, but I can't stop the corners of my mouth from turning up into a smile. What's gotten into him?

His large hands bracket my face. "You are so breathtaking, Zinneerah," he says, every word dipped in syrupy adoration. "God, I love you so much." Then, as if that wasn't over-the-top enough, he tilts my chin up with one finger and *winks*. "Wait right here. I'll be out in a sec."

I nod, mostly because I've forgotten how to speak, and watch as he strides back into the classroom.

Before the door even fully shuts, I hear him shout, "I am in love with my wife!"

Mortified, I cover my face with my hands, but I can't stop the laugh that slips out.

He's absolutely ridiculous.

And he's absolutely mine.

GROCERY FOR THE DAWAT

All-purpose flour

Granulated sugar

Powdered sugar

Ghee

Heavy cream

Vanilla extract

Condensed milk

Semi-sweet chocolate chips

Fresh paneer

Cardamom pods

Fresh berries

Cinnamon sticks

Saffron strands

Rose water

Baking powder

Cashews and almonds

Basmati rice

Red lentils

Chickpeas

Cumin seeds

Coriander powder

Garam masala

Turmeric powder

Fresh cilantro

Green chilies

Fresh ginger

Garlic bulbs

Tomatoes

Onions

Chicken (Bone & boneless)

Plain yogurt

Ice cream (please?)

NO. ⟶

YES.

RAEES...

Yes, Mrs. Shaan?

fine.

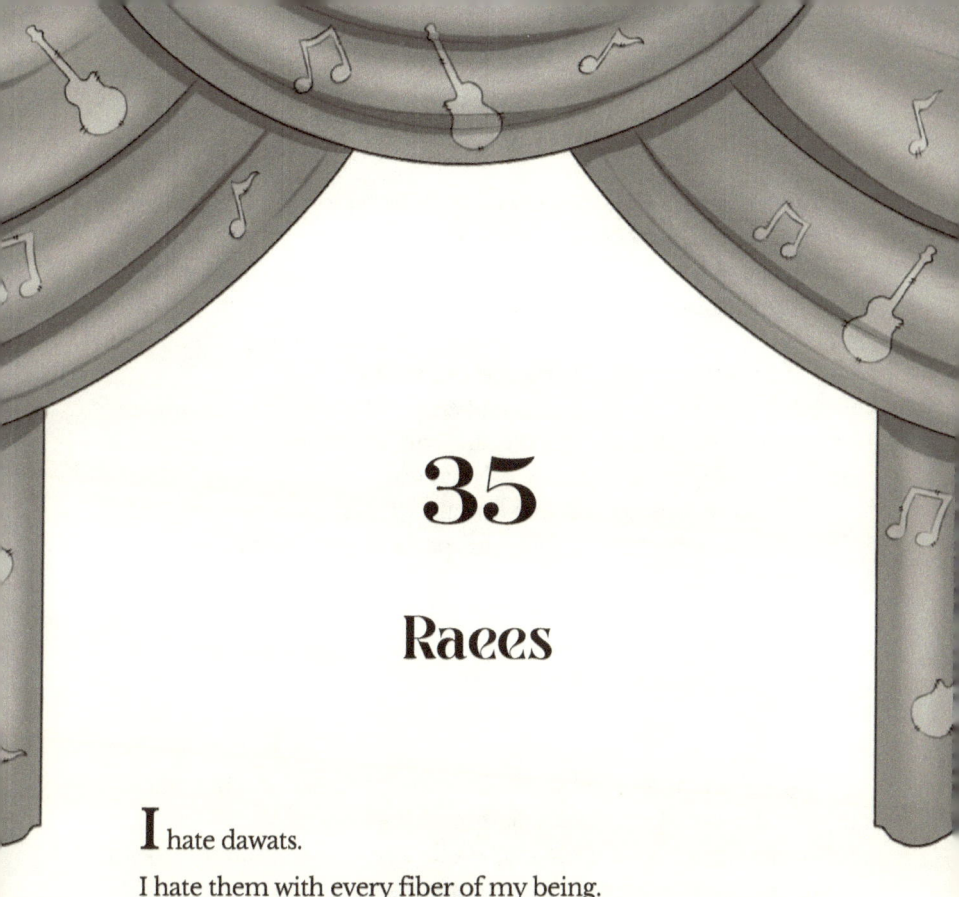

35

Races

I hate dawats.

I hate them with every fiber of my being.

If there's a hell tailored just for me, it's a dawat.

Growing up, they were always a three-ring circus, and Baba was the ringmaster, cracking the whip and showing off his prized acts—his exotic cars, his bulging bank account, and the latest multi-million-dollar home he sold to whichever socialites he loved surrounding himself with. He'd parade Mama around like his greatest trophy, never mind that she was his partner in the business, the engine keeping it running.

No, in Baba's world, her accomplishments were just an extension of his.

Ramishah and I had our own roles in this freak show: the star attractions for the aunties and uncles. Cheek-pinching fodder for relatives who still saw us as toddlers, even when we were teenagers. *"Beta, how's school? What are you studying? Why aren't you engaged yet, Ramishah? What's your five-year plan?"*

Interrogations that turned every conversation into an interview.

Meanwhile, our cousins got to run around outside like actual kids. Not us. We were stuck, held hostage in the living room, sitting up straight, asking for permission to go to the bathroom, terrified that leaving mid-conversation would offend some Aunty who thought she had the right to dictate our futures.

And then, once the aunties had emptied every dish, the uncles had downed the chai, and the cousins had left crumbs all over the carpets, the real show began: Baba's scolding.

If we were lucky, it was just verbal: criticizing our posture, our inability to fake interest in whatever sports or political debate was happening.

If we weren't lucky . . . well, Ramishah would storm out of the house before it got ugly. Mama would take the hits, both verbal and physical. And I stood in the line of fire.

So, there you have it. I'd wipe the whole tradition off the face of the earth if I could.

Zinneerah tugs at my sleeve, holding up a spoonful of cream custard. Her dark-brown kurtha, threaded with gold and black floral embroidery, glints under the kitchen light. A crown braid rests neatly on her head, her loose side-bangs curled just so.

Her inquisitive, obsidian eyes search mine. "What's wrong?"

I force a smile. "Nothing."

"Liar."

No point dodging. I exhale, raising a hand that shakes just enough to betray me. "Fine. I'm nervous. See?"

"Why?"

"These parties . . . nothing good ever comes from them." I tip my chin up, silently asking her to feed me the custard she's been fussing over. She obliges, sliding the spoon into my mouth. The sweet, creamy taste lands like a sugar bomb on my tongue, and I hum appreciatively. "Incredible."

She grabs a napkin and leans in to dab at my mouth, like I'm some spoiled prince incapable of wiping my own face. I let her. Why not?

"You know my social battery drains faster than most people's," I say. "But I'm not about to leave you alone with those vultures. That's a promise. After the dawat is over, I'll stick around to clean, and make sure you've eaten something before bed. Deal?"

Her pupils dilate, her lips part, and a flush of red creeps up her cheeks.

I love that sort of reaction. Especially to my confession last night. She looked like a cherry pie left too long in the oven, ready to blow. And then, she bolted. No words. Just a blur of motion as she fled the kitchen.

I didn't take it personally. I've been collecting her signals for a while now. I've got a jar full of them, and it's overflowing. It's only a matter of time before she comes clean.

Before she admits she loves me, too.

Until then? I'll wait patiently.

Ding!

The doorbell pops our bubble. It almost feels like the opening bell of a boxing match I forgot to train for. *Game face, Raees. This is it.*

"Hey." Zinneerah finds just the tips of my fingers. "You'll be fine."

"*We'll* be fine," I say, because the idea of going into this alone is unbearable.

She hooks her pinky around mine. "Together," she promises.

I maneuver around the gesture, and intertwine our fingers, holding on.

And then I open the door.

Shahzad's waiting on the other side like the human embodiment of a guard dog—a glowering, broad-shouldered sentinel armed with what might be the deadliest glare known to mankind. Or, more accurately, *my*kind.

"Raees," he clips out.

I smile. "Shahzad, how are—"

Before I can finish, he brushes me away like I'm a house fly, and wraps his sister in a bear hug. "Hey, sweetheart!"

I didn't know it was possible for him to sound . . . jolly?

He doesn't stop there. He starts signing, and none of it's meant for me. *I want you to know, you are welcome to divorce this ass and come live with me.*

I scoff before I can stop myself. The sound escapes loud enough to draw his attention. *This ass can understand you.*

"*How?*" he asks, clearly not expecting the answer he's about to get.

I smile because at this point, what else can I do? "I learned ASL last year so I could communicate with Zinneerah."

My wife stands at my side, blushing. "He's better than me."

"No one's better than you at anything," Shahzad fires back, dropping the grizzly-bear act for all of three seconds to soften his voice. Then, just as quickly, he pivots, eyes back on me like a hawk circling its prey. "You cooked everything?"

"I did."

"From scratch?"

"Yes." Sir? General? Mr. Arain? I feel like I should address him formally. "I hope you enjoy it."

"Don't tell me what to do." He holds my gaze like this is some kind of standoff. Then, with a puff of his chest, he marches off into the living room like a commander inspecting enemy territory. But before he's out of earshot, he tosses one more grenade over his shoulder. "You two still sleeping in separate rooms?"

I sigh. "Ye—"

"No," Zinneerah cuts in. She steps forward, arms crossed, daring him to challenge her. My darling wife, everyone. "We're not. He's my husband. Get that through your thick head or I'll personally kick you out of my house."

A moment of silence for Shahzad's ego.

He glares, his jaw tightening like he's biting back about fifty different arguments. But, to my surprise, he doesn't push it further. Instead, he grumbles something unintelligible and storms off, probably to sweep the living room for hidden cameras or poison traps.

Zinneerah exhales and taps my shoulder. *I'm sorry.*

"No, don't be," I tell her, giving her shoulder a reassuring squeeze. "I'm sure he'll be distracted the entire night dealing with our families."

Her face falls slightly. *They don't like him.*

"Oh." I think back to the scraps of information Dua mentioned about how Shahzad had distanced himself from the Arain family after their father passed. The details were murky at best, but it was clear the split had left scars.

I glance toward the living room, where he's currently inspecting a bookshelf with a frown, and something inside me shifts.

I'll do my best. I'll make sure no one gives him a hard time tonight. If that means I have to block, tackle, or charm my way through a few conversations, so be it. Friendship points if it earns me some extra goodwill with him.

Soon, the doorbell's working overtime, chiming like a broken record as wave after wave of guests flood in. Some of these faces are straight out of my childhood—fixtures from my mother's dawats. Others are strangers from Zinneerah's side, faces I'm still working to match with names.

I'm running a relay between the front door, the kitchen, and the dining room, but the one constant? Zinneerah's hand in mine.

"You want some water?" I ask as we duck into the kitchen for a moment of peace.

She nods, looking like she's on the verge of collapsing. I grab her mug and toss in some ice cubes.

There're a hundred conversations in every corner of the house, the air-conditioning is doing its damnedest to keep our anxiety at a low, and we've been poked and prodded by aunties and uncles with their usual, private questions.

"Zinneerah beta, when's your voice going to get better?"

"So, kids? How many? I suggest three. Boys, of course. Cheaper that way."

"No honeymoon? Are you running low on money?"

"Raees, you're going to let her work? But she's a musician? Haye, no income in that. Better to stay home like a good wife."

"And teaching, Raees beta? Is that really going to support a family? I have a nephew in IT. I could pull some strings. Just say the word."

Oh, and then the cherry on top: *"Your father would be so proud of you, Raees."*

I keep Zinneerah tucked into the corner of the kitchen, shielding her from the crowd like a bodyguard. She sips the water, but her hands are trembling, and she spills a little on her kurtha.

I grab a napkin, wiping the spot, then gently dabbing at her chin.

"How much longer?" she whispers.

"I'm asking myself the same question." I sigh, leaning against the counter. "But we haven't even served the food yet. Brace yourself."

She rubs her temples. "Food. Now. Or I'm taking hostages."

I smirk. "On it."

The second I lift the dish covers, the kitchen transforms into a war zone.

Mostly thanks to the stampede of sugar-fueled kids tearing through like we're rationing food in an apocalypse. Zoha's the only polite one in the lot, actually shaking my hand and greeting me like a civilized human being, no parental arm-twisting required. I almost want to give the kid a medal.

"Great party, you two!" chirps Dua, already juggling a plate stacked with kebabs and pulao. She sniffs at her food. "The flavor's almost suspiciously competent. Did you follow Alina and Azeer's method?"

"We cooked it ourselves, believe it or not," I say proudly.

Dua grins and sniffs her plate again. "Well, it's either really good or I'm starving. I'll let you know in my mental Yelp review later." She slaps my shoulder and skips off toward the living room, where—*oh, man.*

Shahzad's staring at me with those deadpan eyes of his. I can't tell if he's plotting a murder or just spacing out. He leans toward Azeer, muttering something under his breath, and then they both give me the once-over. *Slowly.* It's high school all over again, and I'm the guy who just walked into the cafeteria butt-naked.

"Zinneerah, meri jaan!" Maya Aunty sweeps in, and plants kisses on both of Zinneerah's cheeks, her ruby lipstick leaving evidence of her affection. "You've outdone yourself with the food," she coos, stepping right in between us. "You should've told me you could cook this well. It would've saved me all the time I wasted teaching you."

I see Zinneerah open her mouth to deny the claim, but before she can, I rest a hand on her shoulder.

"And how are you, Raees?" Maya Aunty turns to me now, hands clasped in front of her. Her eyes, however, are on the crowd, scanning for some minor social infraction to pounce on.

"I'm great, Ammi-ji."

"Good, good. And is Zinneerah giving you any trouble?"

I glance at my wife. Her shoulders are hunched, fingers fidgeting nervously. All I want to do is take her hand, kiss it, and whisk her upstairs where we can breathe.

"She isn't capable of it," I say.

Maya chuckles wryly. "First time I've ever heard anyone say that," she mutters, giving my wife a little shove on the shoulder.

My jaw clenches, and it takes every ounce of self-control I've got not to step between them or shove her right back.

But then her sharp eyes narrow on me. I don't back down. I even throw in a smile. It's petty, but it feels good. "Are you close with your father, Raees?"

And there goes my confidence.

Damn her. She knows how to land a blow.

Zinneerah steps between us before I can even respond. "Stop being a child." Then, in a move that makes my chest swell with pride, she lifts her chin. "This is my house you're standing in, and I won't have you disrespecting me *and* my husband." She falls into a fit of coughs, and presses a hand to her mouth.

Instinct kicks in, and I guide her gently toward the kitchen. "Let's get you some water." I cast a glance back at Maya. "We'll talk later, Ammi-ji."

"*Stay*," Maya orders. My feet annoyingly freeze.

Zinneerah gives me a frustrated sigh, and signs, *It's okay. The sooner you listen to her, the sooner she'll leave us alone.* She throws her mother a tattered, pained look before quietly heading to the kitchen by herself.

My chest hurts hearing her cough, but thankfully, Shahzad is already by her side, his hand on her arm, guiding her to sit. At least she's not alone here.

"So, you haven't consummated yet," Maya says.

I choke from her very bold statement.

I wish my mother was here to handle this woman. She wouldn't hesitate to put her in her place for asking such a private question. But no, she and Ramishah are busy entertaining our relatives at the dining table, laughing and pouring chai as if everything is rainbows and sunshine. So, it's just me standing here, trying to keep my cool.

"With all due respect, Ammi-ji, what happens between me and my wife is nobody's business but ours."

Maya doesn't flinch. Instead, she gives me one of those patronizing, no-nonsense smiles that makes my blood pressure spike. "I'm her mother, Raees. It is my right to know if my daughter is fulfilling the obligations of her marriage."

"I can assure you that Zinneerah and I are content in our marriage. And, respectfully, whether we are or aren't is not anyone's business. No matter the familial ties involved."

"She's almost thirty, Raees," she hisses. "Everyone's asking why she hasn't announced a pregnancy yet. Tell me, how many people here have asked you that question tonight?"

I meet her gaze head-on. "I didn't marry Zinneerah to turn her into a child-bearing machine," I state firmly. "And it's not my decision to make. I'll wait as long as she wants me to. However long that may be."

"We're not getting—"

"'Any younger'? Right. Noted," I interrupt, my patience finally starting to fray. "But that's not my problem, Ammi-ji. Your daughter is my wife. She's under my care and protection now. And if you ever stopped treating her like livestock for five seconds, maybe you'd see what I see—a talented, ambitious, incredible woman who deserves better than the way you speak to her."

Her eyes thin, head shaking in disappointment. "I hope you don't speak to Zinneerah like this."

CRAZY LITTLE THING CALLED LOVE

I can't help the dry smile that pulls at my lips. "The only person I hold higher than my mother and sister is my wife." I take a step forward, placing a hand on her shoulder, and leaning down so we're eye-to-eye. "And speaking of respect, let's review, shall we? Tonight alone, you've disrespected your daughter, her capabilities, and, if you ever push my wife again, it'll be the last time you walk through our door."

Her mouth opens, maybe to snap back, but I raise a brow—just one—and she clamps it shut.

"Respect is a two-way street, Ammi-ji. If you want it, learn how to give it," I say, fixing her dupatta in place. "Now, have a great rest of your evening."

Without waiting for her to recover, I turn and walk away.

36

Zinneerah

Chai is poured, steaming and slightly over-sweet the way everyone likes it.

I set out the sponge cake and butter cookies, which I'm proud to say turned out decent enough to avoid critiques from the aunties.

Out on the patio, the kids are tearing through jelly and custard, while the teenagers hover in doorways, sighing loudly and asking, "Can we go now?" every five minutes.

But the stubborn adults have settled in at the dining table with the determination of detectives at a crime scene. And, surprise, surprise, the case they're solving tonight is our marriage. Because apparently, dissecting someone else's life over chai is the universal law of every couple's first dawat.

Then there's Raees' cousin, Tariq, unfortunately from his father's side, who's just borderline annoying. Thirty going on fifty, with the confidence of a man who calls himself "an alpha" but still hasn't figured out why he's single.

Tonight, he's decided to double as an amateur journalist.

"So," he starts, leaning back, "how's married life treating you two?"

Raees, bless his soul, doesn't even look up. He just grabs his fifth butter cookie and goes, "Well."

Tariq stares at him. "Seriously? You can give us more than that, man."

Aunty Lubna waves her hand at Tariq. "Oh, leave him alone. You know Raees isn't much of a talker. He's always been shy. When he was little, all he did was hide behind his Rosy's like a little chooza." She even does the universal pinch-the-air gesture, as if she's holding Raees' imaginary baby cheeks.

Alina snorts from down the table, her green tea halfway to her mouth. "Is that what we're calling grown men these days?"

Raees is anything but a baby chick. If we're assigning animal traits, he's more of a Labrador retriever with an insatiable sweet tooth. Loyal, slightly goofy, and very food-motivated. But, I'll admit, there are occasional moments of chooza behavior. Like when he turns those big, brown eyes on me and smiles lopsidedly, asking for brownies at eleven in the evening.

Shahzad, seated conveniently to my left, mumbles, "I could name a couple of other farm animals that suit him better."

I elbow him hard. His ribs are apparently made of granite, because he doesn't even flinch.

"Actually," Ramishah pipes up, "Raees wasn't a chooza. More like a chamgadar in training." She tilts her head, clearly enjoying teasing him. "He turned his room into the Batcave when we were kids, and dragged me out of bed for midnight Monopoly tournaments like some kind of nocturnal weirdo. And let me tell you, if you've ever seen a baby bat, that was him. Tiny, scrawny, and constantly regurgitating."

Those who know what the word 'regurgitating' means chuckle around the table.

"Thanks for the charming imagery," Raees mutters, deadpan, as he reaches for yet another cookie.

"What was Zinneerah like, Maya?" Uncle Rasheed, Rosy Aunty's little brother, questions.

Mama cups her mug, her fingers grazing the rim as Shahzad and I both turn to look at her. She doesn't meet our eyes, and picks at the layer of malai floating on top, her face unreadable. "For a middle child, she was loud," she says. Our eyes meet for a second before she looks away again. "She used to look through my closet all the time, just to annoy me. And she loved watching me do my makeup. I taught her how to apply kajal properly." Mama presses her lips together for a moment. "There wasn't a single day she didn't sing. Always singing around the house."

She shifts in her chair, clearly uncomfortable with everyone's eyes locked on her like she's giving some sort of press conference. "I don't know," she finishes with a shrug. "She was closer to her father. If he were here, he'd give you a better answer."

"That was lovely," Raees says, breaking the silence. "Now I know who to thank for my wife's eyeliner skills."

I blush, offering Mama a smile. She just takes a long sip of her chai. Kindness is a once-a-year allowance for her, and she's already over budget.

"Can I ask you a question, Zinneerah?" Tariq says, zeroing in on me with the kind of sugary smile that gives you cavities just by looking at it.

I restrain a sigh and nod.

"What exactly did my cousin find charming about you?"

The table goes quiet, except for the faint scrape of Raees' thumb still brushing over my knuckles. Or it was—because the second Tariq's question's out, the soothing motion stops cold.

I glance around, wishing, for once, that Dua and my friends were here. They'd have plenty to say to Tariq and wouldn't mind saying it loudly. But they're outside with the kids. And Alex and Ophelia were spooked off the moment Mama showed up.

"Her eyes, obviously," Alina says.

"I think it's her smile," Azeer adds. I try to muster a smile for him in return, but it comes out a little wobbly. "See? Perfect."

"Or," Alina says again, with a raised brow at Tariq, "the fact that she's one of the most down-to-earth humans I know." She leans back in her chair, crossing her arms smugly. "I can see why she caught your eye, Raees. You've got great taste."

Raees looks at me, his seriousness softening into that crooked grin. And, like clockwork, I melt.

"That's all very sweet and all," Tariq says, "but weren't you two arranged?"

"Your point?" Shahzad tosses his hat into the ring. "Arranged or not, they're happy together."

That's . . . surprisingly sweet after the threatening aura he's been brooding around with.

But Tariq's like a dog with a bone. "I didn't say they're not happy together. I'm just wondering what the hell they even have in common if they're arranged?"

Azeer steps in. "Raees and Zinneerah had a whole year to get comfortable with one another," he explains. "Whereas Alina and I had, what, a week? Sure, we were at each other's throats most days, but if you asked me to walk through fire for her now, I wouldn't hesitate."

"And we met under the worst possible circumstances," Alina chimes in, her lips curling into a small, knowing smile.

Relatives on my side nod in agreement, clearly reliving the infamous food fight at Iman's wedding. Alina and Azeer's "meet-cute" involved flying Gulab Jamuns, overturned biryani trays, and chunks of lemon cake everywhere. Dua hasn't touched a rasgulla since she got slammed in the face with one.

"Whatever." Tariq dismisses the subject. "Married life isn't for me."

"Oh, we've been trying to find a girl for him," Lubna Aunty sighs, as if her life's greatest burden is Tariq's refusal to leave the singles club. "But so far, no luck. Those WhatsApp groups don't help either."

"Marriage is for miserable people, Amma," he declares.

"Surprised you're still single," Ramishah retorts.

He glares at her. "You're married to a white guy. Should you even be talking?"

She doesn't flinch. "Half the man you'll ever be."

"Ramishah," Rosy Aunty warns.

How old is Tariq again? Thirty? Thirteen? He has the emotional intelligence of a used tissue.

"Anyway," he says, raising his voice to steer the conversation back into his petty little playground. "In case I needed another reminder why I'm never getting married. Exhibit A." He gestures toward Raees and me like we're a sideshow act. "Seriously, how do you even communicate?"

"Haan, that's true," Batool Aunty, Mama's cousin, agrees. Of course, it's out of the goodness of her heart. She's always ready to deliver a eulogy, even when nobody's died. "I don't understand why you're quiet, Zinneerah beti. Kuch bol bhi lo. Baat karo hamare saath."

It's not like I don't want to speak with them, but I've hit my quota for the evening. The argument with Mama earlier left me with just enough fuel to sit here, sip my chai, and focus on not throwing a butter cookie at someone. At Tariq.

"It's her choice," Raees responds on my behalf. His words are aimed at Batool Aunty, but his eyes don't leave his cousin Tariq, who's two seats down and already smirking like he's plotting his next line.

"Quiet wife, happy life," he says. *There it is.* "Believe me, Raees, you'll understand what I mean when she starts running her tongue again."

The words are a punch to the gut, but I don't flinch. Not outwardly, anyway. Instead, I inhale silently and drop my gaze to a piece of napkin on the table. However, my face muscles twitch, and I know everyone can see it.

Raees straightens in his seat. "Tar—"

"Men like you are the reason behind a woman's silence," Shahzad mutters. In Urdu, no less.

The elders gasp dramatically, hands clutching hearts like he just cursed the family name. Murmurs spread like wildfire, most of them directed toward Mama, who is now sitting ramrod straight.

My lovely, reckless brother leans back, his arm casually draping across the back of my chair.

I nudge his knee under the table, shaking my head at his absolutely absurd decision to throw that line out here, especially in front of the aunties.

He doesn't give a shit.

Fair enough.

"Oh, look at that!" Tariq snaps back. "Another player who doesn't even have the power to speak at this table, let alone sit at it." He leans forward, his smirk widening. "Didn't you disown your family, Shahzad? Couldn't handle being a man after your dad died, so you ran off and abandoned your sisters and mother?"

It's like a match to a gasoline-soaked rag.

I don't even realize I'm half-rising from my seat until the thought of dousing Tariq's smug face with my scalding Earl Grey flashes through my mind like an instinct.

Shahzad plants his cup down so hard it nearly cracks the saucer.

His jaw tightens, and his tongue presses against the inside of his cheek as he lets out a scoff that's somehow more terrifying than any words he could have thrown back. The options are simple: deliver this man straight to hell, or rise above it and not play Tariq's game.

And then the choice is made.

"I don't think you'll have the power to speak at this table when I cut your damn tongue out!" The table shakes as Shahzad slams his fist down, hard enough to rattle the silverware and send a collective gasp rippling through the room.

"Okay, now!" Alina shoots up from her chair like a fire alarm just went off, grabbing Shahzad's arm and yanking him backwards. "Let's go get some fresh air before you break the furniture—"

"No." Shahzad doesn't budge. He looks directly at Tariq, his hand twitching to rip the skin from his face. "Apologize to her."

My pulse skyrockets.

I dart a panicked look toward Rosy Aunty, who's held protectively by Ramishah, clutching her mug like a self-defence weapon if this turns into an actual bloodbath.

My hand shoots out to grab Raees', holding on like a sinkhole has opened underneath my seat.

"Apologize for what?" Tariq stands, his lanky frame swaying slightly as he pushes his hands into his pockets. "For speaking the truth?" His eyes are bloodshot, burning with a wildness I can't believe I hadn't noticed before. He lets out a manic laugh, taking a step closer to my brother. *Oh, my god.* He's on something. How am I just noticing this now? "Go ahead, asshole."

"Tariq!" Lubna Aunty shrieks, grabbing at her son's arm. He jerks it out of her grasp.

Shahzad's nostrils flare, his breath coming laboured as his fists curl tight at his sides. "*Apologize,*" he emphasizes, which makes it a hundred times more dangerous. "While I'm still being nice."

My heart's in overdrive, thudding so hard it feels like it's about to launch itself out of my chest and onto the table. I force myself to speak. "Please, Shahzad. Sit down. Just let it go."

But my brother doesn't let go of things. And right now, he's looking at Tariq like he's seconds away from driving a knife straight through his arrogant face.

"He will apologize to you in private," Mama grits out, but still holding on to a brittle veneer of politeness. It's for show, but I know her too well. Beneath that façade, she's seething. She probably wants to tear Shahzad's voice box out with her bare hands—or, honestly, even Tariq's at this point. "My son—"

"Not your son, Maya," Shahzad interrupts, a bitter chuckle rolling out of him. The elderly are on the precipice of a stroke. "And I don't need you controlling what I can or can't do. You lost that privilege the day you decided to become a mother."

"*Shahzad!*" Alina hisses, her nails digging into his arm in a last-ditch attempt to rein him in, but he doesn't waver.

"I'm not leaving until he apologizes." Shahzad's focus snaps back to the slimy, drugged-out bastard.

And because he's the human equivalent of kerosene at a bonfire, Tariq grins wider. "This," he says, throwing an arm out, "*this* is the family you married into, Raees?"

He barks out a laugh, turning toward Rosy Aunty like she's the audience he's playing to. She flinches, shrinking into Ramishah's side. After everything she's endured—being humiliated day in and day out by her husband and his family—I don't blame her for freezing up from his nephew's stupid act. "I mean, shit, you didn't have the guts to work things out with Saira?" He continues, now fully leaning into his performance. "At least she came from money."

"Oh, for fuck's sake!" Ramishah shoots up from her chair, palms slamming onto the table with enough force to rattle everyone's chai cups. "If you don't sit your ass down in the next three seconds—"

But Tariq's beyond reason now. Drunk on his own toxicity and whatever else might be in his system. "The golden boy!" He places a hand on Raees' shoulder, who's still as a statue, staring at his mother. "The apple of everyone's eye here," he says, ruffling the top of my husband's hair, "married Helen fucking Keller." His fingers tangle together as he mocks my ASL. "That's me saying, 'No offense, sweetheart.'"

I can feel the heat rising in my face as tears prick at the corners of my eyes. I don't even think about it. I let go of Raees' hand to quickly swipe at my cheek, trying to hide the evidence before it spills over. I refuse to give this prick the satisfaction of seeing me cry.

"Tariq, sit. Down!" Lubna Aunty continues with her protests.

Mama jumps in to stoke both men's flames. "Sit down, both of you!"

Shahzad won't sit the fuck down. He's calm and composed, which is the worst of all signs of danger. "Apologize, motherfucker."

Tariq snaps. His hand flies to the nearest glass on the table, gripping it with the clear intent to throw—

Raees stands abruptly and grips Tariq's wrist, twisting it so harshly the glass slips and shatters onto the table.

Chairs scrape. Voices yell. Feet shuffle backward.

But I can't focus on anything else except Raees, who pins Tariq's arm behind his back. He knees him in the shin, and Tariq collapses with a groan, folding awkwardly onto the ground. Right in front of me.

He lets out a guttural whimper, his other hand scrabbling at the table leg for support, but Raees doesn't let him move an inch. He looms over him, towering and terrifying.

"Apologize," Raees asserts, dangerously quiet, and I forget how to breathe. "To my wife." He looks so relaxed, holding his cousin in place. "And to my mother."

My mother-in-law and I exchange looks, and neither one of us recognizes the man before us.

This isn't my husband. This isn't the man who laughs too loudly at his own jokes or sneaks extra cookies when he thinks I'm not looking. This man is someone else entirely. His face is stone. And his eyes . . . they don't blink.

Raees presses down on Tariq's wrist, forcing his shoulder forward, lower, until he's bowing in my direction. The whole scene feels unreal, like I'm watching it happen from outside my own body.

"I'm sorry, Zinneerah!" Tariq yells, his voice cracking into something pitiful and small. "I-I'm sorry, Rosy Aunty!"

The moment the words leave Tariq's mouth, Raees lets go with a sharp shove, sending him sprawling sideways. He lands awkwardly, his hands scraping against the shards of glass littering the floor.

Raees' eyes find mine, and just like that, he's back.

His shoulders relax, his grip on the moment softens, and suddenly he's himself again.

The man I know. The man I love.

Without a word, he reaches for my hand, his fingers threading through mine.

And before I can think, before I can weigh the million conflicting emotions churning in my chest, I hold on. Tight. Clinging to the only piece of driftwood left in a wreckage. I know if I let go, we'll both sink.

I should be terrified. My legs should be moving me far, far away from him. My brain should be screaming for me to run for the door, to hide from the dark thing I just saw take hold of my husband. The oblivion in his glare, the ferocity simmering beneath his soft skin, the powder-white knuckles. All it would've taken was one more word from Tariq, and Raees would've buried him.

But I don't feel any fear. Not even close.

I feel safe. Shaken. Weak. Exhausted to my very core. The only cure is a bed and a year's worth of rest.

The voices from outside start to flood into the house now—high-pitched, nervous murmurs that grow louder with every passing second. The kids rush in first, then my friends, then Dua, all of them looking from Raees to Tariq and back again, wide-eyed and worried.

Raees turns toward them, and for the first time, he seems to see himself through their eyes.

His hand slips from mine. Slowly. Almost like he's pulling away from the edge of some unseen cliff. Whatever remaining darkness had claimed him disintegrates, scattering like ash on the wind. His shoulders sag, his breaths come in sharp, uneven gasps, and suddenly he looks fragile.

His eyes shift to Tariq, who is now being helped up by Lubna Aunty, her small frame stooped with concern. Blood smears on Tariq's hands as he winces, keeping his gaze far from my husband.

Raees steps forward to help, but Tariq stiffens, flinching as if he might lash out again. Lubna Aunty pulls him close, her arm curling protectively around her son, and together, they shrink back—away from Raees.

Away from us.

I look around the room, my throat dry as paper. Every single relative gathered here wears the same expression: fear.

I see it in their eyes, in the way they shift uncomfortably on their feet, in the nervous glances they cast at Raees.

Why? Why are they looking at him like this? Like he's a monster? Like he's done something unforgivable? He was standing up for me. Tariq had it coming. He provoked us, rambling on with that self-righteous attitude, spitting venom with every word. And now, because Raees finally pushed back, they're afraid of him?

I glance at my husband, at the way his chest heaves, at the way his hands fall uselessly to his sides. And my heart aches. He just wanted to protect me. To stand up for me when I didn't have the strength to do it myself.

But none of them see that. None of them care. They just see the shove. The glass. The blood.

And all I see is a man who loves me enough to face the consequences.

"—looking just like Umar," mutters an uncle from somewhere behind me. *Umar?* Raees' father? My stomach tightens at the name.

Rosy Aunty steps forward cautiously. "Raees . . ."

But my husband is lost inside his head, his breath hitching as he stumbles over broken apologies. Muttered more to himself than anyone else. His eyes dart to me, searching, desperate.

I move toward him instinctively, ready to let him know I'm fine, that I'm not scared, that I'm with him no matter what. But before I can reach him, he turns and marches up the stairs without a word.

Ramishah's voice cuts through. "Take your children and see yourselves out on your own," she snaps. Then, softer, to our friends, "Please, make yourselves at home. The living room is all yours."

But I'm not paying attention to her.

My focus is on Tariq, hunched in a chair, his mother fussing over him. Lubna Aunty plucks shards of glass from his palm, dabbing at the blood like he's a child who scraped his knee on the playground. And the bastard sits there, wincing and grimacing, playing the part of the wounded hero so perfectly it's laughable.

It's *disgusting*. He deserved what he got. Every single second of it.

I glare at him. He doesn't look at me, of course. He won't. He can't. Coward.

Before I can stop myself, I nudge his foot with mine.

He startles slightly, finally looking up, and I lift both my middle fingers, the corners of my mouth curling into a smirk. "No offense, sweetheart," I say vehemently.

He flinches, his jaw tightening like he wants to say something back, but Lubna Aunty grabs his arm before he can.

"All right, let's sit down," Ophelia whispers beside me, her arm sliding gently around my shoulders to pull me away before he can swing at me.

I shrug her off without a second thought.

My feet are already moving, carrying me toward the stairs.

I need to see him. I need him to understand. *I'm not them, Raees. I don't see what they see.*

I need him to know that I'm still on his side.

Always.

37

Zinneerah

Raees' bedroom door is locked.

Knocking twice, I say, "It's me, Zin—" My throat tightens mid-sentence, and I cough, the tears I've been holding back scratching at my voice.

I haven't been publicly humiliated since my last relationship. It all came crashing down so fast, but Raees had a quicker reaction time.

"Raees," I whisper, pressing my forehead against the cool wood of the door. "Please. Open. Let me in."

Nothing.

Seconds pass; conversations become farewells. A minute; front door opens and closes. Five minutes; children are asking, "Is Uncle Raees okay?" Ten minutes; everyone and their judgment, their little looks and quiet criticisms, are out the door.

Twenty minutes, and I still stand here. Still hoping.

I can't bring myself to leave. Not until I know he's okay. Not until he knows I'm okay.

Soft footsteps behind me interrupt the silence. I glance over my shoulder to see Zoha creeping up the stairs, her small hands curled around Rosy Aunty's fingers. Of course, they sent a child knowing I'd send the rest of them away.

"Is he okay?" Zoha asks.

"I don't know," I whisper honestly.

"Give him some time," Rosy Aunty says.

"I don't want him to deal with this on his own." My chin trembles. Hot tears spill down my cheeks before I can stop them, and I swipe at them hurriedly with the underside of my palms.

"Oh, Zinneerah." Rosy Aunty reaches for me and pulls me into a warm hug, wrapping me in the kind of softness only someone like her can offer. "It's okay, jaan. Everything's okay. You're safe with us."

And suddenly I'm crying harder. I don't feel okay. Everyone downstairs stripped away me and my brother's dignity piece by piece while Tariq cackled through it all. And now Raees is upstairs, hiding, thinking he's the villain of this story.

She rubs circles onto my back, shushing me gently. "You know," she says, "Raees has loved you for many years from the sidelines."

I freeze, jerking back to stare at her through blurry, tear-streaked eyes. "What?"

She smiles knowingly, her hands bracketing my face with that motherly tenderness I've never quite gotten used to. "It's about time he tells you. I can't keep the secret any longer."

As if on cue: *click.*

Rosy Aunty steps back. "Let's go," she whispers, herding my niece back toward the stairs.

"Good luck," Zoha chirps over her shoulder, flashing me an encouraging smile before they disappear.

I wipe at my face again, quickly, and take a shaky step back as the door opens just a crack. It's dark inside. I can barely make out the shape of him in the shadows.

"Can I . . . come in?" I ask.

The door opens a little more in response.

I step inside his room and am greeted by pitch blackness, save for the streaks of gold from the sunset slicing through his sheer curtains, billowing from the fresh breeze.

Raees doesn't say anything. He just walks to the bed, and I follow, watching his figure slump down.

The room is dead quiet, except for the whistle of the wind and my own awkward breathing. I want to say something, but I don't even know where to start.

And then, finally, "I'm sorry," he whispers hoarsely. "I'm so sorry."

I remain quiet.

"I promise you, I don't lose my temper like that. I don't." His words spill out like he's been rehearsing them for twenty minutes and still can't get it right. "But what Tariq said about you wasn't something I could just ignore. I couldn't control it." His hands drag down his face, and he looks up briefly, only to drop his gaze again like the floor is more worthy of his attention. "I take full accountability. Completely. And I promise you this: no more outsiders in our home for the next year. Hell, maybe the next decade. I'll handle it. All of it. You don't have to see people like that again."

I stand, not saying a word, and pull him into a hug. Just like that.

His head falls against my chest, and I bury my nose in his hair. Mint and citrus, faintly damp from sweat. I hold him tighter.

I wasn't always like this. For years, it's been the opposite. After I was found by my siblings like a lifeless corpse with broken blood vessels in my eyes and one and a half lungs keeping me alive from the car crash, my brain just rewired itself into thinking touch was dangerous. Even hugs from people I loved felt like too much. It wasn't their fault; my body just didn't know the difference between affection and suffocation anymore.

But with Raees? It's different. It always has been.

"Can I hug you, too?" Raees whispers, cracks between his permission.

"Always."

Swiftly, he cocoons his arms around my waist.

I nearly bawled from Tariq's disgusting remarks, from my brother's persistence, from Mama trying to save face instead of showing a bit of empathy toward me and Raees.

Raees, who didn't hesitate. Raees, who saw someone disrespecting me and took charge. Not in a sadistic, self-pleasuring sense, but rather self-defence. He protected not only Shahzad, and his mother, but me, too. I'm not scared of him. Not even a little.

I draw circles on my husband's back.

Baba used to try and calm me down like this. After an off-key note ruined my riff during a rock solo. After my voice cracked during my first talent show, right in the middle of my so-called "big moment." After every stupid little thing that wasn't worth crying over.

After his aneurysm.

I tilt Raees' chin up, and the moment I see his face, I almost forget how to breathe. His eyes are bloodshot and puffy. His lips are swollen, his cheeks streaked with tears and sweat, his whole face like some tragic painting that makes your heart ache just to look at.

"Are you feeling better?" I ask.

He sniffles. "I think so."

"Okay." I nod, then tilt my head. "Do you want another hug?"

A placid chuckle. "Fair warning, Zinneerah. I'll grow addicted to them."

"Fine by me." It's the truth. I feel so close to him right now. So safe and comfortable.

"Darling," I murmur. "Call me that again."

Wonderment brightens his face. His dark brows mellow out, that lopsided grin curls at his mouth, and his lovely, large hands seek mine. "Okay, darling. Does that work for you? Zinneerah darling? Zinnie darling? Light of my life?"

Something in my chest tightens. Not because it's too much, but because he's sitting here trying to make me feel better. Sitting with this guilt for twenty minutes, spiraling, tearing himself apart over what everyone thinks of him.

What did I ever do to deserve him? To deserve this man who defends me without hesitation and still finds the strength to pick me up when he's the one who's breaking?

I sit down beside him, curling myself around his arm, and placing my chin on his shoulder to admire him. "You give the sun a run for its money."

His tired, half-closed eyes crinkle as he smiles. "You give the moon a run for its money."

"You love the moon." I've lost count of how many pictures he's sent me of the moon—crescent, full, half, or just a blurry white smudge too close to the horizon.

"I do," he says, his voice raspy. "I love her."

"Me, too," I whisper, my heart pounding in my chest. "I love the sun so much." My hand moves on its own, brushing a stray strand of hair from his forehead, tucking it neatly back where it belongs. "I am completely in love with you, Raees."

His throat bobs, and I hear the audible gulp before he croaks, "You do?"

"I do," I say the most obvious thing in the world.

"You're sure?" His voice wavers, and his gaze locks onto mine like he's scared I might be joking.

I lean in, pressing my lips to the curve of his shoulder, never breaking eye contact. "I'm sure."

Raees swallows harder.

"And . . ." I trail off, kissing his shoulder again, softer this time, "I want to take you out. On a date. This Friday. Dinner at home. You cook, I bake. After that, we can go swimming."

His breathing grows erratic. "I think I'm having a heart-attack."

"Why?" I laugh, lacing my fingers with his. "Because you've loved me for a while?"

His head snaps back. "How did you—"

"Years? Months? Weeks?" I tease, raising my eyebrows.

Raees shifts, reaching toward the bedside table and flicking on the lamp. The sudden light makes me squint, but I finally catch the way he's staring so longingly at me. "I wanted to tell you."

Tell me, I sign, *and I'll tell you everything. Last night we cry sad tears.*

He nods, sniffling hard, wiping at his eyes with the back of his hand. "Yeah. Okay. I'd like that." He pauses, then adds, with a shy smile, "How about we order sushi?"

I perk up like a starving meerkat. *You hate sushi.*

He shrugs, that crooked grin creeping onto his face again. "I'll eat vicariously through you."

Ice cream for you.

Raees laughs quietly, pressing his still-wavering hands to his chest. Then he lets out a long, theatrical sigh, one hand reaching up to cradle my cheek. "My wife, indeed."

After washing up and throwing on comfortable clothes—me in an oversized cardigan and skirt, Raees in a hoodie that makes him look more like a grad student than a professor—we head downstairs.

The living room is alive with our circle of friends in cleanup mode.

Alina, Alex, and Dua are locked in some kind of trash-dunking competition, tossing red cups into garbage bags while Azeer "coaches" them. Zoha and Juliette are tag-teaming the dining table, obsessively scrubbing at what I'm pretty sure is a design in the table rather than a stain. Shahzad and Ophelia are dusting the floorboards, and Ramishah and Rosy Aunty have claimed the kitchen sink, chatting as they tackle the mountain of dishes.

Raees clears his throat next to me.

Everyone stops in their tracks.

I glance up at him, noticing the slight adjustment of his glasses. He's about to switch into his "professor mode." Sure enough, his posture straightens as he takes my hand in his.

"Thank you all," he begins, like he's delivering a lecture, "for helping us tonight. I'm sorry you had to witness . . . all of that. The harassment from my relatives was unacceptable, and I can assure you they won't be invited to our home again." He pauses, glancing at me briefly before adding, "In fact, we won't be hosting any more dinner parties. As of tonight."

I nod firmly to punctuate his statement.

Our friends exchange glances.

"Are you both going somewhere?" Alina asks, her eyebrows raised as she gestures to our clothes.

"We're picking up sushi and ice cream," Raees replies. I notice he's avoiding eye contact with the guys in the room, choosing instead to focus on a landscape painting that's hanging above Dua's head.

"Oh!" Zoha bounces on her toes. "Can we come, too, Uncle Raees? *Pleeeease?*"

Before he can give in, Azeer scoops her up, pinching her chin. "Not tonight, baby. Tomorrow, I'll take you to get ice cream, okay?"

"That's too bad," Alex mutters, half-heartedly tossing another red cup into the trash.

"Damn it," Alina grumbles, shoving her trash in the bag with unnecessary aggression.

Raees, ever polite, turns his attention to Shahzad, who's still sweeping the corner of the room. "Is it okay if we step out for a couple of hours?"

Shahzad doesn't even look up. His attitude is pissing me off given Raees' bravery an hour ago. God, does my husband actually have to cure cancer to win his grouchy-ass over?

"It's fine, Raees Bhai!" Dua grins as she smacks Shahzad on the back with a little too much enthusiasm. He stumbles forward and shoots her a glare, rubbing his shoulder. "You two go have fun. Eat enough sushi to bankrupt them. Go wild with the ice cream. We'll be out of here before you're back."

Raees nods, looking slightly relieved. "I'll leave a spare key under the mat." He looks down at me with those honey-brown eyes. "Shall we?"

I smile up at him, letting my fingers do the talking. *Take my hand.*

His brows lift, a smile gracing his lips as he laces his fingers through mine. Then he squeezes—once, twice, three times. The signal we've used a hundred times before. "Don't let go," he whispers.

I move my hand across and downward. *Never.*

True to their word, once we're home with a platter of California rolls and two tubs of ice cream—strawberry cheesecake and birthday cake, the essentials—the house is so quiet it's almost eerie.

Everything is spotless. Mopped. Vacuumed. Dusted.

Raees washes his hands at the sink while I scoop the ice cream into one comically oversized bowl. "I don't know why I even bothered making friends outside our amazing circle," he says. "Still, I should probably try again. The couples at Amina's birthday party seemed nice."

"Fun day," I reply, tearing into a soy sauce packet with my teeth like a barbarian. "But don't start conforming yourself to other people's standards."

"I wouldn't dream of it," he says, coming up behind me. "Especially since I won't be interacting with these 'others' for a long, long while."

His hand presses against my back as he picks up a sushi roll. He sniffs it, doing his best to hide the disgust crawling across his face. "Mmm, delicious."

I scowl playfully. "Liar."

"Here, let me help." He takes the ice cream bowl and sushi platter out of my hands. "Dining table or couch?"

I point at the couch because obviously.

"Good call. I don't think I'll survive sitting at the table for a while." He sets everything down on the coffee table and sits on the floor, patting the space beside him. He even grabs a cushion and props it behind my back because he's just that kind of man. I want to marry him again on the spot.

We crack our chopsticks and start eating like two very hungry, very stressed-out people who are convinced—correction: who *know*—food can solve all problems.

Raees abandons his tempura halfway through to attack the ice cream, then circles back to some plain rice, then back to the ice cream. It's weird, but it's also Raees, so it tracks.

"Try some." I plant a sushi roll on his bento box. "And don't sniff it. Just eat it. Be brave."

He picks it up like it's a live grenade. "Are you sure this won't kill me?"

"Only one way to find out."

Deep breath in, he carefully places the roll into his mouth, chews once, and immediately regrets every choice that led him to this moment. His face turns squeamish like he's just swallowed poison, and he starts shaking his hand wildly, flailing his hands at me for a napkin.

I tut three times, handing him a tissue paper to spit it out on. "You owe me one roll."

Raees grabs the ice cream bowl like it's a life raft, and takes a giant bite. "I love you, Zinneerah, and I love your favorite foods. But I do not, and will never, love sushi. I'm sorry. I'm weak."

I pop a roll, scrunching up my shoulders and exaggerating a moan. "Mmm! Delicious. A little piece of heaven."

"Whatever rows your boat, darling."

I stare at him, the wasabi burning my sinuses because I ate too much in my desperate attempt to stop my face from glowing red.

Then, out of the blue, "When's the last time you went to Studio 365?"

"Uh . . ." I blink. "A few days ago. It was empty. Martin retired, and now his son's running it. Or was. He's selling it. Not enough money coming in." I pause, the thought leaving a weird ache in my chest. "I always wanted to work there. You know, as a baker."

"Part-time baker, full-time performer?" he asks, knuckles resting against his temple as he watches me.

My smile grows. "You watched me perform there?"

"Zinneerah, I have been in love with you for six years," he says. "So yes, I've watched you perform countlessly."

Did I just hear what I think I heard?

Raees Shaan. My husband. *Six* years? Six entire *years*?

What. The. Hell.

Is my face still functioning? Can I form words?

"Six . . . years?"

He leans back, grabbing a napkin to dab at the corner of his mouth as if this is a totally normal dinner conversation and he hasn't just upended my entire understanding of our relationship. "I should probably start from the beginning."

I'm frozen, chopsticks forgotten in my hand.

"You were in your second year of university," he says, "and I was in the middle of my PhD." Okay, accurate so far. I'd started performing that winter semester. Nerves in my throat, sweaty palms gripping my guitar. But how did he know that? He notices my look, like he's reading my thoughts, and holds up a hand. "Saira and I had met up to discuss her infidelity at Studio 365. She'd been rambling—excuses, apologies, you name it—but I wasn't listening. I couldn't. I was so overstimulated by the lights, by the noises. I was spiraling. It was like all the progress I'd made in therapy just evaporated. I thought maybe I'd had too much coffee, but no, it was more than that."

I press my lips together, knees pulled up to my chest now, watching him intently.

"I needed something—anything—to pull me out of it," he continues. "A plate, a mug, the clock on the wall. You."

I inhale sharply. "Okay . . ."

"You were sitting on a stool, adjusting your guitar, the one with that little sparrow decal on it. You were smiling at the audience, but I could tell you were nervous. Your hands were shaking. And then you introduced yourself, and I caught myself memorizing your words like I'd need to recite them back later."

I stare at him, my heart thudding so loudly I'm sure he can hear it.

"Then you started singing 'Somebody to Love.'" He exhales, head shaking in disbelief. "And I knew, right there and then, I was gone. Completely and utterly gone."

My hands fly over my mouth. That was my very first performance at the café. My voice cracking on the high note, my hands shaking so hard I nearly played the wrong chords. Two days later, I met Alex and Ophelia. But apparently, I'd also indirectly met my future husband.

That's bone-chilling.

"I left as soon as you finished performing," Raees says. "And then I sat in my car listening to the song on repeat. I played it in my old apartment, in the shower, in bed—basically anywhere I could sit and wallow. I was still trying to process the fact I'd been cheated on after putting myself out there, but I couldn't get your voice out of my head."

He reaches over and rests his hand on my knee, his thumb brushing back and forth. My brain is already going haywire, and now I have to deal with his touch?

How am I still breathing?

"I went to every coffee night after that," he continues. "I figured out you performed on the weekends. By then, Alex and Ophelia had joined you, and the three of you were doing covers. You always took lead vocals. Sometimes, you'd get a solo, and it was always a Queen song. Always. And I'd sit in the back, making playlists of every song you covered. I thought maybe, one day, I'd have the guts to start a conversation with you."

I stare at him, my thoughts spinning like a hamster in a wheel.

Everything . . . would've been so different if he'd just walked up to me. Or if I'd noticed him. I mean, I wasn't shy back then. Far from it. My confidence came alive on stage. I could've easily walked over, given him a flirty little smile, maybe even asked him out. But no. I was too caught up chasing my dumb fantasy of dating an underground punk-rock guitarist.

A fantasy that turned toxic fast.

A fantasy that stole my voice.

"I wasn't stable back then," Raees mutters, pulling me back to the present. "The first time I saw you, it felt like lightning. You were all I could see; all I could think about. I forgot I was even in a relationship. I forgot that I'd just been cheated on. I forgot that I was barely holding myself together." He shakes his head. "I wasn't capable of another relationship, Zinneerah. Even if—*if*—I had a chance with you, which seemed impossible because you're you and I'm me, I couldn't have dragged you into my mess. I wanted to be better for you. I needed to be emotionally available before I even thought about taking that leap." Suddenly, sadness creeps into his voice. "But by the time I thought I was ready—after two years of watching you from the sidelines—you disappeared."

I suck in a sharp breath. Two years? He waited two years and still cared about me after I imprisoned myself into a relationship that drained every ounce of joy out of my life? "You . . . waited? For me?"

"Every day," he whispers. "Every weekend, I'd come back to Studio 365, hoping I'd catch sight of you. Alex and Ophelia were still there for a while, so I asked Alex once if she knew where you'd gone. And you know what she told me?"

"Uh-oh. What?"

"'She's taken. Try your luck elsewhere, buddy.'"

I huff a dry chuckle. "That's Alex for you."

"It crushed me," he says, though there's a smirk on his lips now. "But that's when I realized, if I was going to find you again, I'd have to figure it out myself." He leans forward, his head tilting slightly. "And as luck would have it, Dua ended up in my class."

This handsome, geeky sneak. "You asked her about me?"

"Not directly," he explains. "Her last name caught my attention. I'd seen her at some of your performances. I wasn't about to interrogate her and look like an idiot, so I bided my time." He shrugs, all nonchalant. "Turns out, I'm a bit of a mastermind when it comes to you."

I laugh, shaking my head. "That's one way to put it. Stalker might be another."

"Dedicated admirer, darling," he counters smoothly.

Oh, man. I'm gone. Absolutely, hopelessly gone for this man.

And he's still got more to explain. "A few months before we met, I went to the campus gym where I knew the volleyball team practiced. It was an excuse to talk to Dua about her academics or whatever—"

I hold up a hand to stop him. "You're so proud of yourself right now, aren't you?"

"You have no idea," he laughs, grinning like a kid who just found out it's pizza day at school.

I laugh, too, because I can't help it. "Go on."

"Anyway," he continues, "I pretended I was having the worst day of my life while I was talking to her. Just sulking, looking all moody. You know, the classic 'tragic professor' act."

"Very convincing, I'm sure," I say dryly.

"And Dua, being Dua, asks, 'Are you feeling okay, Professor Shaan?'" He pauses for dramatic effect, and I hold my breath. "And me, being me, said, 'Oh, my mother's forcing me to get married.'"

My mouth falls open. "You did *not.*"

"Oh, I absolutely did!"

"What did she say?"

"She said, 'Same with my sister!'"

I snort. "Dua doesn't sound like that."

"She does."

"She doesn't."

"She does," he insists.

I concede. "So that was it? That simple?"

"I'm not even at the best part," he says, and now he's grinning like a golden retriever that just found a room full of tennis balls. "After she said that, I knew. I was mentally, emotionally, and financially ready to marry you. She showed me a picture of you, and without hesitation, no shame whatsoever, I tell her, 'I'm bringing my mother over tomorrow.'"

I blink at him. "You—*literally* the next day?"

"Next day," Raees repeats, completely unbothered by how insane that sounds. "And, well, you know the rest." He takes my left hand and kisses my knuckles. "Took you long enough to finally be mine, Zinneerah Shaan."

I feel my grin stretch so wide it might actually break my face. How do you not smile when someone confesses something like that? I'm holding it together until his pining, relentless love, patience, the fact that he waited six fucking years hits me like a freight train.

My face crumples, and before I know it, I'm shaking with sobs.

"Wait, what—? Why are you crying?" Raees panics.

"I'm sorry," I manage, burying my face in my hands. I can't stop now. "I'm so sorry, Raees."

"For what?" He leans in, brushing his hand over the top of my head, down to the nape of my neck. "How many times have I told you? Never apologize to me."

"Still . . ."

"Oh, darling." He pulls me close, holding me against his chest, his fingers combing gently through my hair. "Where did you go, Zinneerah?"

I clutch the back of his sweater, holding onto him like my life depends on it. *Six years.* He waited six years for me. Six goddamn years of believing I was worth it, that I'd come around, that I'd say yes. I wish we'd met sooner. I wish we'd had those years back.

Maybe in some other universe we did. Maybe we met in a world where our hearts and bodies weren't broken yet. Maybe we fought dragons together or piloted spaceships or stole robotic empires. Maybe I was a ghost, and he was the only one who could see me. Maybe we were superheroes. Or villains. Or anything else. But wherever we were, whatever we were, whoever we were, we were together.

I take a deep breath of his scent, of home, of the oasis I landed in after a hellish journey through the desert.

I pull a folded note out of my cardigan pocket.

For my friends, and for Professor Daniels, I'd written about my "disappearance," on my Notes app.

But for Raees . . . for him, I hand wrote it, re-wrote it, sitting on my closet floor in the middle of the night, surrounded by crumpled sheets of unfinished songs.

I sign, *Can we lay down?*

Raees nods and grabs a few cushions from the couch, tossing them on the floor. When he stretches out, I curl up next to him, resting my head on his arm. His other hand brushes over my shoulder, pulling me closer. I drape an arm across his chest, holding him tightly.

He glances at the two folded pages in his hand, then at me.

I nod, closing my eyes as he starts.

For once, I don't feel scared about what he's going to find there.

I just feel him.

Here.

Now.

Us.

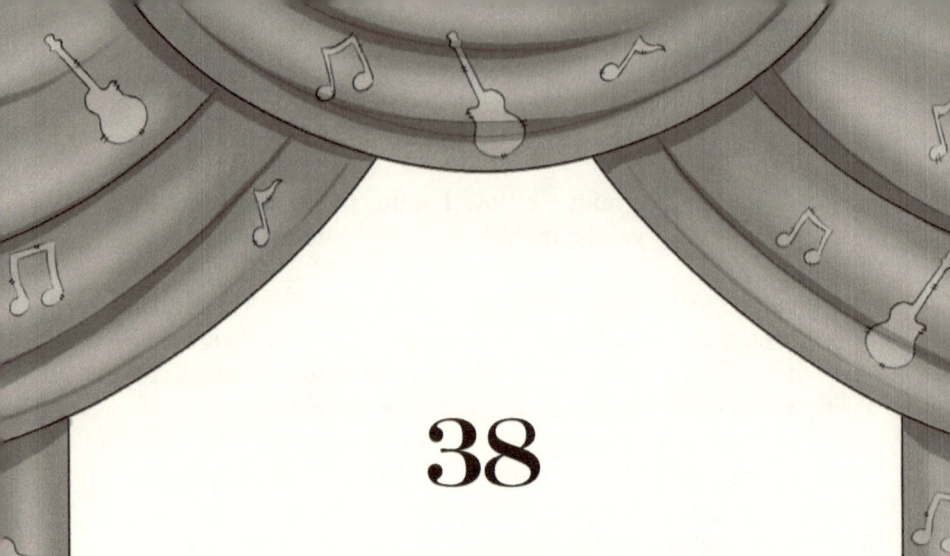

38

Raees

Raees, I'm finally writing a song by myself!

Crazy, right? Surprise, surprise.

These days, I'm finding it a little easier to breathe. A little easier to exist. But there are still those stupid, sneaky moments where I wonder if all of this will blow up in my face. That I'll say or do something so astronomically dumb it'll ruin everything. I don't know what it is. I'm just a fuck-up.

Good things don't last for people like me. That's the ugly truth I've been carrying around for years. And now that I have the best thing that's ever happened to me—aka **YOU**—I'm terrified I'll screw it up. That I'll push you so far away, you'll find yourself standing in some dark corner wondering what the hell you ever saw in me.

I know it's irrational. I know it doesn't make sense. But anxiety's a bitch like that. My head's like a washing machine stuck on the spin cycle. I overthink. I catastrophize. And sometimes I get this horrible thought: What if the best thing I can do for you is protect you from me?

Let me explain.

You know about my Baba passing away. That's where everything started falling apart. Mama returned to Lahore because abandoning us is all she's ever been great at. Shahzad leaving for culinary school made it worse, like ripping out the last support beam holding our family together (I still sometimes hate him for it).

Cue the rebellious phase.

When I turned eighteen, I'd had enough. Dua and I packed our things and left. She was just starting high school. I had no plan, no clue how to raise my baby sister, but we made it work. Thanks to Azeer and his family, we found this little shoebox of an apartment outside the city. It wasn't much, but it was ours.

I used the money Baba left me in his will to put myself through university. Scholarships and bursaries did the heavy lifting. Shahzad helped, too, when he could. I was building a life for us. Independence. Freedom. I didn't need Mama anymore. I was chasing what I loved, pouring everything into my music.

But, like I said, good things don't last for people like me.

I have this problem, you see. I cling to people who show me affection. It's like I'm constantly trying to hold onto that tiny sliver of love I had growing up, and I'm terrified that if I don't love someone back with the same intensity, I'll lose them. That I'll be abandoned.

That's how Damien happened.

I thought opening up to him about my past a week into our relationship was brave.

In hindsight, it was stupid.

At first, he was everything I wanted. Twenty-nine. A fellow musician. Supportive. Encouraging. He made me feel seen. Like I was the center of his universe. He'd listen to my songs, let me crash at his place whenever Dua's boyfriend stayed over. He treated me like I was his whole world.

Then came diner dates where we shared fries and laughed until our stomachs hurt, late-night drives with the music on full blast, windows down, yelling the lyrics to every song, mostly his band's songs. We stayed on the phone until we fell asleep, and he'd surprise me on campus with breakfast just because. We even wrote music together. He'd pluck out a melody since he was a guitarist, too, and I'd write/sing the words.

Then the dates turned into debates. Arguments about where we were going, who we were going to be since I was only twenty. The late-night drives turned into screaming matches, voices louder than the music, and once, he threatened to open the car door while speeding down the highway. He started getting into stupid fights at bars that left his body bruised for weeks. The long, sweet phone calls became abrupt five-minute conversations he'd cut short because he "had friends over." He'd show up drunk on campus, crying, begging for forgiveness. And then, when I didn't forgive him fast enough, he dumped one of my compositions in the trash, and said it wasn't good enough. That I wasn't good enough.

After that, the debates turned into destruction. Actual destruction. Of furniture. Of my things. Of me. He once smashed his guitar into a wall during a fight over drinking from his mug. The drives became reckless, with him slamming the brakes to scare me or swerving so close to the edge I thought we'd go over. He caused a near-collision once, spraining his wrist right before a big show, and somehow, that was my fault. The bar fights were now aimed at me. His fists. His hands. He crushed my phone against the pavement because he was convinced I'd been talking to another man. It wasn't another man. It was my father's voicemail. He didn't care. He disrupted one of my classes, staggering in drunk and screaming at me in front of everyone, calling me names.

But the worst of it—the absolute breaking point—was my birthday.

He'd slapped me the day before because I told him I wanted to invite Dua to dinner. I didn't want to be alone with him. I was too scared, Raees. I needed her there. But he wouldn't allow it. He wanted me all to himself.

To "make it up to me" he took me out to eat Mexican food. It was pouring rain that night, and he was already pissed off because of the weather.

I had ordered ahead to make things easier. My birthday, and I had to do the planning. I had to pay. And still, it wasn't enough. He was impatient, starving, snapping at me the whole ride. Then he demanded I feed him while he drove. I refused. I told him it was dangerous, that we could eat when we got home.

He didn't like being told what to do.

He forced me to undo my seat belt then wrapped it around my throat, tightening it.

And then he grabbed the back of my head and slammed my forehead into the dashboard.

Everything went black.

When I came to, my head was pounding, blood dripping down my face, and he was laughing. He kept saying he was going to kill me. Over and over. He said he'd dreamt about murdering me in my sleep. He said he had friends who could make the evidence disappear.

And then, in the middle of one of his twisted rants, he lost control of the car. The tires screeched. The car spun. And then we slammed straight into a traffic light.

He hit two women and killed them both.

No, three women died that night.

Whatever was left of me—the me who laughed, the me who sang, the me who dreamed—I died right there in the passenger seat.

But unlike those unfortunate souls, I woke up.

With broken ribs. Broken fingers. And a voice that barely worked anymore. My larynx was damaged in the crash. I couldn't sing. I couldn't cry. I couldn't scream. I couldn't even laugh at how absurd it all was. I was alive, but I wasn't really living. I was a ghost in my own skin.

The withdrawals were the worst.

I was diagnosed with insomnia, PTSD, severe depression, and anxiety. My life became a cocktail of medications I couldn't pronounce, online therapy sessions I could barely sit through, and days that bled into nights where I was too scared to leave my apartment. Some days, I couldn't even leave my room. Most days, I couldn't leave the closet I was holed up in.

I stopped eating. My throat felt like it was on fire every few days, and I'd choke down water just to keep myself from passing out. Every attempt to speak felt like trying to squeeze sound out of lungs that didn't work. What came out instead was this pitiful puff of air.

I couldn't let anyone touch me. I couldn't meet anyone's eyes. I was disappearing into myself. The only thing I really did back then was shower in water so hot it felt like my skin might melt, and I swear I cried fifty oceans dry in those first two years until I couldn't see straight.

But the medication started helping. A little. And the speech therapy was impossible at first, but it started to make a big difference too. I began whispering again then mumbling. Barely there, but it was something. Eventually, I took baby steps toward being human again, doing the things I used to love.

The first time I left my room, Dua sat me on the couch and cried. We watched TV together in silence because I still couldn't really talk, but for the first time in what felt like forever, I didn't feel like I was drowning.

The first time I left my apartment, it was snowing. I stood on the stoop, staring at the sky for an hour, letting snowflakes land on my face. I didn't move. I just stood there, breathing in air that didn't feel so suffocating anymore.

I started eating properly because Shahzad stayed with me for months to take care of me. He planned my meals, sat with me while I ate, and made sure I had something in my stomach at least once a day.

After two years of avoiding physical touch, he was the first person I hugged. We were in the kitchen. He made me a grilled cheese sandwich, and when I reached for him, he just hugged me. I broke down right there on the kitchen floor. He cried too. The next day, I hugged Dua for the first time. More tears—happy ones, I promise. She started sleeping in my bed after that, curling up next to me like she was holding me together.

I didn't sleep much, but those nights with her by my side, I managed an hour or two. Sometimes I'd wake up clawing at the sheets or accidentally scratching her skin during a nightmare. She never complained. Not once.

Three years passed. I still couldn't sing, but I was beginning to imagine a proper life again. Then, just as I was starting to feel like maybe I could take bigger steps, get a job or something, Mama came to visit.

Shahzad was there, thank God. He'd vowed never to speak to her again, but he broke that vow for me. He kept his composure as he explained why I couldn't speak, spinning some lies about a fatal throat infection because he knew the truth wouldn't help me.

Mama bought it. She believed it. Then, as if that wasn't enough, she began setting up marriage matches for me.

I didn't fight. I didn't argue. I didn't have it in me anymore. I didn't have the fire, the confidence, the motivation to say no. I didn't want to play guitar anymore. I didn't care about a career. I didn't want anything. I just wanted to escape her. And if marriage was the way out, then fuck it.

She brought me match after match, each one worse than the last. I rejected them all, though not because I was brave or had some great plan for my life. I rejected them because they gave me reasons to. One tried to force me to talk when I clearly couldn't. Another grabbed my hand without asking. One trashed his own mother and sisters like it was a personality trait. Another flaunted his wealth like it was supposed to impress me. A few just rejected me outright.

Mama didn't care. She just kept bringing more. Because, to her, my life wasn't mine. It was hers to control, and as long as I stayed under her thumb, I'd never really be free.

Mid-year, I met you.

Surprisingly, for once, it wasn't Mama's matchmaking obsession that led to you. Dua did. You were the last option. (Sorry, but hey, you won, so take it as a compliment.)

To be honest, I didn't like you when we first met.

But that was on me, not you.

You smiled too much. You laughed at Mama's terrible joke, you even had the audacity to eat every single one of my favorite chocolate biscuits Mama put out.

Every. Single. One. >:(

You said yes to the proposal immediately. But I didn't. I wasn't going to make it easy for you.

So, your mom and mine locked us in my living room together, like some kind of social experiment, to "get to know one another." I figured you'd start talking immediately. Like, a lot. Just chew my ears right off.

But you didn't.

You didn't force conversation. You didn't crowd me. You didn't fidget with your fingers, or shake your leg, or play games on your phone to pass the time. You didn't wander around the room making comments about the picture frames or try to crack a joke about the Teletubby costume I wore when I was three. You didn't even try to have a staring competition with me.

You just sat there. Quiet. For a whole hour. You let me sit in my silence without asking for anything from me.

"How'd it go?" Mama asked when you left. Dua was shaking with the anticipation of my answer.

I remember watching you open the passenger door for your mom, making sure she didn't bump her head, and then driving off. That told me everything I needed to know.

"I want to see him again," I said, and walked back to my room.

And here we are now. In this house. Our house. Married. You, the one patient, precious person who accepted me for exactly who I was. I don't even know how to explain how much that means to me. Someone I cannot bear to lose without losing myself.

I've always believed Baba raised me to be a kite. Wandering, colorful, honed to float through skies, seasons, storms. But even kites are tied to strings, aren't they?

The first sign of snapping was when Baba passed away.

The second when Shahzad left.

The third when it was just me and Dua trying to survive.

The fourth was Damien.

The fifth was forgetting who I was before all of it.

And just like that, my string was gone. I wasn't tethered anymore. I was free-falling toward the sun like Icarus.

But you? You didn't burn me.

With my ex, everything was about control. About power. He smiled like a prince but turned into a monster behind closed doors. He told me I was too loud, so I stopped speaking. He told me I was too opinionated, so I stopped arguing. He told me I was too much, so

I started becoming less. When he pushed me, I said sorry. When he shoved me, I said sorry. When he hit me, I still said sorry.

I thought that was love. I thought love was giving everything and getting nothing back. I thought love was walking on eggshells and making yourself smaller so the other person didn't feel threatened. I thought love was pain.

But then you showed up, and I realized I was wrong.

There are pieces of me I thought I'd lost forever. Parts I'd buried because I thought no one would ever be safe enough to let them out again. But somehow, you brought them back. You made me love me.

You brought me back to life, Raees.

And I know life hasn't always been kind to you, either. I know people haven't always been kind. I know you think you've been walking through the world alone, but you haven't.

Not anymore.

Now, I'm here. Right beside you.

You don't have to keep trying to make people like you. You don't have to stay quiet when someone talks over you. You don't have to brush off the hurt when you're wronged. You don't owe anyone that.

It's okay to teach me things I don't know. It's okay to ask me to teach you things you don't know. It's okay to need space sometimes (but if you take too long, I will get clingy. Consider yourself warned).

You don't need to change. You don't need to prove anything. All I want is for you to stay exactly the way you are. That's the best sweater you can ever wear.

I love you, darling.

Yours forever,

Zinneerah Shaan.

The ink smudges where my tears hit, blurring the word 'sweater.'

Finally, I fold it back up and tuck it into her cardigan pocket, glancing at her as she snores, completely unaware of the mess she's made of me.

Carefully, I slide my arm out from under her and sit up, legs crossed, staring blankly at the little white skulls on her black socks.

My mind is empty, wiped clean. Nothing else exists.

Just Zinneerah. Only Zinneerah. Always Zinneerah.

I clean up the coffee table, sniffing and wiping at my face like the lovesick, sensitive fool I am. I pack the rest of her sushi into the fridge, stack the cushions back where they belong, and then I scoop her up and lie back on the couch with her in my arms.

Zinneerah exhales quietly, her nose brushing against the crook of my neck, her arm instinctively wrapping around it like she's meant to belong here.

I brush her hair back from her face, piece by piece, until I can see her fully.

My lips press to her forehead and make home there, whispering, "I love you, too," against her skin.

August 20th

If you were a kitchen utensil, what would you be and why?

I think I'd be a rolling pin. Simple, but useful. I like the rhythm of rolling out dough, and it's something I've always had in my kitchen. What about you?

A cast iron skillet. Solid, dependable, does a little bit of everything. Not flashy, but it gets the job done.

That's kind of how I feel about you and the skillet. You're always making sure we're fed, like it's second nature to you. I feel lucky to have that.

And I feel lucky you're the rolling pin. You bring order to my chaos. I just throw stuff in a pan and hope for the best. I could never do what you do in the kitchen.

You make it sound more special than it is. It's just... rolling dough. You make full meals, sauces, everything from scratch. That's something I could never do.

Yeah, but rolling out dough isn't just rolling dough. It's knowing how to make something beautiful out of something messy.

And you don't just 'throw stuff in a pan.' You make food that feels like home.

You know, I like the idea of us being a skillet and a rolling pin. We're not the same, but we work together. You bake, I cook.

It does. And for the record, you're the best skillet I've ever known.

And you're the only rolling pin I'd want in my life.

♥ ❤♡♥♡❀♣♥♥♡ᵾ♡♥♥❤♥♡♣♥♡♥♥♡♥♥❀♥

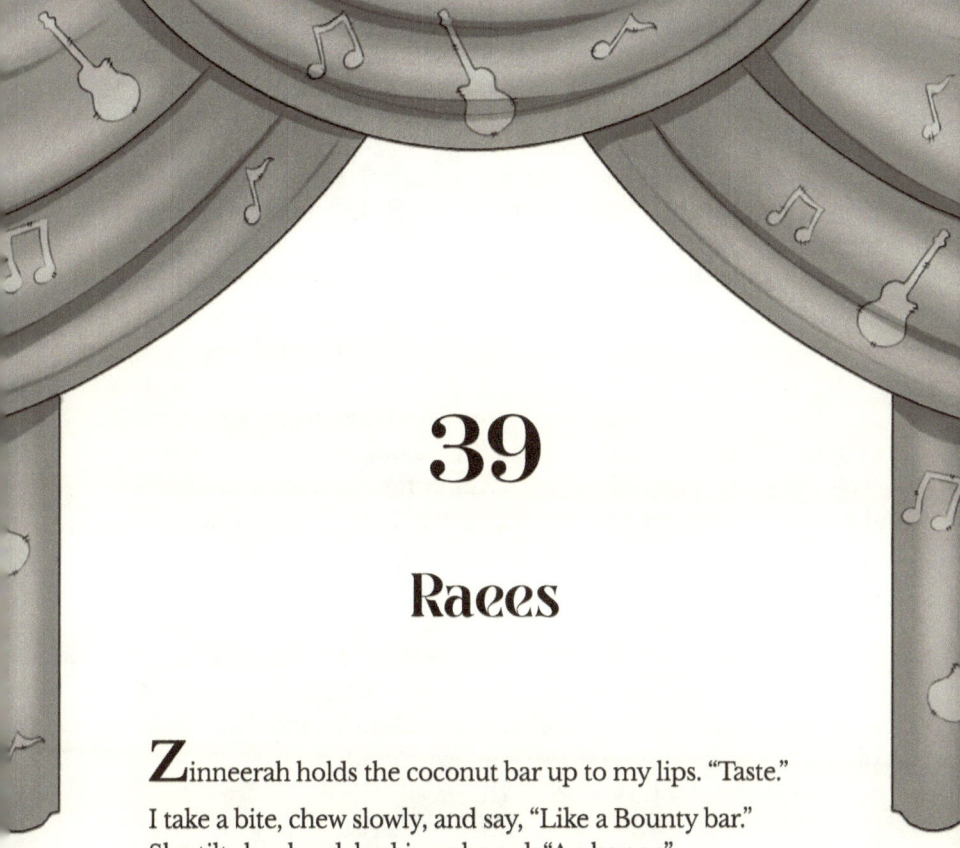

39

Raees

Zinneerah holds the coconut bar up to my lips. "Taste."

I take a bite, chew slowly, and say, "Like a Bounty bar."

She tilts her head, looking pleased. "An honor."

I blow on the garlic glaze, cooling it down just enough before holding the spoon out to her lips. "Taste?"

She leans in, takes it in one quick slurp, and nods thoughtfully as she swallows. "More salt."

I chuckle. "Good thing we're having a date at home. No awkwardly flagging down a waiter for salt."

"Salt is on the table."

I stop stirring, pretending to look up at the ceiling in thought. "Oh, right. That's how restaurants work. It's been a while."

"Me, too," she says softly, leaning into my arm, her hands curling around it. "But you brought the restaurant to me."

I can't stop smiling down at her. "And you brought the bakery to me."

Her brown-painted lips twist into a scowl. "You go to bakeries all the time."

"Yeah, but I like this one better." I pinch the little dimple in her chin just to tease her. Her nose scrunches up, her shoulders following in this cute little way she does whenever she's trying not to laugh.

And then she's off again, fluttering away to sprinkle more coconut flakes on the bars, muttering something about how they need to look presentable even though it's just the two of us.

God, I'm so lucky.

It's been two weeks since the sushi-and-ice-cream post-dawat cooldown. Two weeks of this beautiful, unholy domestic bliss that feels too good to be real. I'd given Zinneerah the master bedroom, so the next day we spent hours merging my clothes in her closet. My razors next to her bottles of Ramishah's expensive-smelling serums. My National Geographic magazines right next to her vinyl.

We drive to campus together, come home together, cook and eat together, and somehow make it through movie/documentary nights without arguing with each other over what to watch. I water my plants while she FaceTime's Alex and Ophelia, and then we do our night routines and collapse into bed.

I don't want this cycle to end. Ever.

We head out to the patio, where she's already hung the fairy lights she couldn't stop talking about last week. They're strung up along the fence and canopy, making the whole space look like something out of a whimsical fantasy movie set.

She sets down the drinks, and I pull out her chair. She tucks her skirt beneath her as she sits, and when I finally settle across from her, I can't help but just stare at my wife.

Zinneerah looks incredible. Hair down. Smoky eyes. Dark lips. God, what did I do to get this woman to marry me?

On second thought, I really shouldn't be asking myself that question.

"Hey," I say.

"Hmm?"

"You're beautiful." Because staring at her isn't enough. She needs to know every second.

Zinneerah freezes, fork halfway to her mouth. "You're beautiful."

"So I've been told."

"Oh? By who?"

"My mother."

She snorts and reaches across the table to pinch my cheek. She does that a lot when I say something she doesn't have a better comeback for. "You're impossible."

"And you're incomparable." I kiss the back of her hand.

She points at her plate with her fork. "So is this. Everything you make is incomparable."

"Thank you, darling." I squeeze her hand, giving her knuckles a soft peck. "You know, I bought your wedding ring the moment I decided you were going to be my wife."

"Is that so?" She narrows her eyes at me. "And when was that?"

"A year into knowing you existed," I admit, brushing my thumb over the little diamond on her ring. "I was drowning back then. Depression is like a tide. You think you've washed up on shore, safe for a while, and then it drags you right back under. But you . . ." I bring her fingers to my lips. "You were my anchor. You pulled me out. Slowly, yes, but you did it. And I'll never be able to thank you enough for that."

Her cheeks go pink, and I can tell she's trying not to look at me. She glances at the pool instead, her lips quirking into this bashful smile that makes my heart happily jump around.

I grin. "Now that I don't mind swimming in."

She lets out a sweet, airy laugh. "The weather's perfect tonight."

"Perfect for swimming after dessert," I say. "Oh, before I forget, will you still accompany me to Professor Wei's retirement party, my lady?"

"Of course, my lord," she says in an impressive English accent, swiping a piece of salmon off her plate. "Dress code?"

"Human clothes."

"Damn," she mutters with a straight face. "Guess I'll have to return the Joker costume."

I choke out a laugh so loud the neighbors probably hear it.

"And it fit so well, too," she adds, chuckling into her palm, and I swear it takes everything in me not to reach across the table and kiss her right there.

After dinner and dessert, we head up to our room to brush the taste of garlic and salmon out of our mouths.

She continues brushing, and I just follow her around like the puppy I absolutely am when it comes to her.

I stand behind her as she leans over the sink, watching her reflection in the mirror. "Don't take this the wrong way, but I've never realized just how short you are."

She pauses mid-brush, turning her head just enough to glare at me, toothbrush dangling out of her mouth. "I'm five-nine, idiot."

I grin and step closer, bracing my hands on either side of the sink, caging her in. She's got toothpaste foam at the corner of her mouth, which shouldn't be attractive, but somehow, on her, it is. "And I'm six-five. So, darling, to me, you're snack-size."

Zinneerah rolls her eyes so hard it's a miracle they don't fall out of her head, but a smile appears on her lips. She tries to keep brushing, but when I lean down to press my lips to her shoulder, she rolls it back.

I kiss her again, smiling against her skin, because this is my favorite version of her—playful, pretend-annoyed, but secretly loving the attention.

She just stops mid-brush and signs with one hand: *Let me brush my teeth.*

I chuckle, straightening up. "Fine, fine." I pat her back and drop a quick kiss on her temple as a parting shot. "I'm gonna go change into trunks."

It takes me maybe a minute to change into my plain black swim trunks and throw on a robe.

When I come back, I expect her to be ready, but instead, I hear the shower water running.

I drop onto the bed with my Switch to kill time. Twenty minutes later, I've beaten six strangers in global mode on Mario Kart 8—absolute domination, by the way—and the shower finally turns off.

"You do realize you're gonna have to take another shower after swimming—" I start, but my sentence dies the second she steps out of the bathroom.

She's wearing a black swimsuit—bikini, one-piece, doesn't matter because my brain refuses to categorize it. All I can register is the sight of her long legs, the way the fabric dips down her chest, and her robe hanging loose at her sides.

And that's when I notice the situation happening with my body. Fantastic.

Zinneerah strides forward like she's got no idea what she's doing to me, but I know better. She snatches the Switch out of my hands and tosses it onto the bed. "Geek," she teases, smirking as she grabs my wrist and pulls me to my feet in one quick motion. "Teach me how to swim?"

"Distracting," I whisper, "you are."

A snort. "Okay, Yoda." She's already dragging me toward the door before I can come up with a better response.

We head downstairs and out to the pool. The air is cooler now, but I barely notice because all my attention is on her as Zinneerah shrugs off her robe. She folds it neatly onto one of the chairs by the pool, and for a second, I can't stop staring. Her back, her legs, the way she moves—it's hypnotizing.

She turns to face me, catching me mid-stare. "Aren't you going to, you know . . ." She gestures vaguely at my robe.

I blink, scrambling for an excuse. If I take off this robe right now, I'm going to humiliate myself.

She tilts her head, and I swear, she knows exactly what's going on.

"Need help?" she asks, so innocent it's criminal.

"No, no. I've got it."

I turn around to save whatever's left of my dignity, loosening the robe and carefully folding it before placing it on top of hers. I make sure to hold it strategically in front of my lower region until I'm absolutely sure I've calmed down enough to face her. "There. All set. Let's go inside."

I take her hand, trying not to grin like an idiot as I lead her toward the pool. I step in first, the cold water hitting me just above the waistband of my swim trunks. It's still freezing despite warming it in advance.

Zinneerah follows, hesitating at the edge before stepping down sideways. My hands are there instantly, holding her.

She shivers as the water splashes her knees. "It's freezing . . ."

"You'll get used to it," I say, even though I know she's about five seconds away from calling me a liar.

She edges further in until she's submerged up to her neck. Her teeth are chattering, and she's scowling like I've just dragged her into the Arctic. "This is awful. Why do we do this to ourselves?"

I laugh. "Because it's fun."

She glares. Man, my wife is adorable when she's mad, but then again, she's adorable doing just about anything.

"Let's stay here for a bit," she mumbles.

I nod, leaning back to let the cold water creep higher on my shoulders. "Do you want to try the deeper end?"

She blinks at me like I've lost my mind. "I'll drown."

"I'd never let that happen." I take her hands, pulling her gently toward the middle of the pool.

She grabs onto my biceps for support, her fingers squeezing. "Oh. Firm."

I lick the self-satisfied smirk off my lips. "Thank you. Judging by how you've been ogling, I'm pretty sure you already know that."

She sighs. "I do. I ogle you all the time."

We chuckle in unison.

"But so does every woman," she mutters. "It's relatable, yes, but pisses me off sometimes. Like, can they be any more obvious?"

I pause us right as we're at the threshold of the deep end. "You don't think I'm irked when other men ogle you?"

"Nobody ogles me."

"Zinneerah, I ogle you in my dreams. And guess what? I'm ogling you right now."

"Your ogling doesn't count."

"Well, it should. Who cares about other people when we have each other to ogle?"

She frowns, and I realize maybe this isn't just some passing comment. I never predicted her to be this possessive over me. Given the look on her face, I can tell this has been eating her up alive for some time.

I lift her chin. "You're a vision, Zinneerah. I've been wearing glasses since I was sixteen, but you're the only woman I've ever seen this clearly. My eyes? They're only for you. My heart? Only for you. Every part of me is yours. So don't you dare look away from me, all right?"

Her eyes pop open.

"Perfect." I cup her cheek, and she leans into my hand without hesitation, her fingers wrapping around my wrist like she can't let go.

I tug her forward another inch, but before she can respond, her footing gives way, and she slips.

She crashes into my chest with a little yelp, her arms looping around my neck instinctively. I don't even blink before my arm curls around her waist.

"I've got you, darling," I assure, and I feel her exhale against me.

Her grip on me tightens. "I can't feel anything under my feet. It's terrifying."

"That's because you're short," I tease. "My toes are still touching the ground."

She pulls back just enough to glare up at me. "Show-off."

"Perks of St. Thomas Secondary's varsity volleyball team," I say, adjusting my grip on her as we float lazily through the pool.

Zinneerah tilts her head back to look at me, eyebrows raised. "Volleyball?"

"Oh, yeah. The coach practically begged me to join. Apparently, tall guys were in short supply—no pun intended. I didn't have a clue what I was doing at first, but the team helped me out. They'd stick around after school to teach me how to spike or we'd meet up in the park for pickup games. Once I got the hang of it, I became their secret weapon. Mostly service aces and blocks."

She chuckles, and her eyes light up like the fairy lights around the backyard, and I swear I'd say anything to keep her looking at me like that. "Have you told Dua?" Her fingers idly twist a piece of my hair at my nape.

I shake my head. "I haven't told anyone, actually. You're the first."

Her grin widens. "I played soccer in middle school."

"Yeah? How was that?"

"I sucked," she says bluntly, and I laugh.

"Couldn't have been that bad."

"No, Raees," she insists, trying to hold back a laugh of her own. "I sucked for real. Like, they didn't even want me to come to prac—" She turns her head to the side, coughing into her arm, and I immediately rub her back.

"And that's your talking quota for the night," I say. "Let me get you some water."

She shakes her head. *I'm fine*, she signs.

"You sure?"

Another nod.

"All right, then," I say, smiling. "How about a piggyback ride? You can hug me from behind."

She nods again, and I walk us over to the shallow end so she can climb on. Her arms wrap around the front of my neck, and her chest presses against my back as she settles in.

"Good?" I ask.

She gives me a thumbs-up.

I take us back out into the deeper end. "You know," I say, glancing over my shoulder, "you can use my body to sign. I'll get what you're saying."

Another thumbs-up.

"I've been meaning to ask," I say, turning us in a slow circle, "have you written any new songs lately?"

My songs?

"Yeah."

A few. No words. Only music. Not performing. My secret.

I grin. Of course, they are. "Will I get to hear you play anytime soon?"

Her nod is enthusiastic. *After swimming?*

"Will it be an original?"

Zinneerah's expressive eyes glaze over my face. I wasn't able to read what she was thinking before, but it's all so clear now. *I play you my new song.*

Guess who just won the lottery, ladies and gentlemen? "Don't mind me if I record you like I'm watching you play soccer."

Zinneerah giggles and leans in, pressing a quick kiss to my cheek.

It catches me off guard, but I don't mind. She's gotten so comfortable lately, curling into me without hesitation, wrapping me in back-hugs, resting her cheek in my palm when I'm driving, letting me kiss her shoulders, her hands, the top of her head.

And as selfish as it is, I want more. So much more.

We finish the swim and head upstairs to rinse off the chlorine. Zinneerah ducks into our bedroom's bathroom, and I take the guest room I slept in before. By the time I'm done—gray sweats, white tee, towel-dried hair—she's already sitting on our bed.

She's in that black satin bathrobe of hers, the one that drives me insane, tuning her black acoustic guitar with the golden sparrow etched on it. And just like that, my head's already spinning, because look at her.

She sees the foolish grin plastered on my face and mirrors it right back, patting the spot in front of her.

I happily oblige, sitting cross-legged in the middle with her. She presses her finger to her mouth, then her ears. No talking, only listening. "Understood."

Zinneerah lays the first strum that I recognize as the C chord. She rubs her right fingers together, takes in a lungful of air, then starts plucking at the metallic strings.

I see the concentration drawing on her face, the slight furrow of her brow, and the serene smile that follows every chord.

It's incredible how she communicates through her music. Each note feels like she's speaking directly to me. I can feel her emotions, her thoughts, her heart. It's like she's telling me a story, our story, without a single word.

Her fingers move so gracefully, dancing across the strings. She makes it look effortless. She *is* effortless.

I feel a lump in my throat, my heart swelling with an overwhelming sense of love and admiration.

She's always had a way of touching my heart, but this is something entirely different. It's like she's opened a window to her innermost thoughts and feelings, allowing me to see and feel what she cannot say.

The melody shifts, becoming softer, more intimate. It feels like a caress across my cheek, a raspy whisper of love. A lullaby and a confession all at once, and I know, without a doubt, this is ours.

This is her love.

Her fingers slow, and the music fades gently.

She opens her eyes and looks at me, a question in her gaze. I don't need to speak to answer her; she can see it in my smile.

I take her hand in mine, and press a kiss to her fingertips, still warm from the guitar strings. "Beautiful," I murmur.

A soft blush dusts her cheeks. *I'm glad you like it.*

"*Like* it?" I chuckle, placing my palm on the side of her neck. "You have no idea what that did to me. You transported me to another world."

She bites her bottom lip. "I wanted to do something special for you." I might combust right here and now. "That song . . . it was for you, Raees."

"For me?" My voice cracks. "You're serious?"

She nods. *Every note was for you. Because you inspire me. You make me want to create beautiful things.*

"I don't know what to say," I mumble, blinking as tears gather on my waterline and slip down freely.

"You don't have to say anything," she reassures me, reaching up to cup my cheek tenderly, thumb wiping away my tears. "You deserve every bit of it and more."

I lean into her touch, relishing the warmth of her hand against my skin. "You always know how to make me feel like the luckiest man alive."

A soft sigh escapes her lips, and she leans in closer, our breaths mingling in the space between us. "Raees," she whispers, "there's something else I want to share with you."

My heart races in anticipation, wondering what else she could possibly have in store for me. Perhaps another song? Maybe a Mario Kart 8 match that I've been secretly hoping for? "What is it, darling?"

She takes a deep breath, her gaze locking with mine as she searches for the right words. "I want us to consummate our marriage."

40

Raees

Mentally, I'm undergoing anaphylactic shock.

Hyperventilation.

Heat stroke.

Heart palpitations.

Blood pressure levels exceeding time and space.

Zinneerah's speaking words, waving her hand in front of my face.

I see her. I always see her. I'm aware of her nearness, her every breath and blink. But right now, I can't hear anything except the thunderous sound of the overwhelmed organ inside my chest.

"—ees? Raees? Hello?"

"May I . . . kiss you?" I ask.

Her brows arch for a split second. *Oh, no.* What did I actually say? Was it kiss you or kill you? God help me if I accidentally said kill you. Not the most ideal thing to say given that she wants us to have sex for the very first time.

Oh, man. I'm going to have sex for the very first time.

I'm not prepared. I don't have any protection. I don't know the steps. I always covered my eyes during sex scenes in movies—reflexively, even now. How do I make her feel good? How do I make this comfortable for her?

Zinneerah cups my face in her hands and lowers my head, staring deeply into each one of my eyes like she's checking to make sure I'm still in my body.

"Did you hear what I said?"

"N . . ." I make a strangled sound. "No?"

"Kiss me," she whispers in the space between us.

My head dips forward automatically, guided by her touch.

"You don't have to be nervous," she says.

How does she do that? How does she look at me like she's peeling away all the layers, seeing everything I'm too afraid to say out loud? It's unnerving. It's comforting. It's her. And it's the reason I need this to be perfect. Because *she* deserves perfection. *She* deserves more than the fumbling mess of a man I am right now.

My hands tremble as I lift them, finding her face the way she found mine.

My palms settle against her cheeks, and her skin is the finest silk. Her eyes flutter closed, and there's a peace in her expression that undoes me. Her trust in me is infinite, and I feel every ounce of it in my bones.

And then, finally, I close the distance.

The first touch of her lips against mine is so soft it almost doesn't feel real.

It's just a brush, a featherlight contact that sends a shockwave down my spine. Her lips are warmer than I ever could've imagined, and they fit against mine so perfectly that it steals what little breath I have left.

Is this okay? I wonder. Am I doing it right? I'm too aware of every second that passes, every minuscule shift of pressure. I don't know if I'm supposed to move, or if I'm supposed to wait for her to move, and suddenly it feels like my entire body is one big, clumsy question mark.

Just start moving, dumbass.

My lips press against hers again, a little firmer this time, and she doesn't pull away. That's good, right? That means it's good.

I draw back, just barely, and catch the faintest flicker of her eyelashes as they flutter open halfway. It makes me want to kiss her again, so I do.

Again and again.

Sweet, small pecks that feel simple to me, but her lips part a little more each time, like she's inviting me in, encouraging me to keep going.

My hand, which I don't even remember lifting, moves without permission, settling lightly on her thigh. But before the panic can take over, she leans closer, pressing into me, her lips molding to mine like she's saying, *Yes. Keep going.*

I press harder, testing the waters, and I hear it—a faint, quiet little sound from her throat, like a sigh. It's so soft I might've missed it if I wasn't this close. But I am *this close*, and it wrecks me.

Her lips part completely, and I follow her lead, my tongue sliding hesitantly into her mouth.

God.

God.

She meets me halfway, her tongue brushing against mine, and what's having a functioning heart and lungs anymore? I can hear myself breathing too hard, too fast, but I don't care. She tastes so good.

I don't think I'll ever stop wanting more.

A groan builds in my chest and slips out before I can stop it, and she reacts instantly, somewhere between a sigh and a whimper. It's the most addictive thing I've ever heard. My hands tighten on her face, my fingers pressing into her cheeks, holding her there like she's the only thing keeping me alive.

We kiss for what feels like forever.

Time doesn't exist anymore.

There's only the push and pull of her mouth on mine, sometimes soft and tender, other times hungrier, more insistent.

Her hands slide into my hair, and when her fingers tangle at the base of my neck, tugging lightly at the roots, I let out a low, shaky breath.

I don't even realize when it happens, but suddenly she's shifting, adjusting, moving to straddle my lap. My hands move of their own accord, sliding to her lower back, pulling her flush against me.

I feel her bathrobe slip off one shoulder, and the glow of her skin leaves me breathless.

My lips leave hers, trailing down to her jaw, then lower, finding the delicate curve of her neck. I press a kiss to the slope of her shoulder, my mouth skimming over the dip of her collarbone. When I reach the faint, faded scars on her neck, I hover over them, hesitating.

She doesn't pull away.

Instead, she breathes out slowly, tilting her head back even further, giving me more. Giving me everything.

Softly, my lips press into her skin. Her hands slide from my hair to my shoulders, her nails scraping lightly through the fabric of my shirt. My mouth moves down to the hollow of her throat, then just below her ear, finding the fragrant scent there.

"You are so beautiful," I murmur the truth against her lips.

Reaching for her bun, I undo it with careful fingers, watching as her hair spills loose around her shoulders.

It's soft as silk between my fingers, and I can't stop myself from threading my fingers into the dark, damp strands.

I remove my glasses and toss them aside, kissing her deeper, quicker, hungrier. Our tongues meet again, sliding together in a way that makes my head spin.

And then she pulls back. Just slightly. Just enough to let her hands move between us.

My breath catches when I realize what she's doing.

Her fingers undo the knot of her robe with ease, and the silk parts like water, slipping from her shoulders and pooling around her waist.

I blank for a second.

She's bare. Completely bare, her skin glowing in the soft light, her chest rising and falling with each slow breath.

My gaze lingers on the soft curve of her breasts, the way her skin seems to flush under my stare, the goosebumps that rise the soft hair on her arms as the cool air brushes over her.

My hands twitch at my sides. I don't know where to touch her first. I don't even know if I'm allowed to touch her. She's so beautiful it doesn't feel real.

I can feel her watching me, and when I force my eyes back to hers, I realize I've frozen. Completely frozen. I can tell by the quirk of her lips that she's noticed.

She takes my hand and carefully guides it up, placing it over her left breast.

My breath shudders out of me, and my fingers tremble as I take in the soft, small weight of her in my hand. Her nipple is hard under my palm, and my fingers flex instinctively, moving on their own. I can feel her rapid heartbeat thudding against my hand, and it makes mine go haywire.

"Is this okay?" My voice comes out more as a rasp than anything else.

"Mm-hmm." That little sound, the quiet approval of it, sends a rush of heat straight to my groin.

I kiss her, pouring everything into it—the awe, the need, the gnawing hunger that's been building for years.

My other hand comes up to her jaw, holding her steady as my thumb brushes her cheek. Her lips are wet and swollen, and I can hear it now, the soft, slick sound of us kissing, and it's driving me crazy.

My lips find her shoulder again, brushing over her skin, and I begin trailing kisses across her collarbone. I take the risk, and flick my tongue out, tasting the faint saltiness of her skin, and the breathy sound she makes in response is enough to undo me.

Then she moves.

It's subtle at first, just a slow, unconscious shift in her hips as she settles herself more firmly in my lap.

But then she does it again.

And again.

Her body rocks against mine, her soft curves grinding against the hard length of my erection, and I have to bite down on my lip to keep from making a sound.

The friction is unbearable.

Painful.

Perfect.

It sends bolts of pleasure racing through me, and I can feel every small movement she makes—the heat of her through the thin barrier of my clothes, the way her body fits against mine like she belongs there.

My hands slide to her waist, gripping her tighter, and I have to clench my jaw to keep from losing control.

"I—" My words stick in my throat, and I have to swallow hard before I can force them out. "I don't have any condoms."

She stops, her hips stilling against me, and my stomach twists. But then she leans back just enough to meet my eyes, and her lips pull into a smirk. "I don't think your mother kept the receipts for all the baby clothes she bought."

There goes my sanity.

I kiss her again, my hand threading into her hair and tugging her closer, like I need to fuse myself to her. I swallow the pitchy sound she makes as I guide her back, laying her down against the pillows. The bed shifts beneath us, and all I can think about is how perfectly she fits under me.

Her hands roam my back, her fingers slipping under the hem of my t-shirt and dragging against my skin.

It sends a buzz down my spine, and before I even realize it, I'm yanking the shirt off and tossing it somewhere behind me.

The second I feel her bare skin against mine, her breasts pressed to my chest, my whole body tightens.

I'm going to lose it.

I'm already losing it.

I kiss her bottom lip, then her jaw, then her throat, each one coming faster, messier, as I make my way down over each breast, kissing the soft curve of them, flicking my tongue over one hardened nipple, then the other.

Her breathing stutters, and I can feel the way her body is starting to respond to me, little by little, her chest rising and falling faster beneath my lips.

I keep going. Down her stomach, where I leave kiss after kiss, letting my hands slide along her waist, my thumbs pressing into her hips. She shifts under me, her thighs parting slightly, and my focus locks in.

I settle between her legs, my hands skimming up her thighs. Her skin feels impossibly smooth under my fingers, but there's no time to stop and think about it because my brain is racing ahead, panicked and needier all at once.

I press my thumb to the center of her slit, the heat of her searing against my skin, and my brain whites out for a second. "How do I make you feel good here? Please. Tell me."

Her breathing hitches, her chest rising sharply as my thumb starts to move, tracing over her with a confusing pressure. I watch her face, searching for anything—any reaction, any sign that I'm doing this right.

"Take my hand," I murmur. "Guide my fingers."

Her eyes meet mine, and for a second, I see the trust that makes me feel like I'm about to explode. She takes my hand, her long fingers wrapping around mine, and guides me exactly where she wants me.

When my fingers find her clit, her breath catches, and her hips twitch slightly against me.

Her gasp is like gasoline poured over a fire.

I press harder, circling the sensitive spot the way she showed me, and her head falls back against the pillows, mouth parting as her breathing quickens.

"Is it okay if I put my mouth here, darling?" I tilt my head down to press a soft kiss against the apex of her thighs

Zinneerah's fingers thread through my hair. "Please," she breathes out, and the sound of that single word nearly sends me over the edge.

I press my tongue flat and drag it up the length of her.

Oh, my god.

Oh, my god.

Oh, my god.

A low hum resonates through me. She tastes like the rarest ecstasy. Something sweet, salty, and heated, something I never knew I'd crave until now. God, I'd stay here forever, drunk on her, if she'd let me.

She squirms beneath me, her thighs brushing against the sides of my face, her hands tightening in my hair. Her gasps grow louder, breathier, and I swear to God, I could get off just from the sounds she's making.

My lips close around her clit, sucking softly at first. Her fingers tighten in my hair as her hips jerk off the bed, her breath catching in little gasps that make it impossible to think about anything but her. She's coming apart for me. *For me.*

Must be on the right track.

I suck harder, letting my tongue work in tandem, and her reaction almost knocks me out of my own head.

Her hands pull at my hair, her thighs trembling against my shoulders, forcing me to pull back. I glance up, confused, but she's already pulling me back down. "No, please. Again. Faster. Put your fingers inside. Middle and ring."

"Understood," I mutter, sliding my hand between her legs.

I push my ring and middle fingers inside her, my breath hitching from how . . . tight it feels. But she's practically inhaling my fingers as I probe deeper and curl them upwards.

God help me. She feels incredible.

I glance up at her flushed face, her lips parted, hair sticking to her damp cheeks and collarbone. She's a beautiful mess.

Her hands tighten in my hair, and her voice comes out wrecked. "Raees—I—"

"What?" I ask, panicking for a second as I pull my fingers out. "What's wrong?"

Her eyes fly open, wild and desperate. "Put them back in," she scolds. "Do that again. Please."

I blink, then smirk. "Got it."

I slide my fingers back inside, curling them upward the way I know she loves. Her back arches, her chest rising as she lets out a sound I want to record and listen to every night.

Goddess, indeed.

I thrust my fingers deeper, hitting that spot again, and she gasps, clutching her left breast. "More. Don't stop. More."

My thumb moves to her clit, circling in rhythm with my hand, and she's trembling so much I'm worried she's about to faint from the overstimulation.

I halt, glancing up at her flushed face. "Are you all right?"

She doesn't answer. She probably can't hear me past the rush of her own pleasure.

I smile proudly to myself. I'm actually doing this. I've only ever dreamt of touching Zinneerah's body this way. Her scent, her smile, her voice, her eye-contact—they're all triggers of making my blood hot. I want to please her this way, see her naked and heaving because of my fingers and mouth, every single day. And now that I've gotten a taste of her, I don't know how I'll ever stop.

I slide down and put my mouth back on her, pushing her knee further apart so I can dive deeper. My tongue moves in sync with my fingers, and the way she reacts, the way she trembles, melts into the sheets, grips the back of my head, makes me feel like I can die happy right here.

She's whispering my name like a prayer.

Over and over again.

Raees, Raees, Raees.

And when she crashes, I'm right there, drinking every bit of her as she falls apart in my hands and mouth.

Her fingers slide through my hair again, softer now, her breathing uneven but slowing.

She coughs lightly, her chest still heaving, and I lift my head to look at her, needing to see her face. "What?"

"You," I whisper, grinning a little as I take in the flush on her cheeks, and the way her lips are curved in a blissed-out smile.

"Me?"

"You. Only you." I lower my mouth to her skin, kissing her waist, her ribs, the underside of her breast. Every inch of her is mine to worship. "Always you, darling."

She touches my face, her fingers brushing against the corner of my mouth. "You've got a very skilled mouth," she says, smiling lazily. "You sure that was your first time?"

I laugh, pressing a quick kiss to her sternum. "First time," I say. "But definitely not the last."

Her fingers brush over my lips, tracing the curve of my smile. They trail down my neck, my chest, slow and sure. When her hand finally dips lower, settling near my pelvis, my breath stalls. I'm not proud of the pathetic noise I make when her fingers trace the waistband of my boxers, toying with me, but there's no dignity left in my body anyway.

"Is it okay if I touch you with just my hand?" she asks.

I shudder. "Only if you want to."

"Oh, I want to." Her breath feathers against my ear, and then she goes lower, her hand sliding beneath the waistband. "But you have to stay really still for me. Can you do that?"

"Yes," I whisper brokenly. Fuck, this is really happening.

"Good." She tips up her chin. "Kiss me."

I press my lips to hers because there's no version of me that wouldn't. She could ask me for anything right now, and I'd give it to her without a second thought.

I groan against her mouth, something between a gasp or her name, and she pulls back just enough to look at me.

"Oh, my god," she murmurs, her hand tightening slightly as she strokes me once, testing. "You're so big . . ."

Worry seizes me. "Is that . . . good?"

"For the sake of my mobility? Probably not." She starts slowly, her hand stroking me with just enough pressure to make my vision blur. Her thumb slides over the tip, pressing down. "But I can't wait to take all of it."

My arms tremble as I hold myself up over her, trying not to collapse from the way she's undoing me with nothing but her touch, and her words.

"I haven't even started, and you're already breathing so hard," she quips, her lips curving into a sly smile.

"My love, are you seeing me for the first time?" I chuckle raggedly. "This is how I am every time around you."

"I see you," she murmurs. And then her strokes get faster, her grip firmer, and my lungs are working overtime just to keep up.

I can't think. Can't focus. My hand tangles in her hair, needing something to hold onto.

But then I meet her eyes, and it's game over.

Those eyes—fuck, those eyes. They've had me trapped since the day I saw her, and right now, they're looking at me like I'm the only man who's ever mattered.

A whimper slips past my lips, unbidden, and I barely manage to choke out her name. "Zinn—"

"Shh." She cuts me off, pressing her lips to my jaw, her strokes picking up just enough to make me gasp. "No talking unless you're going to tell me how good I'm making you feel."

"You're . . ." My voice cracks embarrassingly, and she laughs again, the sound going straight to where she's handling me. "You're making me feel insane," I manage to choke out.

"That's right." Her free hand cups the underside of my jaw. "You don't have to think, Raees. Just let me take care of you."

Her strokes become firmer, her hand twisting and sliding in a rhythm that feels so good, I'm not even sure I'm still breathing. She alternates between slow pumps and quick movements. Her other hand doesn't stop, cupping and squeezing in ways that send jolts of pleasure through my entire body.

I groan again, my head falling onto her shoulder, hips bucking.

"Stay still," she orders, and my entire body obeys without question.

"Yes." I gasp. "Yes. Anything."

"Come," she whispers. "Do it for me."

I'm barely holding on, but I need to be sure. "Are you sure?"

She doesn't answer. She just tightens her grip and tugs, hard enough to pull the last shred of control out from under me. "Do it, Raees."

And I do.

I come apart in her hand, my body shuddering as she continues stroking me, her name falling from my lips before I kiss her.

It's overwhelming. My head spins as the realization crashes over me: this is Zinneerah. This is my wife. The woman I used to watch perform at our café, the one who turned all my miserable days into something brighter just by being in the same room. And now she's here, touching me, kissing me, telling me to come undone for her.

As soon as I catch my breath, I shower her face with a hundred kisses, the sound of her husky laughter making me smile. "Where did you learn that sorcery, woman?"

"The girls group chat."

"Probably shouldn't have asked."

She presses her palms against my chest, gently pushing me back. "Now sit up," she says. "It's easier this way."

"Whatever you're comfortable with." I sit up against the headboard, still completely paralyzed by her.

Zinneerah straddles my lap again. She holds my face in her hands and gives me three seconds to taste that infectious smile. Her hand travels down my chest and grips my cock. Standing just a few inches, she centers it at her entrance and slowly sinks down.

I groan from the sudden sensation in the scenery. She's being stretched out widely, sighing softly, cursing quietly, nails digging into my shoulders.

My head rests back on the wooden panels. I'm hallucinating. I must be in some sick, lucid wet dream. She feels wet and hot, smells like mint and flowers, rasps out my name and kisses my skin and touches me endlessly.

"You're so big," she grits out, head dropping on my shoulder. Her body heaves like she's worked manual labor in mid-July. "I swear I can feel you. Up to my stomach."

I run my hand down her back. "Take it easy, darling."

"Can't look down. Is it in?"

I peer for her. "Not yet."

"What? It feels like it's in."

"Just the tip, I'm afraid."

Zinneerah exhales. "I'm so bad at this."

"No, you're not. Take a deep breath and slowly lower yourself on me." I cup her face in my hands, feeling the heat of her skin. She practices her breathing, her nails marking my shoulders. "That's it, darling. You're doing so good."

Zinneerah is fully seated onto my lap.

"Is it okay?" I ask.

She nods her head. "I'll start moving now." She takes my hands and places them on her hips. "You can touch me anywhere."

I nod, feeling sudden shyness creep up on my face. "You, too."

Zinneerah bites her bottom lip, beginning to roll her hips forward. She hisses through her teeth.

"We don't have to do it in this position," I assure.

"Let's try." My stubborn wife continues rolling forward, and while it's the seventh heaven for me, I can tell she's in extreme pain from the penetration. "No, shush." She closes her palm around my mouth before I can speak. "I can do it."

I sigh into a smile.

Zinneerah seeks a comfortable pace, working her hips back and forth. She breathes through her parted lips. Once again, I stare mesmerized. I want to kiss her neck, lick her nipples, flick my tongue over her clit until she's writhing and numb from her tenth orgasm. Is it possible for a woman to have that many orgasms? With the right partner, I'm sure. I hope I'm right.

"Hurts," Zinneerah whispers, pushing herself to an extent where she winces. I'm not going to allow her to suffer while I'm kicking back my feet and letting her work everything out.

"Hold onto my neck," I say, figuring out the best solution. "As tightly as you can."

Zinneerah listens and wraps her arm around my neck, her chest pressed firmly against mine. My palms grab the mounds of her bottom and roll her forward without her having to put pressure herself. She arches her back a bit, breathing my name into the deep canal of my ear.

"Does it feel better now, darling?" I ask.

She nods.

"That's good. I only want you to feel comfortable. No need to push yourself to please me." I give her body a rest and grip her hips, thrusting up into her. She jerks with each push, breaths coming out choppy. "Is this good?"

"Yeah. So good."

I cup the back of her head, my chest feeling fuzzy and airy from her soft voice. I kiss her temple. "Like you said, darling, we have the whole night." My hands slither down to her back and lift up her hips. "I have to make sure my wife is accustomed to my size before I take her in a hundred more ways."

Zinneerah squeezes the life out of my neck. She grips the back of my hair and cries out airy moans. I continuously work myself inside her, the movements growing quicker, faster, sharper. Sometimes I'd stop and roll her forward, or thrust deep inside her until she's limp like a rag doll against my chest.

Somewhere along the whispers of my name, the nails carving into my skin, her lips kissing the side of my neck, she comes crashing down.

"There we go, darling. You did so well, see?" I say, undoing her arms around my neck. She's absolutely flushed and panting and half-asleep. I kiss her open mouth, snaking my hand behind her nape. "God, I want to kiss you every millisecond of my life."

"Me, too."

Minutes pass of us just kissing like high school sweethearts before she whispers, "But, Raees, you didn't—"

"It's okay," I say, pecking her upper lip. "Pick a comfortable position."

"I don't . . . I don't know any. It's my first time, too."

I lick my lower lip. "Should we Google this?"

"Google sex positions?"

We stare at one another.

We break out laughing.

My lips capture her smile three times, and she hugs me tightly before looking around the bed for any ideas.

"Okay," she says, determined about something. "I'll get on all-fours."

"What's that?" I ask.

Zinneerah tilts her head. "All fours? Hands and knees?" She raises a brow. "Right? That is all-fours, isn't it?"

"Okay." I nod vigorously. "Okay. Yeah. I can—Yeah. Cool. All-fours. Hands and knees."

She chuckles, kissing me suddenly. "You're a dork." Another kiss. "My dork."

Well, I'm even happier now.

I lay her down and slowly pull myself out, peering at the white, stickiness between her legs. She cuts my admiration short by turning around on all-fours and giving me a shy smile over her shoulder. Nothing about her position screams shy, but she's got me blushing like a schoolboy.

I lean over her and sweep her damp hair aside, kissing below her.

Carefully, but honestly, clumsily, I slip back inside her. "Does this feel good?" I whisper.

A soft moan. "So good."

With a kiss to her shoulder, I straighten my spine and hold onto her hips.

I run my hand down her vertebrate and caress her back. She's so soft and bronze-skinned and kissable everywhere. I want her to sleep naked with me every night so I can admire every line on her body. There're even faint pale-pinkish circular marks on different spots on her back. As I peer closer, I realize they look awful lot like cigarette bud burns.

My jaw clenches. That fucking bastard is lucky he's rotting in prison or else I would've finished an entire clip through his brain.

Ignoring the pulsation of my anger, I curl my arm around her waist and bring her up so her scars are glued to my chest. Turning her face to the side, I kiss her lips, holding her gently by her jaw. Her tongue caresses mine, sucking and pulling, and tearing me apart with her taste.

My ministrations grow in pace with the color of her knuckles holding my forearm. I caress her breasts, squeezing them and pulling her nipples, sliding down to her clit again. Her head falls back onto my shoulders, black eyes peering up from her lashes.

I kiss the side of her neck and return her to her position on her hands and knees. I pull out of her, quickly turning her onto her back. "Zinneerah?"

"Yes?"

"You've ruined me."

I drive myself back inside her.

Her back arches off the mattress. I take that opportunity to place a pillow under her for comfort. My palms plant on either side of her head, careful to avoid her open hair, and my hips thrust into her without breaking the fast tempo.

The bed creaks beneath us from the impact, sounds of skin slapping against skin loud enough to fill the room, she's sighing and gasping for air, holding onto my biceps.

"Do you want me to stop, my love?" I ask softly, noticing the tears welling in her eyes.

"No, no, *please.*"

I cup her cheek and kiss her tenderly. "That's my girl. You're doing such a great job for me. Just a little more, okay?"

"Mm-hmm." She bites her bottom lip, eyes squeezing shut as I take it home.

I feel myself getting closer to the finish line. "Hold me."

She locks her arms underneath mine, nails running down my back as I fuck myself further into her.

"Look at me, please." I plank with one arm and use my free hand to cup her cheek, wiping the tears that escape them. "I love you, Zinneerah. I fall in love with you every day. You're the love of my life."

She nods, lips wavering. "You're the love of my life, Raees." She lifts her head and kisses me.

That's all it takes for me to crumble down with her.

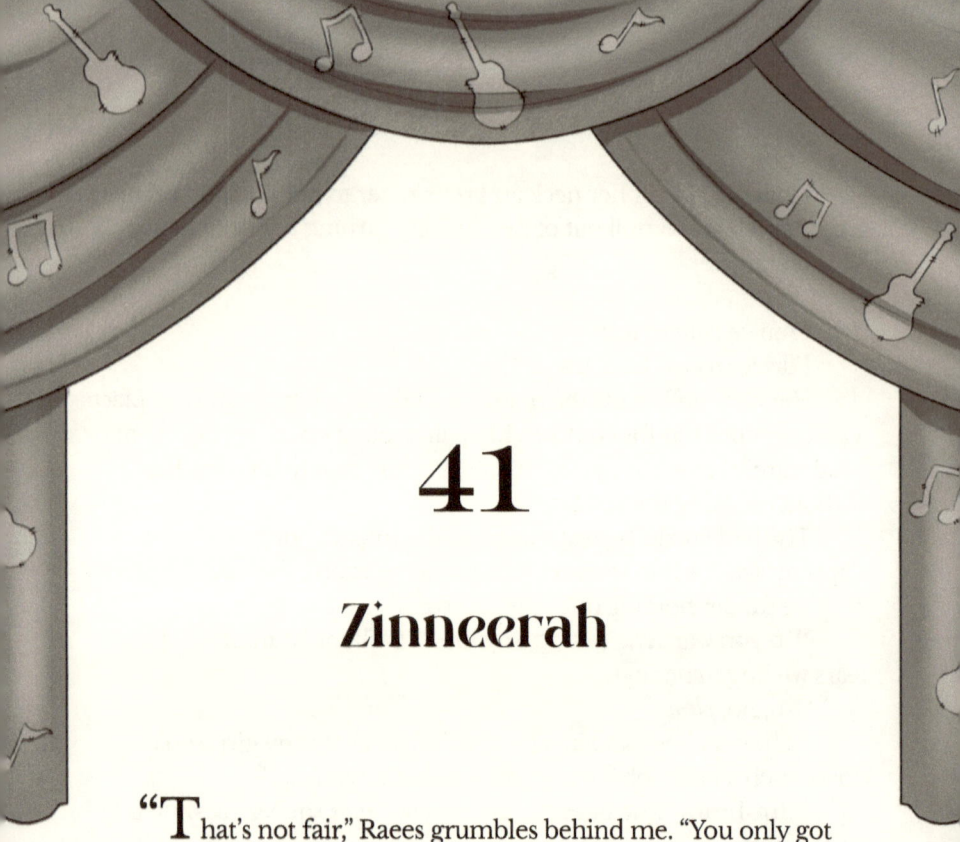

41

Zinneerah

"That's not fair," Raees grumbles behind me. "You only got the red shell because I avoided getting that box."

"Sucks to be you." I hammer the buttons on my controller, Daisy speeding ahead of Yoshi like a pro. All that's left now is Mario—Raees' conventional choice—who's annoyingly holding onto first place. He's right there in my sights, blocking my glorious victory lap.

I drive through another item box.

Red shell. Again.

I cackle and hit the gas. *This is it*. My heart's racing. I'm about to take him down. The comeback of the century. Raees, the so-called undefeated champion of Mario Kart 8, is going down. "C'est la vie—"

Daisy gets slammed by a red shell. My *own* red shell.

"No!" I choke out, flailing in disbelief as Yoshi, that green little fraud, barrels past me. Then Toad. Then Donkey. Then the rest of these pixelated idiots, all whizzing by as if they were waiting for this exact moment to ruin my life. I'm too stunned to even press the 'X' button, my thumbs frozen. "I was so close . . ."

Why does it actually feel like someone just snatched my dream out of my hands? I might cry. Over Mario Kart 8.

This is where my life is now.

Raees' soft hand lifts up my chin so we're both looking at the television. Most likely showing off his win.

But no.

Yoshi won. Followed by the rest of the idiots.

And Mario and Daisy are in the very last place.

I turn my head to look up at him. "But you're world record?"

"I already won," he says, leaning down to kiss me softly. My insides melt. They hurt, mostly, but they melt. "And every day for the past six years."

Something tells me he isn't talking about Mario Kart 8 anymore.

I groan, leaning back against his chest in defeat. "I really wanted to win," I mumble, glaring at the screen where Yoshi's annoying, little victory animation is playing on loop. "Fucking Yoshi. I hate him."

Raees chuckles, the sound rumbling against my back. "You did red-shell him in the previous round, darling."

"So?" I snap.

He doesn't argue, just chuckles under his breath, his thumb tapping at the controller as he starts a new game. Meanwhile, I disappear into the blanket like it's a cocoon and I'm the weird caterpillar that's fallen completely in love with him.

I take a deep breath and, *oh God,* the smell of him—teakwood and woodsy, like he's just strolled deep out of a forest. It suits him. He smells exactly like the kind of man who'd rescue me in one of those ridiculous fantasy movies, shirt unbuttoned, all brooding and heroic. I want to live in his scent. Build a house in it. Maybe a little garden out back.

And, well, I sort of did.

After we'd finished—still panting, my brain barely functioning from whatever wizardry we just did with our bodies—Raees didn't even hesitate. Not a word, not a single question, just scooped me up like I weighed nothing and carried me straight to the bathroom.

He started the shower first, made sure the water was perfect, then plopped me down on the fancy shower bench I used to make fun of because what's the point of a bench in the shower? Now I know. That's the point.

He washed my hair, and then my body. Every inch of me, careful and patient. And when he wasn't making me feel like a damn goddess, he was stealing kisses.

And honestly? I wanted to jump him all over again. My brain was a full-on circus of sinful ideas, and I was ready. But my body had to tap out, especially after that tiny bit of bleeding. Did that bother him? Nope. Not even a little. He wasn't even disgusted or scared—just cleaned me up with a smile.

And if the bar wasn't high enough, he dried me off with the gentleness of a librarian handling an ancient manuscript and started rubbing lotion onto my arms and legs.

Who is this man? Some kind of a robot husband? Because while he was out here being all sweet and attentive, all I could think about was unwrapping the towel slung low around his hips and showing him just how much I appreciated his efforts.

I bury my face in my hands just thinking about it.

He gets me flustered every damn time.

The way his fingers felt braiding my hair afterward, or how he just held me there, arm around my waist, while we brushed our teeth. He carried me to the armchair afterward, settling me down, then started tidying up the room, asking, *"Hey, do you want to play Mario Kart 8 with me?"* as if he didn't just fuck my soul out of my body.

I'm doomed. Absolutely doomed. I love him. Oh, my god, I love him. It's not even a regular kind of love. It's the kind that makes me feel like my heart's about to explode like a pinata, sending colorful, sweet candy flying all over our carpet.

Our.

That's our word now.

"Do you still want to play as Daisy?"

No. No, I do not.

Not when I can't stop thinking about him. Not when it's past one in the morning, and we literally had sex like, what, an hour ago? We need sleep, or we're going to show up to his co-worker's retirement party tomorrow looking like a pair of zombies who crawled out of bed.

I turn around between his legs. "Sleep."

Raees smiles, his damp hair covering those lovely eyes. His sculpted chest on full-display. And goddamn, somebody should outlaw him from wearing grey sweatpants around me. "Sleep, it is."

He puts down the controller and shifts off the bed to turn off his Switch. Then he comes back, slides in beside me, and shuts off the lamp.

We're facing each other now, his arm looping around my waist, our legs a knotted mess. I try to look anywhere but at him since I can feel his eyes on me. Even in the dark, my face heats up, like he's my first high school crush.

The moonlight beams through the curtains, and hits his face just right, accentuating the unfair angles of his jawline and cheekbones. The man is insufferably beautiful, and he's so unaware of it.

I rest my hand on his cheek. "What are you thinking?"

He shrugs. "About you."

"So, nothing new."

A chuckle. Deep and raspy. "I don't know. I always find something new about you."

"Yeah?"

He nods. "Like, how you would cry after a twelve-year-old child in Tokyo red-shelled you."

I make a show of turning around. "Goodnight."

"I'm kidding." Raees pulls me close and presses a kiss to my forehead. I snuggle my face near his neck, wrapping my arm around it. "It's not just that. Like how you count the geese crossing the road. Or how you've turned our freezer into a tater-tot graveyard because you felt sorry no one's buying them at the grocery store."

I lift my head to look at him. "You notice that?"

"Of course I do," he says, his eyes soft as his hand moves in slow circles on my back. "Why wouldn't I?"

"I don't know," I whisper. "I just . . . no one's ever noticed that stuff before."

"You're full of these tiny rituals," he murmurs, brushing his lips against my temple. "You'll whisper a quick apology to our plants if you knock into them, or eat the chips with the green stain first because you think they feel rejected."

My cheeks warm, and I let out a laugh, trying to play it off. "I don't even realize I'm doing half of that."

"Well, no one's looking at you the way I do." He tilts his head down, his lips brushing my hair. "It's my favorite part of being with you, you know? That I'll never run out of things to learn about you. You're infinite."

I tip up my chin to kiss his own. "And you're ridiculously cute."

"And you're ridiculously loved."

"And you're ridiculously cheesy."

Raees' eyes glimmer. "And I ridiculously want to kiss you now."

My lips curve up. "With all due ridiculousness, please."

Raees chuckles, and before I know it, his mouth is on mine. His hand slides up under my sweater, fingers finding my skin. But he pulls back way too soon. "We have to sleep."

"We do," I agree, even though I'm lying through my teeth.

We can't stop staring at each other's lips. His gaze flicks down, then back up to my eyes, and I know mine does the same.

"Because we're responsible adults."

"Totally responsible."

"Playing Mario Kart at one in the morning."

I lean in and kiss his bottom lip, cutting him off. His hand presses me closer to him, fighting a losing battle with his own resolve. "We make the rules," I whisper against his mouth.

"You're right." His fingertips graze down my waist, sending a shiver through me. "Rule number one: we sleep on time."

I kiss him again, because, honestly, I couldn't care less about his stupid rules right now. "Whatever you say," I mumble, barely pulling away.

"Rule—hey, rule number two," he tries to say, laughing at how clingy I'm being. I don't care. I'm kissing his cheeks now, his jaw, anywhere I can get. "Listen, darling."

I pout. "What?"

"Rule number two," he breathes out. "When you're feeling better, there's not an inch of this house I won't take you on."

Oh. My. God.

My entire body feels like it's on fire. My core clenches, and I start kissing him again like it's my life's mission, my hands all over his chest, his neck, threading through his hair. If I wasn't so sore right now, I'd shove him off this bed and make him prove that statement right here, right now. The floor? The kitchen table? The hood of our car? I don't care.

"You're so—" he starts, trying to break away from my kisses, but I'm not letting him off the hook. I peck his cheeks, his jaw, his nose. Whatever's in range. "You're just so eager, huh?"

"For you?" I say, smirking. "Absolutely."

Raees rolls onto his back, and I immediately throw myself on him. My hands are all over his face, kissing him everywhere like a woman on a mission.

He grins, lopsided and lazy, and his hand drifts to my back, fingers tracing my spine. "How long are you planning to keep this up?"

I kiss the tip of his nose. "Forever." Then his cheek. "And ever." Then his chin, and his forehead for good measure. "And ever." I plant another kiss on the curve of his brow. "And always." If I had the precision, I'd be aiming for each individual eyelash.

"I'm so lucky."

"And so handsome," I murmur between kisses, and then I lean down and give him the loudest, most obnoxious smack of a kiss right on his lips. Enough to make him laugh, *full-on* laughing, his body shaking beneath me.

I grab his face like I'm holding a holy relic and stare at him in disbelief. "Seriously, dude. How are you even allowed to walk around this planet?"

He can barely breathe through his laughter now. "What's gotten into you?"

"For starters, you."

And now I'm laughing, too, and he's laughing harder, and I want to capture this moment. The sound of his laugh. The way it makes me feel like the luckiest person alive. If I could, I'd record it, break it into chords, turn it into some masterpiece song I could play forever.

When he finally catches his breath, he shakes his head and says, "Dua was right. You are very clingy."

I raise an eyebrow, mock-offended. "Is that bad?"

"No," he blurts out. "No, never. It's—I just didn't think—I mean, I—"

"Why are you stuttering?"

He closes his eyes, probably hoping to escape my scrutiny, but a slow smile stretches across his face anyway. When he finally opens them, there's a soft glow in them. His knuckles brush against my cheek. "I love when you ask me that question, you know."

I tilt my head, genuinely curious now. "Have I asked you that before?"

He doesn't answer—at least, not with words. Instead, he tugs me into him, locking me in place, and tucks my head under his chin.

"Rule number three," he says, his voice muffled against my hair, "you can't be clingier than me."

"Why not?"

"That's my job."

"Our job," I correct. "Equality in clinginess is important."

He laughs quietly, his chest rumbling beneath me, and his hand finds the back of my head, his fingers threading into my hair.

My eyes flutter shut on their own. I could sleep like this every night. On him, in his arms, listening to his heartbeat.

"You're the best thing that's ever happened to me, Zinneerah," he whispers.

"You're the best thing that's ever happened to me, Raees."

He pulls the blanket over us, tucking us in a cozy little fortress against the world.

I snuggle closer, burying my face in the curve of his neck, breathing him in. He presses a kiss to the top of my head, and I hear him let out this long, tired exhale—like he's finally at peace.

And just like that, the two of us fall asleep. Together.

FUCK MARIO KART 8!!!!!!!!!!!

But I thought you liked playing it
with me....

I do, Raees. I just hate those little gremlins who always
kick my ass.

I'm sorry, darling. Would you like me to
contact Nintendo to create a level specifically
catered to your skills?

Are you making fun of me right now?

NO! Oh, my God. No, never.

Yes, you are! You literally sound sarcastic through
writing.

Okay, you got me. How can I make it up to
you? Would you like a kiss?

.... stop writing and give me ten right now.

I'll give you twenty for each one of your loss.

UGH, I HATE_____

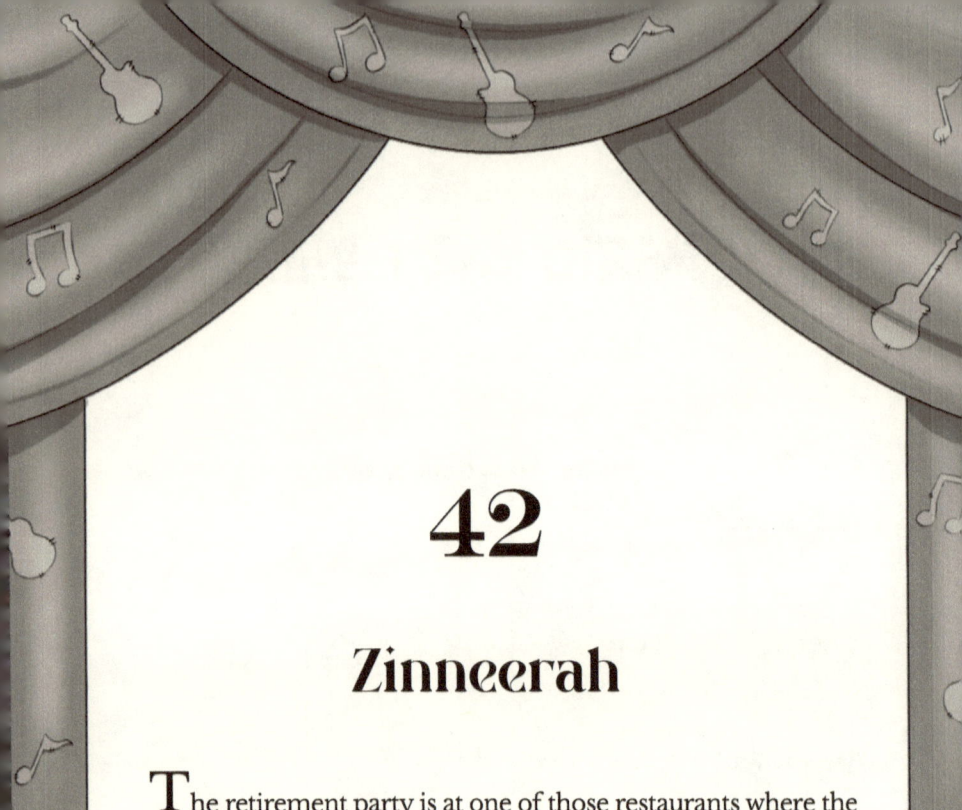

42

Zinneerah

The retirement party is at one of those restaurants where the appetizers alone could bankrupt me if I so much as looked at the menu too long.

Raees holds the door open for me, looking every bit dashing. He's in a black suit that fits him too well, with his hair slicked back, though a few rogue strands have rebelliously fallen onto his forehead. Took me twenty minutes of pleading and a little bribery cupcake to get him to wear his glasses tonight. It's the best decision I've ever made in my life.

As for me? I'm in a black dress with a corset bodice. The sleeves cinch around my wrists, and I even dug out my heels so I don't look like a child trailing after him. (Still barely make it past his shoulder, but it's the effort that counts.)

Raees intertwines our fingers, and I glue myself to his arm as we follow the hostess through a labyrinth of perfectly polished round tables. The air hums with soft jazz from a live band tucked into a corner, mingling with the quiet chatter and the clinking of wine glasses. There's a bar off to the side where couples and friends are seated.

"Who picked this place?" I ask.

"Professor Holmes," he says. "She's friends with the owner."

"Woman of taste."

We're finally led into a private seating area tucked against the wall, and the second we step in, the room goes quiet.

All fifteen pairs of eyes swivel toward us like they're synchronized swimmers. The chatter dies instantly, replaced by a chorus of greetings aimed at Raees.

Well, almost everyone. At the far end of the table, Saira is texting furiously on her phone, clearly unbothered by our entrance.

I glance up at Raees to gauge his reaction, but he's already chewing the inside of his cheek. Mild discomfort. He spent the car ride here practicing social cues after the absolute disaster of the hockey game weeks back.

"Good evening," he says, awkwardly clearing his throat. "Uh, I'd like to introduce you all to my wife, Zinneerah. She'll be performing at the summer festival next week."

Every single time he introduces me with pride in his voice it feels like my heart is about to sprout wings.

A chorus of "Nice to meet yous" echoes around the table as we make our way toward our seats. Hands are shaken, smiles are exchanged. The women compliment my dress, my hair, my very existence. One of them even asks where I got my earrings, and I lie shamelessly, saying they're vintage when I absolutely bought them off a clearance rack in my freshman year of university.

"All right, settle in already. Tonight's about Wei," Professor Holmes announces. She waves a hand toward the man of the hour; a short East Asian man with a jolly smile.

Raees pulls back my seat with a small nod, while I notice a few of the plus-one wives at the table giving him side-eyes with a little too much enthusiasm.

Ogle away, ladies. This one is forever mine.

Raees leans in. "I'm going to speak with Professor Wei for a bit. Are you all right by yourself?"

I nod. "I'll survive."

He kisses the top of my head, and strolls off toward the man of the hour.

I smile politely at anyone who accidentally makes eye contact with me.

The woman sitting next to me turns and sticks out her hand. "I'm Jenna, or better known as Professor Adams. Raees and I co-taught a lab together last year."

I shake her hand. "Zinneerah."

She gestures to the man next to her. "This is my husband, George."

George barely glances up, too deep into a thrilling conversation about bait with another man at the table.

Jenna curves towards me "You know, we were beginning to believe you didn't exist."

I blink. "Oh? Why's that?"

"Because Raees never talks about you," pipes up an agitating voice from across the table. Saira. Of course. I forgot she was here for a second. "We thought he wore the ring as an accessory," she adds with a shrug that makes me want to reach across the table and adjust her attitude.

"In his defense," Jenna interjects quickly, "he *is* a very private person. Almost like a hermit in his shell. You'd expect someone like him to be a social butterfly, but nope. Too bad, eh?" She nudges me with her elbow, and my gaze drops there before lifting up.

I stare at her. "Is there anything wrong with that?"

Jenna freezes mid-smile, like I just slapped the coffee cup out of her hand.

"Honest question," I say, raising an eyebrow.

"I think you're misunderstanding what she means," Saira cuts in, ever the self-appointed spokesperson. She puts her phone on the table, screen up, and—oh, look, her lock screen is a mirror selfie. I rest my case. "We're only looking out for him."

I laugh, tonguing the inside of my cheek. "Right. If you hadn't cornered my husband at that game with your nonsense, or ignored him the rest of the night, maybe you'd know him better by now." I tilt my head and give Saira a pointed look. "He shouldn't have to carry the whole burden of socializing when you already know he struggles in a crowd. That's not his fault. And I'm certainly not going to let him apologize for it." I pause, reach for my water, and take a long, slow gulp. Then I set the glass down and finish sweetly, "Oh, and I suggest you look out for yourself, Saira."

Jenna flushes a lovely shade of pink, flicking her eyes nervously toward Saira, whose expression could rival a department store mannequin.

Finally, Jenna clears her throat and says, "We're sorry for what happened at the game. It was stupid of us to cheer him on. I swear I deleted the video as soon as he left."

Ah, yes. Because deleting a video is the universal symbol of remorse. Not like anyone bothered to stop and actually check on him afterward.

"The past is past," I state.

Jenna nods, eager to escape this conversation. The table falls silent, save for other people's chatter.

Just in time, Raees returns and sits at the far end of the table. He looked relieved when one of the professors pointed out where our seats were, and so am I.

I take his hand. "So, how'd it go?"

"I've never seen a man so happy to retire," Raees says, shaking his head. "Apparently, he's planning a backpacking trip across Europe with his wife and son. It was almost inspiring enough to make me want to retire, too."

I arch a brow. "You're closer to that age."

"You and your ageist remarks never fail to amuse me," he shoots back, grinning. "I should dye my gray hair—"

"Do that and you're sleeping on the couch until the color fades."

His laugh bursts out, loud enough to turn a few heads, but he doesn't care. If anything, he looks even happier, completely oblivious to the curious glances that flicker our way. Raees gets so caught up in whatever moment he's in that the rest of the world ceases to exist. Right now, that "moment" happens to be me, and I'm not complaining.

When the menus arrive, I take one look at the prices and nearly choke on my own spit. *Forty dollars* for truffle fries? Are they cooked in melted gold or something?

Raees, meanwhile, flips through his menu like it's a bedtime story. His hand finds the back of my neck, his thumb brushing slow circles over my nape. It's sweet, sure, but it's also distracting as hell. I can't even concentrate long enough to find something that doesn't cost my entire savings.

I tap his leg under the table. "What are you getting?"

He shrugs. "The salmon sounds good. I've had it here before. It's nice."

The salmon he's talking about costs a hundred and ten dollars. I blink at him like he's just announced he's buying a yacht. "It is a little pricey, Raees."

He looks up again, this time with a brow raised. "Is it?"

I lean in. "The cheapest thing on this menu is truffle fries. Forty-dollar fries, Raees. I don't think you understand the level of food inflation we're dealing with here."

He stares at me for a second, then raises an eyebrow so high it might detach from his face. "You're joking."

"I'm not joking," I say, deadpan, pointing at the fries on the menu. "I'll just get these."

His face twists into something between offended and horrified. "My love, under what possible circumstances have you convinced yourself that you're paying for your own food?"

"I don't want to spend your money."

Raees exhales, placing his menu down. "Zinneerah, how many times have I told you: my money is your money. If you want, I will happily buy this entire restaurant just to make my point. It would be a fantastic investment."

I snort. "*You're* joking."

"I'm not," he says. "My mother is one of the most successful realtors in this city. You don't think I dabbled in purchasing properties in my twenties?"

"Properties?" I repeat, my brows shooting up. "Plural?"

"Yes. Plural. I own an entire residential complex."

My jaw hits the table. "*Own*? Like, you own it outright?"

"Yes." He looks so proud of revealing he's a secret landlord. "I needed a hobby, so I studied for a real estate license and shadowed Ammi-ji at her firm. I started selling and purchasing properties with her when I was 22. It kept me occupied."

I stare at him. "You just casually own a complex. That is a hobby for you?"

"Was, darling."

It's at this moment that I realize I know a lot about Raees, but I also know absolutely *nothing* about Raees. I guess this is what they mean when they say arranged marriages are a slow process. You don't know everything right away; you learn it piece by piece. I always hated that idea because of my parents' disaster of a marriage, but Raees somehow changes my mind about it every single day.

"What else do you own?" I ask, crossing my arms and narrowing my eyes.

"Hmm." He reaches for the water pitcher at the same time Saira does, their hands bumping awkwardly.

"Oh, go ahead," she says.

"It's fine." He's already starting to stand. "I'll get another."

"Sit down, sweetheart." I grab his arm and pull him back into his seat. I yank the water pitcher toward us, pouring two glasses before pushing it back into the middle of the table. Then I lean back, crossing my arms as I turn to him. "What were you saying about properties?"

Saira's line of sight is conveniently blocked now.

Raees grins, his eyes crinkling at the corners. "You're very possessive," he says, amused.

"And you're still dodging the question."

Raees watches me, that smirk of his pulling at one corner of his mouth.

"What?" I question.

"You know what."

"I don't." I do.

He takes a sip, and sets it down. "I own a complex building, a vacation house that's rented out, and a detached home that's also being rented by a family."

I blink. "Well, okay then."

"You didn't think I was dirt poor, did you? We live in a detached home in the most expensive neighborhood, with a home theater and five bedrooms."

I shrug, because what am I supposed to say to that? "Your money wasn't important to me when I married you. It was important to my mom, sure. But I'd love you even if we had to live in someone's shed."

"A shed?" He chuckles, leaning back in his chair. "I'll build us one. A treehouse, maybe?"

"Oh, I've always wanted one. Maybe a treehouse for our future kids?"

His eyes twinkle, and then he's rambling. "I can picture it already. You and I bicker over nails and wood panels while the kids "help" by spilling paint everywhere."

"Useless little gremlins."

Raees laughs, his eyes crinkling at the edges as he leans in and presses a quick kiss just above my brow. "Pick whatever you want to eat," he says. "Make it the most expensive thing on this table."

"If you insist."

I order the vegetarian ravioli, truffle fries, and a side of Caesar salad. Raees goes with salmon, garlic rice, and some fancy mango sparkler that I'm immediately planning to steal sips from.

As we wait for our food, the conversations around the table shift to Professor Wei, who's the star of a talk show. Jenna tries to throw Raees a bone, directing the spotlight his way. But my socially awkward husband clams up, responding with sentences that are maybe five words long, tops: "I love my students." "It's been a good year." "Yeah, they're kind."

The table seems satisfied enough with his monosyllables, especially since he's smiling. I'm just sitting there grinning so hard my cheeks hurt, because every time he opens up even a little, it feels like watching someone coax a kitten out of hiding with pieces of tuna.

He's getting there, though. Slowly. The longer the night goes, the more comfortable he looks.

When the food arrives, I point my fork at his plate. "Can I try some of the rice?"

"You don't have to ask, my love," he says, already scooping up a spoonful, and bringing it to my lips.

I take a bite, and it's like angels are singing on my taste buds. "Oh, *wow*."

"Good?"

"Incredible. I get it now. Worth the price of a lung."

Raees chuckles and says, "I'll try making it at home for you," before offering me another bite.

I happily take it. Then I stab a piece of ravioli, hold it up for him, and watch as he leans in to take the bite. There's a bit of cream sauce left on the corner of his mouth, and without thinking, I swipe it away with my thumb and lick it clean.

"Surprised I'm actually enjoying tonight?" he asks after swallowing.

"Pleasantly," I chirp, nudging his shoulder with mine.

He grins shyly, lowering his gaze. "I thought everyone would avoid me, you know. I've been avoiding them ever since the game. That's why I'm glad you're here. If I was alone, I don't think I'd have said a single word tonight."

I slide my hand across the back of his chair and hold out another bite of ravioli for him. He doesn't hesitate, leaning forward to take it, his eyes meeting mine like it's just us at this table and not an entire room of people.

"You're doing so well," I say, pinching his cheek lightly because he's too adorable not to tease. "Seriously. Everyone's instantly charmed when you smile. You should try it more often."

He presses his lips together in this shy, sheepish way that only makes me want to pinch his cheek again. "I'll think about it," he says, feeding me another bite of rice.

"Those two look like they're in their own world," Professor Harrison comments, his voice cutting through the chatter from three seats down.

"It's the newlywed bliss," Professor David chimes in, raising his glass. "Now that the spring term is winding down, are you two planning a honeymoon, Raees?"

Raees nods politely. "We haven't decided on a location yet. For now, we're happy just enjoying our home. No need for a hotel."

"Hotels are the fun part," George winks as he lifts his wine glass.

"I'll drink to that," Jenna adds, clinking her glass with her husband's.

"Jesus, you two." Professor Holmes groans, shaking her head. "Let's keep it G-rated, yeah?"

Wei chuckles, raising his glass toward us, and then turns to me with that warm, professor-y look that makes you feel like a student even when you're not. "I have to admit, Zinneerah, I haven't seen Raees this happy since he was my student years ago."

I glance at Raees, whose cheeks turn the same shade of pink as the rosé slush Jenna's been chugging all night.

"I agree, Professor," says Saira. Out of nowhere. She's sitting there with her fifth little cocktail glass, obviously tipsy, glaring at me. "Nothing says 'happiness' like rewriting history."

I glare back at her. "Guess it just takes the right person."

Raees chokes on his water.

What? I'm not going to be subtle about it, either.

Holmes, bless her oblivious heart, doesn't catch the tension. "Raees has always been a little grouch like me. Well, no, I'm the bigger grouch. We can all agree on that, can't we?"

The table laughs, and Holmes keeps going, now waving her fork like a magic wand. "But, Zinneerah, let me tell you—there's a light in his eyes now. A skip in his step. Honestly, he was practically shitting rainbows and sunshine every time he talked about you for the past six years."

Saira's head snaps so fast in our direction. "Six years?"

Raees looks like he wants to disappear into the tablecloth. He's so uncomfortable it's almost painful to watch, and the only reason he doesn't immediately nod and confirm it is because she's sitting there, suddenly sobered up.

"Now *that's* love," Professor Benedict says.

And that's Saira's cue. She throws back the rest of her cocktail, slams the glass on the table like she's declaring war, and mutters something about excusing herself before storming off.

"What's her deal?" Jenna leans over and whispers to me.

I give her my best polite smile, and shove an entire ravioli into my mouth before I say something I can't take back. Luckily, the table's attention shifts to Wei talking about his first date with his wife, and I don't have to fake any more interest in Saira's dramatic exit.

Raees isn't as lucky. He hasn't touched his salmon in a while, and now he's just staring at it, prodding at the rice.

Finally, he sets his fork down, exhales, and turns to me, smiling. "Do you want to stay here? Or go home?"

My brows furrow, head tilting as I brush a strand of his hair from his forehead. "You sure?"

"It's over, Zinneerah. I've gotten my closure," he whispers. "I don't owe her one."

A smirk begins at my lips. "Damn right." I pick up a truffle fry and feed it to him. "Time to go home. Watch movies, or documentaries. Whatever you want."

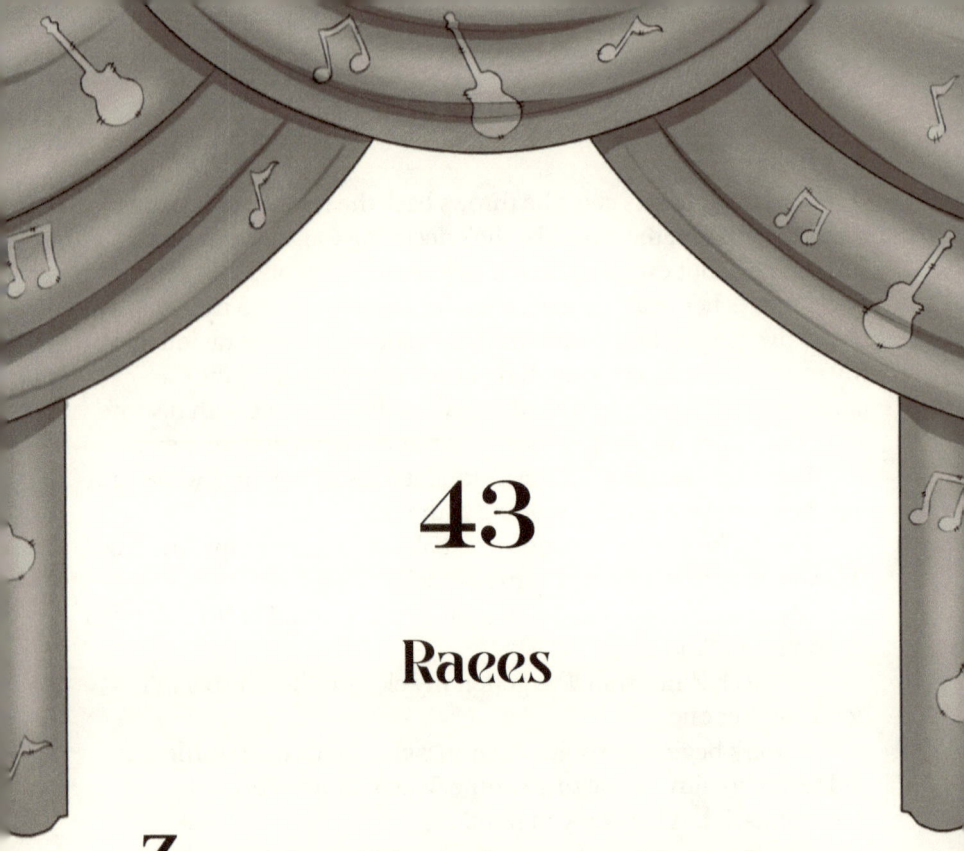

43

Races

Zinneerah lays with her head on my lap while I work my fingers through her thick, silky hair. She's so unaffected by the gore and guts split opened on the screen, chuckling and pointing out the cheap VFX.

Meanwhile, I'm about to vomit the salmon I had hours ago.

She slaps my knee. "This is my favorite scene." The villain breaks the skull of the hero's best friend between a refrigerator door, then throws his body inside an industrial sized beef grinder. "He's going to eat it."

On second thought, I *am* going to throw-up. "I can't watch this anymore."

"What?" She pauses the movie and looks up. "Why? You said you liked horror movies."

"I don't," I say, glimpsing at the paused scene of the man's flesh being minced out. "I'm sorry I lied."

"The DVDs . . ."

"I bought them to make you feel more at home."

Zinneerah raises her head from my lap. She sighs into a smile, pressing a gentle kiss to my cheek. "You don't have to lie to impress me. It's adorable that our choices are different." She returns to the home screen. "Let's watch a documentary."

"Are you sure?"

"You need a change in scenery."

"Okay!" I take the remote from her hands and switch to YouTube. She blinks at my sudden change in mood, then starts chuckling. "There's this documentary on whales that I used to watch as a child with Ramishah. Would you like to watch it with me?"

Zinneerah nods eagerly, sliding her arm around my neck and resting her head on my shoulders. I pull her legs onto my lap, looping my arm around her waist and giving her a kiss on the forehead before hitting play. "Why do you like whales so much?"

The narrator's deep, monotone voice starts explaining migration patterns, and I gesture at the screen. "That. Right there. Majestic, inspiring creatures."

She snorts. "Big, sad creatures that eat krill by the bucketload and look like they'd sink a ship by accident."

"That's a feature, not a flaw."

"So, your favorite animal is basically the ocean's clumsiest vacuum cleaner?"

I glance at her. "And your favorite animal is what? A squirrel, maybe?"

"No. Penguins." She grins, leaning back against me.

"Penguins?" I scoff. "Whales rule the ocean. They can hold their breath for an hour, travel thousands of miles without GPS, and some of them can communicate across entire oceans. Meanwhile, penguins waddle ten feet and fall over."

"Majestic, itty-bitty creatures, migrating thousands of miles," she parrots, biting back a laugh. "Very inspiring."

"Penguins are literally nature's slapstick comedy act," I counter. "They're cartoon birds come to life. Hello, *Penguins of Madagascar*?"

"First of all, don't bring my sons Skipper, Kowalski, Private, and Rico into this," she snaps, jabbing her finger in my chest. "Secondly, penguins mate for life. Isn't that sweet?" Her voice turns sugary in that fake way she knows drives me nuts. "Maybe that's why I like them."

"They're fine," I say begrudgingly. "But they're no whales."

"Whales aren't sexy."

"Whales don't need to be sexy, Zinn—" I stop because suddenly, she's pressing her lips against my cheek. Not a quick peck, either. One of those slow, wet kisses that drag across my skin.

"That's not fair," I say, but my voice cracks halfway.

Another kiss, right under my jaw this time. Her hand slips behind my neck, pulling me closer.

"Zinneerah."

"Hmm?" She hums, pretending to be innocent while her lips trail to the side of my throat.

"I'm trying to explain the majesty of whales," I protest weakly, tilting my head because, let's be honest, I'm not trying *that* hard to stop her.

"And I'm trying to explain the majesty of this," she murmurs, her teeth grazing my skin.

"I had—" I swallow hard. "I had a whole thing about blue whales and echolocation—"

"Tell me about it later," she says, softly nipping the flesh around my neck.

"You don't even care about whales."

"Oh, I care." She presses a kiss to the corner of my mouth. "Just not about whales."

"Darling . . ." I'm holding onto some thread of sanity here, but it's slipping fast. "You can't just—"

"Can't just what?" she purrs, that wicked grin of hers beginning on her maroon-painted lips. She knows exactly what she's doing, the little menace. She doesn't even care that I'm trying to make a point, that my nerd brain is still halfway thinking about baleen and migration. "Can't just kiss you?" She gets up on her knees and straddles my lap, blocking my view of the screen. "Can't touch you?" She snatches my glasses, sliding them on with a curious tilt of her head, only to rip them off seconds later. "Damn, boy. How are you not walking into walls?"

"Okay, wow," I say, exhaling like I've just run a marathon. "I didn't realize this was a coordinated attack. Was this premeditated, or—"

"Premeditated," she says without hesitation, tilting her head to meet my eyes. There's a gleam in hers that tells me I'm done for. "I saw my opportunity when you said the word krill."

"That's absurd. No one gets turned on by krill."

"No one else has you." She lowers her head down and kisses me. Fully. Decisively. Ravishingly.

And, yeah, I've got no argument. None.

The narrator on TV is still droning on about humpback calls, but I don't even hear it anymore. All I know is my wife.

My hands slip to her waist, pulling her closer, anchoring her right where she belongs—on top of me, stealing all my thoughts and making damn sure there's no room left for migration patterns.

Her fingers slide into my hair, tugging just enough to make me groan against her mouth, and the sound must do something to her because she deepens the kiss, her nails dragging along the back of my neck. It's not gentle. It's not slow. It's her. All bite, and no breathing room.

Her ridiculous guitar ringtone explodes from the nightstand.

"Don't," she says, catching my hand as I reach for it to end the call, but the contact name stops me short.

"It's Shahzad," I say.

"My brother's call holds no importance to me right now." She kisses me, her giggle muffled against my mouth.

But the phone keeps ringing.

"Let the call end," she whispers.

"If I let the call end, he'll end me."

"Raees."

"Zinneerah," I say, laughing breathlessly. "Shahzad's not going to stop."

Miraculously, the call ends.

"See?" She grins, sliding down my sweatpants, and sliding her hand inside. "Problem . . . solved."

It rings again.

I groan for many reasons, tossing my head back. "For fuck's sake. Just take the call, my love. It'll be quick."

"Quick?" she repeats, offended. "Quick? Do you even know my brother?"

"Yes, I do. And I know if you don't pick up his call, he'll take a flight here to talk to you."

She gives me an adorable pout that she probably thinks makes her look pissed off. "Fine." She snatches it, swiping to answer. Putting it on speaker, she tosses it back onto the nightstand. "What?"

"Wow," Shahzad says flatly. "A 'hello' right off the bat. I'm touched."

"Hi. Yes. Hello. What do you want?" She gets off my lap, and I almost reach out to pull her back.

"You don't sound busy."

"Oh, I am busy." Zinneerah removes her underwear, suddenly, and I nearly choke. She crawls back onto my lap, kissing down the curve of my neck. "Pull it out," she whispers in my ear.

I'm in heaven.

"How's the café renovations?" Shahzad asks, completely oblivious.

"There aren't any renovations yet," she snaps, stifling a moan as I help her sink down on my cock. "Raees—only bought it three days ago."

I shudder as she nips my earlobe. "Stop."

"Sorry, what was that?" Shahzad says.

"Start. It's starting." Zinneerah slams her hand over my mouth, glaring as I smile against her palm. "Still early days. Why are you asking?"

"I'd like to speak to him."

"Why?"

"Just give him the phone. I know he's home—I have his location."

"He has my location?" I whisper, confused but oddly charmed.

She stops rolling her hips. "What the hell? Why do you have his location?"

"I have my ways, Zinneerah," Shahzad says. "It's for safety. I care about him, maybe five percent less than I care about you."

Okay, I just want to end this conversation now. "Hello?"

"That was fast," Shahzad says monotonously.

"Zinneerah said you wanted to speak—"

"Thank you," he cuts in.

I glance at her, and she shrugs, equally confused, then continues casting her magic like I'm not speaking with her brother at all. "F-For what?"

"For taking care of my sister. I didn't say it after the dawat. I was still a little shaken up from your asshole cousin."

"Fair enough," I manage, pressing my lips together as the sensation builds up inside me.

"But I'm saying it now. Thank you, Raees. You've made her happier than I've seen in years. And that's all that matters to me."

Zinneerah looks at me, a small smile pulling at her lips. I kiss her forehead because I don't know what else to do with all the love crammed into my chest.

"You don't need to thank me for doing what's my right," I say, halting her movements for a second. "But I appreciate the sentiment. And I'm thankful to you as well, for taking care of her when I couldn't."

Shahzad clears his throat. "Yeah, well. It was my right as her brother."

I'm still buried inside her, and her breath hitches as I shift slightly, adjusting her hips. The woman takes it as a green sign to start moving quickly.

Her grin widens as I shoot her a warning look to slow down. Thankfully, she does, and just starts kissing my neck. "We've cleaned out the guest—guest room for you and Nyla."

"No need," he says. "We're staying at Azeer and Alina's. Apparently, they're fighting again, and Nyla's forcing me to mediate."

"She did write, 'Never piss off a pregnant lady,' in our group chat," Zinneerah says, amused.

"Yeah, well, Alina's planning to move to a townhouse, and Azeer's refusing to leave the penthouse. So, that's that."

"Call me if you need reinforcements," I offer. "And let me know if you change your mind about staying here. Also, dinner after the concert?"

"Normally I'd say, 'Don't push your luck,' but . . . I like you now. So, yeah. Dinner sounds great."

How sweet of him.

"Anything else?" Zinneerah asks, clearly ready to end this.

"Yeah," Shahzad drawls. "Exactly why is Raees in the same room as you—"

"Goodnight." She ends the call with a smack of the screen and tosses the phone onto the coffee table.

"You're horrible," I laugh out.

Zinneerah grabs my face. "Just fuck me, Raees."

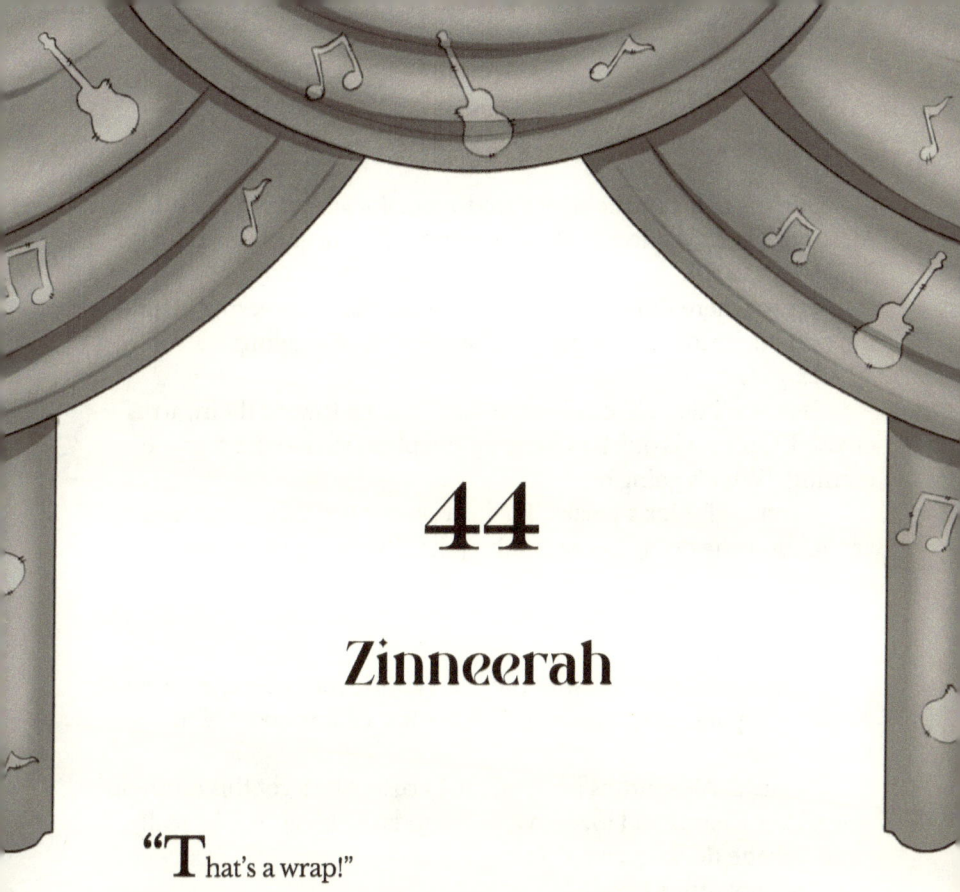

44

Zinneerah

"That's a wrap!"

Professor Daniels and his symphony break into applause, patting themselves on the back.

Our little trio soaks it up, too, with Alex leading the charge. She's hugging everyone, throwing out cheek kisses, and promising Studio 365 after-party plans like she's campaigning for mayor.

"Ladies, gentlemen, and non-binary babes," Alex begins, sweeping her arm theatrically, "it has been an honor for Ophelia, Zinneerah, and me to be part of your team. I was five when I discovered the xylophone, and since then . . ."

She's about to launch into a 30-minute Ted Talk, and I don't have the attention span to focus.

Ophelia's phone buzzes in her pocket. She catches my eye and gives me a quick smile. "Be right back."

She tugs Alex by the sleeve mid-monologue, cutting her off. Alex looks betrayed for all of two seconds, then decides she has bigger fish to fry.

From where I'm standing, I can see the pair whispering behind the curtain, heads close together. There's a lot of giggling.

Suspicious.

Because I don't like being left out, I march toward them, arms crossed. Ophelia is quick to hang up the phone when she sees me coming. "What's going on?"

"Nothing!" Alex squeaks. Then she clears her throat and tries again, this time doing her best sultry alto. "Nothing, babe. Just chilling."

I narrow my eyes at her, then flick my attention to Ophelia. "You sure?"

"Of course," she says with the calm confidence of someone who's absolutely lying. "It was Juliette. She was just calling about, you know—the—"

"Crush!" Alex jumps in. "Yeah, the crush. She's got this crush on one of her friends and loves to give us updates. It's adorable, really."

"Juliette doesn't have a phone."

"School office phone."

"She's using a school office phone to tell you about some crush when she should be in third period right now?"

"Yes," Alex squeaks.

I tongue the inside of my cheek. "Uh-huh. And why wasn't I involved?"

"Because . . ." Her face scrunches, trying to invent a decent lie on the spot. It's painful to watch. "Because she doesn't talk to married people?"

"Oh, for fuck's sake," Ophelia mutters, running a hand through her hair. "Why don't we just discuss this over Studio coffee, yeah? It's been a long day."

I decide not to push it. For now.

"Fine. I'll pack my guitar. Let's go after." I walk back to my case, pulling out my phone to check messages from Raees. Nothing yet.

The thought of him sends a hurricane through my stomach. Not butterflies—a full-blown storm of tingles. My cheeks are sore from smiling, thinking of all my mornings waking up tangled in him, his adorable habit of measuring our hands, then deciding at the last possible minute that we're having sex instead of getting out of bed.

He wasn't lying when he boldly declared there wasn't a single inch of the house where he wouldn't have me.

We've done it everywhere.

Last night, it was the piano. My hands on the keys, his hands on me, and a symphony of wrong notes marking every thrust. The day before, it was the kitchen island. He made this ridiculous sound while eating my molasses cookies, and I lunged at him like a starving animal. The day before that, the pool. The day *before* before that, the theater room, where we tried to finish his whale documentary. We didn't, but he definitely did.

I didn't know my happiness could reach such a pinnacle. I'm grateful for my siblings, my best friends, and my husband. I am alive because of them. I live for them. And, I've started living for myself, too.

I snap my guitar case shut and run my hand over the golden sparrow engraved into the wood. *Baba, I miss you. I wish you could see me now.*

The girls and I take the winding path down to Studio 365, talking about the concert this weekend, songwriting at my place, and a road trip to California we'll probably take in two years. Still, we like making the plans.

"Ah, shit!" Ophelia hisses as we reach the café. She's been glued to her phone since we left the music building. "It's my insurance company calling."

"Oh, shit. Mine too!" Alex dives for her bag.

I squint at both of them. "Okay, that's it. What's going—"

"See you inside!" She grabs my shoulders, spins me around, and shoves me through the café doors.

I stand there for a second, watching them sprint toward the parking lot like they've just remembered they left their stoves on.

Something's going on and I hate that I'm not a part of it.

The café is dead. Not calm or quiet. Dead. No customers, no baristas in sight. Maybe they're hiding in the back. Maybe they gave up on the whole thing and walked out. Business hasn't exactly been booming for Studio 365 lately.

I cross my arms, surveying the empty tables. "Well," I say to no one in particular. "This isn't suspicious at all."

I walk up to the counter and tap the little silver bell. Once, twice, three times. I'm not even hungry. I'm just terrified of missing out. Did I do something wrong? Say something wrong?

"You're here!" Raees bursts out of the kitchen doors, holding a chocolate milkshake in one hand and a plate of oatmeal cookies in the other. He plops them on the counter in front of me. "For you, my love."

I gasp. "Raees, what—?"

"This is yours, too." Then he's nudging me toward the center of the café. "And those tables. And the chairs. The windows, the counters. Empty cups, plates, utensils—all yours."

I blink. "Huh?" *Am I hallucinating?*

Now we're in the back kitchen, surrounded by grinning employees who are all staring at me like I'm the guest of honor. "Meet your new team," Raees announces, motioning at the staff.

I stare at him. "*What?*"

He dangles a key in front of my face. There's a black guitar keychain attached to it. Before I can take it out of his hand, he takes my palm, places it there himself, and curls my fingers over the cold metal.

"Raees," I whisper. My head is spinning. My husband, this handsome, geeky lunatic, just handed me a key. To what, exactly? Studio 365? Did he—*did he just buy it out?*

"Oh no!" Penelope, one of the waitresses, says, sounding horrified. "She's crying! Someone grab the napkins!"

I am crying, but I don't need napkins. I need Raees' sweater to soak up the mess. Which is why I dive into his chest and let it all out, smothering my face in the soft fabric while he holds me.

"Do you mind giving us a minute?" Raees says, laughing lightly. There's some scuffling, some excited whispers, and then the sound of the kitchen doors swinging shut. "I'm sorry if I overwhelmed you—"

I cut him off by yanking him down for a kiss. He melts into it, his hands already at my waist. Then, in classic Raees fashion, he lifts me, and sets me on one of the counters, his smile glowing against my lips.

I hold his face in my hands. "What did I do to deserve you?"

"Exist."

I groan. He's so sweet, I could devour him right here and now.

"*And*," he continues, grinning, "because you're my wife. Because you deserve everything in this world, and more in the next one. Because I love you, I appreciate you, and I know you'll thrive running your own place. Somewhere you can bring baking and music together. It's everything you've always wanted."

I am so in love with him.

I smack a loud smooch on his forehead and wrap him up in my arms, burying my face in his neck. He presses a kiss under my ear, his hand smoothing over the back of my head. "I don't know how to run a coffee shop," I mumble into his shoulder.

His laugh rumbles through me. "That's why you have your staff. You've already got the most important parts down—you make the best coffee I've ever had, and your teas can solve world peace. You're a great cook. You can win every season of *Bake Off*. And you already know how these coffee nights work. Bring in other artists and help them grow. There's so much you could do with it now that it's yours. You can even rename it if you want."

Oh, my god. He's insane.

I almost believe him. No, scratch that—I *do* believe him.

Maybe I can make this place work. It's the only spot on campus where I ever felt comfortable instead of some impostor version trying too hard to blend in. "I'd like to keep the name. For nostalgia purposes."

Raees draws back to kiss my forehead. "As you wish, my darling."

I brush my lips over his knuckles. "Help me?"

"Always. Whatever you need. I've got connections in major magazines. Foodie articles, café reviews—whatever puts us on the map. We'll figure it out."

We.

I look up at him and let it sink in; the way he's already got solutions lined up like chess pieces. "I love you."

"I love you more."

"I love you most."

"I love you most-est-est-est—"

"Up and at 'em, lovebirds!" Alex's voice interrupts the moment. "It's picture time! Fifi's got a red ribbon, and everything. I swear she's been planning this since Tuesday."

Raees helps me off the counter, his hand catching mine.

Out front, the staff is gathered in a semi-circle. Ophelia's holding one end, Alex the other, and someone hands me a shiny pair of scissors that could definitely double as a murder weapon in a pinch. Penelope adjusts the camera that sits on a tripod, playing around with the settings then gives us the cue.

"Do it with me," I tell Raees, holding up the scissors.

"Are you sure?"

"Yes," I say, grinning. "Don't act shy now. You'll ruin your reputation."

He laughs under his breath, takes my hand, and opens the scissors with me. "Ready?"

"With you?" I glance at him, my grin widening. "Always."

Snip.

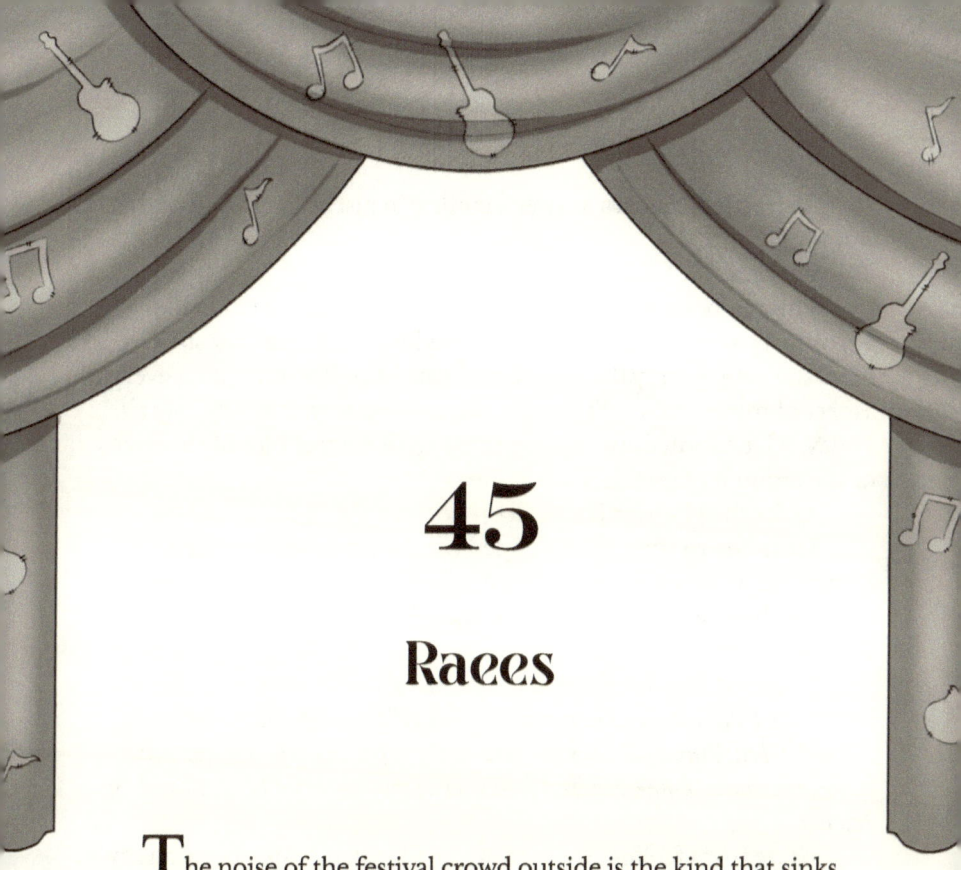

45

Races

The noise of the festival crowd outside is the kind that sinks into your bones when you're near a stadium on the brink of a show.

Out there on the football field, bands are tuning instruments, cheerleaders practicing flips, the audience filling the bleachers, and sound techs yelling into mics.

Backstage, there isn't much of a difference.

Zinneerah is stunning, as usual. Alex has done something to her long hair, turning it into waves that cascade down to her hips. She's dressed in black baggy jeans, a tank top, and a leather jacket, standing at the communal dressing room mirror as she adjusts her eyeliner or touches up her dark-red lipstick.

In the background, Ophelia is helping Juliette with her homework, though Juliette's attention keeps drifting to the ballerinas rehearsing for their performance.

"How do I look?" my wife asks, glancing at me through the mirror.

"Perfection," Sahara answers, cutting in just as I say, "Out of this world."

We glare at each other.

This has been the standard dynamic since Sahara landed in Toronto. I haven't seen her since the wedding, but now that she's here, she's apparently decided to dedicate herself to critiquing every aspect of my existence. Yesterday, she took issue with my tie. My *tie*. Today, it'll be something equally riveting, like my choice of shoelaces or the amount of cream in my coffee.

As for the glaring? That's all on her.

From the moment she stepped off the plane, she's treated nitpicking my knowledge in Zinneerah-ology like it's her new hobby. Even Shahzad wouldn't stoop to some of the things she's managed to find fault with.

Zinneerah likes her apples in wedges, not slices. Zinneerah likes her socks folded into balls, not flat. Zinneerah likes her pillows fluffed in the morning, not before bed. Zinneerah likes her pens in the cup holder faced up for easier access, not down. Zinneerah likes a quarter of cold water for her bath and the rest hot.

Aside from feeling like a failure of a husband, she's been on my personal case, too, trying to change the way I do things for myself.

Like when she caught me trying to brush my teeth this morning: *You should squeeze the toothpaste from the middle, not the end.* Or when she was checking out the guest bathroom: *You should place the toilet paper roll facing under, not over.* When she examined me tying my shoelaces: *You should do double knots, not single.* And when she was going to use our television: *You arranged the remote controls in the wrong order on the coffee table.* We have two controllers—one for the television, the other for the soundbar.

What's the damn order?

And Zinneerah is just soaking up the attention from both of us.

Alex walks in with her band members, bypassing the pre-show nerves in the room and heading straight for the snacks table. She grabs a bowl of chocolate pretzels and announces, "One of the staff told me there are five hundred people in the audience."

Zinneerah freezes. "What?"

"You heard me," Alex says, popping a pretzel into her mouth. "They just cut the line at the ticket booths. Full house, people!"

My wife's eyes dart to me. Her hand finds mine, and her pout is nothing short of a weaponized plea for reassurance.

"You're going to be fantastic," I tell her, letting my hand settle on the back of her neck. My thumb traces the slight tension in her jaw, trying to soothe it away. "You've practiced every day for six weeks. You've got Alex, Ophelia, and everyone who loves you cheering you on. I'll be right there in the front row if you don't want to look at anyone else." Her lips tremble into a half-smile, and I lean in, brushing a kiss to them. "I'll be there to witness your magic as always, darling."

She exhales a shaky breath and pulls me into a hug, her arms looped tightly around my neck. Her fingers weave into the back of my hair, trembling, and I can feel her heart racing against me.

"You're going to be fine," I murmur into her ear. "You've already made all of us proud. You've made your father proud." Her grip loosens just a little as she presses closer. "If you can't look at me, look at the sky. Look at him. You know he's watching you tonight."

Zinneerah nods, a soft sniffle escaping her as her hands slide down to my shoulders. *Thank you*, she signs.

"Don't thank me, my love. I'm always here for you."

She frames my face with her hands as she kisses my cheek. Twice. "Front row. Nowhere else. Understood?"

"Nowhere else," I promise.

She grins, leans in for one last kiss—on the lips this time—and wipes the maroon smudge from my mouth with her thumb. "See you in a minute," she whispers, winking before turning to follow Alex and Ophelia out of the room.

"You've got lipstick on your cheek," Sahara says without pulling her eyes away from her phone.

"And I wear it with pride."

She raises a brow at me, says, "Azeer could learn a thing or two from you on being a better husband," and walks away.

I suppose I'll take that as a compliment.

When I reach my seat in the front, it's a battlefield. Alina and Azeer are sitting as far apart as possible, with Shahzad and Nyla acting as a buffer. Zoha is next to Alina, chatting away with Juliette, who's engrossed in recording everything on her iPad.

Lovely.

"Everything all right?" I ask, sliding into the seat between Shahzad and Azeer. Immediately, I regret my choice. The little ones would've been better company. They'd happily talk about Nintendo and LEGOs instead of dragging me into what's clearly a marital Cold War.

"How are you, Raees?" Nyla leans forward, her rose-gold hair catching the sunset. "I'm sorry I missed your dawat. I was at a fashion show in Shanghai."

"I'm well," I reply. "Don't worry about it. You dodged a disaster anyway."

Her lips press together in sympathy. "I heard. I'm sorry. You and Zinnie didn't deserve that."

Tariq's face flashes in my head. He's been on my mental hit list since we were children. "I wouldn't have cared if it was about me. But no one disrespects my wife and walks away from it."

"Damn right," Shahzad mutters, his arms crossed as he scans the growing crowd behind us. It's an open-field festival at the SLU stadium, and he's on high alert, probably spotting snipers or fraternities.

I glance at Azeer. He's also sitting with his arms crossed, jaw clenched, and sporting the pout of a man who's clearly been banished to the doghouse. I try for neutral ground. "And you? Excited to be a father—?"

"Don't talk to me," Azeer snaps.

I close my mouth, biting back a laugh. Alina must've really done a number on him.

"Stop being a dick," Shahzad says, not even looking up from his vigil.

"I'm not being a dick."

"Yes, you are. Just answer his question. Not everything people say to you is an attack." Shahzad leans back in his seat, cursing his cousin out under his breath. He only lightens up when Nyla distracts him by having him take pictures of her.

Azeer lets out a long sigh, his jaw unclenching enough to throw me a sideways glance. "I am excited."

"That's great news," I say. "One day, you'll have to give me tips."

Azeer's lips twitch into something resembling a smile—or maybe a snarl. "Well, according to my wife, you're the gold standard of husbands. So, you won't be needing any advice from a dick like me."

I raise a brow. "Why are you and Alina fighting?"

He turns his head fully now, glaring at me like I'm the one who started the war. His mouth opens, then shuts just as fast. "Mind your own business, Raees."

I hold up my hands, palms out. "Sure thing. Just keep in mind, when Zoha eventually writes a memoir, she's going to include every fight you and Alina ever had, and it's going to sell millions."

That earns me another side-glare, but he doesn't reply.

My gaze drifts to Alina, who's fidgeting with her wedding ring, her eyes fixed on her lap.

She looks . . . *un*-Alina-like.

People love to gossip about her and Azeer's marriage, like their constant bickering is proof the cracks are about to split wide open. I never bought it. She's the only one who can put a dent in his ego. But now, with the pregnancy and everything she's gone through with her epilepsy, I wonder if it's all taking a toll.

If I were him, I'd be next to her. Asking if she needs water, or food, or if she wants to head home. The strobe lights on the stage are about to fire up. It's too hot out here. She looks drained.

I lean forward toward Nyla. "Do you mind switching seats with me, please? I need to catch up with Alina."

Nyla shrugs. "Sure."

We swap, and as I settle down, Alina's picking at a scab on her thumb.

"Hey," I say.

She glances up, startled, then forces a smile. "Oh. Hi, Raees." She gestures toward the stage. "Excited to see Zinnie?"

"Of course. She was nervous backstage, but I talked her through it." I nod toward the staff clearing the stage for the ballerinas. Two minutes until the show starts. "What about you? Excited for the baby?"

Her hand drifts to her belly, a glimmer of hope in her eyes. "So excited. Just . . . nervous too. The whole giving birth thing, you know? And losing my good looks. But that's the trade-off, right?"

"Alina, who cares about appearances when you're growing a human being? You're beautiful now, and you'll still be beautiful after. And I'm not just saying that because I'm your family."

Her smile falters. "I don't know."

"What do you mean?"

She shrugs, muttering, "I don't know."

I lean forward, resting my elbows on my knees. "Talk to me. What's wrong?"

She shakes her head, her chin trembling. She wipes at her eyes with the back of her hand, but it's no use. Tears start falling.

I slip my handkerchief from my pocket and place it in her hands. "Whatever it is, you know you can come to Zinneerah and me anytime, right? I'll cook whatever weird craving you've got, and she'll bake something overly-sweet to cheer you up. We'll put on a movie, or break out a board game, or whatever you need."

That pulls a small smile from her.

I raise my hands out. "Or, hey, if you need to get out of the house, you can help us with Zinneerah's café renovations. Bring Zoha, too. She'll love it."

Alina dabs at her eyes, nodding. Her gaze shifts to Zoha, who's off in the corner vlogging with Juliette. For the first time tonight, her smile feels genuine. "Zoha's the only thing keeping me sane at home right now."

I take her fingers. "Look, I don't know what's going on with Azeer, and I'm not going to pry. But I know this—you're strong. Stronger than you give yourself credit for. And things will work out. Sometimes it just takes a little patience. Believe me, I waited six years for Zinneerah. Now I'm her husband."

She squeezes my hand, her other dropping on top of mine. "You're a good man, Raees. A very good man. Zinnie's lucky to have you. She deserves it."

"You're too kind, Alina." I grin. "If I'm good, you're brave. Braver than most."

Her smile widens, bright enough to chase away the grey clouds in her eyes. "You're like the older brother I never had. It's just hard sometimes, being the eldest daughter, you know?"

"I wouldn't know," I say, "but Ramishah would back you up on that one."

That earns a laugh.

The microphone feedback cuts through the air, startling both of us. Alina jumps slightly, and so do I.

The host apologizes and redirects everyone's attention by launching into his opening speech. A brief history of Saint Lawrence University, a few words about the festival, and then it's time to introduce the sports teams.

First up: their prized volleyball team. Dua runs onto the stage alongside Zayan and the rest of the squad, their navy-blue and gold varsity jackets gleaming under the lights. She scans the crowd and spots Nyla, who's waving like a madwoman. Dua waves back with twice the energy. Shahzad, ever the proud brother, has his phone out, recording every second of her red-carpet moment.

The host starts rattling off each team's achievements from the spring season, and as expected, the volleyball team gets the loudest applause—they've got the most trophies.

Once they jog off the stage, they climb into the bleachers to join the rest of us.

"Hello, hello!" Dua chirps, practically bouncing as she sits down between Shahzad and me. Or tries to. Zayan sits first and just pulls her onto his lap like she's a backpack. The two of them laugh and banter with Shahzad like old buddies, leaving me to wonder just how close these guys really are. And how can I get to that level with Shahzad?

It's fine, though.

I don't feel left out. I'm used to being the odd one out in this group—an outsider in a family of friends who grew up together. Still, they always make me feel like I belong. Maybe it's because I've known Dua as my student for two years, and I've known Zinneerah even longer, though from a distance, for most of it.

"Oh, Raees bhai!" Dua claps my shoulder, practically knocking me forward. Goddamn, she's got strength. "I totally forgot to tell you. Professor Holmes cornered me the other day to talk about that internship. You know, the one you asked her about? First off, thank you so much for that. I didn't get the position, but it's all good—she said I could train with one of her friends instead. I'll basically be writing articles for my sports blog, and they'll proofread and critique them for me. It'll be great for my portfolio."

I didn't expect Holmes to go out of her way like that, especially since Dua isn't her student. The thought makes me a little proud. "That's great news! Let me know if there's anything else you need."

"Oh, please. You've done plenty already," she says, grinning. "You're literally the best professor any future journalist could ask for. Seriously, everyone loves you. I mean, I already love you because you're my brother-in-law and everything, but still."

"Nice save," I say.

She laughs. "You're a G, bhai."

"A G?"

Her face falls. "And I've lost him."

It seems that teasing me about my age is a family sport.

The next two hours pass in a haze of performances. Ballerinas, dancers, singers, even a stand-up comedian who tries too hard to make a joke about the student center food. There's pie-ing professors, a dog that somehow bolts across the field mid-performance, and even a public *"Can I be your boyfriend?"* proposal from a football player.

Then my phone buzzes. Alex's name flashes across the screen.

I answer quickly. "Yes?"

"Your girl's throwing up everywhere, Professor!"

I'm already on my feet before she finishes, ignoring the girls, and Shahzad, calling after me as I make my way down the stands and towards the women's locker rooms.

470

Outside, I spot Ophelia checking her watch.

"Is she inside?"

Before she can get out a response, I push through the door. "Zinneerah?" I call.

"In here!" Alex exclaims from one of the stalls.

I move past her and find my wife hunched over a toilet bowl, her face pale and clammy, with mascara stains running down her cheeks. "Get me a bottle of cold water and some tissues," I say to Alex before kneeling next to Zinneerah, gathering her hair in my hands. "Are you okay, my love?"

"No," she rasps, leaning back against me, completely washed-out.

Alex hands me tissues, and I use them to wipe her mouth as gently as I can. "It's okay. I'm here."

"Move," Sahara's voice cuts through the room as she steps inside, already holding two water bottles. She doesn't so much as glance at me before crouching down beside Zinneerah. Unscrewing one of the bottles, she presses it to my wife's lips. "Drink."

I take the bottle from her and tilt it carefully, helping Zinneerah take a few sips. From the way she winces, I assume her throat must be inflamed from vomiting. "It's okay," I whisper. "We've got you."

"Let's get her off the floor," Sahara says.

I slip my arms under Zinneerah and lift her, settling us on the bench with her resting against me. "What happened?" I ask, looking between Alex and Sahara.

"She was fine one second," Alex says, wringing her hands. "Stuffing her face with sushi at the buffet, then bolted to the bathroom."

"She loves sushi," Sahara and I say at the same time.

"I know!" Alex squeaks. "I didn't poison her, okay? I don't even know what happened, but, like, we need to fix it. We're about to hit the stage in T-minus ten minutes."

Sahara crouches and grabs Zinneerah's face in her hands, muttering something that I'm sure isn't polite. "Change of plans. Your band's going first. You three will go after."

"But the symphony's set up," Alex protests. "They're literally tuning up as we speak!"

"I'll deal with them." Sahara gets to her feet and levels Alex with a look. "You and the curly haired one are coming with me." Then to me: "You stay here. Don't move her."

With that, she's gone.

"Raees," Zinneerah whispers.

"I'm here." I wipe her mouth and give her another sip of water, though she taps my arm after the second. "You're fine. Take a minute. We're rearranging the setlist, so no pressure." I rest my hand on her head, pressing a kiss to her hair. "You'll be good to go. Just breathe, okay?"

"It was a matter of time I threw up," she whispers. "I've been nauseous for days now."

"Use ASL. Don't overwork your throat."

"Raees."

"Yes, darling?"

"Look at me."

I look at her. Her hands are on my face now, her thumbs brushing my cheeks. "What is it?"

"I'm late."

I frown. "You're not late. You've got, what, thirty minutes before you're on stage—

"Oh, my god." She groans, rolling her eyes. "You adorable, adorable idiot."

"What?"

"I'm late, Raees. As in no period. A week late."

Oh.

Oh.

The realization drops on me like an atom bomb.

My brain scrambles, pulling up old memories of my sister Ramishah calling Ammi-ji and me with the exact same phrase. Right before she announced she was *pregnant.*

"You're pregnant?" I manage.

"I am."

I stare at her, stunned.

"You're going to be a dad," she mumbles.

My head feels like it's been wiped blank. "Test?"

Without a word, she pulls out a crumpled paper towel from her pocket, carefully unwrapping it to reveal *three* pregnancy tests lined up like trophies.

Positive. Positive. Positive.

"I was going to surprise you after the concert," she says.

My eyes are wet now, my chest growing lighter, and she's laughing—her hoarse, scratchy laugh—like it's the funniest thing she's ever seen. Her hands are back in my hair, pulling me closer, and I can barely think straight.

"I'm going to be a dad," I whisper.

"Let's keep it a secret for now," she says, sipping from her water bottle.

"We have to baby-proof the house."

She freezes mid-sip and stares at me. "You're joking, right?"

"And clear out the third guest room. We can make it a nursery—no, no, wait, the baby will sleep with us at first. We'll need a cot. I'll find one tomorrow. And we should start looking at baby names. I've already got a few in mind, but I'm open to suggestions—"

"Raees!" She grabs my face, laughing so hard she's coughing. "The baby is the size of a sesame seed right now, and you're already clearing guest rooms?"

"Precautions."

She clears her throat, succumbing to ASL. *Seven months. At least.*

I almost say, "Who cares?" but think better of it. "Then I dedicate these next seven months to you, my love. Whatever you need, I'm here. I'll even force HR to give me maternity leave."

They won't.

"Doesn't hurt to try."

She kisses my cheek, then stops, sniffing the air. Her eyes drop to the wet speck on her t-shirt. "Crap."

"Take my shirt."

She stares at me like I've grown a second head. *I'm an extra small.*

I pat down her hair. "Yes, I'm aware. If you get to mock my age, I get to mock your height."

She rolls her eyes. *In clothes.*

I kiss her forehead. "Now, seriously. Take my shirt. I'll wear your leather jacket. That is an extra-large, isn't it?"

Her love of oversized clothing works in my favor for once. She nods, crossing to grab the jacket off the stall door. I shrug out of my shirt while she pulls hers over her head. Her cheeks go pink, and mine do, too. My wife is stunning without or without clothes.

I button her into my dress shirt. It's a little ridiculous how big it is—long enough to brush above her knees—but she makes it work, rolling the sleeves to her elbows. I slide on the jacket, which zips up perfectly.

Zinneerah gapes at me, wide-eyed. *You look so good.*

"Do I?"

She steps in, unzipping the jacket enough to show the white tank I've got underneath. Her fingers sweep through my hair, leaving it messy. "My rockstar."

"All right, darling. Rinse your mouth out, and we'll head back to the dressing room to fix your makeup."

Her lipstick is smudged, her mascara streaked, and I can feel my blood rushing south. Not that it's a rare phenomenon.

Unbelievable.

We're going to be parents.

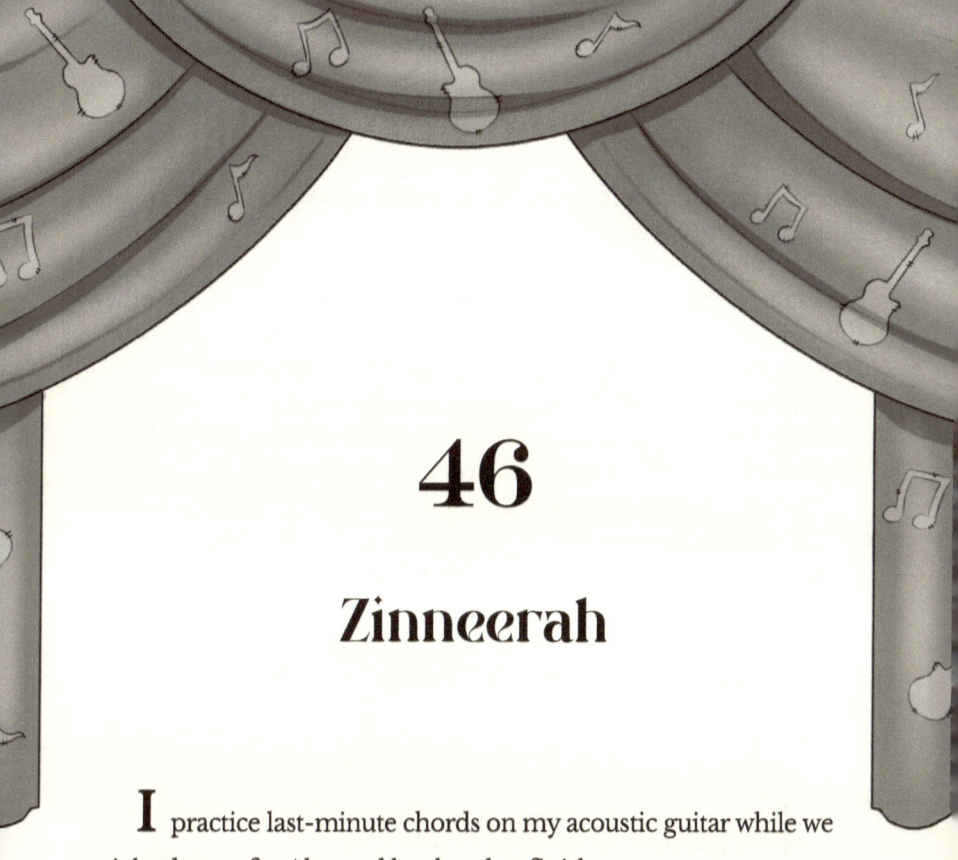

46

Zinneerah

I practice last-minute chords on my acoustic guitar while we wait backstage for Alex and her band to finish.

My fingers move automatically, hitting the notes, though my mind's somewhere else. Sahara's sitting next to me, fanning a piece of paper near my face like it's going to fix my nerves.

"Drink," she orders, handing me a bottle of water like I'm incapable of hydrating myself.

I sigh but take it, because fighting Sahara is a losing battle. Always has been. She dabs a tissue against the back of my neck and my cheeks like I'm a toddler, and when I finally set the guitar down, she grabs my hands and starts massaging my fingertips.

She's so much like Raees sometimes, it's scary. It makes me love her even more.

I practically raised her. Azeer and Shahzad were too busy being "cool boys" when we were growing up, which left her under my watch. She was this wide-eyed kid, still delicate from losing her parents, clinging to anything stable, which just so happened to be me.

I decided right then and there that no one would mess with her. Ever. I'd keep her safe, even if it meant being overbearing.

Not that Sahara ever let herself be pitied. She took that shaky, vulnerable version of herself and bulldozed right over it. While other kids her age whined about recess or argued about whose turn it was to play video games, she was burying herself in books, absorbing everything like her life depended on it. And when she got tired of books, she tried her hand at every hobby under the sun. Her only mission was—*is*—to outdo Azeer in every possible way.

Spoiler alert: she succeeded.

Now, Sahara is one deal close to becoming a marketing billionaire. And not to brag, or anything, but I did teach her long division, so I'm claiming at least one percent of her success.

"Did you tell him?" she asks, still glued to her phone but somehow multi-tasking with rubbing circles on my back with her free hand.

I nod.

"And?"

"He already wants to baby-proof the house."

She snorts, shaking her head. "He's insane."

"I love it."

"And I'm warming up to it," she admits, nudging my shoulder. "But I'm jealous. He's stolen all your attention. There's no space for me anymore."

"Oh, don't start." I roll my eyes. "You'll always be my baby."

"Don't call me that."

"My baby," I tease, reaching over to pinch her cheek. "But you are. Always will be."

Sahara groans but doesn't pull away. Instead, she puts her phone down and threads her fingers through mine. There's a softness in her face that she tries to hide when she glances away.

"What?" I ask, bumping her shoulder.

"Nothing." A shrug. "I'm just happy for you. That's all."

Sahara hates being pressed about her feelings, so I let it go. Instead, I lean my head on her shoulder, swaying her side to side with the rhythm of the music coming from the stage.

The Femme Fatales' performance is winding down. The crowd roars as they finish, soaking up their cheers like it's oxygen. Alex blows kisses, waves, and basks in the standing ovation while the girls bow behind her. Even when the curtains start to close, she refuses to leave the spotlight.

That's Alex Watanabe for you.

"That was exhilarating!" she says when she finally skips over to us, vibrating with post-show energy. "Even the frat boys knew the words! I saw them dancing in the bleachers."

"Incredible job," I whisper, pulling Alex into a quick side-hug. She smells like sweat, her favourite vanilla-caramel perfume from Walmart, and home.

We dodge out of the way as the symphony retakes their seats, instruments whining and screeching with last-minute tuning. Ophelia, who was replaying our songs in her headphones and tapping the floor with her drumsticks, gets up and joins us.

"You girls ready?" she asks, dragging us into a huddle. "This is it. Sophomore-year dreams, in front of a real, big fucking crowd."

"Hell yeah!" Alex squeals.

"And we're going to kill it, right?"

"You're *asking* us?" She cocks her head. "Fifi, are you nervous?"

"Terrified."

"You know what always works for me?"

"I don't ca—"

"A big, wet kiss on the mouth." She lunges at Ophelia, lips puckered and obnoxiously loud kissing noises erupting from her mouth. Ophelia shoves her away, laughing, but Alex clings on like a barnacle. "See? See? Instant confidence booster!"

"Focus," I cut in, adjusting my guitar strap. "You both know your cues, right?"

Alex snaps a salute. "Daddy Daniels will count us in."

"I swear to God, I'm gonna kill you," Ophelia mutters.

A tech appears and starts strapping us into mic packs and earpieces. I hate these things. They always feel like I'm about to be electrocuted on stage.

"Don't overthink it," Alex says, patting my cheek like a coach psyching up an amateur boxer. "I fucked up several chords while performing, but no one noticed. Except for my girls. You'll be fine."

"Yeah . . ." I nod but keep fidgeting. My fingers feel stiff. I catch a faint whiff of sandalwood from Raees' shirt and tug the collar up to my nose. It helps. A lot.

"Let's go!" Ophelia grabs my arm as the host's voice booms across the auditorium, introducing us as the final act.

"Good luck!" Sahara shouts from behind us.

I blow her a kiss before taking my spot behind the left speaker. My electric guitar feels heavier from absorbing all my nerves.

Alex shakes out her hands and plants herself at the mic stand, tuning her strings. Ophelia cracks her knuckles and rolls her shoulders before giving the toms a few experimental taps.

We exchange watery smiles.

This is it.

Everything has been leading to this moment. Our first performance since getting back together as The Cryptics.

I take off my wedding ring, rolling it between my fingers before threading it onto my necklace. It settles next to the little gold 'Z' charm Baba gave me when I was thirteen, the one swore I'd never take off.

If you can't look at me, look at the sky. Look at him. You know he's watching you tonight.

I glance up, hoping Baba's perched on some invisible balcony seat in heaven, watching with a crinkled smile, and nodding along to the melody. I know he'd be proud.

I wipe my damp palms on my jeans, flex my fingers, and grip the pick. The strum is quick—just enough to make sure the amps are responding. They hum back at me. Good enough.

The host is finishing up his intro. I catch snippets—"reunion," "comeback," "beloved band"—like we're heroes coming back from war.

In hindsight, yeah.

Professor Daniels steps onto the pedestal. "Good luck to you all, and let's just have fun." He glances over at us, his wrist rolling in small circles before flicking upward.

"Zinnie," Alex calls to me. "You've got this, okay? You're unstoppable."

"You, too." I smile before my focus snaps back.

The curtains start to part, revealing the audience.

My earpiece clicks on, and the metronome begins its steady count—*4, 3, 2*...

Professor Daniels begins conducting.

Ophelia pounds out the first drumbeat.

The symphony quietly picks up the melody.

Alex begins singing the first line.

And I strum the strings for the first time in front of a public audience.

As we dive deeper into our setlist, I've finally stopped acting like I'm glued to the floor. The first three were stiff—mostly Alex hopping around, slinging her arm around my neck, bumping into me to loosen me up. Meanwhile, I was planted in my little square of the stage.

When I glanced back at Ophelia during the second song, she was already in her element, headbanging so hard I was half-worried she'd snap her neck. She always does that when she's nervous, just throws herself at the music.

By the fourth song, I'm there, too, jumping, strumming, feeling the thrum of Alex's bass and the crowd's roar like a second heartbeat. It's like the whole field woke up. People are off the bleachers, rushing the stage. Every single person out there is admiring us.

I even spot Zoha's on Azeer's shoulders, and right next to her, Juliette's on Raees' shoulders, screaming my name like a maniac.

Alina, Nyla, and Dua are down front, arms around each other, bouncing on their toes, and when I point my pick at them, they lose their minds.

Shahzad is front and center, holding his phone steady as he films me, with Raees' phone in his other hand. He looks like a proud dad at a recital.

I fall right into the solo, and for once, I don't overthink it.

It's just me and the guitar, and my family.

The last song pulls everything back down.

Alex slides onto the piano bench, and I grab my acoustic guitar, sitting on the stool we dragged out just for this moment. Ophelia keeps a soft rhythm in the back, and then the violins join in during the bridge.

It's exactly how we planned it when we wrote "Arcadian" back when we were twenty. I still remember sketching the melody on a napkin at Studio 365 and sprinting to Alex's dorm. We fleshed it out in twenty minutes flat. No talking, just playing.

The song still hits me.

It's about being innocent and free, about pretending you'll never have to grow up. Pretending you can stop time just by wanting it badly enough. I wonder if the crowd feels it the way I do. If they understand what we're trying to say.

It's hard to perform it now, standing here in front of five hundred swaying bodies, knowing the mess my timeline has been. Harder still to keep playing when my eyes land on Raees.

But then he raises his hands, signing: *I love you to the moon and back.*

I follow his gesture, glancing at the pale moon dotting the dusky sky. My chin quivers as I mouth back, "I love you more."

He grins and signs: *I love you most.* Then he winks.

I play the wrong chord. C instead of F. The mistake makes my stomach flip, but I keep going, hoping no one noticed.

Except Alex, of course. She glances at me, smirking, but continues to belt the last chorus.

I shoot Raees a quick glare, but it doesn't stick.

His lopsided grin is impossible to fight, and I end up smiling back before the song pulls me in again.

The after-party is hosted in the royal suite at Sun Tower Hotels.

We're sprawled across the bed and floor, eating room service off mismatched plates while conversations bounce around.

Zoha sits on my lap, scrolling through her iPad. "Look, Zinnie phuppi! This is when you started playing the guitar!" She shows me a three-minute video. It's mostly her screaming into the microphone. "You were so cool up there! I want to play the guitar now. Can you teach me?"

"Absolutely," I say, tucking one of her braids behind her ear.

"I'm going to learn the drums," Juliette announces from Ophelia's lap. "We can start a band."

Zoha gasps, spinning toward Alina. "Mama, can I start a band with Juliette? Please?"

Alina chuckles. "Of course, butterfly. You're already amazing on the piano."

"You know, I play the piano, too," Raees adds, sitting beside me and taking Zoha's hand. "Can I join your band?"

"*Yes!*" Zoha screams, bouncing in my lap. "A million times yes! We need a groupie."

Alina and I freeze.

My eyes shoot to Ophelia, who's struggling to keep a straight face. Alex doesn't even try—she just raises her champagne glass and downs it.

"*Where*," Alina starts carefully, "did you learn that word?"

Zoha points. "Alex."

"Alex," I say, deadpan.

"What?" She shrugs, utterly shameless. "It's just a bunch of best friends following their favorite band around. Right, Zoha?"

"Exactly!" My innocent, *innocent* niece grins.

"So, no more hanging out with Alex," Alina declares. "Until you're twenty."

Alex winks at Zoha, who giggles and sticks out her tongue.

"What are those two plotting out there?" Nyla says, jerking her chin toward the balcony. Azeer's smoking while Shahzad pats his back like he's delivering bad news.

"Az is probably whining again," Dua calls from the bed, where she and Zayan are playing some co-op game on their phones. Sahara should've been here, too, but duty called, as always.

"Baba whines a lot," Zoha mumbles, crossing her arms.

"Zoha." Alina shakes her head. "Family matters, butterfly." She changes the subject fast. "How about that performance, though? Holy cow, you girls slayed out there."

"Literally." Nyla steals a grape from the fruit platter. "I was ready to flash you three from the crowd."

"*Nylana!*" Alina hisses, eyes wide.

Nyla covers her mouth, realizing her mistake. Every pair of eyes shifts to Raees. Zayan snorts under his breath because he gets it. My husband? Not a chance.

"What's going on?" Raees asks, pushing his glasses back up.

"Oh, you sweet, clueless fool," Alex says, hugging his arm. "Never change, Professor."

"I really don't get it," he whispers to me.

I kiss his cheek.

"Got it," he concedes, happily. My sweet, clueless fool, indeed.

Shahzad and Azeer return from the balcony. My brother drops onto the floor next to Nyla, hooking an arm around the front of her shoulder, while Azeer heads to the bathroom. When he comes back, he plops down beside me, phone in hand, scrolling through emails.

Zoha pinches her nose dramatically. "Baba, you stink. Wear a perfume. You know I hate that smell." She scrambles off my lap and onto Alina's, burying her face in her mother's neck. "Mama smells better anyway."

"If Shahzad can quit," Nyla says, giving my brother a pointed look, "so can you, Azeer."

"I'm not Shahzad," Azeer says, pocketing his phone. "I don't have a million hobbies to relieve stress."

Alex leans forward like she's been waiting for her chance to cause trouble. "Well, if I may, there's always—"

"Nope," Ophelia and I cut her off in perfect unison.

"Tough crowd."

"Speaking of," Ophelia says, turning to Alina, "congratulations. I heard you're pregnant. If you need motherhood tips, feel free to hit me up."

"Thank you," Alina says quietly. Too quietly. She's never this reserved. Never a mumbler. It's weird.

Dua pipes up. "Are you going to have a baby shower?"

She shrugs. "I'll think about it."

I glance at Raees, catching him staring at Alina with the same frown I'm wearing.

I tap his shoulder, and sign, *Is she okay?*

He doesn't answer out loud—just gestures toward Azeer with his chin. *Fight.*

I raise an eyebrow. *How bad?*

Raees sighs. *Verbal.*

The others are too caught up in their own conversations to notice as I lean toward Azeer. "You're taking a leave to help Alina, right?"

His eyes are glued to reading an email. "The last few months, yeah."

I cross my arms. "Azeer, you *run* the hotel. You could disappear for nine months, and it would still be fine."

"I just need to be in the office for the first three months to finalize the plan for our resort," he mutters. "But apparently, my wife thinks that's unreasonable."

"The woman's pregnant after two years of talking herself into it," I say. "Give her a break."

Azeer looks at me like I've just suggested he quit entirely. "Zinneerah, I love you deeply, but you wouldn't understand."

Huffing, I pull my purse onto my lap, and dig around until I find the wad of tissue I've stashed in there. With a flourish, I unwrap the three positive pregnancy tests and hold them up for him to see.

Azeer freezes, staring at the sticks like they might explode. "You're *pregnant*?" His voice comes out about three octaves higher than normal.

The room erupts instantly.

Shahzad chokes and blubbers his drink back into the cup.

"Holy shit!" Nyla gasps.

"F-off!" Alex grabs my wrist and stares at the tests like she's checking for herself. "Oh, my god! She's actually pregnant!" She starts passing the stick around.

Raees and I smile at their smiles, holding each other close as our friends gawk like we just announced we're moving to Mars.

Nyla and Dua are the first to crack—full-on sobbing. The remainder are stunned, clinging to each other's arms like they might actually fall over while sitting.

"Congratulations," Shahzad whispers, finally handing me back the pregnancy test sticks. "I'm so happy for you." He cups the back of my head and kisses my forehead—once, twice, three times. His signature of saying, "I love you."

"We're going to have babies side by side!" Alina shrieks, gripping my shoulders. "Oh, my god. Our kids are going to be best friends!"

Before I can process that, she lunges at me and takes us both down to the carpet.

There she is. The Alina I know.

The girls pile on top of me in a flurry of hugs and kisses, pinning me to the floor. Dua's mascara is streaking down her face like war paint, but she's grinning through the tears. The little ones start patting my stomach like they're searching for the baby already.

"Hello, baby!" Juliette chirps.

Raees claps his hands once. "All right, let's give her a chance to breathe, yeah?" He pulls me to my feet, keeping his arm firm around my waist. "Uh, I'm not much for speeches, which is ironic given my profession," he says, earning a round of laughter. "But Zinneerah and I are incredibly grateful to have you all as our family."

I nod, wiping the corner of my eye. "Seriously. Thank you all so much. We already know this baby isn't just going to be loved by us. It's going to have all of you, too."

Dua lets out a loud sniff and starts fanning her eyes. "I swear, if I cry again, it's over for me."

"Well, this calls for dessert, then." Zayan rolls out of bed, already moving toward the minibar, making sure to give me a hug on the way.

Azeer stands up and quietly migrates toward Alina. He drops down beside her, throwing an arm around her waist. She looks up at him, those doe eyes all soft and forgiving. He presses a kiss to her forehead, and she melts against him like butter on toast.

I watch them, smiling to myself. Next time they argue, Nyla better announce she's having a baby. Actually, scratch that—we'll just play a YouTube playlist of baby announcement compilations until they cave and make up.

"You okay?" Raees whispers.

I nod, but he catches my overwhelm settling in after the announcement.

He threads his fingers with mine and helps me stand. "We'll be back in a few," he says over his shoulder as we step out onto the balcony. He closes the sliding door behind us, the noise from the room muffling instantly.

I lean against the railing, the cool, August air fanning against my skin as Raees steps behind me, wrapping his arms around mine. He pulls me close, and we watch the golden-pink horizon slowly sink into twilight.

"I can't believe I'm going to be a mom," I murmur. At the same time, he says, "I can't believe I'm going to be a dad."

We laugh softly, and he kisses my cheek, his lips like home for my skin.

I lean back into his embrace, holding onto his forearms. "Raising a girl scares me."

He rests his chin atop my head. "Why?"

"My mother," I whisper. Who had once again abandoned me the morning after the dawat. Sometimes, I wondered what she was doing in Pakistan all by herself. "Raees, what if I turn out like her?"

"You won't," he says, tilting my face up to meet his eyes. "You won't, Zinneerah. I could say the same thing about my father if it's a boy, but I know I'm nothing like him. And you? You've worked too hard to let history repeat itself. We're going to be the best parents this universe has ever seen." He dips his head, kissing me softly. "This will be healing for both of us."

I turn around to face him fully, wrapping my arms around his torso. He cups my face in his hands, his thumbs brushing over my skin.

"Did you ever imagine we'd get to this point?" I ask. "Because I didn't."

"Never," he says. "If someone had told me that I'd be marrying the woman I've loved since forever and having a baby with her, I would've cried. Then probably laughed. But mostly cried."

"I still can't believe you liked me for so long without saying anything."

"Liked you?" He grins. "Zinneerah, I *loved* you. Six years of loving you quietly, and I'll love you for the rest of our lives, loudly."

My eyes sting, tears threatening to fall. This man is made of glitter and gold. "I didn't think it was possible to be loved like this."

"Neither did I," he whispers brokenly. "But you proved me wrong."

"You proved me wrong, too," I whisper back.

Raees kisses me again, and I sink into him as my back touches the railing. He's soft yet feverish, a bit of a moaner like me. If I'm not kissed by this man every five minutes, I'd die.

"My god, you are breathtaking," he whispers. "Absolutely breathtaking. See? I'm all out of breath because you've taken every single one." He makes me laugh and then steals it for himself.

"Zinneerah Shaan?"

"Yes, sweetheart?"

He signs, *You are the love of my life.*

I kiss the corner of his lips. "Raees Shaan?"

"Yes, darling?"

I sign, *You are the love of my life.*

January 10th

Okay, I've been thinking about names. If it's a girl—and I really hope it's a girl—I think we should go with something timeless, like Yasmine. What do you think?

You're already assuming it's a girl? What if it's a boy?

Then I'll be just as happy. But a little girl? I can already picture us saying it a thousand times a day: 'Yasmine, time for dinner!' 'Yasmine, don't eat that!' It feels right, doesn't it?

It does. But if it's a boy, we'll need to have this whole discussion again.

Deal. But for now, we're officially team Yasmine. Are we gonna tell people, or keep it a secret?

Team Yasmine, it is. Just between us.

You know this means she's going to be a total baba's girl, right?

We'll see about that. She might be a mama's girl instead.

Then I better start clearing my phone storage now to make room for a trillion pictures of my beautiful girls.

I'm only three months pregnant, Raees. You've got plenty of time for that.

I still need space for pictures of my first beautiful girl, too. Bedroom. **NOW.**

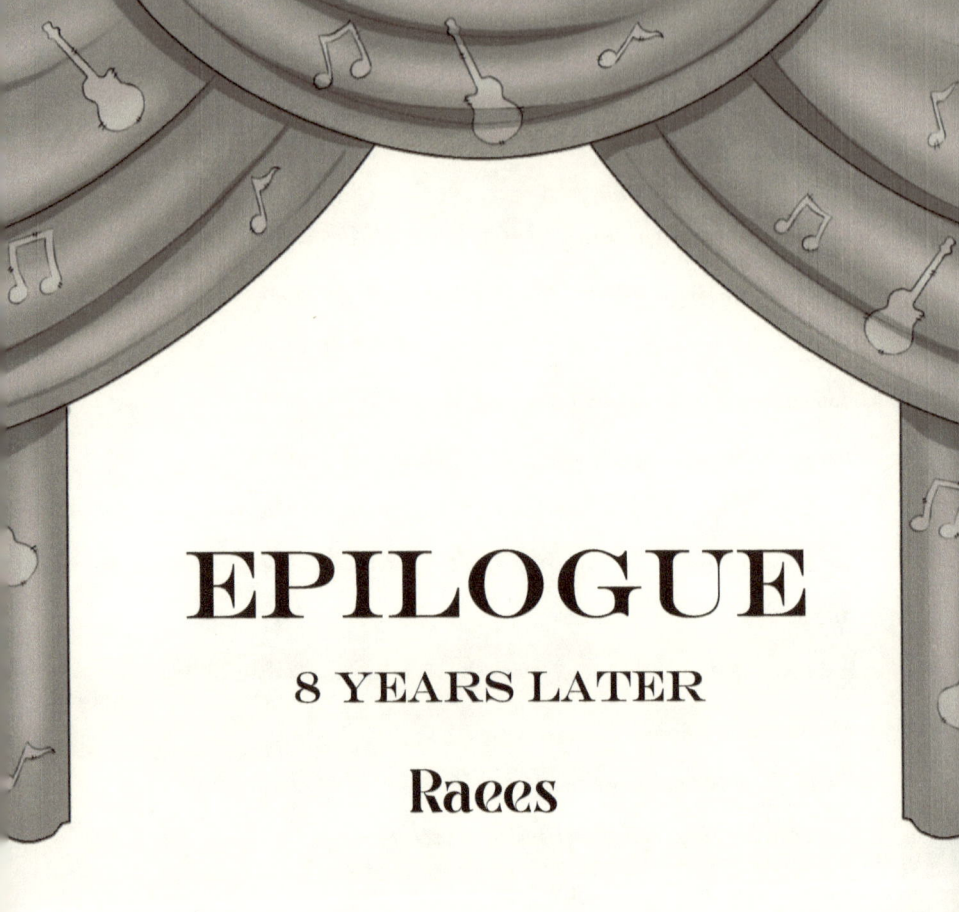

EPILOGUE

8 YEARS LATER

Races

"**D**id you just red-shell me, Princess?"

"Sorry, Baba, but there can only be one winner!" Yasmine chirps, pushing the console keys as she zooms past to take first place reign.

Zinneerah growls under her breath, drifting her motorcycle with Daisy on it, and accidentally driving it over the grass that lowers her speed. "This is rigged."

I chuckle, tossing a banana peel behind me. "Enjoy."

"What—? Ah, shoot!" She takes the banana bait, her motorbike spinning around. Her rank drops from fifth to tenth in a matter of ten seconds while I reach for first. "That's not fair. I'm your wife. You need to treat me with respect."

"Outside Mario Kart 8, absolutely."

She pinches my nose when I start laughing.

"Shush, parents," Yasmine hisses. She sniffs the air, then sighs wistfully. "You two smell that?"

I sniff the air, brows furrowed. "Smell what?"

"My victory."

Zinneerah and I exchange quick looks over our daughter's wild mop of black curls, stifling our laughs.

Yasmine has a very peculiar way of speaking, and it's gotten very theatrical since she joined her drama club at school.

The other day I caught her sneaking into my office to borrow my Oxford dictionary, then laid on her bedroom floor, reading through it. In a span of three hours, she completed definitions from letter A to K. She also inherited Zinneerah's flawless baking skills, and I personally had a pink apron customized with her name on it, and a matching one for my wife in black. Each time I see them baking together, I become all mushy.

Aliza lets out a soft tiny moan from where she's sleeping inside her crib, cozied with two fluffy pillows, her yellow blanket, and a Bluey stuffed-toy that Amina gifted her when she was born two years ago.

Something raises the hair on the back of my neck.

I look at my wife, frowning as she stares at the T.V. screen and her red Switch remote. Nope. Can't allow that. "Give it to me."

"What?"

I give her my remote to play as Mario while I take Princess Daisy. "I'll bring up your rank."

"But I'll lower yours."

"I lied. I also like respecting you inside Mario Kart."

"Either way, you're both losing," Yasmine sing-songs as we reach the final lap.

Zinneerah blows me a kiss. My cheeks ache as I stare at her, down to our little girls, and our matching pajamas and socks. We really haven't set a limit on how many children we want. If I could have a thousand—"Raees, move!"

I blink out of my daze and find Daisy immobile and at twelfth place. "Oh, shoot."

"God, I should've never switched with you." Even though *she's* got Mario in ninth place.

"You're one to talk." I drift around the corner and collect Bullet Bill for a boost. "What will the little kids in Tokyo think of me when they see I've descended the charts?"

"What will *your* kid think, Baba?" Yasmine retorts, closer to the finish line.

I shrug. "Just how cool her baba is."

"The coolest." Zinneerah chuckles, dropping me down to tenth place.

I press my lips together. *Don't cry, don't cry, don't cry*—she crashes into another barricade. A curse nearly slips past my lips. I've gotten her to sixth place, and she's brought me down to the last.

Donkey-Kong takes the victory.

"Let's go!" Yasmine rockets from our bed, doing a victory dance by waving her arms in the air. "Kick butts, take names, suckers! This calls for some ice-cream."

Silence encompasses Zinneerah and I as we quietly get our characters to finish the lap.

A tiny "I'm sorry" leaves her lips.

I stare at the screen then at her big, black eyes gleaming at me. And she's got me trapped again. "I'd rather be ranked number one in your heart, anyway."

She smiles and all my worries of losing my ranking vanishes.

Inching closer, she kisses me, tasting like the chocolate-fudge cupcakes she baked for dessert. Aliza had squished it between her hands and eaten it messily before knocking out from the sugar rush. Seeing the chocolate all over our daughter's face reminded me of my pictures as a baby.

Speaking of pictures, my entire camera roll is filled with Zinneerah and our girls—so much that I had to purchase an extra terabyte. Every tiny thing they do, from giggling to trying to crawl to kicking ass at Mario Kart 8, I'm there with my phone with the camera ready to roll. Whenever I'm having a bad day, all I have to do is whip out my phone and scroll through the pictures, and boom: sayonara temporary depression.

Aliza stirs from the side, rubbing her eyes with the back of her hand.

"And that's the end of the game," I say, shutting off the television and switching on the projector lights that display the twinkling stars on our bedroom ceiling. I help Zinneerah stand up. "Why don't you go use the bathroom first?"

She nods, ruffling my hair and entering the space.

"Yasmine?" I call.

Her voice comes down from the kitchen a second later. "Jee?"

"Just a little scoop, okay? You've got school tomorrow."

She laughs. "The education system cannot control my need for sweets, Father."

I blink. *Okay, that's normal.*

I stretch back on the sheets and stand up, looking down at Aliza in her sleeping cot. She breaks into a smile when I tickle her under her neck, thrashing her legs. "Good evening, my heart. Have you woken from your fourth nap?"

She starts blabbering. "Baba—Bab—" Aliza's a talkative baby, blabbering non-stop at three months, learning to wave, and differentiate between her aunties and uncles. The person she's most comfortable with aside from her parents is Nyla. Probably because her fashion-designer Aunty gifts her with the best dresses, headbands, and sleeping onesies.

"All right, let's get that diaper changed." I pick her up and lay her down on the changing table. When Yasmine was born, we built the nursery inside our room by buying a small bookshelf, making a play corner, and moving the crib next to our bed—though she enjoyed sleeping between us before she moved out into the room next door, and broke my heart.

Now, it's Aliza's turn.

"Staws!" She exclaims, distracted by the twinkling lights moving above.

"Yes, stars. Good job, baby." I quickly change her into a fresh diaper and zip up the onesie again, giving her a flurry of kisses all over her adorable, round face. "All right, go strut." I set her down on the ground, and she goes padding off into her play corner.

Just like Yasmine, she came trained. Only cried for the first few weeks in the beginning, eats all her meals without throwing a fuss, sits in a stroller without begging to be let out, loves sweet treats, and is constantly vying for attention even when I'm showering her with it every day of her waking second. *Unlike* Yasmine, her first word was 'Mama.'

Speaking of my angel, Yasmine appears, licking the ice-cream remnants around her lips. When I give her a no-nonsense look, she just bursts into a big grin and hugs me around my waist.

"Manipulator," I grumble.

"Magician," she says, tilting her head all the way back. "Because my hugs are magical!"

I chuckle, bracketing her round face with my hand and pressing a kiss to her forehead. "Go brush your teeth."

"Can I sleep with you guys tonight?"

My heart swells in my chest, and I swear I almost cry. The thought of my daughters moving out for college, or getting married—*No*. I can't put myself through that pain just yet.

"Absolutely, you can," I whisper. "Go. Hurry. Bring your stuff."

She giggles and skips off to her room.

Zinneerah walks out of the bathroom, enlightened by the sight of Aliza awake.

"Mama!" Our daughter pushes off on her palms to stand and waddles over to Zinneerah, stretching forward to be in her mother's arms now. "Up, up, up."

"Rude," I mumble, feigning a pout. "Have you forgotten who changed your diaper, young lady?"

"Don't worry." Zinneerah feigns a scowl at Aliza, tapping her tiny mouth. "She's only excited for milk. Needy little princess."

I chuckle, dropping a kiss on the top of both their heads, and grab the bottle on the nightstand to hand it off to my wife.

Zinneerah grabs my wrist before I can go to the bathroom. "No, come here." She puckers her lips, and I wholeheartedly kiss them. "One more." I can see where our daughters get their clinginess for affection. To be fair, I am the clingiest of them all. So, I give her two more.

I give her a third, long kiss on the lips then a small smack to her ass making her gasp and give one back.

Chuckling to myself, I enter the bathroom and sigh contentedly. I've never been so happy in my life.

After doing my usual routine, I drop my clothes in the hamper and step into the shower, washing off today's work, and my newfound love for gardening.

I'm planning on a vegetable and flower garden around the backyard. Yasmine said she'd help and has already written out notes. Very helpful notes, actually. We're in August, so we've been a little hesitant to plant anything because of winter. Zinneerah says to just do it as a practice so by the time the snow's gone, we'll be able to build my greens quickly. I've bought a bunch of succulents for the kitchen window to take care of. Aliza almost chewed one when I showed it to her. She'll chew anything except her silicone teether.

Maybe I should get her some gardening toys. Just imagining Aliza in a straw hat and tiny gloves with a little plastic watering—okay, change of plans: I'm buying her gardening toys tomorrow.

When I return from the bathroom, I find Aliza giggling with her small legs bunched up and reaching out for the flower-rattle toy Zinneerah shakes, planting kisses over our daughter's face every time she captures it. Yasmine lays next to her sister, reading . . . well, the dictionary.

I lay down beside Yasmine, both our babies in between, and watch them, wiping the trail of drool leaving Aliza's lips. Every time Zinneerah leans down, she takes it as a sign to kiss her mother's cheek. "Stop trying to steal my girl," I say, covering Aliza's mouth when Zinneerah leans low again.

My wife raises a sassy brow. "Me or her?"

"Her, obvious—*ow*."

Zinneerah taps my head with the toy and I feign pain by sobbing. Aliza watches amused then looks back to her mother then to me. "Stop being a big baby. Isn't your baba a big baby, Minnie?"

"Precisely," Yasmine mumbles.

"Is that a new word you've learned?" I ask, laying my head back on the pillow to see where she's progressed. My eyes widen. "You're already halfway through 'S'?"

"Oh, my god?" Zinneerah's head snaps up, too. "That's amazing, baby!"

Yasmine shrugs. "It's no big deal."

"To us, it is." My wife squishes her cheeks and lays a loud kiss on her left one. "My little nerd. Just like your father."

Yasmine giggles, scooting closer to me. I rest my arm underneath her head, patting her stomach. "Can we go book shopping?"

"We went last week," Zinneerah says, letting Aliza shake around her rattle. "Don't tell me you've already finished the series we bought you?"

"Guilty as charged." She licks her index finger and flips to the next page. "Alina Aunty took Zaid shopping for toy cars yesterday, and he's got a million already. Just saying."

"Well, you're going to wait—"

"No need," I butt in. "I'll take her."

Zinneerah glares at me. She lifts her hands to sign: *Stop spoiling her.*

So, I sign back, *Books. Not drugs.*

As for the spoiling her? She's the eldest daughter, and the one I spent every day taking care of while Zinneerah recovered from postpartum depression. With Aliza, we've split the duties. But Yasmine was attached to me before Zinneerah felt safe enough to hold her again.

"It's okay if you can't afford it," Yasmine says, snapping her dictionary shut and giving it to me to put away. "Thank you."

"We're not broke," Zinneerah defends. "Your mother runs a successful café, and your father's the dean of the English department. We can buy you a hundred books."

Yasmine breaks into a toothy grin. "Perfect!"

I choke on my laugh as my wife stammers, trying to recover from the well laid trap our daughter laid out. I can't help but pull her close to my chest, kissing her head through her thick curls.

Zinneerah narrows her eyes, shaking her head. "You got me good there, Princess Yasmine."

She feigns snoring.

I chuckle, bringing the blanket up with my feet while Zinneerah gets up to get her guitar from the closet. The girls cannot sleep until their mother plays at least one song. With Yasmine, I used to play the piano while she was strapped to my chest to put her to sleep. Then, Zinneerah decided to take over the duties with her guitar to get closer to her, and now it's become a ritual.

She tunes the strings and gives them a long strum. Our daughters are already watching with fascination.

"This one is for my favourite people in the whole universe," Zinneerah says, blowing a kiss in our direction. She starts plucking the strings to "Love Of My Life" by Queen, one of Aliza and Yasmine's favorite ballads in the car. They're both 80s classical rock junkies like their parents. Train them while they're young, you know?

Aliza's eyes are already droopy as she gazes at her mother. Those excited legs and arms deflate. Only soft gurgles and sighs leave her along with a yawn or two.

Yasmine curls up like a cat in my arms, smiling softly as she murmurs the lyrics, then slowly . . . slowly . . . snoring.

Somewhere between Zinneerah's freestyling, they fall asleep. She sets the guitar aside and kisses their foreheads, setting the blanket up to their chests.

My wife and I stare at one another.

I reach out and cup Zinneerah's cheek, bringing her in for a kiss. "You're my number one girl, but you've got some serious competition, woman."

"I'm the favorite parent, so."

I snort. "Is that so?"

"You didn't carry them for nine months." Zinneerah fixes Yasmine's curls from her face, tucking them behind her ear. "Children are naturally closer to their mother's."

"You know what?" I surrender with a sigh. "I agree. I was glued to my mother's side when I was little, too. But you should know, girls are naturally closer to their father's."

"I do," she replies with a sympathetic smile. "Good fathers, though. Baba was excellent, and after his death, I tried to seek the exact love in someone else." Her fingers brush over Yasmine's black dust of curls. "I don't want her to grow up and make the wrong choices like I did, Raees."

"You didn't—"

"I did," she says, caressing her knuckles over my cheek. I give the underside of her wrist a kiss. "Until I met you, I did. That's why I want us to give Yasmine and Aliza as much love and more as we possibly can. I want them to be able to talk to us about anything before turning to their friends for advice. I want them to meet someone who's able to protect their hearts and not let it shatter for eternities. I don't think both of us can bear the sight of our babies having their hearts broken."

My throat constricts. If someone dared to break my girls' hearts, I'd break them before the thought could even enter their brains. That goes for our future children as well. I would never allow a single tear to fall from their eyes unless it's falling off a bicycle when learning or accidentally touching a hot pot.

"You're right," I say, clearing my throat. "You're always right. We're not here to follow our parents' footsteps. We're going to walk our own path. A proper, healthy, loving path." My thumb brushes over Aliza's chin to wipe away more drool. "So that when our children look back, they'll find us standing there." My eyes meet my wife's glistening ones. "Together."

She raises her hands and signs: *Together.*

I raise up and kiss her forehead. "You're a wonderful mother, a loving wife, and a talented, hard-working woman. Your mistakes, your past, your scars, they don't define you. Just like mine don't." My fingers tuck the strands of her behind her ears. "I couldn't have asked for a better soul than yours, darling. My heart belongs with you."

Zinneerah slides her hand behind my nape and kisses me deeply. She smells like fresh soap and citrus and baby powder. "You're the love of my life."

"You are the love of my life, and every lifetime after." Then, I hold up Aliza's small hand and kiss it. "And you are also the love of my life, my heart." Lastly, I curl my arm around Yasmine's waist, drawing her close to my chest. "And you are also the love of my life, Princess."

Zinneerah places her hand on Aliza's stomach. "Goodnight, sweetheart."

"Goodnight, darling," I whisper.

I close my eyes and dream of the first night I saw Zinneerah all over again.

ACKNOWLEDGMENTS

The Sun Tower series is officially complete, and I couldn't have imagined a better couple to close it with than Raees and Zinneerah. They hold such a special place in my heart. Out of every couple I've written (including the ones in my WIPs), they remain firmly at the top. Two broken souls healed by the profound love and admiration they share for one another. I'm absolutely obsessed, and honestly, I wouldn't have it any other way.

First and foremost, a huge thank you to my beta readers: Alanna, Halimah, Kaitlyn, Kiera, Meghan, Rosana, Rooha, Saniya, Ramishah, Ranah, Raania, Simran, and Zinneerah. Your invaluable feedback and support made it possible to deliver this series the way it truly deserved to be. You've helped me so much, and I love you all with my whole heart. Consider yourselves officially invited to my next hundred projects—you're stuck with me now!

To Coz K.A., you are an absolute creative genius. Thank you for designing the stunning covers that brought this series to life. Your talent and magic put my books on the map, and I'll never stop being grateful for that. P.S. If you haven't read her book Airay yet, what are you even doing?

Lastly, to my mom, my biggest fan—thank you for your unwavering love and belief in me. To my friends, who cheer me on every time I share what I'm writing, you have no idea how much that means. And to you, my incredible readers: you are the reason this journey as a writer has been so fulfilling. Your endless support has been everything to me, and I can't wait to spoil you with more stories soon.

With that, I bid you farewell (for now.)

With all my love,
Noor

I'm Noor Sasha, a twenty-something-year-old, and I write about wealthy (for the most part), pretentious men who are explicitly over-the-top pathetic for their girlbossing, gaslighting, and gatekeeping women. If you're in the mood for arranged marriages, forced proximity, desperate pining, second chance romances, nemesis to lovers, and heated sports romance with a leading cast of diverse characters.

Instagram: @authornoorsasha
Twitter: @authornoorsasha
TikTok: @authornoorsasha
Goodreads: Noor Sasha

www.ingramcontent.com/pod-product-compliance
Lightning Source LLC
Chambersburg PA
CBHW030541020726
47494CB00005B/1444

* 9 7 8 1 7 3 9 0 0 7 3 3 1 *